I0668206

The wall wasn't finished and the village was doomed...

Geffrey woke to the sound of thunder. He sat on his cot, rubbed his eyes, then stumbled into the living area and threw open the shutters. No, it wasn't raining. Not even lightning in the sky. But there was thunder, nonetheless.

It was getting louder.

Sounding closer.

He turned to see his father, adjusting his nightshirt, stumble into the room.

"What is it, son?" he said. "See anything?"

"Nothing," Geffrey said, still squinting into the night.

Then, suddenly, Hugo bolted toward the window. "Get dressed," he said in a commanding tone. "Wake your mother—now. Hurry."

"What is it?"

"The Norse marauders! They have returned!"

His eyes wide with fright, Geffrey dashed into his parent's room, shook his mother awake, then returned to his cot where he dressed. His father had donned his clothes and stood in the doorway of their house. Geffrey scrambled to his side, peered through the small window.

In the far distance, he could see the dark figures, riders on large destriers. As before, they carried torches that burned bright against the dark sky. The ground around their home trembled from their horses' hooves pounding the earth.

"Roust the villagers," Hugo ordered his son. "Tell them to grab their weapons and be prepared to defend Lochwald."

The year is 1059, and Norse marauders raid and plunder Geffrey's small Normandie village of Lochwald. Standing in the midst of burning rubble, he finds his father murdered, his mother and fiancé nowhere to be found. Geffrey is taken prisoner to slave away in the iron mines in distant Saxony. After he saves the lives of men trapped in an underground cave-in, Geffrey is promoted to work in the forges, making and fabricating steel weapons to be used by the Norsemen. With the aid of several friends, Geffrey escapes the mines and returns to his village where he rebuilds the family home. When soldiers of Duke William of Normandie come through the village recruiting men for the duke's army, Geffrey and his friends join and are caught up in the duke's plan to conquer and become King of England...

KUDOS for *Hastings*

In *Hastings* by Richard Edde, Geffrey is a citizen of Normandie who is captured by the Norsemen when his village is pillaged and burned. Just a young man at the time, he sees his father murdered. His mother and fiancée disappear, and he has no idea whether they are alive or dead. He is taken as a slave to work in the mines for the Norsemen, but he and three friends escape, only to be caught up in William the Conqueror's quest to claim the English throne. Set in 1059, the story has a ring of truth hard to find in historical fiction. Well written, fast paced, and full of surprises, I found it hard to put down.~ *Taylor Jones, The Review Team of Taylor Jones & Regan Murphy*

Hastings by Richard Edde is the story of a young man who is a teenager in 1059 in Normandie, when the Norsemen invade and ravage his village. Geffrey's father is murdered, his mother and girlfriend are missing, and he is taken prisoner and sold as a slave to work in the mines for the Norsemen. After some time in the mines, the overseer discovers that he was a blacksmith's apprentice, and Geffrey is promoted to work in the forge. From there, he and three friends escape and return to Normandie, building a new home on the ruins of his old one which was destroyed when the village was burned. When William, the Duke of Normandie, gathers an army, Geffrey and two of his friends join the duke in his campaign to win the English crown. Seeking adventure and a better life, they find a lot more than they bargained for...Edde really did his homework on this one, giving it a rare authenticity. Along with marvelous character development, an intriguing and solid plot, and plenty of surprises, *Hastings* is one that historical fiction fans should love. ~ *Re-*

gan Murphy, The Review Team of Taylor Jones & Regan Murphy

Other Books by
Richard Edde
and
Black Opal Books

Blood of Brothers
Trinity

The Yeti Series

Yeti
Yeti Unleashed
Yeti Reborn

H♦A♦S♦T♦I♦N♦G♦S

RICHARD EDDE

A Black Opal Books Publication

GENRE: HISTORICAL SUSPENSE/SAGA/WAR & MILITARY

This is a work of fiction. Names, places, characters and incidents are either the product of the author's imagination or are used fictiously, and any resemblance to any actual persons, living or dead, businesses, organizations, events or locales is entirely coincidental. All trademarks, service marks, registered trademarks, and registered service marks are the property of their respective owners and are used herein for identification purposes only. The publisher does not have any control over or assume any responsibility for author or third-party websites or their contents.

DEDICATION

For Cathy

Soul Mate, Critic, Lover

EPIGRAPH

Once the sword is loosed,
it becomes impossible
to lay it down.
~ Anonymous

Honor is simply the morality
of superior men.
~ H.L. Mencken

PART I

LOCHWALD

CHAPTER 1

Lochwald, Normandie, 1059 AD:

They appeared out of the east riding powerful destriers, the animals snorting and charging, their hooves thundering against the earth throwing clods of soil high into the air. Silhouetted against the rising sun, the raiders' features were obscured by shadows and steel helmets.

A shout rang out in the tiny hamlet of Lochwald, the villagers scurrying through the early dawn mist in advance of the oncoming marauders. The men, on their way to nearby fields, hurried home to protect their families and property while women boarded up windows and locked their doors. The village was in a panic.

The warhorses were large powerful animals and carried their riders easily at a gallop. As the marauders sped through the village, Geffrey managed a glimpse of them. They wore chain-mail tunics under black cloaks and steel helmets with a guard that extended over their noses. Each rider carried a large shield and spear. Long battle-axes protruded from the leather belts of a few. The rider at the head of the column wore a leather strap over a shoulder with a sword and scabbard affixed to it. From beneath his helmet red eyes glowed as if on fire.

Norsemen!

Pulse pounding in his neck, Geffrey stood in the doorway of his father's blacksmith stable and scanned the main road down through the center of Lochwald. In the distance, he saw that a number of homes were ablaze, the flames and black smoke punching into the pale slate-colored sky. With the initial alarm, his father, Hugo, left his place at the forge and sprinted back home to check on Oriel, his wife. A taste of metal filled Geffrey's mouth and he ran, following his father, toward home.

As he did so, he passed men and women lying dead in the streets. A few villagers wandered about dazed, as if struck by a club. Blood ran in deep rivulets down the well-trodden main road. While the Norse raiders continued their ransacking of Lochwald amidst the cries and screams of women and children, men on large black mounts touched their torches to each building. Geffrey watched in silent panic the fires spreading from house to house. The east end of the village was an inferno.

Geffrey's home was located on the far west end of Lochwald, around a hundred meters from the center of town and the blacksmith stable. His lungs burned, screaming for air, during the run toward home. Halfway there, the band of marauding Vikings overtook him, knocked him to the ground. Choking on the dust that swirled around him, Geffrey raised his head long enough to watch them charge past his home and out of the village. Death and destruction in their wake. Amidst the shouts and screams, Geffrey watched as his fellow villagers—people he knew and loved—die by sword and spear. Or trampled. The horses whinnied, the marauders shouted. He didn't dare move. He lay with his head buried in the dirt, a silent prayer for God to save his family on his cracked lips.

In an instant, the raiders disappeared into the mist-covered forest.

Clambering to his feet, Geffrey continued his run home. He bolted through the front door, found his mother unharmed and their home untouched. Standing in front of the family hearth, his father held her in his arms attempting to console her. She sobbed uncontrollably in Hugo's chest while his father was at a loss for words. He held her in his massive arms, patted her. His mother's eyes were red and swollen. Geffrey had never seen her like this.

"Oh Hugo," she stammered, tears streaming down her cheeks. "Why? Why?"

Geffrey stepped into the small house built of wood and a thatched straw roof. It embarrassed him to see his mother weeping so he turned to leave.

"No need to leave, Geffrey," Hugo said, his thick powerful arms still caressing Oriel. "We have no secrets in this house. Besides, at sixteen, you are almost a man. It won't hurt you to see your parents comfort each other."

"I didn't mean to intrude," Geffrey said. "Is mother all right?"

"I am fine, my son," his mother said, breaking from Hugo and drying her eyes with her apron. The raiders—they are gone?"

"Yes, ma'am," Geffrey said. "They rode off to the west. Father, why do the Norsemen persecute us so?"

"Because they are infidels, Geffrey."

"Infidels?" Geffrey had never heard his father use such a word.

"They have strange foreign gods," Hugo said. "They are not the God of the Roman Christian Church. We believe in the one omnipotent God whose incarnate son was Jesus Christ. And the vicar of the One True Church is our Pope in Rome."

"They hate us because we worship a different god?" Geffrey had difficulty with his father's reasoning.

"Yes. They desire to conquer all Normans and make our homeland their own."

"Why don't we fight?"

Oriel returned to her hearth, removed two loaves of bread from the smoldering coals, and placed them on the wooden table. She continued to labor in the kitchen as the two men talked.

"Let's have some of your mother's fresh bread while we talk," Hugo said, placing an arm around Geffrey's shoulder and escorting him to the table. They sat and he watched Hugo cut thick slices of bread and spread them with large dollops of butter. Geffrey listened as he munched the warm dark bread.

Hugo was a short, squat, heavy-set man with dark black hair and gnarled hands and fingers from years of smithing. He possessed deep-set dark eyes. His face softened as he spoke.

"Fight with what, son? We Norman peasants don't have the necessary weapons to mount a successful campaign against the invaders. Our ruler, Duke William, spends his time trying to consolidate his power so the concerns of mere peasants such as the villagers of Lochwald are as far from his mind as the stars. He has bigger fish to fry."

"I have heard the man is a bastard," Geffrey said, a smile forming on his lips at the mention of the word.

"Geffrey!" Oriel scolded. "You know better than to use that word."

Hugo laughed and nodded. "It's all right, my wife. The boy is a man, after all." He winked at Geffrey. "Yes, that is true. William is the illegitimate son of Robert, known as The Devil, who was Duke of Normandie long before you were born, and his mistress Herleve, the daughter of Fullbert, a tanner of Falaise. His enemies call him The Bastard or simply, The Tanner."

"Have you ever seen him, Father?" Geffrey was delighting in the story.

"Once," Hugo said. "When you were a small child I travelled to Alençon to purchase some lace for your mother. William was there with his retinue. He was a tall, thickset man with reddish hair, which receded from his forehead. He appeared to be average height. His voice was rasping and guttural. William had that look of possessing considerable leadership skills and courage. I have heard tell that he is devout and inspires loyalty in his followers, but that he is also ruthless and cruel."

"I would like to meet him one day," Geffrey said. "I still don't understand how, just because people have different gods and worship them differently, they have to make war on each other."

"I'm not sure I can explain it to you, son," Hugo said. "It is a question best put to our village priest, Father Ives. He would be more likely to have an answer than I."

"Maybe I will ask him after Sunday Mass," Geffrey said, gulping down the last of his bread.

"Well, enough of this idle chatter," Hugo said, rising from the table. He licked the butter from his fingers, ambled to Oriel, and kissed her on the cheek. "Let's go see if we can help our friends bury their dead."

With that, Geffrey kissed his mother and followed Hugo out onto the main road where a grisly scene greeted them.

Lochwald was a small hamlet located in the northern duchy of Normandie on the banks of the River Skye. There was a single hard packed dirt road that served as the village's main thoroughfare with a number of smaller streets splintering off at odd angles from it. A few merchants had their businesses in the center of town—the baker, dressmaker, and apothecary. Besides the merchants, there were the humbler folk, the craftsmen who were the carpenters, masons, blacksmiths, and others. Every trade had its apprentices, boys bound to remain with some craftsman a certain number of years to learn his business. The master fed and clothed the boy, gave him a home, and taught him. When he had finished his apprenticeship, he became a journeyman, or workman. Of course, each boy was eager to become a master, but before he could do this, he needed make a masterpiece— a piece of work excellent enough to be accepted by the gilds found in the larger towns.

Beyond the village proper were forests and fields where, every morning, the public herdsman drove the cows of the townspeople to pasture, bringing them back again at night. There were also gardens and cultivated fields around the town. Lochwald was not a clean village. Rubbish was heaped up in front of the doors, and pigs roamed about the streets at their own will, leaving a unique aroma to the atmosphere. One got used to the odor and no one seemed to mind. Or care.

Life was hard and the work difficult. It followed the seasons—plowing in autumn, sowing in spring, harvesting in August. Work began at dawn, preparing the animals, and it finished at dusk with cleaning them and putting them back into their stalls.

Most medieval homes were cold, damp, and dark. Sometimes it was warmer and lighter outside the home than within its walls. For security purposes, windows, when they were present, were very small openings with wooden shutters that were closed at night or in bad weather. The small size of the windows allowed those inside to see out, but kept outsiders from looking in. They were built using wattle and daub. Wattle and daub was a composite building material used for making walls, in which a woven lattice of wooden strips called wattle was daubed with a sticky material usually made of some combination of wet soil, clay, sand, animal dung and straw. It was sturdier than straw and provided better insulation from the elements. As with earlier straw houses, wattle and daub houses also made use of a timber frame and had thatched roofs.

Inside the home, a third of the area was penned off for the few animals that lived in the hut with the family. A fire burned in a hearth in the center of the hut, so the air was continually smoky. Furniture consisted of a couple of stools, a trunk for bedding, and a few cooking pots. Peasant food was mainly vegetables, plus anything that could be gathered—nuts, berries, nettles. The usual drink was weak, home-brewed ale. Honey provided a sweetener. If he ate bread, the peasant enjoyed black rye bread.

Blood-spattered bodies lined the main street of Lochwald. Geffrey's neighbors were among those slaughtered by the Norse raiders. An old man sat on his haunches beside the corpse of his wife and babbled an inaudible prayer. People gathered the dead and loaded them into a cart to be taken to the cemetery south of town. Hugo helped load the bodies. Geffrey counted two dozen.

At the far end of town, he noticed the fires, which earlier blazed with an unwieldy ferocity, were now only piles of smoldering embers. The houses that once stood there were now reduced to ashes. A lump formed in Geffrey's throat as a wave of nausea engulfed him. He felt his knees weaken.

Someone touched his arm and he turned to see Rosalind, the village baker's daughter, standing beside him. She was a year younger than Geffrey. Petite, with blonde hair that hung in long loose curls, she was thin, almost skinny. Rosalind had green eyes and dark beauty mark on her right cheek. Geffrey thought she was the most beautiful girl he had ever seen.

"Can you believe this?" she said in a soft voice.

"It's a nightmare, Roz," he said. "Look at everyone. They're terrified. If I only had a sword."

Rosalind squeezed his arm, her green eyes sparkled. "I know. Where is your father?"

"He helped some of the men take the dead to the cemetery. I guess there will be burials later. Your family all right?"

Rosalind nodded.

"Yes. Father was at the bakery and mother was in her garden. Luckily our home survived."

A man wearing a blackened tunic approached them. His face was soot-stained and there were tears in his eyes. Geffrey smiled at the village mayor.

"Giroldus," Geffrey said, taking the man's extended hand. "How did you manage to survive?"

"The butchers raced right by my house," he said, out of breath. "Didn't even give me or my family a second look."

"You are lucky," Rosalind said. "Many people were not so lucky."

"I know, I know," the mayor said. Turning to Geffrey he said, "Where is your father?"

"I believe he's in the cemetery, sir. If you need him, you can find him there."

Giroldus shrugged, wiped his face with a dirty sleeve.

"I need to organize the funerals," he said. "Today is going to be a long and difficult one. And we'll need to find places for people to stay until they can rebuild their homes. It's too much. Too much."

"I'm sure Father will open our home," Geffrey said. "It's small, but we can find the room."

Rosalind took Geffrey's hand in hers. "And my father as well," she said softly.

CHAPTER 2

The mist over Lochwald cleared during the afternoon but low hanging dark clouds filled the sky threatening rain. A cold wind swept from out of the nearby forest and over the plains of the River Skye. Lochwald's remaining inhabitants gathered in the small cemetery on the outskirts of town, huddled in small groups, their cloaks drawn tight around their shoulders. Hand in hand, Geffrey and Rosalind watched as the last of the dead were lowered into shallow graves. When the dark earth had been shoveled in over the corpses, Father Bernardus, the priest from the next hamlet on the River Skye, along with Father Ives, led the shivering group in the Te Deum.

"O God, we praise Thee, and acknowledge
Thee to be the supreme Lord.
Everlasting Father, all the Earth worships Thee.
All the Angels, the heavens and all angelic powers,
All the cherubim and seraphim,
continuously cry to Thee:
Holy, Holy, Holy, Lord God of Hosts!
Heaven and Earth are full of the Majesty of Thy glory.
The glorious choir of the Apostles,
The wonderful company of Prophets,
The white-robed army of Martyrs, praise Thee.
Holy Church throughout the world acknowledges Thee:
The Father of infinite Majesty;

Thy adorable, true, and only Son;
Also the Holy Spirit, the Comforter.
O, Christ, Thou art the King of glory!
Thou art the everlasting Son of the Father."

Finished with the hymn, the townspeople dispersed and trudged to their homes. Geffrey and Rosalind walked together to the bakery where her father busied himself with his baking chores. They sat at a table and talked. The aroma of baking breads and rolls filled the small establishment. Rosalind's soft voice flowed like honey from her lips.

"This has been the worst day of my life," she said. "I can't believe this has happened."

Geffrey took her hand in his. It felt soft, small.

"I'm so thankful you are safe," he said, his voice almost a tremble. He was still shaken from the Norse raid and the memory of the dark horses with their riders receding into the mist weighed heavy on his heart. "I don't know what I would have done if you had been among those killed." He stroked her hand, all the while knowing his were rough, made that way by hours at the forge and hammer.

"I feel the same way about you, Geffrey." Rosalind glanced toward the bakery oven. Her father still had his back toward them.

"I want us to get married, Roz," Geffrey said. "Right away, if your father will permit it."

Rosalind shook her head and frowned.

"Oh, Geffrey," she said, softly. "I don't think Father would allow it. He goes on constantly about how young I am. He—"

"Your mother then," Geffrey interrupted. "Surely she doesn't think you're too young. Wasn't she fourteen when she married your father?"

"Yes, but—"

"Then there you are," he said. "The old man can't be that against something that he himself did. Took a child in marriage."

"Who took a child in marriage?" Rosalind's father said, having now turned and ambled to their table.

Rosalind blushed. Geffrey jerked his hand away from hers. He stammered.

"Er, nothing, sir," he blurted. "We were just discussing the appropriate age for marriage."

The baker wiped his hands on a stained apron and scowled at Geffrey. His eyebrows narrowed as he spoke.

"My boy," he said, "if you two are considering what I think you're considering, just forget it. My daughter has some growing up to do before she becomes someone's wife."

"But, Papa!" Rosalind exclaimed, her voice much louder. "Mama was only—"

"Hush, child," her father commanded. "We'll talk no more about it." He spun on his heels and returned to his table where he commenced to make another batch of dough.

Geffrey stood and smiled at Rosalind then took his leave. He reasoned that her father had always been a man of such definite ideas. He loved everything about his daughter, from the blonde curls on her beautiful head down to her thin dainty ankles. On his way to the blacksmith stable, Geffrey filled his thoughts with what life would be like when Roz was his wife. He didn't care what the old man thought or what his desires were for Rosalind. Geffrey knew this was flirting with disaster, for the baker and his father were fast friends. On Saturday evenings after work, the two men would drink ale and play Nine Men's Morris, usually at Geffrey's house. His mother would make a plum pudding. Sometimes Rosalind and her mother would come for the evening. He wandered into the stable where his father was at work at the forge. Hugo looked up and nodded at his son. "Glad you got back, son," he said. "These spoons Giroldus ordered need to be hammered out. Can you get right to it?"

"Of course, father," Geffrey said.

Hugo's blacksmith stable was a small cramped affair with a hard packed dirt floor and a large door that faced the main street. Hugo worked by 'forging' metal— heating it until partially melted and malleable, and then shaping it with a variety of specialized tools. Using a hammer, the iron could be drawn or lengthened by beating the metal against an anvil. This flattened and widened the metal, thereby drawing it out. A technique called upsetting was used to increase the thickness of the metal in one dimension through hammering the cold end of the object to make the malleable hot end shorter and thicker. To bend the metal it was placed over the horn of the anvil and struck with the hammer to achieve a smooth curve.

Geffrey found his long leather apron and slipped it on over his woolen tunic. It would protect him and his clothes from sparks. Hanging on a nearby wall was a variety of tools—hammers, ax, chisels, tongs, and pliers varying in size for shaping and finishing the metal objects. There was also a hacksaw, which was nothing but a long blade used for cutting metallic sheets. The punch rod, another common tool that was used for making circular holes, lay beside the anvil.

Hugo forged a large range of household items, farm equipment like plows, irrigation equipment, horseshoes, along with tools like hammers, spades that were sought after by people near and far from the village of Lochwald. The basic reason why Hugo was able to make advancements in the technology was because he kept perfecting and upgrading his skills. Consequently, his manufacturing methods underwent several modifications over a period of time.

Blacksmithing began in Syria around 1,500 B.C. with very crude tools of stone to work the metal after it was heated, probably in a campfire. It was discovered that meteorites had iron in them as well as the red layer of rock strata. The raw iron ore was brought to places called bloomeries and melted down for use by the blacksmith to use. The earliest ironworks were located in areas where iron, flux, and fuel were ample and in proximity to each other. This was due to the weight of the ore and fuel needed to work the iron. Early bloomeries were small furnaces built from rocks that could withstand repeated heating. These furnaces looked like beehives with a vent in the top and an entry portal on the side. The raw iron was brought here and placed in the furnaces and heated until it melted. Once the furnace cooled the still, red hot iron *blooms*, as they were called, were pulled from the furnace and pounded into rectangular bars that were folded over and over to produce wrought iron. Wrought Iron had a very low carbon content making it much weaker than steel. But wrought iron's malleability yielded itself to forging and forge welding.

Constructed of brick, Hugo's hearth—the heart of the forge—was at a height convenient for him. Three walls around the hearth prevented the smoke from being blown into the shop by drafts or wind. The three hearth walls kept fuel contained in the hearth with only minor effort and also helped promote a cleaner shop floor. The forge itself had a square interior area with walls that tapered in from front to back.

The hood of the forge was at a convenient level as well and Hugo took care to place the front at a level so that it did not interfere with tending the fire or placing metal in and out of the fire.

Geffrey grabbed the bellows and stoked the fire. The bellows was a device made from wood and leather and pushed air into the fire in order to generate a high enough temperature to make iron melt. It expelled as much oxygen out as it took in and so fed the fire with much more oxygen than human lungs could.

Early in his life as his father's apprentice, Geffrey had the job of operating the bellows, a dull and grueling task that lasted for hours. By the end of the workday his arms and back ached from the repetitive movements. His bellows was constructed from two wooden panels, one with a hole cut in the center. The paddles were connected with a hinge. A leather flap that only opened one way was secured to the hole in one of the paddles. A leather bag was fixed between the paddles and a nozzle set at the head. The air would come in through the hole in one of the paddles when the bellows were pulled apart. When they were pushed toward each other, the air would be expelled out the nozzle and into the furnace's fire.

As he placed several partially completed spoons into the forge, Geffrey thought over the events of the morning and the why of the raid on their humble village. It was something he could not comprehend. Why Lochwald? Why murder so many innocent people who were only attempting to live their lives in peace and quiet. Or as his father would say, they lived in quiet desperation.

He took the tongs and removed a red-hot piece of metal and, with the hammer, began fashioning the business end of a spoon over the anvil. The stable was warm and the labor caused sweat to trickle down his face and neck. Geffrey glanced at his father who worked a spade for one of Lochwald's men.

"Father," he said. "I have been thinking."

Hugo stopped his pounding with a hammer, turned to face his son.

"That is always a dangerous undertaking for a young man," he said and returned to his work.

"No," Geffrey persisted. "The slaughter that happened today has left me sad and angry. I don't understand the why of it. And if Roz had been killed my life would have been ruined, over."

Hugo eyed him over a shoulder.

"So it will be Rosalind, will it? Your mother and I have seen the two of you together."

"Father, I—we—" Geffrey was suddenly embarrassed that he had mentioned Rosalind.

Hugo laughed a hearty laugh and winked at him.

"Ha!" he said. "You do not think your mother and I were young once? That were do not know or understand the yearnings of the human heart? If that is what you think, you are certainly naive and most assuredly mistaken. The baker's daughter has similar feelings?"

"Yes, sir. We wish to be married."

"And her father? What does Ansel have to say about this arrangement?"

"He's against it of course." Geffrey felt his blood start to boil, his anger mount. His head pounded at the thought of Rosalind's father and his uncaring attitude. "The man is an uncompromising buffoon, Father. He simply doesn't remember his own marriage."

"Now, now, Geffrey," Hugo chided. "Don't be so hard on the man. Ansel has worked hard in building a good life for his family, and he doesn't want to lose his precious daughter. You can hardly blame him for that."

"But he wouldn't be losing a daughter," Geffrey protested, patting his chest. "He'd be gaining a son." Geffrey smiled when he finished. He didn't think it was a bad argument.

"Listen, son. This morning's tragedy has left everyone on edge, jumpy. I'm sure Ansel is just worried and fearful over what happened and what may happen in the future. He's concerned about his daughter's safety and well-being. You must understand that. Ansel is not a bad man. In time, he may come around and see things differently. You must remain patient. And become the best smithy you can become."

"What if the Norse marauders return?"

Hugo laid his tools down, turned toward Geffrey. Deep furrows formed between his dark eyes.

"Then we will defend Lochwald. We will fight."

❧❧❧

Toward the end of the ninth century, the raiders from Northern Europe, commonly known as Norsemen, were regularly foraging, raiding, and trading, along the coastline of the Frankish kingdoms. During these raids, the Norsemen became bolder—sailing up the Seine and sacking Paris. Initially the raiders set off from their home villages in Scandinavia and returned a few weeks later with any plunder they had gathered. However, as the raids continued the Norsemen began establishing raiding bases further from home. It was during this time that a grand army of Norsemen invaded England. These bases were often in very good farmland and they quickly grew rich with the spoils of war. And as a result, grew in size.

In 911 AD, the Frankish King Charles, called The Simple, in an effort to reduce the raids and destruction, offered a large amount of land in northern France to a band of Norsemen led by Rollo in return for token obedience to the Frankish crown. During the years of Rollo's reign, the local term for the Norsemen slowly contracted to Norman and this name stuck.

As befitting the descendants of excellent seafarers, the Normans traded with most of the kingdoms and Empires. They provided soldiers to act as a papal guard and not long after the conquest of the Angle's lands—England—they turned their attention to other places, raiding as far away as Italia.

The main identifiers of the Norman invaders were the language they spoke, a variant of Frankish—French, and their tendency to build castles everywhere. Prior to the Norman occupation, both the Anglo-Saxons and the Celtic Britons before them lived in smallish communities built on hilltops. These Hill Forts were the primary means of defense and provided a community central point for refuge.

When Hrolf Ganger made his pact with the King of the Franks, his bargain was that he would accept Christianity and settle his men and as many other Normans as wished to join him in the lands at the mouth of the Seine as a warrior-barrier against other raiders like himself. The population was plentiful but it was mostly the disarmed and ineffectual peasantry. They could not make the slightest resistance to any armed force. The Franks had spent many centuries reducing the warrior mentality of the peasantry, putting it down violently, outlawing the possession of warrior's equipment, and draining off their best into the *gens d'armes* class, the men-at-arms.

Hrolf took the baptismal name Rollo, but most of his followers even when baptized continued to use their Norse names. Not only did the area become known as Normandie, and of the Northmen, but the names of settlements changed in the area. Rollo's forces sent home for their wives as well as their cousins and anyone else who wanted free land and free serfs to work it in return for their fighting skill.

So the Normans of Normandie were very much still Normans, Norsemen, though they acquired the French language for dealing with both their peasants and their overlords. The Normans expanded greatly in numbers, so much so that they ran out of job positions for warriors. Thus, large numbers were available to resettle when some sent back word from southern Italia that there were lands and cities ripe for new overlordship, did anyone come willing to fight and conquer.

By the time of Lochwald's existence, the Norman peasants were a different band of people, different from the marauding Norsemen who were their distant cousins. Their historical heritage didn't matter, however. The raiders cared not that they pillaged poor men, women, and children with whom they shared common ancestry.

CHAPTER 3

The building of a wall around Lochwald was not an easy task. When the men of the village met at the bakery to discuss Hugo's idea that they should defend themselves and be prepared to fight in the event of another Norse attack, the idea of a security wall surrounding the town developed. Hugo spent the better part of three days fabricating picks and spades that could be used in excavating the stones used in building the wall. It would be reinforced with timbers felled in the nearby forest. The womenfolk would keep the men fueled with food and water during the wall's construction.

When Oriel questioned how long the project would take and worried that the raiders might return before its completion, Hugo tried his best to allay her fears.

"You are right," he said. "They can return at any moment. Tomorrow, next week, next month, possibly never. But if we don't start, the wall will never be finished."

"I suppose that is right, but my friends and I will live in fear until it is finished."

"I will help, Papa," Geffrey said. He knew his muscled back and arms could be used in building the wall. It would be good to work alongside the other men.

"For now," Hugo said, "you can be of more help at the forge fashioning weapons with which to defend ourselves. Most households have a few knives but that is all. I want you to begin forging spearheads and axe heads that can be put on wooden staves. When the Norsemen return, we will have something to fight with."

"Do you think they will return?" Oriel said. Bent over the small hearth, she began heating their dinner of vegetable soup with chunks of venison.

"Who knows?" Hugo said. "But it is best to be prepared. Better to have these things and not need them than to need them and not have them."

Geffrey was disappointed in not being allowed to work on the wall like all the other men but he knew better than to argue with his father. Hugo's temper could flare over the slightest provocation and he had been the target of the man's ire many times when younger. He attempted a weak smile and nodded his understanding.

"When will we begin the wall?" he asked.

"Tomorrow," Hugo said. "At daybreak. The men have agreed to start on the east side of the village as that is where the attack came from. It should be the first side to be built."

"How long will it take?" Oriel said. She stirred the pot, tasted the soup, added some salt.

"Maybe four months. We need to be through by the time spring planting comes around. Most of our neighbors can't survive without their crops."

Oriel ladled up wooden bowels of soup and set them on the makeshift table along with the hearty rye bread baked the day before. The three of them gathered at the table and Hugo said grace in the Roman Church tradition. As they ate, Hugo talked.

"Oriel, our son here has seen fit to fall in love. Can you guess the lucky damsel?"

"Of course," she said. "It's Rosalind. It's always been Rosalind since the two were eight years old. Or didn't you know that, Hugo?"

Geffrey felt the blood drain from his face, his stomach rolled. Hugo laughed.

"Of course, my love. But the young man had the temerity yesterday to proclaim his intentions to me. Such brass."

Hugo slapped Geffrey on the back and laughed again.

"I almost have your sweater finished Hugo," Oriel said. "I was at the spinning wheel for the longest time spinning the yarn for my knitting. I just have the sleeves to knit onto the body."

"I'm glad. My old one is getting quite tattered. It has a number of burn holes in it from the forge."

"Tsk, tsk. How many times have I told you to wear your leather apron when you work, Hugo? This one I'm not letting you wear to work."

Hugo hung his head as he shoveled another spoonful of soup into his mouth. Geffrey chuckled at his father getting told off by his mother.

"It's just that the stable gets so hot sometimes and the leather apron makes me hotter."

Geffrey cut a thick slice of the dark bread and spread it with butter. He used a spoonful of honey to top it off. As he ate he studied his mother.

Oriel was a tall woman, taller than Hugo by a couple of inches. She carried herself in such a stately manner that Hugo often remarked she possessed features of royalty. Her long slender fingers worked from sunup to dark but were never rough or stained. She was full-figured, something that Geffrey also noticed in Rosalind. His mother had dark hair and dark eyes and she was tanned from her daily garden chores.

While Hugo was the head of their household, it was his mother's word that was law. In matters of the daily household chores of preparing food, cooking, cleaning, laundry, his mother was the queen. While Hugo earned a living for the family, Oriel decided how that living was to be spent. And in almost all instances, that was the way Hugo preferred it. Every now and then however, he would bow his back and go against his mother's wishes. When that happened, Oriel smiled and acquiesced to Hugo's demands.

Geffrey's parents rarely argued. Their deep feelings for each other was obvious, a fact that gave him hope that he and Rosalind would have such a relationship. He had a strange feeling that their marriage was one that required much effort on each of their part for his father and mother were such different personalities. Hugo was the serious hard worker who thought deeply about the affairs of life while his mother was light-hearted and carefree. She took what came her way in stride. At least until the raid.

Finished with their dinner, Geffrey went to his cot, and changed into his nightshirt. Tomorrow he would begin his work on the weapons.

ℰↁℰↁ

Hugo was one of the original members of Lochwald's community. He was born in the tiny hamlet of Amiens, the son of a farmer. At an early age, he was orphaned when his parents died during a smallpox epidemic that ravaged the village. The abbot of a nearby monastery learned of his parent's death and arranged for Hugo to become an apprentice to Amiens' blacksmith.

The four years of his apprenticeship were filled with long days of hard work. Hugo had little time for idleness or the earthly pleasures of reading, fishing, or playing games with other boys. Since there was only one medieval blacksmith in every village, Hugo learned that he was responsible for making all the required weapons. A variety of weapons and instruments made by a medieval blacksmith included swords and daggers, door nails and knobs, locks and keys, knives, horseshoes, amours and arrowheads, and others. Sometimes he would also make jewelry items as well as torture devices. Another job was to make the tools and instruments used in farming. The heavy block item upon which the hot metals were hammered into shape was called an anvil. Hammers of various sizes were used for different purposes. There were also punches that were used to punch circular holes in the metals. Other common instruments found in the forge of a medieval blacksmith include chisels, axes, Swages, drifts, sledgehammers, and nails.

It was when he had finished his apprenticeship that Hugo decided to wander the countryside and see the world. He had no family so he took his time, eventually ending his journey at the coast. Later, heading south, he came across a family attempting to eke out a living on the east side of the River Skye. They were hospitable and welcomed him so he decided to settle there. Over the following year, more families joined them and Lochwald was born.

Hugo opened a blacksmith stable and soon was busy fashioning farm implements in his small forge. The villagers built a small church and soon a Catholic priest settled in Lochwald along with a carpenter, baker, and stonecutter.

The Norse raiders troubled him. Unless they were able to build the wall before they returned, there was the firm possibility their village wouldn't survive. Hugo heard the priest speak of their common heritage with the Norsemen but to him it didn't matter. The Normans and Norsemen had long since parted in their culture, religion, values. Until now, Lochwald had been spared their fury. But he knew villages all over Normandie had felt the Norse sword and tasted Norse cruelty. He and the others weren't going to let it happen in Lochwald.

CRCR

A cold mist fell on the countryside surrounding the Norse town of Bayeux a few kilometers from the Aure River. The Norse warlord, Brondolf, an energetic, ruthless leader who spent most of his days either raiding surrounding hamlets or drinking ale and seducing Norman wenches, ruled the region. He ruled from his longhouse deep in the forest far from Norman armies.

Gunnvor, Brondolf's second-in-command, stepped out of the dark of predawn and into the longhouse, lit only by the fire in the giant hearth at the end of the building. He strode to the fire, doffed his mantle, a cloak trimmed with expensive fur that he wore to ward off the cold wind. Underneath the mantle, he wore trousers and tunic made of wool. Approaching the hearth, he saluted his jarl, Brondolf. A jarl was the upper echelon of freemen in Norse society and in Brondolf's case, a cunning warlord.

"My lord," he said to Brondolf, saluting the man by crossing his chest with a closed fist. "I have come from the men. They await your pleasure, sire."

Brondolf sat warming himself next to the hearth. It felt good to be out of the winter cold. He was a tall, heavy-set man with straight dark hair that fell to his shoulders. His face was scarred from smallpox he acquired as a child. A large, Roman nose sat between gray, wide-set eyes while his arms were thick and muscled. He eyed Gunnvor with a sardonic smile.

"Come, Gunnvor," he said in a raspy voice. "Sit beside me for a while. I have missed your company."

Gunnvor moved to a wooden chair opposite the warlord and dropped his squat frame into it.

"Of course, my lord," he said.

Brondolf took a large drinking horn, handed it to his lieutenant.

"Have some ale with me, Gunnvor, while I tell you what is in my heart."

He took a pewter pitcher and poured the man a healthy portion of ale, replenished his own horn, then reclined in his chair. It was cushioned with thick furs.

Brondolf's tunic was of the finest linen, its edges embroidered with golden threads in an intricate design. As he settled back in his chair, he stroked his beard then took a hearty gulp of the ale.

"Gunnvor," he began. His raspy voice was in a lower timbre, almost a whisper. "I am growing weary. These raids to replenish our food stores and other supplies have sapped my energy. One day I will no longer have the strength or will to continue."

"My lord," Gunnvor said. "You are still a young man. In your middle thirties. You have a lot of living left to do."

Brondolf took another drink of the ale, looked at Gunnvor through narrow eyes.

"It is not my body, Gunnvor. I can still fight as well as any man—better than most. It is my heart, Gunnvor, my mind. My soul is weary."

"But, sire, you cannot mean this. Myself, your men, we all depend on you. You have led us on many such raids and through many difficult times. Please do not speak of these things."

"If I cannot so speak my heart to you, Gunnvor, to whom can I so speak? I have known you many a year, my friend. I believe I know you. I trust you with my life. So, I ask again, to whom can I speak my mind if not to you?"

"I am yours to command." Gunnvor raised his drinking horn, saluted the warlord with it, gulped down the ale. Brondolf refilled the horn.

"You saved my life, Gunnvor. Remember?"

"Aye, my lord. It was during the battle with Henry, the Frankish King."

"The very same. The son of that pious sonofabitch Robert. I fell from my horse and was about to be speared with a lance when you rode up and did the bastard in with your battle-axe. You pulled me onto your charger—saved my life."

Gunnvor lowered his head, stared at his feet. "If it had not been me, sire, it would have been someone else."

"Not true, friend," Brondolf said. He reached out and touched Gunnvor on his knee. "I would not have lived to sit in front of this fine fire, drinking this stout ale, if it had not been for your quick thinking. But enough of such talk. I want to tell you what is on my mind and I don't want you to interrupt until I am through."

He waited for Gunnvor to nod his assent before continuing.

"Like I said, I'm tired. Weary of all the fighting. I have heard that far to the south there is a great sea whose water is clear, warm, and deep. Where the climate is temperate and the sands are white. It is where I wish to spend my remaining days. Gunnvor, I long for the comfort of a beautiful woman who loves me and will bear me a son. A son whom I can teach to build a boat, to sail, to hunt. I long to sit at night with my woman and count the stars. I desire a life now of leisure and happiness, not constant warring. My bones ache in this cold miserable place and our home in the north is no different. Isn't it odd that a Norseman would grow to hate the cold? Yes, I wish to spend my remaining days bathed in warmth with my wife and son. Is that too much to ask?"

Gunnvor listened to his warlord as instructed—without interrupting. He set the drinking horn on the hearth and leaned forward, his eyes looking deep into the eyes of the man opposite him. Brondolf's eyes were moist.

"My lord, your dedication to our cause and to me and your men has earned you the right to do whatever your heart desires. You have fought well and earned the respect of us all. You are more than our jarl, our leader. You have cared for us, seen to our needs, doctored our hurts, lifted our spirits. For myself, and I believe I can speak for all, we do not wish to see you go. But if you must, may the goddess Freyja go with you."

"There will be time for a few more raids, Gunnvor, while I fill our coffers with gold and other treasures. And when the time is at hand, you will take my place as jarl."

"My lord," Gunnvor exclaimed. "I am speechless. I do not—"

Brondolf stood and Gunnvor followed suit.

"Come, come, my friend," he said. "You have earned the right to succeed me. Now embrace me and let's go make merry with our men."

As the two men embraced, a lump formed in Brondolf's throat.

CHAPTER 4

An early spring day dawned bright and warm with a cloudless sky. Hugo and the men of Lochwald gathered in the road in front of the blacksmith stable waiting for mayor Giroldus to organize them into work details. The tools he had fabricated lay in a pile at his feet. Oriel had risen early and fixed a large breakfast of eggs, porridge, dried fruit, and toasted bread for him and Geffrey, which they washed down with small beer, a thin and weak cousin of mead drunk soon after brewing. Hugo wore his linen trousers and advised his son to do the same for it would be hot and sweaty work.

Hugo was a man short and squat in stature but otherwise big in heart. He first saw Oriel when she walked along the River Skye picking berries. She was only eleven years old at the time but Hugo remembered that her long brown hair and eyes captured his heart. During the times he returned home to visit his mentor, Hugo extolled the girl's beauty and mentioned that one day he hoped for enough courage to approach her. The opportunity came when she stopped at his blacksmith stable and inquired if he could repair an axe that belonged to her father. She carried the heavy axe head with her and as Hugo studied what it would require to fix the axe he summoned the courage to chat with her. Until she became embarrassed and abruptly left the stable.

After that day, whenever he saw Oriel or passed her on the road, he waved and tried to engage her in conversation, usually without success. Hugo talked to other girls in Lochwald, even went in long walks with one, but none ever possessed Oriel's beauty or quiet charm.

One Sunday after mass, it was pure coincidence that they walked together back to their homes. Oriel looked different, a radiant glow on her cheeks. Again, he attempted to converse with her and, as if a miracle happened, she responded. They chatted all the way to her house. Hugo was overjoyed. And from that Sunday onward, they became friends, bonded by a mutual respect and a love of nature. They took longs walks together along the river.

And eventually Oriel became his wife.

Mayor Giroldus arrived and divided the men into four groups—one to venture into the forest and fell trees to be used as timbers, a second to excavate rocks, the third to begin digging post holes on the perimeter of the wall, and finally men to mix the mortar that would be used—a mixture of sand, clay, and lime. As the men began their chores, Geffrey left for the stable and his work.

Hugo was a member of the group designated to dig postholes. It was hard, backbreaking work but he and his fellow workers went about their tasks with good humor, singing or telling stories as they labored under the bright sun. He figured that in order to build a circular wall completely around Lochwald it would require several months' of heavy labor. Most of the families had to eke out a living so construction of the wall would have to be conformed around that necessity. It meant that they could not work on the wall continuously until completed. Could it be done before the next Norse raid? Hugo had no idea but if they didn't begin the wall would never be finished.

The construction plan was to sink timbers several feet into the earth and use them as a framework against which to lay the stones that would be mortared together for added strength. It was a typical stone wall used by many peasant villages in the surrounding area.

Hugo worked shoulder to shoulder alongside his friend, Ives, the village priest, whose small church everyone attended on Sunday for Mass. They dug holes two feet deep and arranged them ten feet apart. Hugo paused to wipe the sweat from his face.

"Ives," he said, leaning in his spade, "I thought you did a fine job at the funerals yesterday. It was a day none of us will forget."

The priest stopped his labors, took a deep breath.

"It is the worst tragedy to befall Lochwald in its history. We and the families of the victims will have to deal with the aftermath, Hugo, for a very long time."

"We are fortunate to have a man of your persuasion in our village."

Ives's smile was a weak one. "I only hope I'm up to the task," he said.

"You have been a tremendous asset to our small village. We are thankful for your presence here."

The two men returned to the dirty work of digging postholes stopping now and then for a drink of cool water. Rosalind strolled among the men with a wooden bucket of water drawn from the village well near the center of town.

Hugo watched her walk up and down the line of workers and understood his son's ardor for the young lady. That she was fair and beautiful there was no doubt. He could sympathize with her father's natural protective instincts toward her for Hugo knew his son was not Rosalind's only suitor. But she seemed determined to love Geffrey and that fact pleased him and his wife. Besides being the most beautiful young woman in Lochwald, Rosalind had a head on her shoulders. His son had met his match where intelligence was concerned.

ຊາຄາ

Oriel labored over the stone hearth cooking the evening meal of venison stew. The previous week while on a
hunting trip north of Lochwald, Hugo and Geffrey had
killed the small deer. She stirred the pot and added the
potatoes, carrots, and onions from her garden. After tast-
ing the stew, she replaced the cover on the pot and sat
next to the fire.

She was terrified when the marauders came. She was
sleeping on her cot and the sudden clamor of the raid
jolted her awake, her pulse pounding. It brought back
memories of a night long ago when she was a small child
and the Franks raided her family's village to the east of
Lochwald. She and her parents escaped being slaughtered
but her older brother was not so lucky. A Frank spear cut
him down when he ran outside to view the commotion.

As a family, they moved to Lochwald where she met
Hugo. Soon after Geffrey was born, her parents died, first
her father, followed a year later by her mother. Hugo was
sweet during her grief months, bringing her flowers and
sweets almost every week.

Geffrey was her pride and joy for he had grown into a
fine young man, respectful of his elders with a good
sense of work. Part of the boy's character, she knew, was
due to Hugo's constant attention but she had a strong
sense of her contributions. She worked diligently to in-
struct her son with reading and writing skills and a fun-
damental knowledge of arithmetic. Geffrey was quick to
listen, slow to speak, sensitive, caring, inquisitive. All
qualities she knew she had worked hard to instill in the
boy. And to his credit, Geffrey responded by becoming a
man of whom she was proud.

Lochwald was such a peaceful quiet village until the
raid. The thought of such carnage never before worried

her, but now the possibility of another Norse attack on them sent her mind reeling and produced an uneasiness in her. A certain disquiet settled upon her soul like an iron weight, pushing her down into despair. She had an unnerving feeling that she would see the raiders again.

Oriel shook off the depressing thoughts and returned to her stew. Hugo and Geffrey would be home soon and both would be starving. Her boy had grown up.

Now he was making weapons so all the villagers could defend themselves. Her son. It was hard to believe. She must be getting older.

One day he would want a wife.

And she would lose him to another woman.

ოჳოჳ

Geffrey pumped the bellows until the forge glowed white hot. In this way additional oxygen was forced into the forge causing the charcoal to burn hotter. One of his duties since he began his apprenticeship was to light the charcoal each morning and get the coals to glowing. Only then could the wrought iron be heated and shaped into the various implements.

The term, *wrought iron*, meant worked iron. From early times, wrought iron was the most commonly used form of malleable iron. This meant that unlike cast iron, wrought iron was not as brittle. Wrought iron had a lower carbon content, which made it malleable, easier to weld. At its peak, wrought iron was used in the manufacturing of nearly everything all over the world.

Due to its malleability and toughness, wrought iron was coveted all over Normandie. In those times, blacksmiths were considered to be as equally important as the local doctor because as the doctor kept the people healthy, the blacksmith kept the town moving. To many people, the blacksmith's ability to transform a seemingly coarse, hard material into something of breathtaking beauty was magical.

Wrought iron essentially was considered a charcoal iron. Charcoal iron was primarily used from the Iron Age and produced through a charcoal fire.

One of the first production methods of iron was with the use of bloomeries. A bloomery was a sort of furnace with a pit and chimney, and featured stone or clay walls for heat resistance. Clay pipes entered near the bottom of the pit allowing airflow either from natural source or through a bellows. Once a bloomery was filled with charcoal and iron ore, it was lit and air was forced through the pipes fueling the fire and heating the mixture to just below the melting point for iron. This forced the impurities to melt and run off while the carbon monoxide from the charcoal reduced the ore to iron in a sponge-like mass. This material was then forged with hammers, further removing impurities in the process.

Geffrey took several pieces of iron and placed them in the forge and while they were heating assembled his tools, tongs, and hammer. He laid them by the steel anvil that weighed over two hundred livres. A yellow-white glow took shape in the center of the charcoal and the iron was lost in the glare. Geffrey couldn't look directly at the glare—it was too intense.

A couple of minutes later, he picked up the tongs and withdrew the iron bar. The end now glowed bright yellow and spit sparks—the temperature well over two thousand degrees. Geffrey laid the metal over the anvil's edge and picked up the heavy blacksmith hammer. A few whacks were all it took to put a nice bend in the bar. He utilized the basics of the blacksmith's age-old craft— bending, flattening, twisting, tapering, and upsetting. Striking a bar to thicken and enlarge its hot end. Periodically, he dropped the piece into a bucket of water to cool and harden it. After the sizzle and steam dissipated, he inspected his handiwork then began the process anew. It was hot difficult work but Geffrey enjoyed seeing the results of his labors take shape.

When the sun was high overhead, Rosalind stopped by the stable with bread, cheese, and a metal tankard of ale. She sat and watched him eat.

"I still don't understand it, Geffrey," she said. "I mean where did the attackers come from? They certainly didn't look like us. They must be foreign invaders to our land."

"I have asked father the same questions," Geffrey said between mouthfuls. "He told me the Norsemen come from the far north. Sweden, Denmark, and Icelandia. They left their homes and sailed across the seas in long-ships to land on the shores of Briton and other parts of Europe and Normandie. They come to raid and pillage, taking whatever treasures they can steal, murdering those who get in their way. Butchers, all of them."

"I have heard them called berserkers," she said in her usual soft voice. "My father says the fury of the berserkers would start with chills and teeth chattering and give way to a purpling of the face as they literally became hot-headed, culminating in a great, uncontrollable rage accompanied by grunts and howls. They bite into their shields and gnaw at their skin before launching into battle, indiscriminately injuring, maiming, and killing anything in their path."

Geffrey nodded.

"Yes, I have heard that too. My father has often said the meaning of the word, berserker, could mean a bare shirt, that is, naked. He says berserkers, as a mark of ferocity and invincibility, are said to fight without requiring armor. The word, however, may also mean bear-shirt, reflective of the shape and nature of the bear assumed by these warriors. More literally, it may refer to protective bearskins that such warriors may have worn into battle. Father said when the berserker rage was upon him, a berserker is thought of as a sort of were-bear or werewolf, part man, part beast, which is neither fully human nor fully animal."

"Oh, that is so creepy," Rosalind said. She gathered the leftovers of Geffrey's lunch and put them in the burlap sack she brought them in. She leaned down and pecked him in the cheek. He blushed.

"I'll be going," she said. "I must get back to the work. My job is to bring water to the men."

"How is the work progressing?" Geffrey said, standing next to her.

"They have got the postholes dug for one side of the wall and a large pile of stones has been excavated. Men have pulled large timbers from the forest. Their work seems to go well."

"Father says it may take several months to complete. With God on our side maybe it will be finished before another raid."

"I heard the men talking about a gate. They were arguing about how large it should be and how to construct it."

Geffrey laughed at her remark.

"Our men argue about everything," he said. "It is their nature, in their blood. Without an argument nothing would be built properly."

"It just seems such a waste of time."

Again, Geffrey laughed. "It usually is."

They stood together for a while, Geffrey lost in the green opalescence of Rosalind's eyes. Finally, he spoke.

"Roz," he said. "Why does your father hate me so? Can he not see that I would make a good husband to you? When I finish my apprenticeship I will make good wages."

Rosalind smiled softly, reached out, and touched Geffrey on his cheek.

"It's not that he hates you," she said. "It's just that he doesn't see either of us as adults. And it's going to take some time for him to accept the fact that I am now a woman and will soon be taking a husband. Sometimes I think he cannot remember when he and mother were courting. It's difficult for him to understand that his daughter feels things as an adult."

"The man cannot remember how he felt at my age?" Geffrey said with an indignant edge to his voice.

"He cannot." She laughed. "But time will mellow him. Mother will see to that."

Rosalind returned to her chores and Geffrey went back to fashioning weapons.

CHAPTER 5

Rosalind had a suitor in addition to Geffrey. Robert was the stonecutter's son and he was Rosalind's age. He worked with his father at the local quarry learning the stonemason trade. The quarry was located several hours by ox-drawn cart from Lochwald on the far side of the River Skye and deep within the forest. After it was discovered quite by accident by a band of roving minstrels when they passed through the village a number of years earlier, Robert's father learned of the quarry, moved to Lochwald and began cutting the stone into useable ones for building. For the past fifteen years he was engaged in his business and two years earlier Robert began helping and learning to become a stonemason himself.

Rosalind knew, as well as everyone in Lochwald, that Father Ives was hoping to build a small cathedral in the village and in all likelihood would employ Robert and his father for the stonework. That meant that he would have a steady source of income for many years, a fact that her father often reminded her. Even though she loved Geffrey and had pledged herself to him, her father didn't care for the blacksmith's son. His eyes lit up however, when he talked of Robert and his promising future.

Masons in Normandie were responsible for building some of region's most notable buildings. Highly skilled craftsmen, their trade was most frequently used in the building of castles, churches, and cathedrals. They belonged to a guild. However, a mason's guild was not linked to just one town as the members of the guild had to move to where building was required. The Mason's Guild was an international one and throughout Normandie and Europe the guild was sometimes referred to as the Free Masons as free stone was the name of stone that was commonly used by masons. It was a soft stone that allowed the masons to complete intricate carvings.

Masons tended to lead nomadic lives. They went where there was employment. Other tradesmen could effectively stay where they were as there was enough trade for their skill to allow them to settle. However, masons had to move on to their next source of employment once a building had been completed—and that could be many miles away.

A mason who was at the top of his trade was a master mason. However, a master mason, by title, was the man who had overall charge of a building site and master masons would work under this person. A master mason also had charge over carpenters, glaziers, and others. In fact, everybody who worked on a building site was under the supervision of the master mason. He would work in what was known as the mason's lodge.

All-important building sites would have such a building that served as a workshop and a drawing office from which all the work on the building site was organized. Anyone who arrived at the building site and claimed that they were a master mason would be tested by the master mason and by master masons already working on the site. By doing this they ensured that quality was maintained— and that they would have a good chance of future building work.

It was the end of the workday and Rosalind walked to her home with all the men. The east side of the wall was about half complete. She surmised it was around eight feet high and two feet thick. What they had accomplished in several weeks looked impressive.

Robert fell into step beside her. His clothes were covered with dirt.

"What do you think of our work so far?" he said, smiling. He matched her hurried walk step for step.

"It's really tall," she said. Rosalind hurried on, picking up the pace of her walking, hoping he would fall back with the men. Unfortunately, he did not.

"Yes," he said. "And my father and I dug the most stones and chiseled them into shape. If it weren't for us the blasted wall could never be built." Robert's eyes lit up with this pronouncement. He laughed.

Rosalind didn't care for Robert's haughty demeanor. It was his most repulsive feature. That and the fact that he smelled like ox dung most of the time. She knew he tended to the family ox each morning, the one that his father used to pull their cart but he could at least bathe now and then. No matter how much Geffrey labored at the hot forge and sweat, he always smelled of lye soap when she ventured close enough to notice. She knew it was because his mother insisted that he bathe regularly. She didn't understand Robert's lack of training in this matter. Personal hygiene was important to her. She couldn't possibly marry someone who smelled of dung.

"Yes, yes, Robert," she said over her shoulder as she ventured ahead of him. "You always seem to have a high opinion of yourself. I suspect you come by it quite naturally."

"Father and I are the only stonecutters in the area," Robert said. "It is only logical that we dig and cut the stones for the wall. No one else has the skills to do it."

"Well," she said, "I'm sure that is important. But the carpenters and blacksmiths have a vital role as well."

"Blacksmiths?" Robert said. His tone sounded conde-
scending. "The blacksmith is only digging holes. Not
much skill involved in that."

Rosalind felt her cheeks burn at the obvious slur but
she continued to walk.

"Geffrey is making tools and weapons in his father's
forge," she said, feeling an urge to come to Geffrey's defense. "He is helping with the wall and working to give
us weapons to defend ourselves. It is much needed
work."

Robert laughed and she felt her cheeks tingle with anger.

"Geffrey will never amount to anything, Rosalind," he
said. "When he finishes his apprenticeship, he will leave
Lochwald. I have heard him speak of doing so. After the
wall is complete and work on the cathedral is begun, I
will be here for a number of years. We will be able to see
each other for a long time."

They came to her house and she saw Geffrey standing
next to the picket fence that surrounded the small yard
and garden. She ran to him, smiling. Over her shoulder,
she noticed Robert walk on toward his own home, a
scowl on his face. She tossed her head, her curls bouncing, as she came to stand by Geffrey.

"I see you were walking with that little fopdoodle,"
Geffrey said. "I'm surprised you would stoop so low,
Roz."

Rosalind turned toward him, her green eyes flashing.
"You are not to tell me who I can walk with and with
whom I cannot, Geffrey. You are not so high and mighty
yourself, you know."

She could sense that her words stung him, an unexpected outpouring of indignation, but she would not have
him think he was lord over her. Just because he desired
her hand in marriage wasn't reason enough for her to al-

ways bend to his will. She wasn't going to allow him to dictate to her with whom she could associate.

"I—I—didn't—" he stammered.

"It's okay, Geffrey. Just please don't think you can control me like that. I won't stand for it."

"I'm sorry, Roz. I didn't mean to offend you. It's that boy is such a fonkin, a little fool. He thinks he's better than everybody, including me. I can't stand him." Geffrey's tone was conciliatory and at the same time, apologetic.

Roz decided to let it rest with that and went inside, leaving Geffrey to contemplate her words.

ℰↃℰↃ

As he watched Rosalind skip away toward her house and waiting Geffrey, acid bile belched into Robert's throat. He couldn't bear to see his girlfriend talking with that churl, a young man content with pounding metal with heavy hammers. He, Robert, was a true craftsman, one destined to become a master mason, one who someday would command the construction of large and beautiful buildings. Growing up in Lochwald and watching his father work the nearby quarry, he had seen the family's status increase. When he finished his apprenticeship in a couple of years and was able to court Rosalind properly, he felt certain she would see that he was the better man. Better than Geffrey.

He was an expert with the tools of the stonemason—pitcher, punch, claw, chisel, lump hammer, and the mallet. The pitcher was the first tool used for roughing out a shape from a stone slab; the punch was used for punching down the stone to a desired height or dimension and was a quick way to eliminate unnecessary stone; the claw was used to bring the surface down to the desired depth, before the final step; the chisel was the final tool used for smoothing the surface and was also used to etch mason's marks to identify individuals so they could be paid for work completed. The lump hammer was used for the initial, heavy work involved in pitching and punching while the mallet, made of hickory, beech, or other hardwood, was used with a lighter touch to finish the stone with a straight chisel.

Robert was learning the complex work with instruments of the stonemason's trade. The compass, or dividers used for configuring arcs and intricate moldings. Artists like his father sometimes depicted Christ as the Supreme Craftsman holding a compass. The set square—the simple tool that ensured that the walls of buildings remained square and true at ninety-degree angles. Finally, the straight edge.

On completion of a flat stone, success or failure depended upon the straight edge lying perfectly flat across the face of the stone. So the use of this tool was a litmus test of the stonecutter's skill. If spaces appeared between the straight edge and the stone, it was evident the stonecutter had cut too deep. If the straight edge seesawed, more cutting was required.

So, it seemed to Robert that he possessed or would soon possess the knowledge and skills that would make him a desirable mate for Rosalind. His future was brighter than the smithy apprentice's future and he was confident that not only would Roz see him and his talents for what they were but her father would also.

A thought struck him.

Win the baker, win Rosalind.

He decided that he would see the baker the following day.

e∽e∽

In the somber, gray light before sunrise, Brondolf's warriors trudged to their longhouse and followed their jarl in his flowing white robes. Guided by the fiery luminance of torches borne by a handful of thralls, the column moved in respectful silence along a narrow path that snaked between the cultivated fields and up the gentle slope to their destination. The ancient oaks loomed dark and ominous against the silvery-gray of the lightening sky as the warriors, still silent, filled the longhouse.

It was early morning of the spring equinox and Brondolf's Norsemen gathered in the longhouse. The occasion was the *blót* sacrifice to *Wödan*, to give thanks for his generosity in battle and to beseech his favors in all future endeavors. It was always important for the Norsemen to be on good terms with the gods. In order to ensure that this was the case they made blót sacrifices. The blót was an exchange, in which they sacrificed to the gods in order to get something back in return—the gods' goodwill regarding weather, fertility, or luck in battle.

A great fire blazed in the hearth at the front of the longhouse while the huge carcass of a bear roasted over its flames. Fat from the animal dripped into the embers producing a tantalizing aroma that filled the longhouse. The animal's hide and fur hung from a nearby pole, a symbol the beast's great strength. Brondolf stood in front of the fire surveying his fellow warriors. He wore an arm ring smeared with the blood of the bear.

"Here me, my friends," he intoned with a great voice. "We are gathered here this morning to give thanks to our god, Wödan, and ask his blessing upon us. As we beseech the blessings of our god, let each of us offer a silent prayer of thanksgiving that he has blessed us and protected us."

With that, Gunnvor took a large bowl filled with the blood of the bear and circulated among the warriors. He dipped a juniper twig into the bowel and splattered each man with the blood. As he did so, Brondolf repeated the age-old refrain.

"From the gods to the Earth to us,
from us to the Earth to the gods.
A gift for a gift.
Hail to the gods and goddesses!"

When Gunnvor was finished sprinkling each man with blood, they held their drinking horns while he filled them full with mead. When all had a full horn, Brondolf raised his with an outstretched hand. His men followed his lead and did likewise.

Once more Brondolf's thick heavy voice boomed through the hall.

"Hear our prayers, O god Wödan.
We humbly beseech you
To look down from Valhalla
Upon your humble servants
With mercy.
All-Father, lord of wisdom,
war and death,
mighty god of all gods
God of gods, lord of earth and sky,
giver and taker of life,
We pledge our fealty with honor
And courage.
In return for your gift of wisdom
We pledge new lands
And new peoples
For your kingdom on earth.
Wödan, May the lifeblood of our
peoples' enemy please and strengthen you."

The prayer finished, after Brondolf drank his horn down in one continuous gulp he had one last word.

"To your feet, my people, and witness our offerings to the All-Father, who has given his sign of acceptance."

With the final pronouncement, the hall erupted in revelry, a raucous noise filled the longhouse. Great quantities of mead flowed freely. Brondolf doffed his white robes and along with his men feasted on the roasted bear. The blot sacrifice was completed.

A gift for a gift.

య౨య

The Norsemen influenced many changes in Europe, but the most important change occurred because of Europe's influence on Scandinavia. They evolved from a polytheistic society to a monotheistic society within three centuries of the introduction of Christianity. Conversion from the old ways occurred as Scandinavians in the Norse age traveled and traded more with Western Europeans and the British Isles. Christianity had already taken a hold in Europe by the time the Norsemen began trade and political relations. Little by little the Old Norse religion was replaced with Christianity until finally at the start of the eleventh century Christianity dominated the old Scandinavian ways.

Iceland was discovered in the year 870 AD by a Norwegian king named Ingolf Arnarson. He gave it the name Reykjavík. The people of Iceland were mainly farmers, sheepherders, and fishermen. They gained more wealth once people began arriving from Norway. The most famous Icelander and Norse explorer was Erik the Red. He was born in Iceland of Norwegian decent. He was a humble man, a farmer, hunter, and fisherman like most of the Icelandic population. Although he was well liked by many, he had enemies. After feeling he had been cheated, Erik took the law into his own hands and murdered a man. For his crime he was put to trial, found guilty. And for punishment he was exiled from Iceland for three years. While exiled, Erik gathered a crew of men and set off to sea.

His plan was to find and explore lands he had heard of west of Iceland. So he ventured west and eventually ran into land. Erik took full advantage of his exile. In his three years he explored every fjord and bay on the southwest coast of the vast unknown country. Upon return to Iceland he named the new found land Greenland. In Iceland he spread word of the lush growth, vast amounts of land, natural resources, and prime fisheries. An important advantage for settlement of Greenland was the region Erik explored was uninhabited. He attempted to entice others to come with him and settle Greenland with the promise of becoming wealthier.

Erik successfully recruited eight hundred new settlers in twenty-five ships to start the emigration to Greenland. Of the twenty-five ships fourteen of them completed the journey. These settlers formed the two largest populations of Greenland, the Western and Eastern Settlements. Waves of other Icelanders and Scandinavians would come and continue to create population growth in Greenland. In 1000 AD, Leif Eriksson was sent to Greenland by the king of Norway to convert it to Christianity. In their low draft boats, Scandinavians who were to be called Norsemen ventured out with swords and axes on quick raids along Europe's shorelines or up rivers. They were back to sea before help could arrive, and with little or no resistance to their assaults they were encouraged to launch more and bigger assaults.

The Norsemen were highly skilled navigators and traders. They responded to economic growth in their own country accompanied with an increase in population, and they were aware of the wealth that existed elsewhere and were inspired to go out and grab some of it. In addition, they were aware of the wealth being stored in monasteries and churches, and these were their usual targets, conveniently located on rivers and near the coast. Most often, they returned home happy with the prestige that their loot inspired, and the success of them inspired even more raiding. The Norsemen send word that land was available abroad. With the growth in population having eliminated the availability of land at home more Scandinavians were willing to venture to distant areas for the purpose of settling down.

The Norwegians kept pushing west, sometimes merely raiding, sometimes also setting up settlements, to the Scottish islands, to Ireland, to northern England. They occupied the Faeroe Islands, Iceland, and parts of Greenland. They pushed south through England, into France, down to the Mediterranean.

The Danes expanded westward along the North Sea coast toward France. They fanned out within France—Paris was sacked—then they went south raiding deep into Spain. Pressing through the straits of Gibraltar and into the Mediterranean, they sacked Luna, a small town in northern Italy, apparently thinking it was Rome. The Swedes traded and colonized around the Baltic. They sailed up Russia's rivers and became the first rulers of the Kievan Russian state then made their way to Constantinople and the Orient. Once there many served as the bodyguards of the Byzantine emperors.

CHAPTER 6

T he work on the wall progressed at a slow pace. The men of Lochwald had their own businesses and work that needed to be done in order that their families might eat. Work shifts on the wall were sporadic and only a handful of men at a time labored on it. The cold of early spring evolved into warmer weather and longer days so Geffrey and his father hoped the work would proceed more efficiently. Digging in the thawed ground was much easier than during the previous month when the earth was still partially frozen.

The Easter Vigil, presided over by Father Ives, was the most sacred of church ceremonies, with a whole host of its own rites—the great fire, the Paschal candle, the singing of the Exsultet, endless readings from Scripture, and particularly, the baptisms of a few of Lochwald converts. After the prayers, the Liturgy of the Eucharist continued as usual. This was the first Mass of Easter Day. During the Eucharist, the newly baptized received Holy Communion for the first time. The prayers offered by Father Ives were ones beseeching the Almighty's aid in building the wall.

The week following Easter saw work on the wall pick up. Most of the men turned out each day putting their backs into the difficult labor involved in the digging, constructing, and mortaring the stones into a structure that would offer them protection from future raids. Working alone in the blacksmith stable, Geffrey forged a num-

ber of spear points and axe blades on which the woodcutter could fashion handles or staves. One morning he was
stoking the forge thinking of Rosalind. She had been
somewhat distant from him the past few weeks and he
wandered if her ardor for him was diminishing. It worried him for he had seen her on a few occasions walking
with Robert.

A shout rang out.

It came from the wall.

Geffrey stopped pumping the bellows and ran out of
the stable onto the road. At the far end of the village a
crowd gathered, shouts filled the air. People hurried from
their homes and businesses toward the construction site.
A sudden panic filled him. His father. Had something
happened to him? Or one of the men?

He bolted to the scene of confusion, legs churning,
lungs burning. When he arrived at the wall he saw two
men lower another man down from the top of it. The
man's left leg was askew and he winced in obvious pain.
His father was one of the men helping support the broken
leg.

"Father," he shouted in an excited voice. "What happened?" On closer inspection, he could see the man was
Giroldus, Lochwald's mayor.

"Giroldus slipped while he was on top of the wall,"
Hugo said, holding the mayor's leg as he was laid on the
ground. "His foot got lodged between the stones when he
fell. His leg is broken."

Giroldus lay on his back moaning, his leg twisted at a
horrible angle. His eyes were glazed over, tears ran down
his cheeks. Ansel kneeled beside him cradling the
mayor's head in his arms.

"Let's get him to my stable," Hugo said. "Geffrey, run
home and bring the bottle of pain reliever that your
mother brewed and bring it to the stable." Turning to the

other men, he said, "Let's go and be gentle with him. Help me support his leg as we go."

Geffrey ran home and gave the news to his mother and what his father requested. She retrieved a small earthen bottle containing the liquid from the cupboard next to the hearth.

"Be careful with this," she said. "It only takes a small amount. Give him too much and he will become delirious."

Geffrey nodded his understanding and ran to the stable with the bottle. When he arrived he found Giroldus lying on the floor of the stable, his father kneeling beside the man's broken leg. The man was still in obvious pain, opening and closing his fists, writhing his head back and forth.

Hugo looked at his son, smiled weakly.

"Have him take some of the liquid," he said in a low, matter-of-fact tone.

Father Ives pushed to the front of the crowd gathered around Hugo and Giroldus.

"What's in that stuff?" he said.

"Equal amounts of radish, bishopwort, garlic, wormwood, helenium, henbane, and hollowleek. Those are boiled with the root of the mandrake plant. It will kill the pain." Hugo motioned to Geffrey to give Giroldus sips from the earthen bottle.

"That is the brew of witches!" Father Ives shouted. "The Church forbids its use. By all that is holy, Hugo, do not give Giroldus that vile concoction."

"Father Ives," Hugo said in a quiet voice. The men gathered around Giroldus looked furtively between him and the priest. Geffrey watched in quiet amazement. Surely, his father would not go against the wishes of the Church. "Father Ives," Hugo continued, "I respect your opinion in all things theological and related to churchly affairs. But when it comes to relieving pain and suffering, you are no more qualified than anyone else. Now stand aside and let me get on with the task of setting this man's leg." He nodded once again for Geffrey to proceed.

With a trembling hand, he held the bottle to Giroldus's lips and allowed the brown liquid to drizzle into the man's mouth. The mayor licked his lips several times and swallowed.

"A little more, Geffrey," his father coaxed.

Geffrey noticed that Father Ives had disappeared from the throng gathered within the stable. He was nowhere to be seen. Geffrey held the bottle to the mayor's lips once more and allowed the liquid to run into the man's mouth. It must be bitter, Geffrey thought, for Giroldus smacked his lips for a full minute.

After what seemed an eternity to Geffrey, Giroldus ceased his moaning and writhing and lay still on the earthen floor. It seemed a miracle. It was the first time he remembered seeing the potion work on someone, and its effects left him bewildered. Did roots and plants have magical powers? Maybe the father was right. Maybe the potion his mother brewed was the concoction of witches that lived deep within the forest. And his father had done the unthinkable—he had scorned the advice and command of the village priest. Surely, there would be repercussions from Hugo's heresy.

Hugo grabbed Giroldus's angled broken leg and while several men held the mayor's shoulders and hips, with a quick jerk snapped the lower leg back into position. Giroldus let out a loud grunt but soon settled back into his deep sleep.

"Fine," Hugo said. "Bring me several thin boards and some strips of cloth so I can fashion a splint for his leg."

When a man returned with the requested items, Hugo placed the boards on either side of the leg and wrapped it with the cloth strips, starting at the ankle and ending above the knee. When he was finished he settled back in his haunches and studied his handiwork. The mayor's wife pushed into the crowd to kneel next to her husband. Her tear-stained face turned to Hugo.

"He is fine, Anne. I just fixed his broken leg, that is all. He is sleeping now and will be all right in a month or two. We will carry him home and put him to bed. He needs to remain in bed for a week then can be up on crutches I will ask the woodcutter to make for him."

The men carried Giroldus to his home and placed him on his bed. His grateful wife gave each man a tankard of ale and kept crossing herself until they left her alone with her husband.

Most medieval ideas about medicine were based on those of the ancient work, namely the work of Greek physicians Galen and Hippocrates. Their ideas set out a theory of the human body relating to the four elements— earth, air, fire and water—and to four bodily humors— blood, phlegm, yellow bile and black bile. It was believed that health could be maintained or restored by balancing the humors, and by regulating air, diet, exercise, sleep, evacuation, and emotion. Doctors also often advised risky invasive procedures like bloodletting.

Medical knowledge derived from antique theory was largely confined to monasteries and the highly educated. For ordinary people, especially those outside towns, it would have been difficult to access professional practitioners. Those in need of medical assistance might instead turn to local people who had medical knowledge, derived from folk traditions and practical experience.

Medieval astrologers believed that the movements of the stars influenced numerous things on earth, from the weather and the growth of crops to the personalities of newborn babies and the inner workings of the human body. Doctors often carried around special almanacs containing illustrated star charts, allowing them to check the positions of the stars before making a diagnosis. Many of these almanacs included illustrations, helping to explain complicated ideas to patients. The diagrams were intended to explain how the astrological formations rule over each part of the body.

In medieval Europe, medicine generally operated within the context of the Christian Church. Hospitals, which cared for the elderly and the ill, were often run by religious orders, which could maintain infirmaries for their own members and operate hospitals for others. Where professional medicine could not help, the faithful often turned to saints, and visited saints' shrines in the hope of miraculous cures. The sick might also turn to the occult—the dividing line between magic and medicine was not always obvious in medieval sources, and many medical practitioners used occult knowledge to heal the sick either by natural means using herbs to treat or prevent illness or ward off danger. As a last resort, family of the sick might turn to demonic magic, with the hope of using diabolical forces to intervene and heal their loved one.

Back in the stable, a curious Geffrey asked his father about the brew.

"I learned it from a traveling apothecary years ago before I married your mother. It is from the science of plants and roots, Geffrey, that man learns how to lessen suffering."

"But Father Ives said the brew was the work of witches. I heard him later. He told others it was the work of Satan."

"Satan doesn't inhabit plants, Geffrey. God would not allow it."

"But he said Satan can invade a person's spirit forcing them to do evil deeds."

"Son, while you were in the stable, did you see anything that amounted to evil?"

Geffrey shook his head.

"Of course not," Hugo said. "We relieved Giroldus's suffering so I could set his broken leg, that is all. The Church assumes that diseases of the body result from sins of the soul. It encourages its flock in this misplaced belief. For that reason, many people do not bother with medicines that can help them. Instead, they seek relief from their ailments through meditation, prayer, and pilgrimages. They pray for supernatural relief of their suffering. For the most part, I do not hold to such outmoded ideas, son."

"It's not heresy then?"

Hugo laughed. "Heresy? I think not. Do you not think God placed these plants and herbs on earth for us to use for our benefit? How noble to relieve pain and suffering through God's gift of nature. And do I not accept the Church's position on sin and morality. Heresy? Ha!"

Later that day when Geffrey sat alone on the banks of the River Skye he thought about what his father had said. And Father Ives's words.

According to the priest, sin consisted of disobedience to the known will of God. The first example of sin described in the Bible came in the story of Adam and Eve, who were placed by God in the Garden of Eden. They chose to disobey God and, as a result, were expelled from his presence and condemned to live in a harsh and inhospitable world.

Father Ives taught the doctrine of original sin, the belief that all human beings share in collective guilt as a result of the disobedience of Adam and Eve in the Garden of Eden. This resulted in the Fall of Humankind, together with an ongoing predisposition to disobey God. Everyone, therefore, needed to be cleansed through baptism, to learn to resist temptation and to live in such a way that, when death came, they would be ready to face God's judgment on their thoughts, attitudes and actions.

Celebrating mass, also known as the Eucharist, was an important sacrament. By taking part in this, believers symbolically shared in the victory paid for, and won by Christ over the power of sin. Through this they could receive the grace, or the undeserved gift, of salvation.

Thinking on it in this way, there was nothing in Father Ives's sermons that would indicate what his father did by offering the potion to Giroldus was against Church teaching. So where did the Father come by the idea that the brew was of the witch's own hand? In all his years Geffrey had never heard his father speak about such matters in such strong language. Was he saying the Church was wrong? Was that not in itself a sin?

Geffrey was thinking on these things when he noticed Rosalind walking along the river's edge, a basket of flowers in her hand. He called out and waved to her. She saw him, waved back, and soon was sitting on the rock beside him.

"It's beautiful here," she said, showing him the basket of flowers she had collected.

"This is my favorite place on earth," Geffrey replied. He pointed to a small waterfall a ways downstream. "I came here often when I was younger. There is a pool of large trout at the base of that waterfall."

Rosalind's look turned serious. "I heard what happened to the mayor," she said. "How your father defied Father Ives in treating him. Something about a magic potion."

"It was not magic, Roz. It was simple science. The effects of medicinal plants that father learned from an apothecary many years ago."

"Some of the townspeople are calling your father a heretic. They are saying that Hugo should be expelled from the Church."

"Excommunicated?" Geffrey's pulse began to pound in his temples at the news. How could people be so stupid? "All he did was set the poor mayor's leg, Roz. He didn't blaspheme the Church, God, or Christ. For heaven's sake are people really that ignorant?"

"Oh, Geffrey," Rosalind said. "You mustn't swear like that, saying 'for heaven's sake.'"

"Tell me, Roz. When I gave that potion to mayor Giroldus, it was as if his pain went away. He quieted down, hardly moaned at all when father straightened his broken leg. A few moments earlier the man was in great pain. So, I ask you—do you believe it was the work of the Devil to relieve his suffering? Because that is what we did."

The sparkle in Rosalind's green eyes dimmed as she contemplated Geffrey's question. He could see she was perplexed by his question for she gazed vacantly into the crystal clear waters of the river rushing past them. After a few moments, she answered.

"To lessen suffering, Geffrey, is a noble thing. But to do it without the aid of the Church? I don't know about that. And I hate to think of your father living outside the blessings of Father Ives and the Holy Church."

CHAPTER 7

Geffrey woke to the sound of thunder. He sat on his cot, rubbed his eyes, then stumbled into the living area and threw open the shutters. No, it wasn't raining. Not even lightning in the sky. But there was thunder, nonetheless.

It was getting louder.

Sounding closer.

He turned to see his father, adjusting his nightshirt, stumble into the room.

"What is it, son?" he said. "See anything?"

"Nothing," Geffrey said, still squinting into the night.

Then, suddenly, Hugo bolted toward the window. "Get dressed," he said in a commanding tone. "Wake your mother—now. Hurry."

"What is it?"

"The Norse marauders! They have returned!"

His eyes wide with fright, Geffrey dashed into his parent's room, shook his mother awake, then returned to his cot where he dressed. His father had donned his clothes and stood in the doorway of their house. Geffrey scrambled to his side, peered through the small window.

In the far distance, he could see the dark figures, riders on large destriers. As before, they carried torches that burned bright against the dark sky. The ground around their home trembled from their horses' hooves pounding the earth.

"Roust the villagers," Hugo ordered his son. "Tell them to grab their weapons and be prepared to defend Lochwald."

Geffrey raced out into the humid darkness and down the road to begin waking the other villagers. Some were already awake and were outside looking toward the thundering sound.

"Get your weapons!" he cried. "An attack is coming! Everyone outside!"

He ran down the main road of the village screaming the alarm. Slowly, much too slowly, candles and lanterns were lit inside the houses. A few men carrying the axes and spears he forged scrambled onto the road.

The partially completed wall posed no barrier for the oncoming marauders. They simply rode around the ends of the wall or their powerful chargers leaped over the shorter portions. Geffrey saw the Norsemen, dressed in their dark fur-edged cloaks covering their chain mail, their metal helmets with nose guards, waving spears and battle-axes. The bearded man in the lead had a long sword raised above his head. His eyes blazed red.

Geffrey knew it was the same raiders who plundered Lochwald earlier.

Hugo was at his side and handed him an axe as the riders thundered closer. Screams erupted throughout the village. Women dragged their children to the refuge and safety of the forest.

Geffrey's heart pounded, his stomach revolted, and his knees weakened. He glanced at his father who stood with his feet apart, the axe gripped with both hands.

"Aim for the horses," Hugo said. "Once they go down, we can fight them on foot. Have courage, my son. If we die this day, it is because God has willed it."

Geffrey couldn't see how God would be interested in saving a massively outmanned insignificant Normandie village from the likes of brutal Norsemen but at the present moment he didn't have time to argue the point. He prayed that if he was cut down it would be a painless death. He swallowed hard, palms aching from the tight grip on the axe.

As the raiders swept into Lochwald, they set fire to the homes they passed. The flames stretched skyward, filling the village with thick black smoke. Soot filled Geffrey's mouth and lungs, tasted like metal. He watched as Robert ran into the street, a club held high in his hand. A passing raider felled him with a blow from his axe, the blade plunged deep into the boy's neck with a loud *thump.* Robert went down and didn't move.

In the middle of town, Geffrey swung his axe into a horse's foreleg causing the animal to pitch forward then fall to the ground. Its Norse rider hit the earth but managed to remain on his feet. Geffrey struck the invader a ringing blow across the helm, denting the metal. The Norseman's knees buckled and he tumbled to the ground. Before he could regain his senses, Geffrey was on him, sliding the blade of his dagger into the exposed skin of his throat, right up to the hilt. Blood gushed from the wound. The marauder gurgled and twitched as the last breath left his lungs.

The center of town became a nightmare. Screams and fighting between the villagers and the raiders continued. Geffrey moved to another Norseman who confronted him with a spear.

The man plunged his weapon at him. Geffrey parried with a thrust of his axe, hitting the man in the arm, drawing blood. The bearded invader growled and lunged at him with the spear. Hugo arrived and hit the man in the neck, decapitating the invader. The sound of metal grinding on bone sickened Geffrey. Soon the smell of burning flesh greeted him. He thought he would faint. Hugo slapped his son on the shoulder and moved off into the thick of the fight.

Geffrey pushed down the fear that tasted like rancid meat in his mouth. He moved down the road where a Norse invader had Ansel by the hair. When he saw Geffrey approach with his axe, he turned to fight. The two men locked in combat. As they circled each other, the man swung at Geffrey with his battle-axe, grazing his arm, drawing blood. Their weapons gleamed in the cool moonlight. Geffrey knew that only one would walk away. His opponent's axe was stained with blood. Geffrey shuffled to the side and awaited the man's attack and, possibly, inevitable death. His opponent charged with a mighty cry. Geffrey dodged to the side in one fluid move. His enemy swiveled in his direction, his menacing eyes blazing red while his dark cloak made the rest of his features indistinguishable. The Norseman sliced through the air with his axe, only to be met by Geffrey's axe. Both weapons met in the air with a resounding *clang*. The man was a master with the axe. Slowly, Geffrey was tiring. His arms felt as if they were made of lead. The Norseman's strength superior to his own and he was winning the fight Geffrey screamed, "If I am to die, I shall fight to the last breath." With renewed vigor, he slashed his blade back and forth. His wound began bleeding openly.

Geffrey stepped aside, turned to his right, and swung his axe, grazing off the man's chain mail tunic. Ansel appeared, struck the Norseman with a club in the back of his knees. He buckled slightly, off his guard long enough for Geffrey to strike him in the head. The blow rang out as the man fell to the ground. Ansel plunged a knife into the man's throat slicing through his windpipe. A gush of air issued forth as the man fought for life. Soon he lay limp in the road.

He glanced about for his father and saw him a few meters away swinging a short sword at an invader. His mother was nowhere to be seen. He had no idea where she had fled after he woke her. The baker was at the far end of the road using an axe against a Norse horseman. Where was Rosalind? She wasn't among the women and children running and screaming in the dark of early morning. Geffrey felt a wave of nausea overtake him and he choked down the urge to vomit.

An invader swept down upon him, battle-axe held high. The charger's nostrils flared and belched steam as horse and rider pressed closer. Geffrey gripped his axe with a firm sweaty hand and waited. The thunder of destrier's hooves pounding the hard ground echoed in his ears. At the last moment, Geffrey jumped out of the way, plunged his axe into the horse's flank. With a loud squeal the animal went down, catapulting its rider into a motionless heap. Geffrey pounced on the man and swung his axe into the man's head.

But the numbers were against the Lochwald townspeople. The Norsemen marauders overwhelmed the small group of Norman defenders. Their town was in flames and once again, men, women, and children lay dead in the main road. He scanned the village for his parents, could not locate them. Hugo was lost in the fighting. His mother and Rosalind were nowhere to be seen. In the gray dawn of early morning twilight, Lochwald lay in ruins. Not a single home or building could Geffrey see that was still standing. Black smoke, smelling of burnt wood and human flesh, lay as a heavy mantle over the ashes. Tears well in his eyes as a tremendous sense of foreboding filled his soul. Where was God in their hour of desperate need? Why hadn't he answered his father's supplicatory prayers?

Strong hands grabbed him and forced him along the road to where the big Norseman stood. The man was heavy-set and muscled, with thick dark shoulder length hair. He had removed his helmet revealing a scarred face and gray wide-set eyes. The men on each side of him pushed him to his knees.

"My lord," the man on his right said, "here is one of the villagers. He killed a number of our warriors."

The big man looked down on Geffrey, a stern scowl etched on his scarred face. Beads of perspiration and soot clung to his head, neck, and arms, his hair matted against his face.

"What name are you known by?" he said in a voice that boomed through the village.

Geffrey's stomach pumped bile into his mouth. He felt as if he would vomit.

"Geffrey," he managed weakly.

"Age?" the man said.

"Sixteen, sire."

The big man stooped and, grabbing Geffrey by his tunic, brought him to his feet. The man towered over him. His breath was foul.

"I am Brondolf," he said. His voice was sharp, gruff. "I am jarl of the Normandie Norsemen. So, Geffrey of Lochwald—what is your occupation? Or do you still suckle at your mama's teats?"

Geffrey felt his face flush at the mention of his mother's breasts.

"I am a blacksmith apprentice," he said, this time leaving off the title of sire.

"A blacksmith, eh?" Brondolf said. "We can always use a man who can forge iron."

"My father is Lochwald's blacksmith. I am his apprentice." Geffrey's tone, initially weak and hesitant, was now stronger. He tried to summon the courage to look the big jarl in the eye as he spoke.

"Where are your parents, my boy?"

"I do not know. I haven't seen them since..." His voice trailed off and he lowered his eyes, stared at the ground.

"We will find them," Brondolf said. To the two men standing next to Geffrey, he said, "Shackle him. Keep him with you."

The men pushed him to one side and tied his hands with rope behind his back. Yanking him to a tree they forced him to sit. From his location, Geffrey noticed that his father's pride and joy, his blacksmith stable was nothing more than a heap of glowing embers. Everything was gone—the forge, bellows, tools—everything.

And at the sight of the smoldering ashes, Geffrey wept.

Brondolf had one of the surviving women of Lochwald identify the bodies of the village mayor, priest, and Geffrey's father.

When Geffrey saw his father's body he sank his head onto his chest and wept. The man who he admired, who taught him the world and its complexities, complained about the vagaries of the Church, lay in a motionless heap. Hugo's vacant eyes stared out through his blackened dirty body. Geffrey couldn't believe his father was dead. He looked to the Norse leader, tears streaming down his cheeks.

"My mother," he said. "Where is my mother?"

Brondolf looked at him through cold, narrow eyes.

"Your mother? Who knows? But one of these men is your father?"

Geffrey nodded and pointed to Hugo's corpse.

Brondolf turned to one of the raiders next to him.

"String these men up from a tree limb and burn them," he said. "And take this swine away from here."

The Norsemen strung Hugo's body and those of Giroldus and Father Ives from a thick tree limb then set them on fire. Geffrey sobbed and turned away as their corpses were reduced to cinders. He couldn't bear the sight of his father's body.

They gathered the few remaining survivors into a small group—only women and children. The men, except for Geffrey, all died defending the village. He didn't see his mother or Rosalind among those assembled.

👁➳👁➴

The caravan of destriers and riders snaked through unfamiliar territory. The narrow path Gunnvor chose led through a dense forest and its brambles and briars clawed at Geffrey's legs. His hands were bound behind his back making it impossible to guide his horse. His was a huge powerful steed, undoubtedly once belonging to a Norseman who was slain back in Lochwald. The horse seemed to have a mind of its own, determined to bump its unfamiliar rider off its back at each opportunity. Geffrey's legs ached from the constant struggle to remain balanced atop the beast.

By the time the sun peeked through the trees they rode out of the forest and onto a vast plain divided by a fast moving stream. Here they stopped while the Norsemen and their chargers quenched their thirst. They kept Geffrey perched on his animal—he got no water. The stream was clear, looked cold and refreshing. What he wouldn't give for a drink. After a few moments while the marauders refreshed themselves they were back on the trail once more. He listened as they regaled each other with stories of the fight and the villagers they killed. Slaughtered was more like it, he thought.

The Norse warriors made their way along the stream until they came to a deep gorge whose east side slanted upward. The stream descended into the gorge and as they ventured up the side of the hill, Geffrey lost sight of the fast moving water.

The path along the edge of the gorge was rocky and narrow. As the riders gained altitude, the horses labored. Geffrey's destrier stumbled, nearly catapulting him from the leather saddle. He struggled to keep his balance without the use of his hands. Down in the gorge below, the stream appeared as a tiny ribbon winding its way through the rocky terrain. Two eagles plunged down through the gorge then soared skyward on the uplifting warm air thermals.

Once past the gorge they were back in a forest of elm and cedar and Geffrey felt refreshed by the coolness of the shade. Wildflowers of purple, white, red, and blue grew in abundance, their sweet fragrance an invigorating diversion to his nose. The grade was slightly uphill while they progressed through the trees. Birds he couldn't identify squawked alarm below their lofty perches. Once, in the distance, Geffrey thought he caught sight of a deer bounding into a thicket ahead of their small column.

His wrists were raw from the bindings, his legs and back ached, the pain shooting up his spine into the base of his skull. He was miserable. He wanted to die.

It was difficult for Geffrey to ride with his hands bound behind him making it necessary to grip his horse solely with his knees and legs. Numerous times during the ride northward he almost tumbled off the back of his charger so that by the time he arrived at the Norse village his legs and thighs screamed with pain. He tried to formulate a mental map of their route but the many twists and turns left him confused so he gave up. The vision of his father's burnt body haunted him all through the ride, tortured him. He wept most of the way.

There had been no need for the last act of the barbarians. Burning a corpse was usually meant to convey a stark message—we are the rulers. Do not dare resist. When he last had seen his father, he was fighting like a man possessed. So, at least he had died with honor. What of his mother and Rosalind? He did not know. He did not see them in the small group that was rounded up and led off somewhere. To where was also a mystery. His gut rolled from not knowing what happened to them or where they were. He uttered a silent prayer that they had not been abused or worse. They rode all through the early dawn hours arriving at the Norse stronghold by mid-morning.

As they approached the village Geffrey noticed that it was located in a forested series of low-lying hills. Somewhere off to the west he heard the trickle of a stream, its size he could not discern. The same two men pulled him from his horse and his knees buckled as he attempted to stand. The ride left him lightheaded and weak.

They forced him to a circular fortress whose ramparts were made of wood and soil. There were four gates into the fortress that were connected to each other by wooden blocked streets, which intersected at the center of the fort. Each gate pointed to the four cardinal points—north, south, east, west. The small outpost, composed of isolated single structures about seven meters long and four and meters wide, appeared impregnable. The roofs were thatched and the walls were simple materials woven together within the posts. The floor of the house was made of packed earth.

The wooden blocked streets inside the fortress divided the fort into four equal parts. Each of these sections held four longhouses making a total of sixteen longhouse buildings within the fortress. The buildings stood in a concentric circle in relation to the rampart on the outside of the fortress. All buildings were built of oak. Geffrey could tell that certain buildings were used for habitation, while others were used as workshops for both blacksmith and goldsmith. A short fence surrounded a cemetery outside of the ramparts.

He needed to rest but the brutish Norsemen pushed him into a longhouse then down to its front by the hearth. His mouth felt like leather from lack of water.

The man who identified himself as Brondolf sat in a large chair covered with animal skins and furs and eyed Geffrey as he approached. His smile revealed black teeth with a wide gap in them. Another man stood at his side.

"Well, Geffrey of Lochwald," he said. "We meet again. Welcome. I suppose you are wondering what is to befall you. I have given that much thought and I must confess Gunnvor here thinks you should die. I admit his idea has much merit. We simply do not have the need of more slaves."

Geffrey's mind wasn't on Brondolf's words for he was still reeling from the sudden confrontation with the man responsible for his father's burning and not knowing what had befallen his mother and Rosalind. But he heard the man's last pronouncements.

"But I have hit upon a great idea, Geffrey of Lochwald," Brondolf continued, "As you are a blacksmith, a man who works with metals, I am sending you to the Norse iron mines at Remmelsberg. There you will work as a menial slave worker. If your God has mercy on you, one day you will earn your freedom and return to rebuild Lochwald. I do not know why I have decided to spare your life, other than we always seem to require more weapons. If you work hard, maybe the overseer will one day set you free. But until that day—I bid you adieu."

With that, Brondolf waved a hand and the two men jerked Geffrey out of the longhouse to where an uncertain future awaited him.

CHAPTER 8

The cart lurched, jolted Geffrey awake. From the gray light forming on the horizon he surmised he was traveling east and dawn only an hour away. He sat upright, looked around. His hands were no longer bound but his wrists were raw and painful. He slouched in a rickety wooden cart pulled by a shaggy horse that had seen better days. Its head hung low as it plodded one hoof in front of the other.

How long he had travelled in the cart he did not know. The hours ran together in a continuous stream of misery. His back and legs ached from the cramped quarters of the small cart. A bearded man sat perched on a seat at the front of the cart and held the reins loosely in gnarled hands. He appeared asleep but a dark cloak draped over his head and shoulders made it impossible for Geffrey to get a look at him. In front and beside the cart two Norse warriors rode on horseback, their chain mail tunics and swords visible beneath their cloaks.

At the edge of the forest they encountered a clear stream where they stopped for the morning meal. While two men kindled a fire, another gathered water. A bearded man eyed Geffrey, nodded.

"You can hop down now, lad," he said in a graveled voice. "Just do us a favor and don't run off. I would have to run you down and put my sword through you. We would lose some good wages."

Geffrey stood, stretched, hopped down from the cart. His bones and muscles ached from the long journey. He ambled to the rising fire. One of the men placed a water-filled metal pot on a rock next to the flames. Geffrey stooped and held his cold hands to the fire. It felt good to warm his hands.

"Where are we?" he said.

"On the road to Saxony, lad," the bearded man said.

"Why? What for?"

"Taking you to the Remmelsberg mines," another bearded man said. He stoked the fire, poured something into the pot.

"I'm sorry, my lad," said the original Norseman. He wore dark tattered clothes. His hands were grimy. "Let me introduce your companions on this trip. My name is Rankin. That man tending the fire there is Noddy and that old geezer in charge of the cart is Biljohn. Don't get cross ways with him cuz he'll carve up your liver and we wouldn't get paid."

Noddy stirred the pot, poured water into pewter tankards and passed them around. Geffrey gulped his water down. Noddy was a short man with a deformed shoulder.

Breakfast was soon ready. Noddy dipped thick sticky porridge into earthen bowls and the men sat around the fire eating their breakfast. Beyond the stream the forest was quiet. The nighttime animal activity had retired for the coming day. The only sound other than the men's quiet chatter was the gurgling of the stream that bounced lazily over bright colored lichen covered rocks. The air was cool, crisp.

"Why are you taking me to these mines?" Geffrey asked. The porridge tasted good. And it was hot.

"Because, my lad," Rankin said after a mouthful of porridge, "Brondolf ordered it."

"But why?" Geffrey persisted.

"Cuz the overlord of the mines paid Brondolf a handsome sum for your services," Rankin said.

At the word *services*, Noddy and Biljohn snickered. They didn't look at Geffrey but kept their eyes on their bowls of porridge.

"Paid for me? What services?"

Again, Noddy and Biljohn snickered.

"The mines are worked by slave labor, my lad. You're to provide the labor."

It dawned on Geffrey that he was being sold into slavery and was being taken to an iron mine somewhere in Saxony to be worked like a dog. At the realization of what his future held, he lost taste for his porridge. He turned queasy. The picture of his father, Giroldus, and Father Ives, their burned corpses hanging from a tree, was etched indelibly in his brain. He would never forget what these bastards did to them. He said a silent vow that if the opportunity of escape presented itself, he would take it. Maybe he could sneak away during the night if they didn't tie him up. He would wait and see.

The warming fire took the chill out of his bones and he began to feel better. The rawness of his wrists still burned but Geffrey felt halfway human. The sun broke over the horizon sending streams of golden light through the trees dappling the ground around them. Overhead, birds began their morning songfest and he heard unseen critters rustle in the underbrush. With the rising sun the morning chill began to fade.

Their breakfast finished, Noddy washed the dishes in the stream, then they continued on. With his stomach full, the jostling of the cart lulled Geffrey asleep. He saw his father and mother standing in the doorway of their home. He was black, burned but alive, and smiling as Geffrey approached them. His father took him into his arms in a passionate embrace. He smelled of soot and burned flesh. Parts of Hugo's flesh hung in large chunks from the white bone. When the two parted, Geffrey's hands held burned clumps of skin.

Rosalind appeared. Dressed in a long white dress, she stood next to Brondolf who had an arm around her. *No, it can't be. Rosalind married to Brondolf?* Then he noticed the man's hand on her stomach—a bulging, protruding belly. Rosalind carried Brondolf's man-child inside her. The Norse warrior looked into Geffrey's eyes then tossed his head back and laughed.

Then, in an instant, they were gone.

Geffrey woke in a cold sweat. The nightmare left him drained, exhausted. They were back among tall spruce trees, the sun near the horizon. They would be stopping soon so he leaned back against the side of the cart and watched the forest go by. It was a different land that they were in. Rankin ordered Noddy to go deeper into the forest in search of game. From atop his destrier the man sneered but took his bow and quiver of arrows then disappeared beyond the trees. They waited in the shade next to a tall pine tree and waited for Noddy but he didn't return. Late in the afternoon, Rankin sent Biljohn to look for the man. Several hours later both men emerged pulling a large deer behind them. Rankin helped the two men butcher the deer and place the meat into sacks for later roasting.

By the time the sun set, they were once again on the edge of a forest. Rankin called a halt for the night. They found a clearing off the path and made camp. Noddy produced the cloth bags that held the venison and the men sat around a large fire roasting the meet. Geffrey sank his teeth into the first fresh meat he tasted in quite a while, savoring the taste while wiping a smear of grease from his chin. They ate and roasted huge chunks of venison late into the night. Before retiring under wool blankets, Biljohn bound Geffrey's hands and feet and fixed him to a tree. He uttered not a word as he worked, occasionally shooting Geffrey a hateful glance through slitted eyes.

After the men were asleep, he labored against his fetters but found them impossible to loosen. He finally gave up and drifted into a fitful sleep.

Rosalind visited his dreams again.

She wandered the forest and he knew she was searching for him. He called to her but she did not hear. He ran to her but she did not notice him. He put a hand on her arm but she did not feel his touch. Something was amiss. Why didn't she recognize him? He looked at her face, could tell she had been weeping. But she smiled when Robert strolled at her side. Robert? No, not Robert. It was Geffrey's place to be at Rosalind's side, not the arrogant little twit. Robert clutched her hand and together they disappeared into the forest.

Early the next morning, they were back on the trail. The sun was not yet up so they ambled in silence, Rankin leading the way across the vast plain that stretched out before them. Being tied to a tree throughout the night left Geffrey stiff and tired. When the sun reached a height high enough to provide warmth, it felt good on his taut muscles. He was finally able to relax a little in the cart.

That afternoon found them at the edge of a small lake where they stopped for a rest. The waters appeared cool and deep. As they reclined in the soft grass near the lake, a stooped grizzled man approached. He carried a knapsack slung over one shoulder and held a gnarled walking staff in one of his hands. Rankin pulled a dagger from his belt when the man was close.

"Hello, fellow travelers," the man said in a strong voice, "May I approach your camp?"

"This is not our camp," Rankin said. "But if you bear us no harm or sorcery, you may join us,"

"I assure you, sir," the old man said as he hobbled near, "that I am neither a sorcerer no a bandit." He continued to stroll to where they were resting until he stood next to Geffrey. His eyes widened when he noticed Geffrey's bindings.

"Have a seat, old man," Rankin said. "Where you be heading?"

"Heading west. My name is Roul. I am a storyteller. And you, where might you be going if I might be so bold as to inquire?"

Geffrey noticed the man gave him another look.

"This man, here," Rankin said, "is an escaped highwayman. We are taking him back for punishment."

"A storyteller, eh?" Noddy said.

"Aye, sir," the man said. "A teller of tales from the other side of the world, strange stories of the Arabian Nights, folk legends of Greece and Rome.

"Please warm yourself by the fire and tell us a story, then."

The man shed his knapsack, lowered himself to the ground with the aid of his walking stick. Seated, he breathed a long sigh. "The story goes something like this. There once was a chaplain who was widely known for his worldly living. Unfitting for a man of his station, the priest indulged in that most worldly of aristocratic pasttimes—the hunt. For his love of the chase, he was nicknamed the *hundeprest*. Well, eventually, he died and was interred at the Monastery of Melrose. For reasons likely related to the man's impious living, one night the corpse of the priest rose from its grave, and unable to enter the monastery, proceeded to wander about the walls, finally making its way to the bedchamber of a certain, illustrious lady it had served whilst living, causing its former mistress much distress with its loud groans and horrib_e murmurs. After this happened a few more times, the ter- ror-stricken woman decided to seek out the help of a nearby friar, pleading with him to offer prayers on her behalf.

"The friar enlisted the help of another friar along wich two powerful, young men, and the four set out to watch over the cemetery that night and to prevent the monster from terrorizing the lady.

"These four, therefore, furnished with arms and ani- mated with courage, passed the night in that place, safe in the assistance which each afforded to the other. Midnight now passed by, and no monster appeared, upon which it came to pass that three of the party, leaving him only who had sought their company on the spot, departed into the nearest house, for the purpose, as they averred, of warming themselves, for the night was cold. As soon as this man was left alone in this place, the devil, imagining that he had found the right moment for breaking his courage, roused up his own chosen vessel, who appeared to have reposed longer than usual. Having beheld this from afar, he grew stiff with terror by reason of his being alone, but soon recovering his courage, and no place of refuge being at hand, he valiantly withstood the onset of the fiend, who came rushing upon him with a terrible noise. He struck it with the axe he wielded in his hand deep into its body. On receiving this wound, the monster groaned aloud, and turning his back, fled with a rapidity in the direction from whence it came. All the while, the admirable man urged his flying foe from behind, and compelled him to seek his own tomb again. It opened of its own accord, and receiving its guest from the advance of the pursuer, immediately appeared to quickly close again. In the meantime, the three who had retreated to che fire ran up, though somewhat too late, and, having heard what had happened, rendered needful assistance in digging up and removing from the midst of the tomb the accursed corpse at the earliest dawn. When they had brushed away the clay cast forth with it, they found the huge wound it had received along with a great quantity of gore that had flowed from it in the grave. And so, having carried it away beyond the walls of the monastery and burnt it, they then scattered the ashes to the winds. These things I have explained in a simple narration, as I myself heard them recounted by religious men."

"Sounds more like a bad dream," Noddy said. "However, I enjoyed the tale."

Rankin removed a coin from his pocket and tossed it at Roul.

"Yes, it was a nice story, very entertaining. Tell me where do you get your stories?"

The old man thought for a moment then his eyes flickered as if lighting upon another tale.

"From the depths of Hell, my son," he said. "And impious living on my part. I have met many a scoundrel and thief along life's journey. They all have a good story to tell."

"You tell a good tale, old man," Rankin said. "Now we must be on our way."

Biljohn jerked Geffrey to his feet and pushed him into the cart. The storyteller rose with animated difficulty, donned his knapsack, made his way beyond the lake, and disappeared.

Midday found them at the city of Reims, built by the Romans before the birth of Christ. It was a large walled city with a number of arched gates manned by soldiers who controlled access of those who desired entrance. Rankin called a halt in front of the south gate. Crowds of people came and went through the large opening in the wall. A throng milled about outside the gate laughing and shouting at one another. Geffrey sat straight in the cart surveying the activity outside the walls. It appeared there was a bazaar on the outskirts of the city where those not allowed entrance to Reims sold their wares and bartered other business.

While Rankin contemplated whether they should enter the city or go around it, a hunchbacked man with a black patch over his right eye hobbled to the cart. He carried a crooked rudimentary crutch under one arm. Rankin wheeled his horse around as Geffrey leaned on the cart's side.

"You men be strangers in these parts?" the old man asked. "Weary travelers in search of a comfortable bed for the night?"

Geffrey noticed the man's good eye twitched uncontrollably and most of his teeth were missing. The few that remained were black.

Rankin slid out of the saddle, stretched his legs. He ambled to the man who cocked his head at Rankin's approach.

"We may have need of lodging for tonight, old man. And a meal to satisfy our peckish innards. What is it to you?"

The old man smiled, spit something from his mouth. "My name is Theobald," the old man said. "If you wish, I can be of service to you gentlemen. I can arrange for you to enter the city and my cousin has comfortable lodgings for a small price."

"Why can't we just walk through the gate ourselves?" Rankin said.

"Ah," Theobald said. "This is a Christian city, sir. And by your dress it is obvious you are foreigners to this land. It is unfortunate, but you will not be allowed entrance unless someone like myself vouches for you and you pay the gate tax. In fact, if I am not too far from correct, you appear to be Norsemen. You will not be welcome in Reims."

Rankin and Theobald haggled over the price for the old man's services until an agreement was reached. Theobald signaled that the little company should follow him to the gate. One of the soldiers stepped forward and Theobald ran to speak to him. As he did, the soldier kept giving Geffrey and the others furtive glances. A frown formed on his face. Geffrey's heart sank. But then, when the old man offered money, the soldier nodded and Theobald waved them on. As they passed, the old man hopped on the cart next to Biljohn. They advanced through the gate and into the city of Reims.

As they meandered through the streets of the city following Theobald's instructions, he gave Geffrey a quick history of the area.

"Reims is a very old city," he said. "Its original name was Durocorteron, meaning round fortress. In fact we just passed through the Durocorteron Gate. When Julius Caesar conquered Gaul, this city allied itself with the Romans. According to the legend, Remus, Romulus's brother who founded ancient Rome, founded Reims. The Celtic tribe who lived in the region might have taken therefore the name of Remes. After the Roman conquest, Durocorteron was integrated into the Roman province of Gallia Belgica and became its capital. During the last century, the Roman Catholic Archbishop of Reims, Adalbero, founded schools here, which taught the classical liberal arts. Remi, bishop of Reims, baptized Clovis, the Frankish king, in a baptistery that is today situated where our cathedral stands. It is thanks to Clovis's baptism that Reims became the seat of the coronation of the kings of France."

Theobald pointed in a direction to turn and the small company ambled down a narrow street lined with outdoor shops, businesses, a few grand homes. The echoes of various animal hooves' on the cobblestone street produced a cacophony of sound. People crowded everywhere, talking loudly, wildly. The sights, sounds, and smells of this strange city overwhelmed Geffrey's senses. He had never seen anything so grand.

Geffrey turned to Theobald who was speaking again.

"The richness of Reims is attributable to its woolen textiles which are famous far and wide and win many awards at fairs and festivals. My cousin, Haveron, is himself a textile merchant and is a wealthy man."

Theobald continued directing them through the streets of Reims, turning one way then another, until they reached a large two-story house that had an arched wrought iron entryway. Flowering vines grew over the gate filling the air with sweet perfume. Geffrey and his escorts waited with the cart while Theobald went inside to locate his cousin. A small courtyard lay beyond the entryway gate and contained a fountain and flower garden. Two large trees gave shade to the courtyard and from his perch in the cart Geffrey noticed a table and chairs next to the fountain.

It wasn't long before Theobald emerged leading a small man with a thin goatee. He walked with a slump similar to guide.

Haveron introduced himself then took the men through the courtyard and into his home. The living area was floored with pink marble and contained several settees with plush pillows. Thick purple curtains covered two large windows. Haveron led the group to a small room that contained four cots. Geffrey collapsed on a bed and the Norsemen followed suit. Haveron excused himself but soon returned with a tray of roasted partridges, smoked fish, figs, and melons. Haveron's wife, a skinny, gray-haired woman with a large hawkish nose, brought tankards of mead. They sat on the cots and ate their fill. The mead was sweet and refreshing.

"Haveron's sister-in-law was recently convicted of sorcery," Theobald said. "His wife's sister. The old hag was expelled from the city. Isn't that right, Haveron?"

Geffrey stared at the man between bites of food. He had never heard of an actual person accused of being a witch.

"Alas, it is true," Haveron said. "Unbeknownst to her family the woman practiced necromancy."

"Necromancy?" Geffrey said, mesmerized by the topic.

"Yes. The blackest of all the black arts is undoubtedly necromancy, the ancient method of communication with the dead. The art of raising the dead and controlling their spirits."

"I have heard of such evil doings," Rankin said. "Things best left unsaid."

"Oh, the woman is long gone from these parts," Haveron said, swallowing a mouthful of mead. "But for a time it was said she was quite active in her arts. I have heard her ritual requirements were extraordinarily elaborate as it was due to the great risks any sorceress might encounter the moment she summoned ghosts and devils from the underworld. These spirits were often quite unhappy at having to make the trip. She conjured up the dead with her magical charms to learn the future.

"Her greatest claim was to offer for sale the demon she summoned, so that anyone could destroy his enemies with evil arts. It is said she enjoyed blood and sacrifices and often touched the bodies of the dead. By her imprecations of the resuscitated dead, she prophesied and answered questions. While she questioned them, she poured blood on the corpse, for demons love blood. Whenever necromancy was performed, blood was mixed with water, so that the dead might be called forth."

"Why would she do such things?" Geffrey asked. His attention was riveted on Haveron.

"For money, of course," Haveron said. "Spirits were sometimes conjured up out of affection—someone missed a loved one who had departed this vale of tears. Sometimes spirits were summoned up because the sorcerer wanted the arcane or secret knowledge that only spirits were reputed to possess. And sometimes—perhaps quite often—spirits were called upon to divulge the whereabouts of hidden treasure hoards. People generally understand that the dead may have lost their lives in the normal sense but that they have gained the ability in the afterlife to uncover all secrets and see into all things."

"So they ran the old woman out of town, eh?" Rankin said. "Good for them."

Haveron and Theobald took their leave and left the men to rest. As Geffrey lay on his cot his mind was filled with images of witches summoning up dead spirits.

Soon they were sleeping soundly.

The house was dark and quiet when Geffrey woke. He scanned the room and saw that Rankin and the other men were snoring. What with the food, mead, and the story of the sorceress, Biljohn had forgotten to secure his hands and legs for the evening leaving Geffrey free to roam about. He crawled off of his cot, donned his shoes, and wandered through the living room toward the front door.

There was no one about. He had no idea where Theobald and his cousin were sleeping. Outside, a breeze rattled the shutters on the living room windows.

Without making a sound, he ambled closer to the front door.

A thought struck him.

He could walk out and never look back. Then he would be free of these bastards. His heart ached for the chance to find Rosalind and his mother. He had no idea where they were but he would not rest until they were located and he was reunited with them. He couldn't bring himself to think of the possibility that they both might be dead.

At the door he hesitated, listened for sounds on the street. Hearing none, he glanced over his shoulder to the interior of the house. There was no movement. No sounds.

He placed his hand on the door latch.

Then he was gone.

CHAPTER 9

The streets of Reims were almost empty. Almost, but not completely. Fragrances from evening cooking fires still hung heavy on the crisp night air. Scents of garlic, anise, balm, lemon, and basil tickled Geffrey's nose as he crept through the streets in search of a way out of the city. A sliver of a moon rode high and shed pale silvery light on the cobblestone streets as he wandered them. Deep shadows between the bazaars and buildings hid whatever sins lurked in their depths.

Confused by the maze of streets and alleyways, he continued on, searching for any landmark that might mark a return to the city's walls. He past the small cathedral and remembered it from the previous day so he must be close to the gate by which they entered Reims. A sense of urgency pushed Geffrey on, him fearful that his escape would be noticed and any moment he would turn to face Rankin and the others. The streets of the city were a confusing patchwork of interconnected streets and alleyways meandering in no particular organized fashion. It was difficult to get his bearings. After passing the cathedral, he could not recall another landmark from the previous day. He was lost, disoriented.

Turning a corner, he bumped into a beggar, the man stumbling among the shadows. The man held up a staff ready to strike.

"Hold on, old man," Geffrey said, grabbing the man's arm. "Which way to the main gate?"

"The main gate?" the beggar repeated. "The main gate is closed at dark. It won't open until sunrise."

"Are there other gates open?"

"None, young man. None until the sun comes up."

The beggar turned and hobbled away. Panicked, Geffrey glanced down the street. There was no one else around. He scurried along a cobbled side street, keeping an eye peeled for his captors. Or soldiers on a nightly patrol. Never having been in a city the size of Reims kept Geffrey in a state of turmoil, his head reeling from confusion and fear of discovery. The street was lined with shops, all closed, but he occasionally caught a glimpse of the market located on the street behind them. He didn't remember passing any of this earlier. Nothing was familiar.

He needed a place to hide until the gates opened. He ran down an alley, found it had no exit. Then turned.

And faced Rankin, Noddy, and Biljohn.

ℰↄℰↄ

The remainder of the trip to Remmelsberg was uneventful. To ensure a quiet ride Biljohn kept Geffrey's hands and feet bound the entire way while Noddy rode in the cart with him and made doubly sure he didn't distract them and escape again. They passed a small fortified town named Nanciacum that they learned was built by Gérard, Duke of Lorraine. A castle dominated the small township.

Proceeding east of Nanciacum they camped in a small copse of trees. The sun was low on the horizon casting the thin clouds with hues of magenta, orange, and purple. A cool breeze wafted through the birch trees while Noddy set about building a small fire. Biljohn pulled Geffrey from the cart and pushed him down against a large rock.

Numb to the pain that earlier shot through his limbs, he stretched his legs, reminded himself that his life as a slave was rapidly approaching. From his seat on the ground, he watched as the men readied the evening meal.

When Rankin squatted next to the waxing flames, Geffrey spoke to him.

"Rankin, what do you know of this place you are taking me? Have you been there before?"

Rankin eyed him with a glower.

"Never before," he said. "Just following orders. But I have heard of the place, sure. It is in Saxony, I believe. King Magnus, the great Norse leader, conquered the Remmelsberg mines. He fought many battles in Saxony and came to rule there for a time. The story goes that after one battle few of Magnus's men were killed, but great numbers were wounded. There weren't enough doctors to care for the sufferers. Magnus himself, therefore, went among those who were whole, feeling the palms of their hands. He chose twelve of these, whose hands were soft, and bade them bind up the wounds of their comrades. Now our people use the mines for a source of iron and steel that are used to make our weapons."

Earlier in the day, Noddy killed a rabbit that roasted over the fire and the aroma of it cooking made Geffrey's mouth water. Other than the meal they had in Reims, they subsisted on porridge and venison during the journey.

"What if the Saxons and Franks run you from their lands?" Geffrey inquired. He gazed longingly at the rabbit, which was turning a golden brown.

"Ha!" Noddy interjected having overheard their conversation. "Never will that happen."

"Noddy is right, my lad," Rankin said. "We Norse are too powerful—"

And too ruthless, thought Geffrey.

"Our fighting tactics are superior to any foe," Rankin continued. He shook his head. "No, we Norsemen are here to stay. Best understand that, lad."

The rabbit was shared by the three men leaving Geffrey to eat the remaining few scraps of venison washed down with a tankard of water. Oh, for a taste of fresh meat, he thought.

The next morning they continued the journey toward the Remmelsberg mines. The weather turned cool for late spring and Geffrey shivered, goose bumps forming on his skin. His arms and legs revolted against the bumping of the cart. He had no cloak or coat to ward off the morning's chill and hoped the rising sun would soon warm his aching bones. The bouncing of the cart jarred his body sending jolts of stabbing pain deep within. He tried thinking of better times, times with his father in the stable, listening to him extolling on philosophical topics, meals with his parents as they laughed together, watching his mother labor at the family hearth. But mostly he attempted to rekindle thoughts of Rosalind, where she was at this moment, what was happening to her, was she thinking of him. The horror of what occurred in Lochwald still resonated in his soul with incalculable sorrow. And contempt for the Norse marauders.

The days passed in what seemed an endless series of camps, scanty meals, campfires, and chilly morning rides in the rickety cart. The landscape consisted of rolling hills punctuated with flat plains of lush grasslands and the occasional forest. Water was in abundance for streams and rivers dotted the countryside.

Geffrey's captors seemed to not care if he was uncomfortable or his wrists were raw and bleeding from his restraints. Riding in a cramped position in the cart didn't allow him a chance to stretch his legs and work the kinks out of his muscles so he spent most of the day contracted and in pain. He dealt with his discomfort by keeping his mind focused on Rosalind and his mother but it only partially helped.

One dreary afternoon when the clouds hung low in dark gloom, they crested a hill. Rankin let out a shout.

"Remmelsberg!"

The small village behind a fortified wall was situated in a glen surrounded by hills covered with small forests interspersed with fields of low-lying green vegetation. Less than a kilometer north of the village, Geffrey noticed a group of wooden structures and narrow buildings. The mines, he figured. In the faint distance he saw men scurrying about the structures, a few disappearing into the earth.

Remmelsberg's gate was open and through it Geffrey caught sight of the town. From his perch in the cart it looked similar to Reims with its cobblestone streets lined with shops. A quick glance as they bypassed the gate revealed crowds of people walking and talking in the village streets.

Biljohn skirted the village, guiding the horse and cart up the squat hill toward the mines. Geffrey's heart pounded in his chest, his gut rolled over, his mouth tasted like metal.

They had arrived.

Without stopping in the village, Biljohn chatted with Rankin who gazed at Geffrey with an evil grin, chuckled. The dirt road was wide and hard-packed from obvious frequent use. The horse labored as it pulled the cart, its plodding steps slow but steady. Biljohn popped his whip over the poor animal's head urging the horse onward.

Closer to the mines, Geffrey was able to see that most of the men were dressed in short trousers, mid-thigh in length while others wore bright red and green tunics and carried whips in their hands. Several wooden towers loomed ahead of them, reaching several stories into a bright sunlit sky. Some of the men bore wicker baskets on their backs that were filled with rocks and they trudged back and forth between the mine entrances to another site where the rocks were dumped into a large pile. Drenched in sweat, their skin glistened, their faces flushed red from the exertion. Geffrey scanned the area wondering what Remmelsberg had in store for him.

Biljohn stopped the cart in front of a dilapidated shack, dismounted and stood at its side. Rankin and Noddy went inside but soon reappeared with a man who shuffled along with a limp. His entire body was scarred from head to foot and half his nose was missing. The man wore his black hair in a ponytail. He limped up to the cart, glared at Geffrey. His face was blackened with dirt and sweat.

"Skroppa, this is your new worker," Rankin said with a sly smile. "Jarl Brondolf delivers as promised."

The man called Skroppa sneered at Geffrey, poked him in the ribs as if testing a piece of meat to see if it was done cooking, then stepped back a step. He carried a baton in one hand and slapped it against his other palm. He stared for a few moments then approached Geffrey.

"Get down out off that cart," he said, his tone cruel, harsh.

Geffrey climbed to the back of the cart, jumped to the ground. Skroppa hit him on an arm with his baton. Geffrey winced.

"You're a slave now, boy," Skroppa said. "You belong to me. Here at Remmelsberg you work when I say, you eat when I say, and you sleep when I say. That clear?"

Geffrey nodded without a word, his arm reeling from Skroppa's blow.

"Good. Now that we understand each other, come

with me. I will get you some clothes and show you where you will bunk." He turned to Rankin and nodded. "Stop by the office and collect your money," he said.

Skroppa pushed Geffrey ahead of him forcing the baton into his ribs as incentive. He cast a long look over his shoulder and saw Rankin and Biljohn turn the cart around and head back down the hill. Noddy followed never looking back. Once they reached a small office constructed of wattle and brick, Skroppa pushed Geffrey into it and had him stand while he located a pair of short linen trousers. He tossed them to Geffrey.

"This is what you wear while you are here," he said. "Do not let me or the foremen catch you in anything else. If you wear anything but those shorts you will be severely punished. When those wear out, tell a foreman, he will see that you get another pair." He tossed a pair of leather sandals toward Geffrey where they fell at his feet on the office floor. "You will wear only these. Anything else and you will be punished."

Geffrey held the shorts, felt the thin material. It didn't seem like much. The men he had seen in arrival at the mines wore only the shorts and sandals. No shirts.

"Now," Skroppa continued, "we work sunrise to dark in the mines, six days a week. You get one day of rest. You eat twice a day, once upon rising each morning and again after work. When the lanterns go out at night you are not to be up. Doing so gets you punished. There are no latrines in the mines so if you need to use the bathroom do so before going to work. There is one water and bathroom break at midday. Having to stop work to use the bathroom during work gets you punished. Talking in the mines gets you punished. Fighting gets you punished. Stealing or fighting with a foreman gets you executed. There is no appeal here. The foreman's and my word is law. Deviate from that law and you will be punished."

Geffrey's head spun from all the rules.

"Get dressed in those short trousers and I will take you to the mines. And be quick about it."

Geffrey quickly changed into the shorts and joined Skroppa for the walk to the mine entrance. Along the way Skroppa gave him a quick overview of the mines.

"Here at Remmelsberg," he said, "there are three vertical shafts sunk deep into the earth. Possibly three hundred feet down. At several levels there are horizontal shafts—we call them galleries. The galleries follow a vein of the iron and it's where all the work is done. The rocks are carried out in baskets."

"What keeps everything from collapsing?" Geffrey asked. They were halfway to the first shaft.

"The shafts and galleries are shored up using wood bracing. You will begin by digging with a gallery crew. It is the lowest level of work and where all new men must start. The highest is the bracing crew for it is the most important. Men's lives depend on solid bracing."

They arrived at the first wooden tower, a large square affair rising several stories into the air. Cross braces secured and strengthened the vertical beams that were a foot on each side. In the ground at the tower's base was a large black hole, the shaft entrance. Geffrey ventured to the edge of the shaft and peered down into its depths. Affixed to one side of the shaft's wall he noticed a ladder descending downward. Every ten feet or so an oil lantern provided enough light where one could see where to place his foot on the ladder.

As Geffrey gazed into the hole, he tried to look beyond the boundaries of the light, into the impenetrable black void. What was down there waiting for him? It seemed as if he was about to descend into Hell, the unfathomable abyss Father Ives mentioned so often in his sermons. Hell was where the Great Imposter ruled. Satan.

It seemed to Geffrey he was on his way to meet the Evil One.

"Get going," Skroppa said behind him. "I'll follow."

Geffrey took a deep breath and stepped into the shaft.

PART II

REMMELSBERG

CHAPTER 10

Remmelsberg, Saxony, 1060 AD:

Covered in grime and drenched in sweat, Geffrey labored most of the day in dim light hacking a hole in the sedimentary and limestone gallery two hundred feet below the surface. There were six other men working this particular gallery, lit only by a few oil lanterns. They spoke in whispered tones lest they incur the wrath of Skroppa. In the weeks he had been forced to work in the mines, Geffrey had seen the overseer's anger lash out at anyone who broke the rules. He used the whip freely and often. Geffrey himself had been caught conversing with a fellow worker and felt the sting of the whip that left large raised welts on his back and arms.

The work was heavy and dirty. Swinging a pick-axe all day left Geffrey exhausted. The other men seemed used to the physical exertion, leaving him wondering if he would ever become accustomed to it. As they dug into the rock, their work resulted in a fine mist of dust that clogged Geffrey's lungs making it difficult to breathe. He set his pick down, took a ragged neckerchief from a pocket on his shorts, and wiped his forehead. He gazed deeper into the hole where his companions labored in silence. Skroppa stood at the head of the gallery, whip in hand, an angry look about him.

When a pile of rocks containing the iron ore piled high enough, men designated as haulers carried them away.

The haulers loaded the rocks in large wicker baskets with shoulder straps affixed to them, hoisted the baskets onto their backs, then carried them out of the gallery. One of the men told Geffrey they hauled the rocks to the smelter on the backside of the mines where the iron ore was crushed and melted down. He remembered seeing the haulers the day he arrived. The entire Remmelsberg operation was enormous, utilizing, Geffrey figured, over a thousand men providing the slave labor.

The thought stung his soul. But that was what he was—a slave. Bought and paid for and now resigned to labor away in dust and dim light until he died of exhaustion or succumbed to the dust. Dust fever. He had heard men speak of it at night while they lay on their rudimentary cots. It wasn't a pleasant way to die, they said. Continual coughing spasms, spitting back large portions of the mountain they inhaled, a high fever that resulted in uncontrollable fits. Not a pretty way to leave this earth, he thought. Then there was blackdamp. If dust fever didn't get you then blackdamp would. He had no idea what it was but apparently it had something to do with the air in the mines. If one breathed too much bad air one would get the blackdamp and die. He realized how dangerous it was to work in the mines. Was that going to be his fate? Probably, if he lived long enough and didn't die from falling down a shaft or from a collapse of a gallery.

Most of the iron used by the Norsemen came from bogs. Called bog iron, they collected the shallow deposits of iron ore from bogs and swamps wherever they lived. Streams carried dissolved iron from nearby mountains into the bog where the iron was concentrated. The bog ore could then be collected by shallow excavation where it harvested in the form of pea sized nodules of bog iron, the raw material that was then melted down. One of the challenges was to get high enough temperatures needed to smelt the iron from the bog ore. This was done by continually feeding the oven from the top with charcoal, a process whereby any Norseman would need to first burn a cartload of charcoal, which took about five days. When completed, the oven was turned over and the bloom was extracted. This consisted of a mixture of low-carbon iron, slag, and charcoal. This bloom had to be processed afterward, in order to cleanse it for residue. Hammering at it for a while caused the impurities and slag to fall away.

But as the Norsemen expanded their territories, the need for more and more iron increased. Bog iron could not keep up with the demand. New sources needed to be found. When they conquered Saxony, they confiscated the small mine at Remmelsberg then greatly expanded its operation. Supposedly the mine was named after a knight named Ramm, who was a henchman of the Saxon emperor, Otto the Great.

Removing rock was a difficult and time-consuming process. Iron was used for most tools. When Geffrey and his fellow workers labored in a gallery, they used an iron gad or pointed bar struck by a hammer that removed the stone in flakes and dust. The gad could be socketed for a handle, held in miners' hands, or gripped with tongs. Geffrey used both single and double-headed hammers weighing fifteen to twenty pounds, fitted with sockets for a wooden handle. Iron picks, with an eight to nine inch curved blade, worked the softer rock. Other iron tools include crowbars, battering rams, and iron wedges.

From the main vertical shaft, horizontal galleries were driven at depth. The galleries followed the veins as they wove underground. The outline of the galleries was rectangular, with a height of around six feet or less and a width of four feet. There were some tunnels that were even smaller, making it impossible for a man to stand upright. Collapse of a shaft or gallery was a constant worry. Skroppa inspected the wooden bracing daily for weaknesses. The bracing crew slept and ate their meals in separate quarters from the others.

The deep mine workings created problems with ventilation, lighting, and drainage. In addition to bad air, the mines were hot. The deeper the shafts and galleries were, the hotter the ambient temperature in the mine. To overcome the problems of heat and toxic gases, the Norsemen followed the example of their Roman predecessors by creating additional air movement through convection. Cutting additional shafts in parallel so that the warmer air from the mine rose and was replaced by cooler air from outside did this. Movement thinned the air. A lighted lamp down the shaft detected gases, for if the flame was snuffed out by the power of a gas, then ventilation shafts were dug next to the shaft on either side. In this way the gas vapors were dissipated through the shafts.

The control of underground water could determine the viability of a mine. This water came from percolation from above the mine, or more rarely, from digging into the sea or a subterranean river. Many mines simply stopped at the water table. Mines that went below quickly filled with water were abandoned. While they were being worked, the Norsemen used several methods for handling the water. They could drive drainage tunnels below working levels, use slaves to bail the workings, or employ mechanical devices. The Romans handed down one such device, the so-called Egyptian screw, which Archimedes invented when he visited Egypt. By means of these devices, set up in an unbroken series up to the mouth of the mine, they dried up the mining area and provided a suitable environment for work. It consisted of a hollow wooden cylinder with a wooden helical screw, the rotor, inside. The rotor had wooden or copper vanes, around a central wooden core, which was attached to the case with an iron pivot. A person, treading on the cleats around the center of the case or turning a crank, operated this screw and raise water from one end to the other.

A whistle sounded in the distance signaling the end of the work shift. Geffrey dropped his pick and trudged with the rest of his crew to the shaft and waited in line for the climb back to the surface. Men from other galleries gathered in the narrow space occasionally pushing or jostling each other for a place in line. A large man pushed Geffrey back and stepped in front of him. The man seemed well over six feet in height, burly, covered in hair and sweat, possessed deep set eyes of coal.

"Excuse me," Geffrey said, irritated at the man's impertinence.

"Yeah?" the man retorted brusquely. His penetrating gaze was a somber one.

"You cut in front of me," Geffrey replied, trying to sound as conciliatory as possible.

The big man punched him in the chest with a fat finger.

"Listen, you little fonkin. Do you not know who I am? I am Jubal. I squash little fonkins like you. Even Skroppa gives me a wide berth."

"Well, Jubal," Geffrey said, summoning his courage, "you still cut in front of me."

"What of it? Jubal said. He chest-bumped Geffrey, stared at him. "I'll be waiting for you after supper if you care to try, little fonkin."

On his way up the ladder, Geffrey tried to envision how a confrontation with Jubal might turn out. With Geffrey squashed like a bug, no doubt. Once back in the fresh air, he stumbled to the dining hall with the rest of the men where he seated himself at a long table. Young and old women, slaves themselves he reasoned, brought their food to them. Geffrey wondered if Rosalind might be among them. He searched the hall but did not see her.

The dining hall was a high raftered building where the thousand or so slaves ate their meals. Filling the hall were long wooden tables with benches that were arranged in rows. After all the men were seated the women carried in trays loaded with food. Tonight, the fare consisted of porridge, roasted wild boar, and dried apricots. No ale, just water to drink. What I wouldn't give for a tall tankard of bitter ale, Geffrey thought.

A young man about Geffrey's age slid into the bench beside him. He was fair with sandy colored hair, freckles, dark eyes, and was missing part of an ear. He smiled at Geffrey.

"My name is Byrun," he said in a whisper, shoveling the porridge into his mouth.

"I'm Geffrey. From Lochwald."

"Yes, I know," Byrun said. "I'm a Norman peasant myself. I heard what happened to your village." He appeared to possess an expression of intensity, forward looking, as if his thoughts were trained on a single entity.

"You did? How?" Geffrey spoke in a low voice while he scanned the dining hall for Skroppa. Talking was forbidden during meals.

"I am from across the River Skye. My village was raided the same day as yours. I saw what happened between you and Jubal."

Geffrey studied the young man next to him. Byrun was not conspicuously tall nor was he conspicuously handsome. His skin was tight and smooth, possessed watery gray eyes. There was something slightly odd about him although Geffrey couldn't quite put a finger on it. Maybe it was the way Byrun seemed to be amused at his situation.

"If it's a fight he wants, then I'll accommodate him," Geffrey said.

"I would not advise that, Geffrey. I have seen the monster fight. He doesn't fight fair. He will hurt you. Maybe even kill you."

"And Skroppa does nothing about it? His precious slaves hurt by a goon such as him?"

"I dunno. I think Skroppa is half afraid of the man."

Skroppa passed behind them, swinging his baton. They ceased talking until he passed on.

"Well," Geffrey said after the overseer was at the end of the row. "If it's a fight he's pushing for, I must oblige. Honor calls for it."

"Honor?" Byrun said in a voice that had an incredulous tone about it. "Where is honor in a place such as this?"

Geffrey smiled.

"My father thought of himself a simple man's philosopher. He said that in a society such as ours, in which the civic onus is placed squarely on the law, it is common for the concept of honor to quickly lose relevance in the shadow of the almighty law. If man has the law, he has no perceivable need for honor or morals or ethics, for it is the law that tells us what is right and wrong. To determine right and wrong in such a way is laziness, and nothing more."

"I have heard that thought expressed before," Byrun said. He ran a hand through his curly hair. "An overdependence on the authority of the law can kill the soul and the greater the dependence thereupon the quicker the death." Byrun continued eating as he talked between mouthfuls.

"To do the honorable thing," Geffrey said, "is to submit the whole of one's being to the belief that there is underlying all human life and interaction and indeed all of existence, a universal sense of right and wrong. Some call it natural law, others objective truth. Regardless of its designation, it remains one and the same—an unalterable code by which all men are not only expected to adhere in their dealings with others, but also by which all men may hold a reasonable expectation to be dealt with by others. To seek to live honorably is naught but to satisfy that innate urge felt inside all men and women when presented with a choice between genuine right and wrong."

"We deal with others as we ourselves wish to be dealt."

Geffrey nodded.

"You are quite the philosopher yourself, Geffrey," Byrun said. He took a large gulp of water. "But how does all that relate to the big man, Jubal?"

"What Jubal did by cutting in line was wrong. I must stand up against that wrong. It's fairly simple, really."

"Personally, I think you're going to get your head bashed in. But I shall watch with interest."

Later that evening in the living quarters, Jubal found Geffrey.

CHAPTER 11

Geffrey and Bynum sat on a cot next to each other chatting about their previous lives before the mines. Jubal appeared, the big man towering over the two, an angry stare on his face. Geffrey shifted on his cot.

"I'm here for the reckoning," Jubal said.

Geffrey stood, eyed the man. Jubal was a good foot taller than him and outweighed him by at least a hundred pounds. His knees trembled.

"You are a big man," he said. "You are right—you can hurt me. I know that. But, by cutting in front of me without asking, you are without honor. Someone should send you a message that you can't do that with impunity." He stood, stared at Jubal. "So, big man, bring it on."

Jubal rushed, his huge arms flailing at Geffrey. The big man lumbered forward, grunting as he did. Geffrey sidestepped Jubal's charge, hit him on the side of the head, sending him sprawling onto a cot. Geffrey pounced on the man, landing several blows to his face, bloodying Jubal's nose. The man grimaced, shook off the pain then struggled to his feet. He peered through the blood, wiped his face with a burly arm, charged again.

This time Geffrey wasn't so lucky. A swinging arc from Jubal's right fist connected with the side of his head, rocking him backward on his heels. Jubal grabbed Geffrey in a bear hug and squeezed, forcing the air from his lungs. He struggled against the man's powerful grip, couldn't breathe. He felt faint. Just when he thought he would lose consciousness, Jubal released his grip, dropping Geffrey to the floor. Dazed, he staggered to his feet. When Jubal swung again, he caught the blow with an arm, twisted it back over his other arm, forcing Jubal to his knees. The giant let out a loud agonizing scream. The large group of onlookers who had gathered to observe the fight cheered.

Both men toppled to the floor, grappling each other, searching for a hold that would end the fight. But Geffrey felt his strength waning. In desperation, he head butted Jubal's broken nose. The man howled in pain and released his grip, freeing Geffrey. He jumped to his feet only to have them taken out from under him by a blow to the knees from Jubal's massive arm. He tumbled on top of the giant who quickly rolled Geffrey over onto his back. The men in the quarters cheered their respective favorites, argued over the possible outcome of the fight. The clamoring became a distant noise in Geffrey's head.

Jubal grabbed Geffrey by the hair and pounded his head into the wooden floor sending flashes of light reeling through his rattled brain. He felt his grip on consciousness slipping as Jubal again pounded his head onto the floor. And again. He was losing it.

"Here, here!" a voice boomed from somewhere in the living quarters. From where he lay, Geffrey had no idea who it was. Then Skroppa appeared, stooping over him. "What is the meaning of this?" he demanded. "Jubal, you know better."

Several of the men helped Geffrey to his feet, set him on a cot. His reeling head began to feel better. He looked around. With Skroppa's appearance, most of the men scurried from the area. Only Byrun remained with him along with Skroppa and Jubal. One of the mine foremen stood next to the door and held a baton.

"I told you," Byrun said. "Told you you'd get your head bashed in."

"Damn you, Geffrey. And you, Jubal," Skroppa said with a snarl. The scars on his body seemed as if they had mushroomed into a deeper red color. "You both shall be punished for this." Turning to the foreman, he said, "Take them to the dungeon. I will be there later."

The foreman and two others took Geffrey by the arms and pushed him out of the living quarters and into the cool evening. He was weak, his legs felt like rubber. They pulled him along the path to a rounded building constructed of brick and stone. Inside, they shoved him down a series of steps into a darkened chamber that smelled of mildew, stale sweat, and urine. Through a swollen eye Geffrey noticed Jubal was not with them. He was alone with the foremen.

They forced him into a corner where Geffrey fell to the floor exhausted. He touched his face, gently feeling the bruises and swelling, wincing each time his fingers probed a different area. Byrun was right, he thought. He got his head bashed in.

A single oil lantern provided the only light in the dungeon. As he surveyed his environs, Geffrey noticed the bloodstains on the floor. There were chains affixed to the walls in several places and the thought formed in his head that the chains were used to bind prisoners to the walls. In the dim light, he watched the foremen who sat at a small table playing some sort of dice game. Once in a while, one would give him an insidious glance.

The dungeon door opened and Skroppa entered. The foremen stood giving him their attention. He crossed the room in three energetic strides. His baton pointed at Geffrey.

"Bring him to the iron chair," he commanded tersely.

The foremen yanked Geffrey to his feet, shoved him

into a smaller room where in the middle stood a large black metal chair. It had a high back and armrests that were filled with numerous holes. There were metal bands that fastened arms and legs to the chair. His stomach churned. His mouth seemed full of cotton.

"Now, Geffrey of Lochwald," Skroppa said. "You will pay the price for such hot-headed behavior. You will learn that fighting here is forbidden."

Geffrey realized that struggle was useless as the men pushed into its cold hard seat and began locking his arms and legs in place. What kind of torture was this, he thought? The chair was hard and cold, caused his skin to bristle.

Skroppa stepped into the room and ambled to Geffrey's side. Connected to the side of the chair was a large wheel. As it dawned on Geffrey that he was to be tortured, fear shot through him like a bolt of lightning searing his heart, as would a red hot poker. A vision of his mother and father raced through his mind. His mother, beautiful Oriel, at work tending the small family garden. His father, Hugo, the village smithy whom the townspeople looked to for steadfast leadership as when Giroldus broke his leg. And dear Rosalind, the love of his life. Where was she?

Skroppa stepped to the wheel beside the chair, a sardonic grin on his lips. He began turning the wheel. He kept an eye on Geffrey.

What is about to happen?

Soon, pain began to seep into his body. Arms, legs, back, and buttocks all felt the stabbing pain. Then he understood the holes. Hundreds of sharp spikes—followed by the progressive tightening of the wheel, protruded through the holes. With each turn of the wheel the spikes were forced deeper into his flesh. The deeper the spikes jammed into his body the more intense the pain. Soon it became unbearable. He felt his shorts become warm and wet as he lost control of his bladder.

Skroppa stopped turning the wheel, ambled around to the front of the chair to face Geffrey. Through tears he saw that the overseer smiled at him.

"Now Geffrey of Lochwald," Skroppa said. "You know the penalty for wanton disregard of Remmelsberg's rules. You wish me to be merciful and stop?"

Geffrey's mind was a blur. He grimaced, then nodded.

"But I am not yet merciful," Skroppa said. He turned the wheel another two turns. Geffrey winced and cried out.

"Please!" he begged.

"My mother figures me to be a magnanimous person," Skroppa said. "Should I show her how magnanimous I can be, Geffrey of Lochwald?"

Geffrey nodded again. "Please," he said, his voice weak, barely audible. "I beg you."

"But I am not yet magnanimous," Skroppa said. He gave the wheel another few turns forcing the spikes deeper into Geffrey's pain-wracked body.

Geffrey could stand it no longer. He cried aloud. "God help me!"

Skroppa stuck his head in Geffrey's face and snarled. "God is not here, Geffrey of Lochwald. God has abandoned you. He no longer hears your pleas."

A dark fog engulfed Geffrey, wrapping him in velvet arms, until the pain no longer mattered.

When he regained consciousness, Geffrey realized he was being carried somewhere. The foremen each had hold of a limb while Skroppa walked alongside. A quick inventory of Geffrey's body revealed it was covered with gaping bloody holes. The pain was intense.

Through the fog of his agony, Geffrey struggled to see where he was being taken. They proceeded down a long hallway dimly lit by a single oil lantern. A musty odor of peat filled his lungs. At the end of the hallway, the foremen stopped while Skroppa retrieved a large key ring and unlocked a heavy oaken door. The men took Geffrey into the dark room, tossed him in the floor. There they left him as Skroppa closed the door behind them. He heard the key turning in the lock.

Alone and abandoned, Geffrey understood the true horror of his predicament.

He wept.

༄༅༄

Jubal was a Romani and as such was called a gypsy by most people with whom he came into contact. The Romani did not have a shared homeland or national identity. They were a people scattered across the globe and whose origins were shrouded in myth and mystery. They kept no written records of their early history. Many saw them as dirty, thieving, and undesirable, others as artistic, romantic, and carefree.

His father, through his quick wits, penchant for giving himself a fake dukedom, and claiming to be on bogus pilgrimages, managed to gain the protection of kings and popes as the family made their way across Europe. No good Christian was going to turn away a traveler with a title or a letter from the Holy Father, fakes though they were.

Jubal remembered with alarming clarity the impression his family made on the Normans, who lived very sheltered, monotonous lives within their tiny villages. To encounter a band of dark-skinned traveling people with black eyes and hair, wearing strange clothes and speaking a strange language was a source of amazement and fear for most medieval folk.

The Romani would set up camp just outside the towns and, among other things, the men worked as horse traders and metal workers while the women told fortunes. The problem was that they also depended on the generosity of the local people. When they felt said generosity was insufficient, they would even the score by helping themselves. They gained a reputation as pickpockets and thieves. Many Romani were arrested for theft, and some were executed for their crimes.

The day he was taken prisoner by the Norsemen, Jubal fought and killed a number of them. In the end, they managed to subdue him and bring him to Remmelsberg. Skroppa vented his anger on the giant of a man, beating and striking him often with his whip to the point that Jubal had permanent scars on his back and shoulders. By the time of his confrontation with Geffrey, Jubal had so much pent-up anger boiling in his soul that the slightest provocation set him off. But inflicting hurt and pain on another human was not part of the Romani way, and Jubal wished to make it right.

☙❧☙

Byrun lay on his cot, worried about the new friend he made in the dining hall. He hadn't had much of a chance to know Geffrey much at all, but he sensed the young man possessed an internal grit and sense of self that Byrun found enviable. He hoped that Skroppa had not broken Geffrey's spirit. Or too many of his bones. Byrun suspected that Geffrey's sense of honor and courage came from a deep well of tenacity instilled by his parents. His friend exuded a quiet confidence that was alluring and enviable, characteristics Byrun wished he possessed.

When Norse marauders overran his tiny hamlet, Byrun was taken prisoner and made a slave in the Remmelsberg mines. Byrun's father was a farmer, and Byrun hoped to follow in his footsteps on the small family farm, but those dreams were shattered when his father, mother, and two younger sisters were brutally murdered as the invaders laid waste to the village.

Once, he was involved in an altercation with Skroppa who, in the scuffle, bit off part of Byrun's ear. Half of it was gone. It bled profusely, but he recovered.

In talking with several acquaintances, he learned that Skroppa did not punish Jubal for his part in the fight with Geffrey. The big monster of a man lay on his cot and bragged how he got the best of a little fonkin. Byrun assumed that Skroppa took Geffrey to the dungeon where he was tortured. He wondered when the young man would be able to return, for he had seen others tortured and they never faired very well. At least for a long while.

The next day after the fight, Byrun went to work. He labored in a different gallery from Geffrey's but figured the work was the same—picking rocks out of the mountain with picks, chisels, and hammers. As he picked up his pick, a man he didn't know approached him.

"May I have a word with you, son?" the man said. He was older, wore a long gray beard, and was stooped slightly at the waist.

"Sure," Byrun said. He noticed the man was missing most of his teeth and wondered how he ate the roasted wild boar they had for supper.

"I watched the fight last night," the old man said. "The one between the young man and the mulish brute, Jubal."

"Not a bad fight initially. The end of it wasn't in Geffrey's favor, however."

"That's the young man's name—Geffrey?"

"It is. Why do you ask?"

The old man shifted his weight onto another foot, peered about, obviously conscious of the ban on talking.

"You are a friend of his? I noticed that you were by his side."

"We just met," Byrun said. "I'm sure Skroppa tortured him last night. I hope he's all right."

"As do I," the man said. "I was hoping I might entertain with you the idea of an escape. I fear I don't have much time left, and I hate the thought of spending my remaining days in this despicable place."

"Well…say, I didn't get your name."

"Jodocus. My name is Jodocus."

"What kind of name is that?" Byrun asked.

"I am from Silesia," Jodocus said. "Me and my family escaped the wars with the Poles, and these damned Norse infidels captured us. I lost track of my wife. Our grown daughter and her infant traveled with us but, alas, I have no idea where they are either."

"I am sorry to hear that. Well, Jodocus, I know of no plans for escape. However, I am willing to entertain the possibility. When I find Geffrey, maybe we can talk again.

Jodocus eyed Byrun and smiled. "Maybe," he said.

CHAPTER 12

Geffrey came to in darkness. Every muscle, sinew, bone, and square inch of his body ached with an intensity he had never known before. As the stone floor came into sharper relief, he realized that he lay in the corner of a small room, a few handfuls of dried straw scattered about. There was no light. He could see nothing farther away than a few inches from his eyes.

He shivered.

He was cold.

He rolled onto his back, felt a rat scamper across his chest. He jumped and the sudden movement shot a white bolt of pain through him again. He winced, grunted.

Where was he?

Ever so slowly, it came back to him. The fight, the torture in the chair, men carrying him somewhere,

To here, possibly.

In spite of the pain, Geffrey pushed himself to a sitting position in the corner and leaned against the wall. He took a deep breath, smelled the dank must of his cell. Yes, he must still be in the dungeon.

How long had he been here? He didn't know but it couldn't be very long for his aches and pains were still much a part of him. Sitting in the dark, he explored his face with his hands. It was swollen about his eyes and mouth. He moved a finger over his torso and limbs feeling each puncture wound—the ones left by the spikes in the iron chair. They had crusted over but were still tender to the touch.

His mouth felt as if it was full of wool, his tongue thick from lack of water. Geffrey smacked his lips and felt them crack. A drop of blood found its way into his mouth, and its metal taste surprised him. He remembered Skroppa fixing him to the iron chair, remembered his diabolical laughter as he tightened the spikes farther into Geffrey's body.

Skroppa. How he hated the man.

Geffrey lay back on the stone floor. Once again black velvet welcomed him into its outstretched arms.

A man dressed in a black cloak escorted him across the river. He couldn't see his escort's face. It was strange but they crossed the water without sinking into its depths. Floated across the river. Once on the far bank, another man took Geffrey by the arm and led him to an ice cathedral where inside, the temperature was just above freezing. A shaking chill overtook him. His escort led him to a large throne in the cathedral's hall. The throne was raised above the floor and on it sat a pale white figure dressed in white robes. The figure's body appeared translucent. Surrounding the throne were a number of seraphim, who bowed continuously toward the figure. Geffrey instinctively knew he looked upon Lucifer, god of Hades.

"Come hither," the figure said, an outstretched bony finger pointed at Geffrey. "Come and receive your judgment."

Geffrey trudged to the foot of the throne, which appeared to be made of carved ice. For the first time, Geffrey caught a glimpse of the figure's face—hideous, grotesquely scarred, and distorted. It looked down upon Geffrey with red glowing eyes.

"Kneel," the figure commanded and Geffrey fell to his knees. "You know my name?"

"You are Satan," Geffrey said.

"And you are here to receive my judgment, are you not?"

Geffrey nodded.

"Speak up!" the figure said.

"Yes, my lord."

"Your sins have been measured and added up. Your judgment has been arbitrated before the council of Hades. You, Geffrey of Lochwald, will spend eternity in the Place of the Damned. You will be alone—forever. From that place there is no exit."

"But, my lord," Geffrey protested. "I always tried to live a good life. Please tell me what my sins were that I should be judged so harshly."

The figure stared at him with the glowing eyes that penetrated to his very core. He pointed a deformed finger at Geffrey. "It is not for you, Geffrey of Lochwald, to know the specifics of your crimes, lest you beg for reprieve. You had your chance, given you by the all-knowing Creator."

The figure's voice was harsh and crackled with evil humor. Geffrey trembled before the throne. "No one should be sentenced," he said, summoning a small bit of courage, "to such depravity without a chance to defend himself. Someone should speak in my behalf."

The figure laughed, its voice echoing throughout the ice cathedral. "You impudent little fool," it said. "As I said, you had your life, your chance. Here there is no further justice. Justice was served prior to your arrival."

A sound startled him awake. God, it had been a nightmare. Geffrey was covered in droplets of sweat in spite of the freezing cell.

The noise came from a metal plate sliding through a small opening at the base of the door. Geffrey crawled to it, and in the darkness noticed that the plate contained a piece of dark rye bread and a small cup of water.

Suddenly, he was hungry. He stuffed the bread into his mouth in huge mouthfuls and greedily drank down the water. Finished, he rolled back onto his back, breathing hard.

The dream left him drained, frightened. Could it portend his future? Once his breathing had returned to normal, he crawled back to his corner. Soon, he was sleeping.

How many days Geffrey spent in the dungeon cell in total darkness, he had no knowledge. There was no way of knowing when it was dark outside or when it was light. When the sun was up or when the moon shone. It must have been more than a week for his bruises healed and the wounds from the spikes dried up. Most of his pains left his body. He was able to stand and amble a few steps about his cell.

The door opened allowing a shaft of light to flood the cell.

Three men entered, grabbed Geffrey by the arms, and hauled him out of the cell. His legs buckled with the brusque treatment. He was in a weakened state. Barely able to put one foot in front of the other, the men dragged him to a room where he faced Skroppa. The bright light momentarily blinded him. He thought about lunging at the man, attacking him, but he was too weak. He just stood there while Skroppa studied him.

"Well, Geffrey of Lochwald," Skroppa said after a moment. "I trust you have learned your lesson. We have rules here, and those rules need to be obeyed. Right? Of course. Since I am a merciful man, I will give you a couple of days to recover your strength, then it is back to work for you. All right, take him away."

Geffrey of Lochwald. Wasn't that the phrase the figure in his nightmare used?

The men gathered Geffrey in tow and pulled him from the dungeon back to the living quarters where they dropped him on his cot, alone. Geffrey sat, feeling some better. His bruises felt less painful but they were still tender to touch. The holes in his arms and legs created by the spikes had healed but left behind a deep-seated ache in his muscles and joints.

He heard the whistle signal the end of the work shift and soon Byrun was at his side. The young man smiled when he looked at him, slapped him on a shoulder. Geffrey winced from the blow.

"Sorry," Byrun said. "I arranged to have the cot here next to you and Skroppa gave me permission to care for your wounds until you are able to return to work." He chuckled. "As long as it didn't take longer than three days. The man's a demon, Geffrey."

Geffrey nodded, smiled at his friend. "I'm glad to see you," he said in a halting voice. "How long was I gone?"

"A little longer than a month. What did they do to you?"

"They—they have a chair," he said, "down in the dungeon. Skroppa called it the iron chair. They fasten you to that chair then cause hundreds of spikes to be driven into your body. All over. Hurt like hell."

"My God," Byrun exclaimed. His face turned sour at Geffrey's description of the torture.

"After that," Geffrey continued, "they threw me into a dark cell. There I remained until now. I was fed bread and water. The cell was pitch black so I never knew when the days began or ended. The rats, Byrun, had the run of the place. Once I awoke feeling one of the bastards nibbling on one of my sores. It was a living hell."

"That's horrible, Geffrey. Was it worth it to fight the big man, Jubal?"

Geffrey's laugh was followed by a coughing fit. "I suppose not," he said. "But at least the big oaf knows I am not afraid of him."

"He has been asking about you."

"Really? Why?"

"Says he wishes to make amends. Says he never wanted you to be taken to the dungeon. Most of us know about that iron chair. It's strange in a way, but you made a lot of friends by your courage, Geffrey. The men look up to you."

Geffrey laughed again and coughed. "It was only a little fight," he said. "And one in which I didn't fare too well either, I might add."

"It wasn't the outcome that impressed everyone," Byrun said. "It was the fact that you stood up to the man for what you thought was right. You called it honor, I remember. And you were willing to suffer the unknown consequences. However bad."

"And that honor nearly got me killed."

Byrun left and returned with a cool damp compress that he applied to Geffrey's face while he lay on his cot. He applied a salve to his healing wounds. While Byrun worked, Geffrey recounted his dream.

"It was unbelievable. I was in a crystal cathedral built of ice. The entire building was transparent. In the center were a large throne and this figure—this icy figure sat upon it. His name, Byrun, was Lucifer, the Devil. And he sentenced me to eternity in a place called The Damned. Alone, all alone. I couldn't bear it. I thought it was real."

At that, Geffrey broke down and wept. Tears mixed with the salve creating a thin paste on his face.

Byrun touched his shoulder. "There, my friend," he said in a soft voice. "Let it out. It's all right. Just let it go."

For several minutes Geffrey cried, more from the release of tension and exhaustion than fear.

When he finally finished with the tears, Byrun wiped his cheeks and smiled. "Feel better?" he said.

"Yeah, much. And thanks for being my friend, Byrun. It means a lot."

"You are welcome. Listen, I met an old man while you were—indisposed." They both had a laugh at Byrun's choice of the word. "Name is Jodocus. He's from somewhere in Silesia. Was escaping a civil war there and was taken prisoner by the Norsemen and brought here. He wants to escape. Asked me to join him. What do you think?"

"I dunno. Maybe we can talk about it later when I'm feeling better. Right now, I'm still pretty weak."

"Of course. Now, relax and rest. If you need anything during the night, I will be right next to you. Just reach out and wake me. Understand?"

Geffrey nodded. When the foremen walked through the quarters later and extinguished the lanterns, Geffrey lay in the dark until sleep overtook him.

ೞೞೞ

Jodocus hated working underground. The work was dark, dirty, and there wasn't much in the way of ventilation. In addition, there were the Knockers. He could feel their presence. Once, he thought he caught a glimpse of one watching him at the end of a dimly lit gallery. He didn't like it.

Most of the miners held a firm belief in the existence of underground creatures and spirits. The belief in such underground supernatural beings developed as a way of accounting for strange mishaps and accidents that sometimes occurred in the mines.

Knockers were the underground equivalent of the Irish leprechauns, measuring about two feet in height, with a grizzled, but not misshapen, appearance. As these creatures inhabited underground mining areas, they were often depicted as wearing miniature versions of standard miner's garb. Their name was derived from the supposed knocking sound produced just before a rock fall or the caving-in of a roof.

Some miners believed that the Knockers were actually evil creatures and that the knocking noise was the sound of their hammering at walls and supports to cause the cave-ins. However, others believed that they were essentially well-meaning sprites and that the knocking was their way of warning the miners that a life-threatening collapse was imminent. The Knockers watched over the mines, and could bring miners rewards or punishments. Some believed that the knocking noises they made would lead miners to a rich ore body. Others believed that the knocking was a warning of danger, but that the miner who first heard it would die. These spirits were believed to be a species of fairies who had their dwellings in the rocks and crevices, but their homes were invisible to mortal eyes.

Another tale Jodocus heard was that the Knockers were the helpful spirits of people who had died in previous mining accidents and that their knocking was a warning to the miners of impending danger. To thank them for the warnings, and to avoid future peril, some the miners developed a tradition of casting the last bite of their supper into the mines for the Knockers.

The constant banging, hammering, and daily beatings of the workers by Skroppa and his foremen were having a deleterious effect on Jodocus. He couldn't deal with much more of the insanity that was the Remmelsberg mines. His wife, daughter, and granddaughter had vanished, never to be seen by him again. He was slowly going out of his mind. He needed fresh air. He needed friends.

Most if all, he needed freedom.

CHAPTER 13

A few days later, Geffrey was back at work in the mines. Back in the familiar gallery, banging and hammering away at the rock. While he was locked in the dungeon, progress of a few feet had been made as the men followed the vein of iron. With the exception of his scars he was almost completely healed of his injuries. It was hard for him to believe that Byrun had spent the last few days caring for him, tending to his bruises and pains, placing cool compresses and salve on them. The young man's compassion touched Geffrey's heart, something rare in this world of tough men and hard difficult work directed by an evil overseer. Since returning to work, he and Byrun talked every night of their hopes and dreams, reliving past lives and loves. When he mentioned Rosalind, Byrun related his own story of losing a fair-haired maiden.

"Her name was Miranda," he said to Geffrey one night as they lay on their cots. "She was the daughter of our town's cobbler. She had long blonde hair, green eyes the color of deep pools, and a smile that reduced me to a bumbling idiot when I was around her. Her father didn't like the fact that my father and I were farmers, said it was a filthy way to earn a living. But we would see each other every chance we got."

"I can relate to that," Geffrey said. "Roz's father didn't like me, either."

"Anyway, one winter, Miranda and I were walking down by the river, talking. We chatted about getting married, you know. We loved each other so much." Byrun's eyes grew misty as he related the story. He found it difficult to continue.

"If it's too painful, Byrun," Geffrey said, "you don't have to go on."

"No, it's all right," he said, drying his eyes with his blanket. "I want to."

Geffrey rose to an elbow as Byrun continued with the story.

"We walked close to the water's edge. Next to the shore the still water had turned to ice. She ran ahead of me, laughing. I tried to warn her that the rocks and ice were slippery but she wouldn't listen. She just kept running down the shoreline, jumping from rock to rock. Once, I remember, she looked back and smiled.

"I shouted again for her to stop, wait for me. But she wandered farther out on a group of rocks, out into where the river rushed into a long deep run. She slipped and fell. Fell into the icy river. All at once the current took her downstream. Her head disappeared. I never saw her again.

"I ran down the river's edge after her, crashing through briars, stumbling over the rocks and boulders until I was out of breath. But it was no use. I couldn't find her."

"That's horrible," Geffrey said. "What happened?"

"I ran back to the village and grabbed the first person I saw to come and help. Soon most of the men were scattered out along the river but alas, Miranda was nowhere to be found. Later that winter, a farmer found her dead body among some fallen timbers a mile downstream."

Byrun looked at Geffrey with tears in his red eyes. Geffrey's heart ached for his new friend.

"Miranda's father never forgave me," Byrun continued. "He held me responsible for his daughter's death, which only added to my own grief and guilt. Later, when the Norsemen raided our village, her father and mother were killed. I guess it all evens out in the end."

"Byrun, I am so sorry," was all Geffrey was able to say.

❦❦❦

One afternoon, as the rock haulers carried basket after basket of iron ore to the smelter, Jubal appeared at Geffrey's shoulder. He jumped when the man touched him, startled to see the big man in his gallery.

"You shouldn't be here, Jubal," he said. "This isn't where you work."

Jubal pushed him to the rock wall. Geffrey's heart skipped a beat.

"Calm down," Jubal said. "It isn't what you think. I've come to tell you that I'm sorry for what I did. I ask you to forgive me."

Geffrey was stunned. The big man appeared sincere. His face had the look of supplication.

"What brought this on?" Geffrey asked.

"I heard what they did to you in the dungeon," Jubal said. "Your friend, Byrun, told me. I want you to know it was never my intent for you to suffer so."

"What happened to you?" Geffrey asked. "They took you to the dungeon as well."

Jubal smiled, a sheepish look in his face. "I have a certain...er, certain understanding...with the man Skroppa. I do the work of three men so when I get into trouble the punishment is not severe."

"Convenient," Geffrey said.

"Your friend mentioned the two of you were going to

escape from this place. If that is so, you will have the need of a man like me. I can be helpful. Three heads are better than one."

Geffrey thought the man somewhat dim-witted and slow afoot. He wasn't sure how much help the giant would be.

"Was it acceptable to Byrun?" he said.

"It was," Jubal said. "Look, I wish to make amends, Geffrey. I want out of this place. It is a place of death." He extended his hand. "How about it?"

Geffrey took the giant hand in his, felt the huge fingers wrap around his own. The grip was firm.

"Sure," he said. "Grudges help no one here."

"If you want, I will allow you to hit my face as often as you like if it would square things between us. I hate to think we can't put this completely behind us."

Geffrey laughed, looked around for Skroppa. He had no desire to return to the dungeon and its horrors.

"Naw," he said. "Don't worry. I believe your sincerity."

Jubal smiled and left him to return to his hammering.

That evening Geffrey mentioned to Byrun the meeting with Jubal.

"Yeah, he said he was wanting to talk to you and apologize after I told him what Skroppa did to you. Even the giant Jubal doesn't care for Skroppa. Or trust him."

Later in the week a deep rumble shook the mountain. The mine galleries filled with dust and the men scrambled in panic.

"Cave-in!" a shout rang out.

The whistle blew, its wailing sound ricocheting through the shafts and galleries. Geffrey dropped his pick and ran to the gallery opening. Men were gathered in the common area two hundred feet below the surface. *My god*, he thought—*a cave-in. Part of the mine has col-*

lapsed. Men must be trapped. He looked around, searching for Skroppa. The man was nowhere to be found. *Has he left us down here to die?* Geffrey thought. The men were talking wildly in excited voices, their animated gestures signaling panic.

"Where's the cave-in?" he shouted above the din. "Where is it?"

Jubal grabbed an arm, spun him around. "Next level up, I think. Let's go."

He pulled Geffrey to the ladder leading to the surface and next level. Geffrey began the scramble up with Jubal right behind. Dust filled the shaft making visibility nearly impossible. The oil lanterns gave off weak lighting, just enough to see a few rungs ahead on the ladder. As the smoke and dust filled his lungs, it became more difficult for him to breathe. He paused, looked back at Jubal. The man's face was covered with dust, barely recognizable.

"Don't stop!" Jubal screamed. "Every second counts!" He pushed Geffrey on the buttocks to get him going again.

Geffrey's legs screamed as he climbed. Rung after rung until he reached the next level. There he was greeted by eerie silence. He stepped out of the shaft and into the common area. The place was full of men standing silent, doing nothing. Jubal climbed out of the shaft and stood beside him.

"Where's the cave-in?" Geffrey demanded.

The smoke and dust were thick, men were coughing and spitting.

A man holding a hammer stepped forward, pointed to a gallery. "Down there," he said. "The gallery gave way. We've been hesitant to go down there for fear of another collapse."

"I'll go," Geffrey said. "How many men are trapped?"

"Possibly a dozen," the man said. "Maybe a few more."

The air in the alcove where the men gathered was dank and heavy, the temperature stifling. Geffrey was appalled at them standing around doing nothing in the face of such an emergency. The faces of most of the men bore impassive expressions as they milled about in silence. With each passing minute, the trapped miner's chances of survival diminished. They had to do something.

Geffrey and Jubal hurried down the gallery until they came to the collapse. A wall of rock and rubble filling the entire gallery greeted them, blocking any further progress. The dust was thick, coating Geffrey and Jubal to where they looked like pasty corpses.

"This is the gallery were Byrun works," Jubal said, advancing to the wall of rocks. "He must still be in there."

"We've got to save him, Jubal," Geffrey said. He began throwing rocks behind them.

Jubal took his lead and followed suit, grabbing the larger stones and tossing them aside. His great strength allowed him to throw them aside like they were mere pebbles. Gradually, as more men entered the gallery, the number of helpers increased.

Geffrey looked behind them, noticed men just standing around doing nothing to help. "Get those men in a line," he shouted. "Form a chain to pass the rocks out of here. Hurry!"

ɛ⁄ɔɛ⁄ɔ

The oil lantern flickered out when the cave-in occurred, trapping Byrun behind a rock wall of large boulders and splintered timbers. He was knocked to the gallery floor by a falling beam. It was pitch black—he could barely see his hand when he held it up to his eyes. His tomb was silent. That was what it felt like, a grave deep underground.

He pushed himself to an elbow and a sharp pain rocketed through is right leg, causing him to catch his breath. He lay there for a moment, breathing hard, allowing the pain to subside before moving on to a sitting position. The small space was filled with dust and it clogged his lungs, choking him. After a coughing spasm, he crawled to the rock wall where the gallery had collapsed and, using his hands to feel the rocks, tried to get a handle on his situation.

It wasn't good.

From what he was able to discern in the darkness, he was trapped, and he doubted anyone would be able to get to him before he ran out of air. The wall that now blocked his escape seemed impenetrable—no one could make their way through it for a rescue. Unfortunately, there was only one way out of the gallery—through the rock wall. He sat with his back against a boulder and tried to figure what he should do next.

He had been near the end of the gallery when the collapse occurred. The area he was in seemed to be no bigger than a large closet. To begin throwing the rocks aside would have him using up the air in the enclosed space faster than if he just lay quiet and waited for help to arrive. It didn't seem the right thing to do however, so he propped himself against a rock, took a breath, and prayed he wouldn't die.

Byrun had heard other workers talk about previous disasters and cave-ins, and he knew the available air in his enclosed space was limited. It seemed counterproductive to use up precious air by trying to dig his way out.

But was it reasonable to do nothing and wait to be res-
cued?

He had an uneasy feeling about his situation. Byrun
tried to quell his racing heart and relax.

But it was difficult.

ℯↄℯↄ

An old stooped man sauntered up to Geffrey.

"I am Jodocus," he said. "I will get the men organized
in a line. My friend Byrun is in there."

"You know Byrun?" Geffrey said while he continued
to move rocks.

"Yes," Jodocus said. "And you are?"

"Geffrey. From Lochwald."

"Yes, Byrun has talked of you. Don't worry, we will
get your friend out of here."

Jodocus limped off and began organizing the remaining men into a line where they began removing rock from
the gallery. Geffrey noticed his stooped stature and wondered how old the man was. The man had a full head of
white hair. His eyes were bright.

Geffrey's hands were soon blistered and bleeding. He
and Jubal weren't making fast progress. The wall of
rocks loomed large as ever. He glanced over his shoulder
and noticed that Jodocus had the remaining men arranged
in two lines, and they were passing the rock from hand to
hand out the gallery. The harder he worked pulling the
rock from the cave-in, the more surprised he was that
Skroppa was not present.

No sooner had he the thought than the man appeared
on the scene, inquiring of the men what had happened,
how the cave-in occurred. His eyes met Geffrey's, and he
hurried to the pile of rocks.

"So," he said, "you were first on the scene, eh?"

"No," Jubal interjected. "We were the only men willing to work. The rest just stood around until that old man over there got them organized." He pointed to Jodocus at the head of a column.

"Yes, Jodocus," Skroppa said. "He's been here for many years. He was here when I came."

"Yes," Geffrey said.

"Do you two need anything? I hate to lose men to these infernal collapses. I have to go and purchase more slaves. It means leaving my wife for a time."

"We could use more men up here clearing these rocks," Geffrey said. "Byrun is trapped in there and must be running out of air."

"And get a hauling crew here," Jubal said. "They can help moving these rocks out of the gallery."

"Of course," Skroppa said. He disappeared into the throng of men. Soon others came alongside and began heaving rocks from the slide out of the way. Haulers arrived and started filling their wicker baskets with rocks and moving them out of the gallery.

For the next hour, they labored away, digging through the wall of rock that blocked the gallery. The sharp edges of the rocks cut and bruised Geffrey's hands. The heavier rocks needed to be pried away with iron crowbars then pushed to the side of the gallery. Soon he and Jubal were drenched in sweat, their skin glistening in the dim light of the torch.

"You think they have lost air in there?" Jubal said. He looked at Geffrey with concern. His hands, too, were bloodied.

"They might still be alive," Geffrey responded. "Especially if there is a ventilation shaft leading into the back part of the gallery. If so, then they are getting fresh air, even if only a trickle. But we still need to hurry."

"I will say a prayer they are alive," Jubal said.

"A prayer?" Are you a religious man, Jubal?" Geffrey tried to not make his tone sound skeptical.

"Of course, Geffrey. I belong to the Roma people, what you call gypsies. We pray to Dei or your Christian God. We have customs that you might find strange, but they make sense to us."

"Like what, Jubal?"

As he talked, Jubal continued to pull rocks away from the collapse. "When a person dies, relatives and friends gather around and ask for forgiveness for any bad deeds that they have done to that person. They are concerned that if such grievances are not settled, then the dead person might come back as an evil spirit and cause trouble. In the past, the widow might commit suicide when her husband died so that she could accompany him during the afterlife. Sometimes, the deceased's nostrils are plugged with wax so that evil spirits cannot enter and occupy the body. Clothing, tools, eating utensils, jewelry, and money may be placed in the coffin in order to help the deceased in the next world. The deceased's possessions are burned, broken, or sold to non-Roma."

"I didn't know," Geffrey said.

He found a small crack between the rocks and stuck his hand in it. It slid in to his elbow without difficulty. He stooped, peered into the crack but saw nothing in the dark hole.

Then a sound.

Like rock banging on rock.

Someone was just beyond the rock wall and they were alive.

Alive!

"Dig, Jubal. I heard them pounding. It's a signal. They're alive."

Jubal doubled his efforts at throwing the rocks off the great pile. Soon he had excavated a hole.

"Get a lantern up here!" Geffrey shouted.

When a light arrived, he took the lantern and held it front of the hole Jubal had made. There was a shout from the other side. He still could not make out anything, even with the aid of the lantern. Geffrey signaled. More men pounced on the rock slide and flailed away, throwing the rocks off the pile.

A hand shot through the hole.

"We're through!" Jubal shouted and a cheer went up among the men. Jodocus hobbled over, nodded. He patted Jubal on the back then returned to the work of removing rock from the gallery.

"Byrun, are you in there?" Geffrey screamed into the opening. "Byrun!"

There was no answer.

The hole enlarged wide enough for Geffrey to crawl through. He carried a lantern with him. On the other side of the rock pile a grisly scene greeted him. A number of men lay dead, scattered about, their bodies crushed and bleeding. A few had their skulls crushed, brain matter drying on the gallery floor. Huge rocks were everywhere. He raised the lantern so its light illuminated what was left of the gallery.

"Byrun!" he called. "You in here?"

The thought suddenly occurred to him that there could be more pockets of men similar to this one. Their work might not be over.

A man stumbled toward Geffrey, his face bloodied.

"Any others alive?" he said to the man.

The man, covered with pale rock dust, ignored his question, kept stumbling forward.

"I said are there any more men alive? Is this the only group of men in the collapse?"

The man acted as if he hadn't heard. He just stumbled to the hole. *Dazed*, thought Geffrey.

At the back end of the gallery he heard a stirring. Someone moving or trying to move. He rushed to the sound. Byrun lay on his side in the midst of the rubble. He moved. He was alive.

Geffrey was on him in a second, assessing his injuries. Byrun looked up at him with a vacant stare.

"Byrun, you all right, buddy? Talk to me. It's Geffrey. I've come to get you out."

CHAPTER 14

I may have misjudged you," Skroppa said to Geffrey who was seated across the small table from the overseer. "May have even punished you too harshly," he added.

The two men were seated in Skroppa's living quarters. His wife brought them each a tankard of ale that Geffrey sipped with measured mouthfuls. It was the first ale he had tasted in two years, and he didn't want to get drunk in Skroppa's house.

"I am not familiar with Lochwald," Skroppa said. "You said that was your home, right?"

"Yes. Lochwald." Geffrey wondered where the question was leading.

"Your parents alive?"

"No, they were killed."

"Oh. Any brothers or sisters?"

"No."

"Not very talkative are you?" Skroppa said. "Oh, well, it's probably the rules we have here against talking until after supper. Did you work there in Lochwald?"

"I was my father's apprentice." Geffrey took another sip of the ale. It was good and bitter.

"And what did your father do?" Skroppa, despite his proclivity for violence and meanness, seemed genuinely interested.

Geffrey decided to answer truthfully. "He was a blacksmith."

Skroppa's eyes widened, and he jumped in his chair. "A blacksmith you say? Well, I do say. It's my lucky day. Why didn't you tell me before this?"

"I don't understand," Geffrey said, surprised that his remark would cause such a stir in the overseer.

"How far along in your apprenticeship were you?"

"I was almost finished."

"What luck," Skroppa said. He was still in an excited state. When his wife reentered the room, he got her attention. "Martha," he exclaimed. "The boy is a blacksmith. What do you think of that?"

The woman nodded without a word, wiped her hands on an apron, and left the room.

"What's the big deal with me being a blacksmith?"

Skroppa took a long pull at his tankard then leaned forward, his elbows on the table. "Nothing, except we happen to be in need of one in the smelter and forge," Skroppa said. "My boy, how would you like to leave the mines and work in the forge? It's located farther up the hill. The men who work there have their own living and eating quarters nearby. What do you say?"

Geffrey thought about it for a few moments. The idea of leaving the mines interested him greatly but he didn't want his friends to think he was deserting them.

"Oh, I dunno," he said. "I have made friends in the mine."

"Who?"

Geffrey wasn't sure if he should disclose who they were out of fear of repercussions by the overseer.

"I—" He hesitated.

"Don't worry, my boy. Nothing will befall them. Now who are they? If they are keeping you from coming to the forge, I might be able to help."

"A man named Byrun. One named Jubal."

"Byrun from Skye?"

Geffrey nodded.

"Byrun who tended to you after your punishment?"

Again, Geffrey nodded.

"And Jubal the giant man? The one you fought?"

Geffrey shrugged. He decided to risk asking a favor of Skroppa. "I would go to the forge," he said, "if my friend, Byrun, could go with me."

Skroppa leaned back in his chair. Geffrey could see the wheels turning in his brain. After a few moments he spoke.

"It can be arranged," the overseer said. "I must admit, my boy, you have brass. What about Jubal?"

"I didn't want to ask for too much," Geffrey said. "But if it pleases you and Jubal agrees—well, that would please me."

"If it means we get another blacksmith in the forge, then I'll gladly agree to your request. I will send Ornolf for you at daybreak tomorrow. He will take you and your friends up the hill to your new work."

"Ornolf?" Geffrey said.

"The forge and smelter overseer. He and I go back a few years. But I warn you, he's a hard taskmaster—brutal, in fact. Cross him and you'll regret it." When he stood, Geffrey did as well. "Just a word to the wise."

Geffrey didn't see how the man could be any more violent than Skroppa.

Back on his cot, Geffrey explained to Byrun his meeting with Skroppa. The young man jumped at the chance to leave the dust-filled mines for the smelter and forge. It didn't matter the work, he said, anything to get out of purgatory. He would get the word to Jubal later in the evening when everyone was asleep.

"How did this come about?" Byrun asked Geffrey. They sat on their cots after the evening meal.

"Skroppa felt beholding to me for saving your life and the lives of the others. I think he was being gracious. But while we were talking, he found out that I was a blacksmith apprentice, and he was overjoyed. Apparently, they are short of smiths up at the forge."

"How did he find that out? You must have told him."

"Yes. He asked about my life in Lochwald and what I did there, what Father did. That's when I mentioned I was my father's apprentice. He was Lochwald's blacksmith. Skroppa seemed very happy at the news."

"So when do we go?"

"In the morning. Ornolf, the smelter and forge overseer, will get us after the morning meal and escort us up there."

"What will we be doing?" Byrun asked. "Anything will be better than the mine."

"Don't really know as Skroppa didn't say. But the smelter is where the iron is burned away from the rock and the forge is where the iron tools and implements are made. I have heard their main output is weapons, but we'll see when we get there."

"I imagine I'll be in the smelter. I don't know anything about smithing." Byrun reclined on his cot, closed his eyes. "Who knows, I might even be your assistant."

"Ha!" Geffrey exclaimed. "I'll require someone with half a brain."

Byrun threw a sandal at him, and they laughed together. Finally, Geffrey thought, they were leaving the mine behind. Whatever the future held in the forge, it would be better than life in the oppressive mines. The work would be familiar, and he would have his friends with him. It had been a number of years since he had last labored over a forge but the work in the mines had strengthened his arms so using blacksmith hammers wouldn't be a problem. At last he would hold smithing tools in his hands once again.

The following morning a short squat heavy muscled man called for Geffrey and Byrun. He had curly reddish hair and beard to match. A bulbous nose sat perched between two beady narrow eyes the color of robin's eggs. In the next barrack they found Jubal sitting in his cot, waiting for them. Ornolf looked up at the tall Jubal and shook his head then quietly led them out of the living quarters and up the hill to the smelter.

It was located in a large wooden building that contained a series of six huge furnaces at one end. A man dressed in similar short trousers to Geffrey's brought baskets of crushed rock and dumped them in a large bin next to the furnaces. Inside, the building's temperature was uncomfortably warm, almost hot. Geffrey noticed that Byrun and Jubal were perspiring.

"The iron ore is brought to an area behind the smelter here and crushed by men using hammers. The crushed ore is brought here and placed in the furnaces you see at the end of the smelter." Ornolf pointed to the furnace as he spoke. Geffrey and his companions watched as the work proceeded in front of them. Ornolf continued his description of the smelter process. "The furnaces are fired with charcoal, which we make from timber found in the forest nearby. The ore is then heated to a temperature that melts the rock away from the metal. It is drawn away by a hole in the floor of the furnaces. We call it slag. The remaining iron is in a soft melted state and is then removed from the furnace."

"That's typical of what we call wrought iron back home," Geffrey said. "Fairly soft and malleable. I have made many tools with it."

"Yes, this is basically a huge bloomery," Ornolf said. "The real magic of our steel begins in the forge."

As they approached the furnaces, Geffrey felt the heat from a distance, noticed the red glow of the fires. The noise of the furnaces and men working was deafening.

Jubal wiped his forehead with his arm, shook his head. "How can one work in this heat?" he said. "This is hotter than in the mines."

"Every two hours, the men here are given a break from working," Ornolf said. "And they have free access to water at all times."

The smelter was a huge operation. Basket after basket of crushed ore was brought to the furnaces in what seemed a never-ending procession. Ornolf continued.

"The smelting process starts with the pre-heating of the furnace. Once the furnace is pre-heated it is filled up with burning charcoal. On the top of this we add a layer iron ore and one layer of charcoal alternately. After about two to three hours, the slag is tapped from the furnace through a slag-tapping hole built into the bottom of the furnace. The slag contains non-iron substances from the iron ore and some iron that could not be reduced from the ore. When the iron bloom is removed, it is compressed on a log with a wooden hammer."

"This is a huge operation," Byrun said.

Ornolf turned and led the three men out of the smelter and across a small yard to the blacksmith stable and forge. The building was a large one with a high rafted ceiling whose beams were of heavy rough-hewn timbers. On one wall were two large furnaces, the forges, each connected to an enormous bellows. Arranged in front of each forge and hanging from a railing were a series of blacksmithing tools. Hanging from a rod within each forge were large earthen pots. They hung over the large charcoal fires smoldering in each furnace.

"Until this forge," Ornolf said as they strolled through the stable, "the only native metal available for our swords and other weapons was the bloomery iron that came from our smelters. This created an end-product replete with slag inclusions and only occasionally formed a hardened steel. This process of crucible steel, which we developed here, makes a remarkable improvement on the bloomery process by placing pieces of iron and charcoal in a crucible and heating it until they combine to form a steel ingot. We then forge the ingots into hard, sharp blades at low temperatures. It is a revolutionary new process. The result is a steel of exceptional strength."

The forges had a rear wall and a pillar of stone at the front of each side upon which a hood was supported. This allowed access both to the front of the forge for normal small or short bars, and long bars could be placed through the sides so to heat the middle of those longer bars while the ends of the bars extended clear out both sides of the forge.

"I have never heard of this way of making steel," Geffrey said. "Where did you come by it?"

Ornolf shook his head.

"I have heard that it came from far away Persia but I couldn't say for sure. We have several engineers here who are constantly trying to improve our process. To improve the quality of our weapons."

"Beginning with wrought iron greatly improves the blacksmith's efficiency." Geffrey said. "He doesn't have to smelt his own iron."

"We want our smiths to be spending their time forging quality blades and other weapons," Ornolf said. "Not doing less technical work."

"These forges are much hotter than my blacksmith shop back home," Geffrey said.

"It is to better melt the iron," Ornolf said. "Get rid of the impurities."

"What will be our jobs?" Jubal said. "It's only slightly cooler in here than in the smelter."

"You, big man, I will put back in the smelter. We need men of your strength."

Geffrey watched Jubal's shoulders droop. At least it was better than the mine, he thought.

"You," Ornolf continued, pointing to Geffrey, "since you are the blacksmith, I will place you in the forge here. Your other friend, I dunno."

"He can work the bellows," Geffrey said. "I had that job when I began my apprenticeship so I can advise Byrun on how it's done. Not too little air, not too much."

"When the steel comes out of the crucibles," Ornolf said, "it is poured into ingot molds. We label that cast iron. Your job as smithy will be to reheat the ingots and shape them into swords and whatever other weapons are called for. I have much experience making swords with this process so I will be your mentor at first. Once you learn our process, you will be allowed to work on your own."

"May we talk to each other in here?" Byrun said.

"Yes, you are allowed. As long as you obey the rules of no fighting or not attempting escape, you may talk to each other. Break our rules, and I'll come down on you hard. If you thought Skroppa was bad, you'll hate me. Break the rules, and I'll be on you like stink. Now, return to your quarters and pick up your things. Then return here, and I'll take you to your new living quarters. Compared with what the mining slaves have, they are lavish."

Ornolf laughed and the trio left the forge.

Geffrey thought his life was shaping up. He was still a slave but at least he was out of the mines.

ℰↄℰↄ

Medieval iron was both soft and brittle. The long inclusions—looking a bit like sausages—found in most medieval swords —were inclusions of slag, the nonmetallic part of the ore that was never separated from the iron. The slag made the iron brittle, which didn't give one a serviceable sword. Medieval blacksmiths didn't make slag-free steel, because their fires weren't hot enough to fully liquefy the iron. But in the Norse era, carbon could only be introduced incidentally, mainly through the coal in the fire, and the only way to remove the slag from the metal was to try to hammer out the impurities with each strike.

Of the thousands of swords from Normandie to the East, all were made from this inferior steel, which gave the Norsemen an advantage with their weapons. Norse swords could slice through the softer weapons of their enemies. Crucible steel swords seemed to be a completely different material. There were none of the long, gray slag inclusions in the swords, the inclusions that make the metal brittle. The uniformity of the steel was a remarkable advancement.

This new revolutionary metal, known as crucible steel, gave the swords capabilities far ahead of their time. But it could only be made by melting iron at high temperatures.

Many Norsemen were pagans who worshipped their weapons and even believed a sword could help a warrior enter heaven. The warriors would come to a special place, called Valhalla, where they would have feasts and fighting. In a warrior paradise, the only way to get to Valhalla was to be a warrior and die in battle, with your sword in your hand. Norse sagas told stories about the swords, how powerful they were. Many of the swords had personal names, sometimes, that were connected to, for instance, a bear or a wolf. By giving it a name, one could also incorporate the power of an ancestor or someone strong into the sword.

The reality of Norse combat was there was not the constant edge-on-edge, blade-on-blade contact. They used their shields in a dynamic fashion. The warriors got in close, overwhelming their opponent with vicious blows. They moved in, hit their opponent's shield. If they didn't do it right, in all likelihood they were killed. The sword was a tool that was used to do things such as warding off blows. It had to be robust and resilient, because fighting was not just about clash, clash, clash. It was a lot more dynamic.

The lack of brittle impurities in the crucible steel yielded swords of unusual flexibility and that was a huge advantage. A Norse fighter was doomed if his sword got stuck in a shield and broke. It took a special steel to withstand such stress and a sword that could do this might even be seen to possess magical powers. Crucible steel blades and their blacksmiths were held in certain esteem, even feared, because of this elemental property of what they were working with and what they were producing. To be able to make a weapon from dirt was a powerful thing. Magic and science had been intertwined throughout human history and crucible steel swords merged mysticism and the advanced engineering of the times.

CHAPTER 15

Geffrey's days in the forge were filled with heavy, difficult work as he labored to learn the strange new crucible process of forging steel into weapons. The crucial process, he learned, was the formation of iron in an earthen crucible. Some type of magic occurred while the iron cooked over the fires, a magic that he didn't understand. He spent hours attempting to figure it out but always was left in the dark. Maybe someday he would understand the strange process but for the present he just accepted it for what it was—a mystery.

Ornolf stood beside him as he grasped an ingot with a pair of tongs and placed it into the forge. Byrun pumped the giant bellows that blew air into it, causing the charcoal to glow red hot. When the metal was soft, Geffrey removed the glowing ingot from the forge and started hammering it flat. The real sweat came when he set about to work the ready metal into a blade. A swordsmith needed to carefully forge a blade. He had to shape and mix metals of different known qualities, some softer for the core or sides, some harder for the edge and point. This was done essentially by sandwiching harder steel around softer iron so that the blade could flex under sudden impact but resist deformation.

With the hammers and tongs that were his trade, Geffrey worked the infant blade, moving the block of glowing metal back and forth between the anvil and the forge fueled by the bellows. He needed the right color of heat to keep the metal at just the right pliability. He shaped his metal while red hot by slowly and repeatedly hammering and reheating until it was the length, width, and thickness he wanted. He had to work the sides, edges, and tang into shape, none of which was entirely identical in its characteristics to the others.

In order to be both strong and light for striking powerful cuts or thrusts against either hard or soft targets, Geffrey learned that different sword blades required not only different lengths and widths but also different cross-sections. Ornolf showed him how to skillfully create these shapes, perhaps in some small way improving his design each time by refining his techniques and incorporating new ideas.

When satisfied with the initial shape, Geffrey was far from finished. A finely crafted sword had to have just the right mix of good steel as well as just the right temper. Heat treatment was the final crucial step that gave the blade its strength and toughness. Heat-treating was the whole process of quenching or hardening and tempering. Tempering was the low-temperature reheating of hardened yet still somewhat brittle steel. Ornolf explained that in essence it's the relaxing of the steel at a low temperature. The higher the temperature or the longer a temperature is applied the more the metal's structure is relaxed, thus making the blade tougher while somewhat softer.

"All this work is not the whole story," Ornolf said. "Each swordsmith's work is slightly different from his peers. The very fact that the consistency and quality of source metals for swords has not been standardized in any way has ensured that each swordsmith must follow his own instincts. A true artisan must judge it from his experience and skill as such heat treatment can ruin a good blade or help save an inferior one."

"This process is much more complex than I thought it would be," Geffrey said one day at the end of their work. He, Byrun, and Ornolf sat by the forge relaxing. Geffrey was hungry.

"There are many different means to make the blade tougher but all of them involve quenching it by soaking the heated blade in water in order to lower the temperature. Quenching is the fast cooling of the glowing hot blade in order to harden it. To ensure toughness and flexibility the blade needs to be quickly quenched in either oil or water. Quenching happens before any tempering. The combined shock of this followed by the slow reheating to a low temperature essentially causes the metal's attributes to change."

"Then you polish the blade and add the hilt, right?" Byrun said, obviously getting bored with all the technical talk between the two men.

"Yes," Ornolf said. "We are experimenting with some blades made with a laminate construction, produced by folding the steel over and over then forge welding at each fold, resulting in layers. In this lamination method we hope that we might be able to refine and make the steel more homogenous. Theoretically, the more the steel is folded the more homogeneous the metal in the blade becomes. The amount of folds would be determined by both the material and the final qualities we are looking for."

"It is a much more complex process than I ever dreamed," Geffrey repeated.

"We do this all for the glory of our god, Wödan," Ornolf said, his eyes brightening at the name of the Norse deity. "Wödan is the primal animating force that permeates all life. He's the will to power that dwells at the heart of the world, by which the cosmos eternally strives to overcome itself, to grow and to flourish and to sweep away stagnation. All the shamans, rulers, warriors, outlaws, poets, and sorcerers who enjoy Wödan's patronage are the highest ambassadors of Ódr, the ultimate and unconditional life-affirming force.

"Wödan is seldom active in a battle but when he is, he can strike his enemies blind in combat, deaf or horrorstruck. Wödan can even cause their weapons to hit like sticks, or make his own men as strong as a bear and go berserk. Wödan also has the ability to travel to remote lands in his or in the memories of others. He can send people to their death or give them an illness. Some people sacrifice to Wödan, give him good promises, and hope by this to gain insight into whether they can win a battle or not."

"The God of we Normans is different," Geffrey said. "My people believe he lives in Heaven and created the world."

"Our idea of Heaven is Valhalla. It is for warriors only. You must die in battle first and be escorted by beautiful Valkyries. After clashing in battle all day long, your cleft limbs and wounds are miraculously restored in Valhalla. Once there, you feast, drink mead, and discuss the battle."

Later after the supper meal, Jubal related his experience in the smelter.

"It is hot," he said, "so very hot in the smelter. But there is light and there is ventilation and there is no dust. Being Roma, I am used to the heat. Most of the time, I load the rock ore into the furnace. It is hard work but not as hard as the mines."

"At least we eat better up here," Byrun said. "We even have fruit to go with the roasted boar and fowl. I would have loved to have a large tankard of ale, however, to go with it."

"But I do not think I can thrive here," Jubal said. "Soon, I must try to escape."

"Jubal," Geffrey said. "I do not mean to sound impertinent but you sound like you have had an education. Where did you grow up and did you go to school?"

"My family is from Moldavia," Jubal said, reclining on his cot. "We lived on the steppes north of the Black Sea. After the Magyar conquest of nearby Transylvania, my father decided to move our family to the Norman region. My mother taught my brothers and me how to read and write the Romani language. She also taught us how to count and add numbers. She told us many stories."

"How did you wind up in this hellhole?" Byrun asked.

"One day my father and I were out hunting. We were far from home in the Cindrel Mountains on the track of a herd of elk when a band of Norse raiders attacked us. There were only a dozen of them but our bows were no match for their weapons. Appearing suddenly out of the mist, they quickly surrounded us, and we were taken prisoner. They tied Father and me to our horses and took us northwest over a mountain pass. When we stopped at a small village, I was separated from my father. I do not know what happened to him. Or my mother or brothers "

"It seems we all have similar stories," Geffrey said."

"One day I hope to find my family," Jubal said. "I pray they are still alive."

❧❧❧

At first, Jubal worked unloading the carts filled with ore brought from the mines. He and a number of other men took the baskets of rocks into the smelter where they dumped them into a large pile. Others had the hot job of putting the ore into the large furnace and siphoning off the iron, the wrought iron, and staking it into bundles ready for transport to the blacksmith stable and forge. It was easier work than in the mines and the men were allowed to talk while they labored, something Jubal enjoyed. He wasn't a gregarious person but did involve himself in the revelry among his fellow workers. The men were constantly trying to best each other with feats of strength, seeing how heavy a basket of rocks they could lift. Jubal usually won.

Smelting was the second of the three basic steps of iron manufacture. Basically, smelting was the process of melting down ore in order to separate its metallic components from impurities. Charcoal, technically charred wood, was the predominant heating source of the Remmelsberg smelter, the abundance of wooded acreage across Saxony making it the easiest and most transportable, if not most efficient, resource for smelting and blacksmithing. Lime flux, usually either limestone or oyster shells, was often added so that it would combine with impurities to create a brittle slag, the residue formed through the oxidation of the iron due to smelting. Smelting took place in various types of furnaces—the Corsican and Catalan forges improved upon the bloomery hearth's design by utilizing more permanent masonry walls on two or more sides. The subsequent Stückoven, however, remained the most advanced furnace, increasing output to as much as three times the earlier furnaces. Its masonry construction reached heights of ten to fourteen feet and often employed a water-driven bellows. The use of waterpower, though, reached its pinnacle in the blast furnace. Although the Chinese developed a water-powered blast furnace whose technology spread as far west as Persia, it is believed that the technology was probably developed independently in Normandie and Germania. The blast furnace's water powered technology increased combustion and allowed the iron to be held in contact with the charcoal, producing steel that was more malleable.

The greatest benefit produced by the blast furnace was that the iron could be handled to produce pig or wrought iron both easily and at will. The term pig iron comes from the image of the molten iron that separated from the slag, ran into a canal of sand, called a "runner," and on into shallow, radiating depressions. The depressions reminded medieval ironworkers of a sow with suckling pigs. Although this choice between pig and wrought iron was possible in some previous furnaces, the quality of the blast furnace's iron greatly exceeded anything seen before, with a much greater efficiency and higher percentage of iron from the ore. The waterwheel powered enormous pairs of bellows that blew through an opening in the furnace. This greatly increased the draft into the furnace and thereby the temperature; higher temperatures meant that the ore was heated to a point where the steel became stronger. Not only the greater efficiency of the blast furnace, but also its ability to run continuously, allowed for a marked increase in output. The water powered blast furnace could run for weeks or even months at a time.

After a few months of working unloading the ore, Ornolf moved Jubal inside the smelter, a promotion of sorts. It was more complicated work—manipulating the bellows, blast furnace, water wheel, dealing with the wrought iron. He suffered minor burns a number of times until he got the hang of it. Each night at supper, he regaled his friends with tales from the smelter.

ℰᏅℰᏅ

During the following months, Geffrey honed his skills

in the forge, fashioning two-handed double-edged broad-swords four feet in length. The hilt and pommel provided the weight needed to balance the blade. Ornolf revealed to Geffrey the Norse secrets of polishing the steel to a mirror finish. Geffrey had never seen such a beautiful finish on metal in his life and marveled at the process.

Tripoli powder, crocus powder, and emery powder were used to polish the finished swords. Tripoli had the fineness of chalk and came from Greece. Crocus powder was brought from Armenia, and emery came from an island in the Aegean Sea. When they were applied to leather and rubbed on oiled steel, they formed a slurry that polished the steel very well.

Later, the swords he turned out were of a variety of sizes—heavy, two-handed broadswords, shorter, thinner one-handed swords, long daggers, and knives. A Norse innovation, the fuller, was a groove that ran the length of each side of the weapon. Its function was to decrease the weight of the blade without diminishing the strength. Use of a fuller allowed a blacksmith to use less material to comprise the blade, making it lighter without sacrificing much structural integrity. The grips were made with a variety of materials, ranging from simple wooden grips wrapped with leather, to elaborately decorated grips wound with wire made from precious metals, or covered with embossed plates of precious metals that Geffrey made for a jarl. In addition to swords, Geffrey learned how to forge the battle-axe. They were light, fast, and well balanced, and were good for speedy, deadly attacks, as well as for a variety of nasty, clever moves. The Norsemen used a wide variety of axe head shapes. Generally, the cutting edge was three to six inches long, but a few had crescent shaped edges nine to eighteen inches long. Sometimes, the edge of an axe was made of hardened steel welded to the iron head. The steel permitted the axe to hold a better edge than iron alone.

Helmets were also made at the Remmelsberg forge although Geffrey was not particularly interested in them. Helmets were made from several pieces of iron riveted together, called a spangenhelm style of helm. It was easier to make a helmet in this way, requiring less labor. The spangenhelm used a single iron band that circled the head around the brow, riveted to two more iron bands that crossed at the top of the head. The four openings were filled with riveted iron plates to create the bowl.

"So, do you think we will ever make it out of here?" Byrun asked as the three men gathered around Geffrey's cot late one evening. The lanterns had been extinguished so they sat in darkness and talked in hushed tones while the other men slept. The only sounds heard were the ones of heavy breathing and snoring.

"I don't know," Geffrey responded. "I hate to think we are stuck here until we die."

"I have lost track of time," Jubal added. "No longer know how long I've been imprisoned here."

"Geffrey," Byrun said, "I don't think I can last much longer. I have thought of killing myself. All I do all day is pump the infernal bellows and watch you work. And talk with Ornolf. I'm slowly going out of my mind."

"My God, Byrun," Geffrey said, his pulse increasing. "Don't do that, please. There's always hope. While we each live, there's always hope. We'll get out of here. I promise. We just need to find a way."

"Where would we go?" Jubal said. "If we managed to get out?"

"Home," Byrun said. "I'll go home."

"I have no home to go back to," Geffrey said.

"Neither do I," Jubal interjected. "We'll go together, Geffrey, and rebuild your village."

"Rebuild Lochwald?" Geffrey's tone was incredulous.

"Of course. Why not?" Jubal patted him on a shoulder, smiled.

Several nights later while all were asleep, Geffrey woke to someone shaking him, whispering.

"Geffrey. Wake up."

It was Jodocus. He appeared pale and sickly in the darkness.

"Jodocus," Geffrey whispered. "What are you doing here? You'll get in trouble."

"I have found a way off the mountain," he whispered. "I believe we can leave this hell."

"How? Where?"

"It's difficult to explain but there's an abandoned mine shaft not far from where I am working. The shaft goes down to a level where a ventilation tunnel leads to the other side of the mountain."

"How did you find this?"

"I don't sleep well at night so, after everyone has fallen asleep, I go for walks outside. I discovered this shaft quite by accident."

"Aren't there guards or sentries posted about the grounds?" Geffrey was now awake. This was good news from Jodocus.

"A few," the old man said. "But I navigated around them without much difficulty."

"Isn't it dangerous?"

"Dangerous?"

"The abandoned shaft. Could it collapse with us in it?"

"Of course it could." Jodocus's eyes twinkled. "But it hasn't so far."

"You think we could sneak out of here at night? Wouldn't we be missed?"

"Listen, Geffrey, by the time they find us missing, we'll be long gone. We could be many miles away by morning." Jodocus's voice rose to barely above a whisper.

"Shhh," Geffrey admonished. "Not so loud."

"Think about it. Talk it over with Byrun and Jubal. We could all get out of here. But we need to do it soon. Before the winter months."

"I will, Jodocus, I will."

Long after the old man left, Geffrey lay awake, thinking over what he said. Was it even possible? Could they manage to get out? What he wouldn't give if it were possible. The possibility of reuniting with his mother and finding Rosalind was enticing. He remembered what Jubal had said, and it applied to him as well—that he had lost all track of time in this place. He had no idea how long he had been imprisoned in the mines. How many months? Years?

Was it possible? Could they do it?

CHAPTER 16

On a warm, moonless midsummer night when the mines of Remmelsberg were silent of the back-breaking toil of digging iron from the earth and fashioning the metal into weapons, Geffrey and his two companions crept out of their sleeping quarters. Standing at the end of the building, Jubal peered around the corner, scanning the grounds for guards. He nodded, and Geffrey led the men to a small copse of trees that stood halfway between the mine towers and the smelter where Jodocus waited.

A soft humid breeze filtered through the birch and pine trees, bringing the scents of smoldering charcoal and the garbage pit to their nostrils. An owl hooted in the distance.

Jodocus nodded as they gathered around him. "There's usually a few guards at each tower and around the smelter and forge," he said in a soft voice.

In the dim moonlight, Geffrey thought Jodocus looked older and weak and wondered if the old man was up to the challenge of escape.

Geffrey scanned the area beyond the trees. In the darkness, his visibility was limited but he could see no guards. But he knew the old man was right—they were out there somewhere.

"The place looks deserted," Byrun said. "We're in luck."

"Don't fool yourself, son," Jodocus said, the furrows

in his face appearing even deeper in the dark. "They're out there. Make no mistake about that."

"Where to now?" Geffrey said.

"We need to get over to the tool shed," Jodocus said. "Then somehow get into the forge."

"The forge? Why?" Jubal's tone sounded troubled.

"I'm not leaving this place defenseless," Jodocus responded. He glanced over his shoulder at Jubal, winked. "I want a sword with which to defend myself."

"Surely the forge will have sentries," Geffrey said.

"Yep. We'll just have to overpower them. And do it without making a sound so as not to warn the others."

"That's why we have Jubal," Byrun said, chuckling, and he punched the man in the arm.

"The tool shed is on the way to the forge. The path to it leads behind that hedge row right there." Jodocus pointed a bony finger at a line of low vegetation off to his right.

"Then, let's go," Geffrey said and he took off, running crouched behind the hedgerow. The others followed.

It was a good hundred feet to the tool shed. The men scurried along the serpentine path as it wound its way, first behind a rock outcropping then continued on alongside the hedgerow. Geffrey had his eyes focused on the tool shed but his ears were locked into the sounds of the night, alert to any unusual sound that might signal a guard walking his post.

They crowded behind the shed while Jodocus surveyed the distance to the forge. Piles of rock ore lined the path and would give them some cover as they approached the stable.

"There's always someone posted at the forge entrance," Jodocus said, his voice now in a whisper. The men could make out the forge's faint outline in the dark.

"I suggest we get to the rear of the forge then make our way to the doorway where we can overpower the bastard." Geffrey pointed the way he advised.

"All right," Jodocus said. "Lead the way."

Geffrey took off, sprinting low behind the piles of rock ore. The distance to the forge turned out to be farther than it looked in the dark, and his lungs burned as he ran, his legs growing weary. He wasn't used to running. As he ran, he thought of Rosalind. If he managed to get out of the mines, would he be able to find her? He didn't know if she survived the attack on Lochwald and was even alive. Maybe she was the concubine of some Norse jarl and had borne him children by now. He remembered a line from the twenty-third Psalm and muttered it to himself. *Yea, though I walk through the valley of the shadow of death, I will fear no evil, for Thou art with me.*

As he made his way to the forge, he kept his eyes on the guard, now visible standing at the doorway. The man looked bored, possibly asleep. Geffrey heard the soft footfalls of Byrun, Jubal, and Jodocus behind him.

Out of breath, the group reached the rear of the forge and rested. Geffrey took a breath, tried to calm his frenetic nerves. He glanced around the corner, saw nothing. The guard must still be at the forge's front doorway.

"All right, Jubal," Geffrey said. "Your turn. Lead the way. When you get to the front corner of the forge, stop. I'll rap on its side to draw the man around and you take care of him. Understand?"

Jubal nodded his understanding. He slipped to the side of the forge, Geffrey and the others following him. Once they reached the front corner, Jubal stopped. Geffrey rapped on the building. They waited.

Nothing.

Geffrey rapped again. Louder.

The guard stepped around to the side, yawning and stretching his arms. Jubal pounced on him like a large bear engulfing its prey. He gripped the man's mouth with a large hand, throwing him to the ground. Geffrey pulled the man's dagger from his belt and, without hesitation, plunged it into the man's chest. The guard jerked several times then stopped, his watery eyes vacant. Geffrey pulled the dagger free and wiped the blood on his short trousers.

Inside the forge, Geffrey led to them to the storeroom where the completed weapons were stored until transported elsewhere. They each chose a dagger and a short sword that Ornolf called a gladius, patterned after the Roman short sword. Geffrey slipped the dagger into his belt and gripped the sword with a tight fist. It felt good.

Back outside the forge, they faced the long trek to the abandoned mine shaft Jodocus said led to freedom beyond the mountain.

The old man pointed to a tower on a small knoll off in the distance. "There it is," he said. "That's the abandoned shaft."

"Good Lord, Jodocus," Geffrey said. "It's a half mile away across open ground. We won't make it."

"Yes, we will," Jodocus said. "Once we are halfway there, the other guards can't see us. Their line of sight is blocked by those trees over there." He pointed to the edge of the forest above Remmelsberg.

"I hope you're right," Geffrey said and he scrambled toward the tower.

He didn't like scurrying across open ground, but it appeared they had no other choice. If Jodocus was right and the shaft did lead to the far side of the mountain, then they might get away undetected. If he was wrong and they were spotted, it would mean torture and the dungeon followed by death. Geffrey put the thought out of his mind, muttered a prayer that the shaft was truly abandoned.

One by one, they scrambled toward the tower. In the open, he felt vulnerable, exposed. He hurried along and kept praying. He was thankful that the moon had slipped behind a cloud, for it made their approach to the tower less likely to be discovered. The grounds were dark, quiet.

When he was on a line parallel with the forest, Geffrey shot a quick look over his shoulder. Jodocus was right—the mines below had disappeared from view. They were out of eyesight of the guards. He continued up the hill, legs burning, lungs heaving.

Finally, he reached the tower and its attendant shaft. The others soon joined him, breathing hard. Geffrey stepped to Jodocus."

"Lead the way, Jodocus," he said. "It's going to be light in a few hours. We need to be far away from this place. And stick your weapons in your belt to free your hands."

Without a moment's hesitation, Jodocus stepped to edge of the shaft and climbed into the black hole.

"We have no light," Jubal said. His voice was halting. "I'm afraid of the dark. We need a lantern."

"No time," Geffrey said. Jodocus had disappeared down the shaft. "Besides we have nothing to light a lantern with. Get going, Byrun."

Byrun scrambled into the hole and began the descent into the darkness. When he was gone from sight, Geffrey patted Jubal in the shoulder.

"All right, my friend. Your turn. Don't worry, I'll be right behind you. And Byrun is below you. Take it slow and easy. Breathe normally. You'll be fine."

Jubal looked at Geffrey with a frightened frown then slowly stepped into the black void. Geffrey watched him until he could no longer see him then crawled over the edge and into black.

Although he couldn't see the rungs of the ladder, Geffrey descended by feel. Below him, he sounds of the others filled the cramped shaft as they descended deeper. The shaft was dark, blacker than black, thicker than a heavy coat. He hoped that his future would begin in this darkness. Prayed a stubborn hope that if he just showed up and tried to do the right thing, the dawn would come and bring freedom. And Rosalind.

Jubal called out. His voice sounded panicked, distressed. He halted his descent. "Help me," he cried. "My foot is caught in the ladder. I'm stuck."

"What's the matter, Jubal?" Geffrey called down to him.

"My foot is caught in a rung of the ladder. It's too dark to see. I don't like being here. Help me, please. I'm getting sick."

Geffrey eased himself down the ladder to where he was just above Jubal's head. The man was a faint outline in the dark.

"Byrun," he called. "Can you see Jubal's problem? His foot is stuck in the ladder. Can you get to it?"

"Just a minute," Byrun called back. His voice echoed off the walls of the dark shaft.

Geffrey heard Byrun climb up the ladder, barely made out his head just below Jubal's feet.

"Yes, I see the problem," he said. "I'll try and free his foot."

Geffrey could tell Byrun was working on the foot for sounds of grunting and movement echoed up the chamber to him.

"There," Byrun called, "I think it's free. Jubal, check your foot."

"It's fine, Byrun. Thanks. I hate this dark. I want out."

"Hang on, Jubal," Geffrey pleaded. "We'll be out of here soon."

After another few minutes of climbing downward, Geffrey heard a sound up above.

It sounded like someone walking over gravel at the shed's entrance.

"Hold on!" he said in a loud whisper. "Stop for a moment."

Geffrey waited, clinging to the ladder. Sure enough, the sound was still there, and it did sound like someone walking up above them.

He waited. His heart pounded in his throat.

A light flickered.

Jessums, Geffrey thought. *Someone has discovered us!*

The walking sound continued for a while, the light flickering above. But no one descended the shaft. After several anxious moments, the light flickered out and the sounds of walking receded into the distance.

"Who could that have been?" Geffrey said to no one in particular.

Soon, they were descending again, deeper in the shaft. In another ten minutes, they stood on flat ground at the bottom. Jodocus limped up to Geffrey.

"Who was that above you?" Even in the dark Geffrey saw the anxious look on the man's face.

"I have no idea. Didn't get a look. I thought you said this shaft was abandoned and no one came in here."

"Well, I was wrong about that, wasn't I, son?"

The others just stood there, staring at the old man.

"The ventilation shaft is back this way," Jodocus said and trudged to the rear of the gallery.

After what seemed like an eternity, Geffrey felt a rush of cool air hit his face. They must be getting closer to the mountain's surface. The tunnel at this point was level and the trek easy. Soon, they were outside.

After the climb down the shaft and trek through the ventilation tunnel, the night air felt good on Geffrey's face. The moon was still behind a large cloudbank. Off to the west was the forest and, in the distance, Geffrey again heard the hoot of an owl.

"Let's make tracks," he said.

He began scrambling toward the trees while the others followed in a single file line behind him.

When they reached the forest, Geffrey didn't stop, his internal compass pointing them in a westerly direction. They were a long way from Normandie. They had no food—were going to have to find it themselves with only their hand weapons to aid them. They were on foot, the hope of finding horses a distant one. They had no map. They had no water, the most precious resource. Without it, they would die more miserable than the rats of the dungeon. Geffrey had no idea what kind of country awaited them. But, for the moment, they were free. Their lives depended upon each other's loyalty. Their future was uncertain.

But west was the direction they needed to travel.

What remained of Lochwald lay to the west.

CHAPTER 17

S kroppa was beside himself. Angry wasn't the word that described his emotion. It was more like utter outrage. The men he had given over to more prestigious work in the Remmelsberg mines had disappeared. *How dare they?*

When they were not at the dining table for the morning meal, the alarm sounded and guards swiftly searched the buildings and every square inch of the Remmelsberg grounds for them. But it was in vain. Geffrey, Bynum, Jubal, and Jodocus were nowhere to be found.

Damn them!

Skroppa called Ornolf to his small office in the mine's main building. The forge overseer was obviously distressed at losing three workers.

"I tell you, Ornolf," Skroppa said, "there's going to be hell to pay if we don't find these men and quick. Once the jarl gets word of their escape, he'll come down on us like a wall of crumbling stones."

"They are bastards," Ornolf replied, spitting his word out as if they burned his tongue. He slapped his hand down on the table that sat between the two men. "And by Wödan's almighty hand, I'll find the bastards if it is the last thing I ever do. I gave that boy, Geffrey, the run of the forge. Taught him what I know. And this is how he repays me."

"Gather four or five of your best guards," Skroppa said, "and your stoutest, best conditioned destriers. I will lead the hunt, and you will be at my side. Together, we will hunt these spit-frogs, and when we find them, we will have our way with them. If that sniggard Geffrey thought the iron chair was horrible, wait until he sees what I have in store for him and his pals."

When the horses and guards were assembled in the main square, Skroppa mounted and led them west. He surmised they would be heading west back to Normandie where Geffrey once made his home. The escapees had a significant head start but were on foot. Hopefully, Skroppa and his men would catch up with them by evening, or the next morning at the latest. As they rode off, with the rising sun at their backs, Skroppa's mouth salivated at the thought of Norse revenge. Wödan would see that they succeed on this hunt.

Skroppa pressed the chargers until midmorning when he called a halt for a brief rest. As the men dismounted and drank from the nearby stream, he and Ornolf discussed the route the escapees might be taking.

"Should we continue on this path, Ornolf, or press on overland?"

"We will make the best time if we stay on this current path," Ornolf said, squinting back into the sun and surveying the ground over which they had come. "It would be their fastest route as well. And if we haven't caught up with them by tomorrow, we can take an overland route going back."

"I suspect you are right," Skroppa said. They had led their destriers to the water and allowed them to drink their fill. "They're most likely wanting to make the best time possible. They're on foot so we should catch up with them unless they're holed up somewhere. You glad to be along?"

"When I was a boy, I dreamed of becoming a warrior. Dreamed of conquering new lands in the name of

Wödan. But, instead I became a blacksmith. Because my father was a blacksmith. This is my chance to be that warrior I dreamed of becoming. I am honored to be a part of it. I hope we can reclaim our honor by capturing these scum. They betrayed your giving them better work."

"If we don't, then I suggest we keep riding. I don't wish to face the jarl," Skroppa said, remounting his charger. "Let's push on."

They alternated walking, trotting, and cantering the rest of the day, stopping only for a quick water break and a chance to relieve themselves. Skroppa was used to running a mine, not spending all day in the saddle searching for escapees. His backside ached and pain shot down both legs. By nightfall, they entered a wide clearing in the forest so they dismounted and made camp for the night. They had not seen a single sign of Geffrey and the others all day.

Ornolf sat with the men and ate jerky washed down with stream water. Skroppa pulled the saddle off his horse and joined them.

"Tomorrow," he said, "we'll spread out and go back overland. Maybe we can get an idea where they are by doing that."

"They're either far ahead or they are somewhere out there," Ornolf said, pointing out into the dense forest beyond their campsite.

"They were on foot," Skroppa complained. "How can they be ahead of us? I think they're between here and the mines. We should run across them sometime tomorrow."

ⲉⲫⲉⲫ

Geffrey adjusted the sword that hung loosely in his belt along with the dagger. He and his friends were camped in the middle of a dense forest. Since they dared not risk a fire, they sat on the ground as darkness descended about them. After traveling overland all day, all the previous day, and most of the night before that without stopping and without food, they were exhausted. The only water they found was a small trickle of a stream where they stopped long enough to quench their thirst.

Geffrey collapsed, with his back against a tree, stared at the stars in an inky sky, and thought again of Rosalind. His heart ached to be near her, smell her perfumed hair, watch the sparkles in her eyes.

Byrun squatted beside him, interrupting his daydream. He pushed a lock of sandy hair from his forehead. "Say, Geffrey," he said, "do you have any idea where we are or how far we've come?"

Geffrey picked up a small stone, threw it into the woods. "I'd say we've come about close to forty miles. As to where exactly we are—I have no idea."

"At this pace, it will take some time to get to Normandie, won't it? On foot, I mean."

"It will. But I'm hoping we will be able to get some horses soon. That would speed up our travel."

"Get them with what?" Byrun said, shaking his head. "We have no money. Steal them?"

"If we have to." Geffrey's tone was matter-of-fact. "I remember a river, a genuine river, being about this far west of Remmelsberg. We should come to it soon."

"What river?" Byrun said.

"I don't know. I just remember it was a large one. There was a bridge over it. I hope we can find it because if we can put the river between us and Skroppa, we might be able to shake him off our trail."

"You think he's pursuing us?"

"Skroppa?" Geffrey's voice took a higher pitch. "You can bet on it. They may be right over that last hill we climbed."

"I hope not."

"Where's Jubal?"

"He and Jodocus are sleeping. I didn't think the old man was going to make this trek, but he's stronger, more wiry, than he looks."

"What are you going to do if we make it back to Normandie?" Geffrey said. He stretched his arms and yawned.

"I don't know. I am sure that there's nothing left of my village across the River Skye, so I dunno. My family is dead, so going back would be a waste of time. My father was a farmer. I was a farmer. I can grow things, Geffrey, so I'll probably find a piece of ground somewhere and plant. What about you? What plans have you, if any?"

"When my village was destroyed by the Norse raiders, I was my father's blacksmith apprentice. We were in the process of building a wall around our small town when they came, burned it to the ground, killed most of the people, including my father, and took me away to Remmelsberg. That's how I got the job on the forge. When Skroppa learned I was a blacksmith, he took me out of the mines and put me in the forge, fashioning weapons. With you. Remember? I'm fortunate, Byrun, a blacksmith can usually find work most anywhere. I do want to return to Lochwald and see if anyone made it back. But beyond that, I dunno. Jubal wants to rebuild the village."

"If you don't mind," Byrun said, "I'll just tag along with you. Who knows? We might make a good pair down the road."

"I'd be honored," Geffrey said.

The next morning, the quartet of men continued their journey westward. Traveling overland and keeping away from the beaten path, Geffrey stumbled upon the river he remembered. It was wide and flowed with a strong current. The heady pungent aroma of river water tickled his nose. Now, they needed to locate the bridge. Jubal scurried north while Byrun went south along the river's eastern bank in search of the crossing while Geffrey and Jodocus remained as a lookout for Skroppa and any guards pursuing them. They knew, as sure as the sun rose each day, that Skroppa was somewhere behind. If they were caught with their backs against the river, it would all be over.

The day dawned clear and bright with only a few cumulus clouds doting the sky. An odor of fish and water wafted from the river to where Geffrey stood while his companions searched for the bridge.

"You making it all right, Jodocus?" Geffrey said.

They paced the rocky shoreline of the river together.

"I'm fine," the man said. "I'm so glad to be away from the mines."

"How long were you there?"

"Ten years, I think. I began to lose track of time lately. I'm afraid my memory isn't what it used to be."

"What are your plans, Jodocus, if we manage to get out of this?"

The old man laughed, his eyes twinkling in the early morning sunlight. "Silesia, my home, no longer exists. Those infernal Poles, led by their king, Boleslaw, an evil tyrant if there ever was one, subjugated many of my countrymen and ruled Silesia as if it belonged to him. I guess it does now. Anyway, I cannot return."

"You are welcome to travel with me for as long as you care to," Geffrey said. He genuinely liked Jodocus's easy manner, his kind way of speaking to others. His experience might come in handy down the road.

"I appreciate the offer. Who knows what lies ahead, Geffrey? It may be that we will need each other's skills and brains if we are to make it to safety."

"Wherever that is," Geffrey added. "These Norsemen seem to be overrunning the country."

"It's funny. To think most of us are originally descended from them a century ago. But that, obviously, is of no matter."

Jubal's yell pierced the morning quiet. He had located the bridge. When everyone gathered at its eastern side Geffrey gave it the once over.

"It looks sturdy enough," he said. "Let's get to the other side."

The bridge was a wooden affair with heavy pilings supporting a trestle-like bracing. The trusses appeared strong and sturdy but the flooring was in disrepair—its boards broken or rotted. The foursome scurried over the bridge, dodging the holes in the flooring. On the western shore of the river, they rested for a few moments.

"Let's drink our fill before moving on," Byrun said. "You never know when we'll happen on water again."

Jubal dropped on his knees and scooped water on his hands and into his mouth. The others did the same. Once they sated their thirst, Geffrey led them into the forest along a narrow path. Birds he couldn't identify squawked their alarm as they progressed deeper. It seemed to Geffrey that the forest canopy was closing in on them, the trees becoming denser, the underbrush thicker.

"I hope that Skroppa gave up pursuing us," Jodocus said. "I never liked the bastard myself. Years ago, he put me in the dungeon for almost a year. I'll never forget it."

"I don't know which was worse," Geffrey said, keeping an eye out, now and then, on their back trail. "The iron chair with their spikes or the dark dungeon cell full of rats. For a while, I thought I might lose my mind."

"Now that I have a weapon," Byrun said, "if I ever see that man again, I promise I will run him through."

"Ornolf wasn't nearly as bad as Skroppa said he was going to be." Geffrey hurried along the path, his legs much better with the night's rest. "He actually enjoyed teaching me the swordsmith business."

"What were they like?" Jodocus asked. "The broadswords, I mean."

"Similar to these," Geffrey said. "I've never seen a finish on swords like these, have you? No, I didn't think so. These swords are stronger than anything ever made before by man and the mirror finish is simply exquisite. These weapons are a true work of art."

"As long as they kill good," Byrun said. "As long as they can kill a man."

Geffrey watched him pull his sword from his belt and take a few practice swings with it.

CHAPTER 18

Skroppa turned to Ornolf, his face red, his neck veins bulging. After searching for most of the day for Geffrey and the other escapees, they were now at a wooden bridge that spanned a wide, fast-moving river. "Dammit, man," he shouted, venting his anger, "we haven't seen the slightest sign of them all day."

"What now? Think we should continue or turn back and spread out?"

Skroppa paced in front of the bridge, looked over its span to the opposite side of the river. Low dark clouds threatened rain. "I don't see any footprints around here," he said. "If they made it this far and crossed the bridge, they did it without leaving any tracks."

Ornolf squatted and peered closer at the ground next to the bridge entrance. "Either that or they managed to cover their tracks somehow. But I can't tell if they swept the ground here or not."

"They couldn't have made it this far," Skroppa said. "I don't relish continuing the search in the rain."

"What then?" Ornolf said. "I agree. I don't see them making it to here."

"Let's fan out overland and head back to Remmelsberg. If we meet up with them, fine. If not, well…" His voice trailed off as he remounted and reined his horse back to the east. He gave a shout to the others, ordering them to spread out.

"At least the forest will afford some protection if it decides to rain," Ornolf said, climbing onto his mount.

As Skroppa kicked his charger into a trot, his mind raced over possible places where the escapees could be hiding. He might have to intimidate a few farmers on the way home if he hoped to find them.

ⲉⲟⲉⲟ

Jubal pointed to the low dark clouds. The wind had picked up and blew out of the north, bringing a cold front from off the English Channel. "Looks like rain is coming," he said to no one in particular. "We might be in for a blow."

Geffrey shot a glance skyward and nodded his agreement. "We ought to find someplace to hole up until this passes over," he said. "I don't care to spend a night cold and wet."

Bynum gave a shout. He had located a small cave in a series of rock outcroppings.

"This should do," Geffrey said. "At least we won't get soaked. Anything living in there, Byrun?"

"I haven't had a chance to check," was his answer.

"Let's build a fire and wait a while," Jubal said. "If anything's in there, it should drive them out. Bugs too."

He gathered tinder and twigs and, using the technique of a fire drill, soon had a small blaze going. Geffrey and Byrun piled on logs they picked up off the ground and the fire roared. Geffrey scouted the area and found a small slow stream where they quenched their thirst. It had been several days since they last ate and their bellies ached. Geffrey felt a weakness settle over him. They needed to find food.

Jodocus set out several small snares and, just before the rain hit, managed to catch a rabbit in one of them.

While he cleaned it, using his dagger, Geffrey fashioned a spit and, as the rain began to fall, the group settled back in the tiny cave and watched the rabbit roast over the fire. Geffrey's mouth watered as the aroma of the cooking meat filled the cave.

"Best meal I've had in a long time," Jodocus announced after several mouthfuls.

"I must admit I was about done in," Byrun said. "Thanks, Jodocus, for getting us this meal."

The man waved a piece of rabbit at him.

"Frankly," Byrun continued, "for an old man, you've done amazingly well in keeping up with us. I'm impressed."

Jodocus eyed Byrun with a cold stare. "Old man, am I?" he said. "Why I'll dance on your grave, you little whippersnapper." He laughed and his stare turned friendly again.

Jubal and Geffrey laughed, and soon they all were smiling and slapping each other's shoulder.

When the rain hit, it came down in sheets. Wind howled outside the cave. Inside, the group, warm and dry and having consumed the rabbit, settled down and soon were asleep.

The dawn came cool, clear, and bright. The storm that blew past the previous evening left the morning crisp and fresh, as if wiped clean of the dirt and grime of the men's lives. As the sun's warming rays filtered through the birch and pine trees, the group made their way west, while Geffrey kept a nervous eye behind them. Worried that Skroppa and his men might descend upon them at any moment, he tried to keep his fears at bay by concentrating on the road ahead.

The path through the forest was muddy and, in places, a quagmire. Geffrey led the men around large deep puddles, often meandering deeper into the forest through briars and thickets before finding his way back to the road. When the sun was high and the temperature had warmed, the sultry air vanished, leaving in its wake a magnificent day.

They plodded west, always west. Soon they stumbled upon a muddy lane. Geffrey decided to leave the path and take the wider road. His comrades followed quietly, not saying much. Late in the afternoon, Geffrey rounded a short bend and noticed a covered wagon mired in the mud to its rear axle. An aging man and a young girl pushed the cart from its rear while a woman sat up front and encouraged a shaggy horse to continue pulling. Closer, Geffrey saw that they made no progress. The wagon was going nowhere.

He hurried to the wagon. The old man gave a start at his approach, and the girl flashed a dark suspicious look at him.

Geffrey felt Byrun at his side. "Hello! Looks like you could use some help," Geffrey said as Jodocus and Jubal gathered around the wagon.

On closer inspection, the faded wooden wagon had large writing on its side. In red letters it said, *MAGICIAN * JUGGLER * PEDDLER OF WARES*. The horse, standing hock deep in the mud, seemed grateful for the rest.

The woman on the wagon seat peered over her shoulder at Geffrey. Her wrinkled face sported a frown. She spoke first. "If you are planning to rob us," she said, "we have no money."

Geffrey thought her voice had an irritable tone. He smiled and shook his head. "I assure you, madame," he said, stepping closer, "we are humble travelers ourselves with no intention to rob or do you harm. We can however, assist you in getting your wagon unstuck. But if you prefer we be on our way—"

"Hold on, now," the man said. He picked his way through the mud to stand alongside Geffrey. "I would be pleased for the assistance."

"My name is Geffrey. These are my friends." As he called each name Jodocus, Byrun, then Jubal stepped forward and smiled, bowed at the waist.

"A pleasant day to each of you," the man said. He patted the girl on an arm. "This dirty little creature is my daughter, Norène. My wife, Miriam, is on the wagon seat.

"Oh, Papa," Norène said, her dark eyes flashing. "I am not a little creature." She stomped out of the mud and onto firmer ground.

"Byrun," Geffrey said, taking hold of the wagon's nearest wheel. "Grab this wheel. Jodocus, you and Jubal get on the far wheel and let's get this thing out of the mud."

Geffrey watched as his companions took their places and, along with him, took a wheel in their hands. "All together now. Push!" He let out a grunt as he leaned his weight against the stuck wheel.

Miriam, up on the wagon seat, cracked a whip over the horse's head and the animal lurched forward, straining against the harness. The wagon wheels moved a couple of inches then settled back in the mire.

"Again," Geffrey shouted. "Push!"

Miriam cracked the whip once more. The animal strained, its legs plodding in the mud. The wagon moved a foot.

"Once more," Geffrey called out. "We've almost got it."

This time, with the pushing by Geffrey and the others, combined with Miriam's coaxing the horse, the wagon moved forward. The animal strained, legs churning, Miriam shouting encouragement until the wagon moved out of the muck and onto firm ground. Miriam drove the wagon farther down the road and into a small clearing in the forest. Quinn and Norène ran to catch up while Geffrey and his friends ambled to the wagon. They were out of breath and stood there panting while Quinn helped his wife down from her perch.

"Thank you, gentlemen, very much," Quinn said. He was a skinny balding man who had an aristocratic air about him. "I believe we will spend the night here. You are welcome to join us and share our evening meal."

Geffrey eyes his companions, who nodded their assent. "My friends have voted in the affirmative," he said. "It will be our pleasure."

As the family started their evening chores with Norène gathering firewood, Quinn building the fire ring, and Miriam searching for dinner items, the men went in search of water. Quinn gave them a wooden bucket.

As they ambled to the small stream, Jubal remarked. "He called us gentlemen. I've never been called a gentleman before."

Jodocus laughed. "Well, Jubal," he said. "Welcome to the aristocracy. How does it feel?"

Jubal puffed out his chest, grinned. "I'm an aristocrat," the big man said.

Everyone laughed.

When they returned with the bucket full of clear water, Quinn had a fire going. Miriam poured some of the water into a pot and set it over the fire. While his wife and daughter prepared the evening meal, Quinn relaxed under a tree and smoked his pipe. Geffrey and Byrun joined him.

"So, where are you men heading?" Quinn asked as he puffed on the pipe, a contented look on his face.

"West," Geffrey said, not sure how much of their story he should entrust to the man.

"Ah," Quinn said, nodding. He rubbed his bald head with the palm of his hand. "Normans. The Norsemen have been on the march lately. Raiding and pillaging. I have heard they have ventured into Italia and have taken lands there."

"And you, my friend. What about you? Where do you go and what work are you engaged in?"

Quinn pointed to his wagon. "As the wagon says, Geffrey, I'm a juggler, magician, and humble peddler."

Byrun chuckled. "Yes," he said. "We had someone like you pass through our village every few months. It was quite an entertainment."

"I can speak and rhyme well, be witty, know the story of Troy, balance apples on the point of knives, juggle, jump through hoops, play the citole, mandora, harp, fiddle, and psaltery." He further advised, "For good measure, I have learned the arts of imitating birds, putting performing asses and dogs through their paces and operating marionettes." Quinn's eyes sparkled at the description.

"Some of our merchants didn't like the traveling peddlers," Byrun said.

"Sad, but true," Quinn responded. "Peddlers have long occupied a minimal position in buying and selling, but we are central to the provisioning of homes and the supply of semi-luxuries. Shopkeepers vilify us as unfair competition that undermine their legitimate trade. Yet, in reality, we offer little by way of real competition as we are relatively few in number and sell only small quantities of easily transportable and non-perishable goods, such as purses, knives, girdles, glasses, hats, and other penny ware."

"And Norène?" Geffrey said. "She is quite lovely."

"You fancy Norène, my new friend? She is fourteen. The ripe age for marriage."

"Oh—well—er," Geffrey stammered, taken aback by the man's remark about marriage. "I did not mean to offend, Quinn."

"You are not offending," Quinn said. "I just mentioned a fact that should be obvious. When you men arrived, I first feared you were bandits. Highwaymen."

"I can assure you," Byrun said, "we are not bandits."

"You never know, these days," Quinn said, smiling. "Between the Norse raiders and bandits, it is risky to travel the roads."

"Yet, you continue to do so?" Geffrey said.

"Yes, it is somewhat dangerous but peddling is my life," Quinn remarked. "I know no other."

Miriam called everyone for supper. They gathered around the fire while she ladled large portions of steaming stew into earthen bowls then passed a loaf of thick dark bread around. The food was good. Geffrey thought he had never tasted anything so delightful. When they had eaten all they could hold, Quinn brought out his flute and played a lively tune. Byrun grabbed Norène by the hand, pulled her to her feet, and danced her around the dwindling fire. She was reluctant at first but soon was smiling and giggling as Byrun paraded her all around the campsite. When the music stopped, she fell exhausted on the ground next to her mother.

"You say you can juggle?" Byrun asked.

"Oh, yes," Quinn said. He picked five colored balls out of a sack and began juggling, keeping them in the air with relative ease.

"Look at that," Jubal remarked. "I never saw anything so—"

"So interesting," Jodocus said.

"I tried it once," Byrun said, "but could never manage to do it. Kept dropping the balls. Say, Quinn, what's the secret?"

Quinn looked at him with a wry smile. "If I told you the secret," he said, "soon everyone would be doing it."

"No, now come on, man. Tell us." Byrun held out his hands in a supplicatory pose.

"Most people," Quinn began," think it's in the catching. But the true secret is in the toss of the balls. One must learn and practice the toss until it forms a consistent arc, always landing in the same place. You start practicing with one ball. Practice, practice, practice. When you finally are able to toss one ball consistently, you can progress to two balls. It's simply a matter of practice after that."

"It looks complicated," Geffrey said.

"It's not, really. Only one ball is in the air at a time. The others are in your hand."

As darkness settled around them, Quinn retrieved his flute and played a melancholy refrain. To Geffrey, Skroppa and his men seemed far away. For the present, he and his comrades were safe and happy. Among friends. And the mines of Remmelsberg were a distant memory.

CHAPTER 19

Geffrey climbed out from under the wagon where he spent the night. Jubal was still snoring but Jodocus and Byrun were already up and lounging by the fire. When he joined them, Jodocus smiled.

"Good morning," he said. "Sleep well under the wagon?"

"Like a baby," Geffrey said. "Where are Quinn and Miriam?"

"Quinn is down at the stream fetching water, and Miriam is in the wagon getting breakfast ready."

Geffrey squatted next to Jodocus and warmed his hands.

"We going to tag along with these folks?" Jodocus asked.

"Might as well," Geffrey replied, "as long as they are traveling west. There's always safety in numbers and the conversation will be stimulating. Besides, I think Byrun has eyes for Norène."

After a breakfast of porridge, everyone climbed aboard the wagon, and Quinn whipped the horse into moving west. Miriam sat between Geffrey and her husband on the wagon's seat while the rest crowded into the wagon's interior. Geffrey was glad he was riding up front, for the inside of the wagon was filled to overflowing with the peddler's wares and his musical instruments. Jubal rode on the tailgate while Byrun made conversation with Norène.

By midmorning, they moved along the edge of a large lake bounded by rolling verdant hills. The sun was warm, a clear cloudless sky overhead. Geffrey chatted with Miriam and Quinn about the life of a traveling peddler and juggler.

"It's a living, as they say," Miriam said. "Quinn has so many talents, it's a natural calling. We've been married so many years I have forgotten a life before him."

"Not much of a living," Quinn added. "But Miriam has always been satisfied with what I managed to provide. And you, Geffrey, you've been reluctant to speak about your life, where you come from. Why?"

"No reason to burden strangers with my problems," Geffrey said.

"We're strangers no longer," Miriam said. "We were so grateful of your help yesterday."

"Of course," Quinn chimed in. "How far you men going?"

Geffrey watched the sun reflect in the lake—shimmering ripples like diamonds on the water. "My village was called Lochwald on the River Skye in Normandie. Norse marauders leveled it. Burned it to the ground. They killed my father, hung his body, and set it on fire. It was the last thing I saw as I was made prisoner by the raiders and taken to the mines at Remmelsberg where I worked as a slave."

"That's terrible," Miriam said. "What about your mother?"

"Never saw her again after that raid. I don't know if she is alive or dead."

They moved around the far edge of the lake and into wooded country.

"I don't know what happened to the girl I planned to marry," Geffrey continued. "Her name was Rosalind."

"A lovely name," Miriam said.

"The Norsemen have increased their raids about the country," Quinn said. "We have been fortunate not to become one of their victims."

"They are a brutal people," Geffrey added.

"What was it like in the mines?" Quinn asked.

"Not good. Slave labor worked the mines. It was dark, dirty, the air suffocating. Workers weren't allowed to talk to each other except at night after supper. Violation of the rules got you tortured and sent to the dungeon."

"Were you ever tortured?" Quinn said sympathetically.

"Yes. Once I was put in what they called the iron chair where spikes penetrated my skin. It was horrible. After that, they shoved me into a dark cell where I stayed for weeks. I almost lost my mind during those dark days. Somehow, by the grace of God, I managed to survive and, after I helped with a cave-in, I was sent to work in the forge. Jubal worked in the smelter. The forge was where I learned how to fashion the swords we brought with us."

"You and the others managed to escape, eventually," Miriam said. She had taken the reins and guided the horse around a large rock outcropping. The forest was not as dense as the one they encountered the previous day.

"Jodocus found an abandoned mine shaft and ventilation tunnel. We got out through it."

"You are on your way back to your village?" Quinn said. "Lochwald?"

"It no longer exists, Quinn, unless there were survivors that returned to rebuild it. But yes, I want to return and see if my mother and Rosalind might still be alive."

"It sounds like an impossible task," Miriam remarked.

"I won't rest until I have found them or learned their fate."

As they passed the rock outcropping three rough looking men stepped onto the road. The horse neighed and Miriam reined to a stop. One man grabbed the reins while the other two approached the wagon. They looked as if they had not bathed in months, sported a month's growth of beard, and wore tattered clothes.

Geffrey knew at once they were highwaymen. Intent on robbery.

"Halt!" one of the bandits shouted. "Everyone off the wagon!"

The taller of the bandits grabbed Quinn and pulled him to the ground. He landed with a thud. Miriam's hand was at her mouth. The man looked at Geffrey and Miriam through narrow eyes.

"Get down from there," he commanded.

Geffrey climbed down from the wagon seat then helped Miriam to the ground. Miriam ran to her husband's side as he was sitting.

"I'm all right," he said, brushing Miriam's hand away from his face. "We don't have much they will want."

Geffrey watched Quinn get to his feet, brush himself off. The bandits, he noticed, had short swords in scabbards at their sides. It was interesting that they were not brandishing the weapons at the moment. What did they want?

Jubal rounded the corner of the wagon.

"Why have we stopped?" he said. When he saw the three bandits, he stopped short.

The bandit who spoke motioned to his accomplice. The man drew his sword and hurried to the rear of the wagon and soon returned pushing Norène, Byrun, and Jodocus ahead of him. The two highwaymen now brandished their weapons in front of the small group.

"Give us your money and valuables," the taller bandit said with a sneer.

Quinn looked about and shook his head. "We don't have much money," he said. "And as for valuables? Look at us. I'm a poor peddler. Did you look in the wagon? See what's in there? Only a few bobbles and some pots and pans. Nothing of real value. I'm afraid you've wasted your time."

"Give us what you've got," the man demanded.

Geffrey stepped forward, his eyes on the man's sword. "See here," he said. "If it's a fight you want, we can oblige you."

"Geffrey don't," Quinn pleaded. "We'll just give them what they want."

"The hell we will," Geffrey said. "Jubal, get our weapons."

In an instant Jubal disappeared to the rear of the wagon and returned carrying their swords, which he tossed to Geffrey and Byrun.

"Now let's see how bold you are," Geffrey called and headed for the tall one, his sword at the ready.

The tall man rushed Geffrey slashing the air with his long dagger. Byrun ran toward the other man as the one holding the horse took off into the forest. Geffrey was not an accomplished swordsman, in fact, he never had wielded such a weapon in his life. But, in this instance, he knew he had the bigger weapon and therefore the advantage was his. He stepped aside from the onrushing bandit and brought his sword down on the dagger with an ear-piercing clang. The man gave him a startled look and was about to strike again when Geffrey thrust his sword into the man's upper arm, drawing blood. The man winced and fell back.

Byrun attacked his man with such ferocity that the man could only attempt to parry the blows from his sword. The man stumbled backward over a rock. Byrun was on him, his sword at the man's throat. With a shrug, Byrun's opponent relinquished his weapon.

While Geffrey's bandit was bleeding from his flesh wound, he continued to slash the air with his sword. With a long sweep of his sword, Geffrey knocked the weapon from the bandit's hand. He stared at Geffrey with hateful contempt, and then he and his companion disappeared into the forest, their swords abandoned.

"I don't think they'll be back," Geffrey said.

Norène, who was watching the skirmish from the rear of the wagon, rushed to Byrun's side.

"Are you all right?" she said. Her dark eyes flashed with fear and concern. "Are you hurt?"

Geffrey and Jodocus both laughed at this display of affection while Byrun assured the girl he was unhurt.

"Well, I don't know about the rest of you," Quinn said, "but I am in need of a nap. Let us make camp here for the night. The village of Brenig is not far and we can make it by midday tomorrow."

With that, he stretched out under a nearby birch tree, pulled his hat over his face, and soon was snoring.

"That man," Miriam said, gathering camp supplies from the wagon, "how he can sleep after all that excitement. It's beyond me."

Byrun and Norène went off in search of firewood for the evening campfire leaving Geffrey, Jubal, and Jodocus to chat with Miriam. Jodocus quizzed her about how she came to meet Quinn.

"Oh," she said, smiling a broad smile that revealed her brown chipped teeth. "Quinn was a juggler and poet for a duke. When the duke was commissioned to fight for the Holy Lands, Quinn left the castle and roamed the countryside. He came to my small village, juggling and performing tricks of magic, and I was taken with him. Against my parent's wishes, I invited him to our home for supper where he played his mandolin and flute. He eventually won my mother's heart as well as mine. He returned three months later and we were married. We had a son but he was killed when our horse kicked him in the head. Quinn poisoned the animal. Norène was born soon after that."

"You have a nice family," Jodocus said. "You've seen a lot of country, I presume."

"I nursed Norène from the Channel to the Black Sea. Yes, I would say I've seen my share of the world."

"She seems like a nice young girl," Geffrey said. "However, she shouldn't get too infatuated with Byrun. He's on a mission."

"Oh?" Miriam said, raising her eyebrows.

"Like me, Byrun is trying to get back home. To see if there is anything left of it and his family. He may be momentarily smitten with Norène but I don't think anything can sway him from this journey we are on."

"Thanks for telling me," Miriam said. "I will have a talk with Norène. I would hate for her heart to be broken just yet."

"Yes," Jodocus said, smiling. "Plenty of time for that later."

 භාජ

Jodocus watched Byrun chase after Norène, and he didn't like what he saw. As a group, the four men were on the run and, as such, needed to be clear-headed and focused on putting as much distance between themselves and Skroppa if the man was chasing them. Not running after a pretty skirt. He decided to speak with the young man.

"She is a fine, lovely girl, Byrun," he said, early in the morning before breakfast. "But, I wouldn't set my cap for her. We have other troubles at the moment."

Byrun shot Jodocus an evil look. "Yeah?" he said. "Like what?"

"Like getting out of this country before the Norsemen catch up with us."

"I doubt if Skroppa is on our tail," Byrun said, tossing his head to one side in a smirk. "Besides, what does an old man remember about love?"

"Oh, I remember. And I understand. However, I would never forgive you if you jeopardized our escape, and I had to return to the mines. You understand my meaning, Byrun?" He gave the young man a stern look.

"We're so far ahead of Skroppa, he's probably given up and returned to Remmelsberg. You worry too much, Jodocus. Relax."

"I will never relax until I am back in Normandie. And I advise you to do the same, Byrun."

With that, Jodocus returned to the cart and finished readying himself for the morning's journey.

※※※

The village of Brenig was a small thriving community consisting primarily of farmers but a number of merchants—blacksmith, carpenter, baker, furniture maker, and wine merchant had their stores along the main road. Located a hundred yards to the north of the village was the tiny monastery headed by Abbot Sewell.

Brenig was a quiet community, untouched in recent years by the violence perpetrated by Norse raiders. The two cobbled streets were in the shape of a Latin cross, with the long main road transected at a right angle by a shorter one. The main road housed the merchants and other businesses while homes of a few of the villagers dotted the shorter limb of the cross.

Abbot Sewell had been the head of the Brenig monastery since its inception ten years earlier. During those years under his leadership the monastery built a church at the edge of town where the villagers gathered on the Sabbath to sing their praises to God and listen to his sermon. The Sabbath service was well attended and for the most part Abbot Sewell was pleased with the work he and his fellow monks did in Brenig.

The monks brewed ale. It was how they earned their living. That and their monthly allotments from Rome. Behind the monastery there was a small farm where the oats and barley were grown—the barley later malted and added to the ale mixture. Brewing varied by the season of the year, with vast amounts produced in December when more than three thousand gallons were brewed and put into large oaken barrels. In the dry month of February, only eight hundred or so gallons were brewed.

Abbot Sewell had one over-arching passion—the building of the small cathedral next to the church. Work had been ongoing for three years. Stonemasons, cutters, carpenters, and builders now lived in Brenig's environs and were the laboring force in the construction of the cathedral. By cathedral standards, it was small, but to Abbot Sewell's eyes it was to be a magnificent glorious edifice. Most of Abbot Sewell's time was spent in the continual effort to raise money to pay the laborers so the building could continue. Sales of the monastery's ale helped but did not defray the entire cost of the project.

The abbot hoped his cathedral would be completed before he died. His one wish was to live long enough to hold a service in the cathedral and see the morning sun stream through the stained glass windows he planned for each side of the nave. Oh, it would be a glorious sight.

One mile from the monastery was the quarry where the stone for the cathedral was harvested and cut. Sandstone, limestone, and basalt were dug from the quarry then master stonecutters carved them into the necessary formations required by the builders. It was a huge undertaking and in the three years the cathedral was under construction the labor force increased to now number over a hundred able-bodied men.

The abbot knew that, for the most part, the men who worked on his cathedral were not religious men. On Saturday nights, they enjoyed drinking, games of chance, and chasing after the village's eligible young women. After a night of carousing, the revelers slept late and didn't give the Sabbath services a second thought. He tried to remain tolerant of such behavior unless there was a fight or accusations of a more serious nature. Then he intervened by terminating the guilty one's employment. Over the years he had added a few souls to his flock but realized he fought a losing battle.

This morning Abbot Sewell was on his way to the farm to check on the progress of the barley harvest. It was a beautiful day, and he was in good spirits.

CHAPTER 20

Brenig, Normandie, 1063 AD:

Geffrey guided the horse and wagon over the cobbled road of Brenig. The village was astir with the activities of daily living—people scurrying about, merchant's doors open for business, a few men with open carts selling their wares. The village was filled with noise, colors, people, and smells of all kinds. The aroma of spices, baking breads and pies, roasting meats floated through the street tantalizing Geffrey and his traveling companions.

"What did I tell you?" Quinn said. "Brenig is a marvelous, crazy town."

Geffrey pulled the wagon to a stop in front of the town's water well, a stone structure enclosing a small pool. A statue of the Madonna stood in the middle and a stone bench lined the well. The travelers climbed down from the wagon and rested.

"I'm going to open for business soon," Quinn said. "Then later we'll have music and magic show. Hopefully, we'll make a little money."

A small crowd began to gather around the wagon so Geffrey, Jococus, and Byrun decided to wander about and see the sights while Jubal remained behind to help Quinn and Miriam. They strolled among the throng of villagers and carts, inspecting what the merchants had for sale. Dogs barked, children squealed, mothers admonished their husbands—Brenig was alive with activity.

At the end of the long road, Geffrey noticed what looked like a construction site. A building of some sort was being erected, its framework jutting into the bright sky. Around the site were dozens of men laboring at various tasks—some hauling stones in carts, some cutting the stones, some mixing mortar. In the middle of this activity was a wide table, on which was spread large sheets of paper. Several men were poised over them engaged in serious conversation. Whatever they were building, it was going to be big, he thought.

Geffrey knew something of stonecutters and their work, for one lived and worked near Lochwald and helped erect the wall—Robert, who had been sweet on Rosalind, and his father. Stonecutters often lived itinerant lifestyles, moving from one construction site to another. They would either be paid by day, or by piece. Piecework was often reserved for new craftsmen or those recruited for short periods. Such craftsmen carved their mark on every stone they cut, to enable them to calculate how much they were owed. With time, maker's marks became a sign of pride and grew more elaborate.

If they were building a stone structure, they would need blacksmiths to forge and fabricate the tools necessary for the work. He wondered if he could get work on this project, whatever it was. He had no money and no horse. If he were going to make it all the way to Lochwald he would need both.

"Maybe we could find work here," he said to Byrun and Jodocus. "We need money and horses if we are to continue on our journey. Quinn told me when they finished here, they would head south for a while before returning the way they came. We will be on our own again."

"I'm for working," Byrun said.

"And finding a place to stay," Jodocus added.

"If we can find the master builder for this project, then he might be able to help. From the size of this project, it looks like they'll be working here for a while." Geffrey searched the work site, decided to approach the men at the table.

They made, their way through the throng of workers to the large table where three men were bent over it. None of them looked up as they stood by the table.

Geffrey cleared his throat. A tall bearded man raised his eyes, stared at him with a penetrating gaze. He suddenly felt weak in the knees.

"Pardon," Geffrey said. "We are looking for work. I am a blacksmith. My friend here," he said, patting Byrun on the shoulder, "has worked with me at the forge. My other friend here is very intelligent. Knows numbers and angles. We have another friend who is a giant of a man. He can lift heavy stones with ease."

The bearded man put down his compass and moved closer to them. He was wiry and possessed a hooked nose. "We can always use good workers," he said. "Where do you hail from?"

"We have been traveling with Quinn, the peddler. He and his family are at the well now selling their wares."

"Quinn, the peddler? Yes, I know him. You say you are a smithy?"

"Yes, I am."

"And there is another with you who is extremely strong?"

"Yes."

"Well, we can use all of you." He extended his hand, Geffrey took it. It was a firm grasp. "My name is Howard. I am the master builder. Welcome to the cathedral at Brenig."

"You're building a cathedral here?" Byrun said.

"Yes," Howard said. "The Brenig monastery is doing the construction. Abbot Sewell will want to meet you. He likes to meet all the workers and welcome them.

"We will need lodging," Geffrey said. "Can you help us with that?"

Howard nodded. "I believe so. The stonecutter has a barn that is not being used at the moment. I can ask him if he would allow you all to stay in his barn. He is a hard worker with a nice family."

"That would be great," Jodocus said. "Any sort of shelter would be fine with us."

Howard led the men over a narrow path beside a garden filled with flowers and an oval pond to the monastery. As they walked, Howard described the construction.

"Construction on the cathedral began about three years ago," he said as the circled the pond and headed up the path to the monastery proper. "The first master builder was a drunkard so I was hired to replace him after a weekend of debauchery and raping several of Brenig's young girls. The villagers almost killed the man. Anyway, the construction has been proceeding slowly as one would predict but it is progressing. The foundation for the nave is laid and the walls are going up."

"How much longer before it is completed?" Jodocus said.

"Completed? Ha!" Howard scoffed. "It will never be completed, at least in my lifetime. If I were to hazard a guess, I would say another thirty years should see it finished."

"Wow," was all Geffrey could muster.

The monastery building was a modest stone affair and it stood on a small knoll that overlooked Brenig. Howard knocked on the large oaken door and a little pink man

wearing a brown robe answered it. His small eyes squinted at the group.

"We are here to see the abbot," Howard said. "Howard, the builder, and some new workers."

"This way," the monk said and shuffled down a tiled
cloister to an office in a far corner of the monastery. He
knocked and entered.

A short, obese, clean shaven man looked up from his
desk. A burgundy bishop's mitre lay beside him. Geffrey
noticed his crozier leaning in a corner. The abbot rose,
smiled." Howard," he said in a deep voice. "Welcome.
What brings you to the monastery this time of day?"

"Three new workers," Howard said. "This man," he
pointed to Geffrey, "is a blacksmith. There is a fourth
man who they say is extremely strong. We can use
them."

The abbot cast a gentle smile at Geffrey.

"Welcome, gentlemen. I am Abbot Sewell, the head of
this monastery. We monks here adhere to the Benedictine
Rule that was established five hundred years ago. You
have heard of the Rule?"

Geffrey shook his head. "I am afraid none of us are
very religious," he said.

"Well, maybe we can change that during your stay
with us," the abbot said, smiling. "The Rule offers people
a plan for living a balanced, simple, and prayerful life. In
it, Benedict tells his monks and nuns that *ora et labor* is
their way—work and prayer—that the Divine Office is
their work or *opus dei,* and the vows of stability, conversion, and obedience are their commitments. These vows
have much to say to those of us not living in a monastery
or convent. Please, gentlemen, have a seat in the chairs
there."

Geffrey and the others sat in leather chairs around the
abbot's desk. A crucifix containing a bloodied Christ

hung on a wall behind the group. A worn Bible lay beside the mitre.

"You're unfamiliar with monastery life, I take it," the abbot said.

Geffrey shook his head. "I'm afraid not, sir," said, unsure of how to address Abbot Sewell.

"We monks sleep in a dormitory," the abbot continued. "Our studying is done in covered cloisters or in the library. Soon, we hope to have toilets with running water to get rid of our waste. The chapter house is where a chapter of rules for our monastery is read out each day.

"It is my greatest desire that Brenig should have a cathedral worthy of its citizens. Our brotherhood is truly blessed to have a man of Howard's knowledge and skill to direct its construction. You will be paid according to your skill and talents. No one here works for nothing."

Howard nodded. "Abbot Sewell oversees the daily life at the monastery here," he said, "but he also spends much time in the raising of funds to build the cathedral, right Abbot?"

"Seems like that is all I do, Howard. But it is a labor of love, as they say. Do you men have lodging?"

Geffrey nodded. "I believe Howard may be able to provide for us. He has been very gracious."

"Yes," the abbot said, "he is a good man. He stays on top of the workers but that is a good thing, I think."

Howard chuckled. "Can't have any slackers, can we? Well, we will take our leave, Abbot." He started for the door.

"Work progressing normally?" the abbot asked.

"There was a major breakdown on the north wall and its flying buttress. The mortar wasn't the correct consistency and crumbled into sand when it dried. It took most of a day to figure out, but I believe we're back on schedule now."

They took their leave of the abbot and Howard introduced them to the stonecutter, Breslin, who agreed to allow them to stay in his barn for a low rent. Howard told them to report for work in the morning so they ambled back to the town well where they found Quinn doing a roaring business selling pots and pans.

Later, the peddler pulled the cart to a stream outside Brenig where Miriam roasted pigeons for supper. Quinn traded a pot for them.

"They brew ale at the monastery," Geffrey told Quinn as they sat on the ground and ate. It's been a long time since I tasted a good ale."

"Ale?" Jubal said. "Fine, fine. I'll be working up quite a thirst in the quarry."

"I'm surprised they don't make beer," Quinn said. "The process is different but beer's taste is much to be preferred."

"How so?" Geffrey said.

"For an ale, the wort, which is the liquid containing sugars and protein extracted from the grain, is not boiled prior to fermenting. For a beer, the wort needs to be boiled with the hops. This seemingly small difference accounts for the taste of the beer. Hops add a measure of bitterness to the beer, and also helps preserve it."

"Never had beer," Byrun said. "I've had a good mead before."

"So, you men are staying in Brenig, are you?" Quinn said as he perched himself against a tree, stoked his pipe. "Miriam and I will be missing you, that's for sure. Norène as well. We'll not say farewell, for who knows? We may meet up down the road someday."

"You've been a good friend, Quinn," Jodocus said, "to allow four strangers into your company. May all your troubles be small ones."

Norène ventured from the wagon and came to sit beside Byrun. Geffrey noticed that she looked at him with a sad look and tears in her eyes. After a few minutes beside Byrun, she jumped up and disappeared into the wagon.

ℰↃℰↃ

The next morning, Geffrey, Byrun, Jubal, and Jodocus each shook hands with Quinn. Miriam kissed them on a cheek and wept as she climbed into the wagon seat. Quinn hitched the horse to the wagon, hopped aboard, waved to them. Norène was nowhere to be seen. Must be in the rear of the wagon, Geffrey surmised.

As Quinn headed the wagon south, a lump formed in Geffrey's throat.

At the worksite, Geffrey and Byrun were assigned to the forge while Jodocus went to the cathedral and Jubal to the quarry.

Geffrey spent the day laboring over a giant forge sharpening tools and fashioning new ones after they broke. The workforce involved in the construction of a cathedral varied considerably in terms of skill. At the lower end of the scale were laborers who performed basic jobs such as transporting building materials, digging for the foundations, or removing earth. Higher-skilled workers linked to a construction site included quarrymen, plasterers, mortar-makers, stonecutters, and masons. Practical considerations determined the work process. Because transport was time-consuming and costly, stones were often shaped in the quarry. Although stone cutting could take place all year, masons, the ones responsible for actually laying the stone, could not work in winter, as frost prevented the mortar from binding the stones together.

During the midday break, Howard dropped by the forge to check in the new workers.

"How are you two doing?" he asked Geffrey.

"Hard at work," Geffrey said. "How does one go about building a cathedral? It seems a gargantuan undertaking."

"It is," Howard said. "After our plan was put in place, the basic building work of the cathedral foundations began. This cathedral's foundations are up to twenty-five feet deep underground, because any mistakes could cause the walls above ground to become weak, particularly once the roof has been added.

"During the laying of the foundations, our skilled craftsmen worked in the quarry where they produce stone blocks to use in the process of building. Up to fifty advanced skilled apprentices work within the quarry with two hundred fifty laborers all under supervision by our master quarryman. The master quarryman is provided with templates for the required shapes from cut quarry stone by the master mason. Individual stones are marked to plan where it is to go once the building began.

"In some sense, a cathedral is like a building made of playing cards, each section leaning on others in some sort of equilibrium. This also determines the stages of the construction. It will be expensive to shore up one part while another is being built, only to have to remove it later. Much of the building process of cathedrals is innovative and experimental. Bits tend to fall down from time to time."

"No wonder it takes so long to complete the building," Geffrey said.

"Cathedrals have large curtain walls filled in with stained glass, walls that do not support the weight of the vaulting and roofs. This cathedral won't be as tall as most. The taller ones have to resist considerable side pressures from wind. The main weight of the cathedral structure is carried downward by the tall pillars that march along the nave and the side aisles. The pointed arch vaulting directs more of the force downward than does the Roman arch, but there remain sideways forces to be managed. Down the marching pillars and bays there are counter-forces from bay to bay, but pressures remain toward the outside, for which solutions need to be found."

"Seems extremely complicated," Byrun said.

"It is," Howard replied. "It's one reason construction takes so long."

✐✐✐

Abbot Sewell sat in his office, reflected on the great cathedral he envisioned for the small community of Brenig. It wasn't that he was an unusually proud or profane man, although in some respects he realized he was exactly that and asked nightly forgiveness for that sin. It was more a sense of duty to God and to his fellow man that he felt compelled to build the cathedral. A vigorous man in his middle forties, Abbot Sewell knew the construction would continue, hopefully, long after he departed this world. He desired to give the building a good start so that nothing in the future would stand in the way of its completion.

St. Benedict's conception of a monastic community was distinctly that of a spiritual family. Every individual monk was to be a son of that family, the abbot its father, and the monastery its permanent home. Upon the abbot therefore, as upon the father of a family, revolved the government and direction of those who were committed to his care, and a paternal solicitude characterized his rule. St. Benedict said that an abbot who was worthy to have the charge of a monastery ought always to remember by what title he was called, and that in the monastery he was considered to represent the person of Christ, seeing that he was called by His name. The monastic system established by St. Benedict was based entirely upon the supremacy of the abbot. Though the Rule gave directions as to an abbot's government, and furnished him with principles upon which to act, and bound him to carry out certain prescriptions as to consultation with others in difficult matters, the subject was told to obey without question or hesitation the decision of the superior. Needless to say this obedience did not extend to the commission of evil, even were any such command ever imposed. The obedience shown to the abbot was regarded as obedience paid to God Himself, and all the respect and reverence with which the brethren of his house showed him was out of respect for Christ, because as abbot—father—he was the representative of Christ in the midst of the brethren. The whole government of a religious house depended upon the abbot. His will was supreme in all things. Yet, as the Rule mentioned, nothing was to be taught, commanded, or ordered beyond the precepts of the Lord.

Abbot Sewell took his role as head of the monastery seriously and the building of the cathedral even more so. He rose from his desk, strolled in silence to the monastery chapel, where he knelt before the large wooden cross. He crossed himself and uttered a silent prayer asking divine help in the magnificent work he undertook.

CHAPTER 21

At night the four men ate with Breslin the stone-cutter and his daughter, Isolde. They relaxed in Breslin's house and listened to the man's progress report on the cathedral while Isolde fixed their supper. As Geffrey sat near the hearth, he admired the girl's slender delicate features, her long blonde hair, blue eyes, and fair skin. She hummed to herself while she labored over the hearth next to him. Every once in a while, he caught a whiff of lilacs—her perfume or the soap she used.

"Yes," Breslin was saying, "We have gradually developed an external system of buttressing, which applies counter-acting force sideways toward the cathedral wall. This resists the tendency of the walls to bulge out from the lateral pressures. There are no lateral forces exerted by the roof, for the roof is framed in wood and cross-pinned to hold it together. But, of course, the wind forces do transmit force laterally. The upper flying buttress redirects the wind forces from the roof and the cloister wall, guiding them downward into the pier buttress. The lower flying buttress performs the same duty, but for the outward lateral forces being exerted by the nave vaulting."

"I have seen the work first hand," Jodocus said. "It's amazing to watch the progress from the inside."

Over a supper of roasted wild boar, vegetables, some kind of cake, and strong ale, Breslin continued his discussion. "Roman arches are fine for spherical domes and barrel roofs, but not for more complex shapes. The arches for an oblong bay must span three different distances, a complex situation. This can be handled effectively by the use of pointed arches, by varying the steepness of the arcs, thus terminating all three arch lengths at the same height above the nave."

"You're quite knowledgeable in how the cathedral is to be constructed," Byrun said, taking a large gulp of ale.

"A stonecutter must understand the intricacies of how the building goes together or it will come down. I hope to become a master builder one day," Breslin said.

"There seems to be a considerable amount of mathematics and geometry involved," Byrun said.

Breslin's eyes lit up and he smiled. "To become a master builder is a long and difficult process. It is not easy. There is much to learn. And as you say, the mathematics and geometry are formidable."

When supper was finished, Geffrey and his companions headed for the barn. There, they readied themselves for bed as dawn came early. A single oil lantern provided light for the barn.

"That daughter of Breslin's." Geffrey said. "She's a fine looking girl. Her hair is like ripened barley. She reminds me a little of Rosalind. And she smells of heaven."

"It sounds as if our friend Geffrey has found someone that has captured his attention," Jodocus said.

Jubal guffawed as he pulled off his boots and lay back in the straw.

"Friends," Geffrey pined. "My friends."

The next day Howard came and found Geffrey in the forge.

"Come with me," he said. "The abbot wishes to see us."

"Why me?" Geffrey said.

"I dunno. Something about tools."

Geffrey followed Howard to the monastery and through the cloister to the abbot's office. Along the way they past several monks engaged in copying an ancient manuscript. Abbot Sewell greeted them with a handshake and smile, offered them high backed chairs in which they sat. "May I offer you some of our ale?" he said. "As a refreshment? We brew the region's best ale, I can assure you."

"That would be fine, Abbot," Howard said.

Abbot Sewell opened a cabinet and retrieved a pewter pitcher and poured three tankards of the ale. Geffrey thought the ale was strong, pungent.

"What do you think?" the abbot said after both men had taken a sip.

"Mighty fine, sir," Geffrey said. "Best I've had in quite a spell. Nice and bitter."

"Now, to business," Abbot Sewell said. "I would like a large chandelier made for our refectory. I would like it to have twenty oil lanterns on it."

"Refectory?" Geffrey said.

"Our dining hall. In the winter months it gets rather dim during the evening meal."

"Twenty lanterns on it?" Geffrey made a quick mental calculation.

"Think you can build it at your forge, Geffrey?" the abbot asked.

"Sure, just draw me out a sketch as to what you want. With my other duties, it might take a little while."

"As long as we can have it by fall and it doesn't impede progress on the cathedral."

"It shouldn't."

"Fine, fine," Abbot Sewell said. "I'll get you a sketch with some preliminary dimensions. Do you and your friends find our village to your liking?"

"Seems nice enough," Geffrey said. "Time will tell, however. Howard and the stonecutter have treated us well."

"They are both fine men," the abbot said. He stood. "I believe that is all. And thank you."

The men shook hands and Geffrey made his way back to the forge and work.

Later that night after supper, Geffrey noticed Isolde walking alone near the family vegetable garden. He caught up with her.

"Good evening, Isolde. That was a nice supper you prepared for us. May I walk with you?"

"You may," Isolde said. "Your name is Geffrey, right?"

"Yes. My friends and I work at the cathedral."

The sun had gone down leaving the dusk cool. A gentle breeze filtered through the garden and whispered through Isolde's golden hair. Once again the scent of lilacs tickled his nose. He walked beside her.

"Yes, I know. Papa told me. But you are not from around here," she said.

"No. I'm from a long way off. I lived in a village by the name of Lochwald. Ever hear of it?"

She shook her head.

"How long have you lived in Brenig?"

"Several years," Isolde said. "We moved here when father took the job at the cathedral. We've traveled all over southern Normandie."

"Building cathedrals?"

"Oh no. This is Papa's first. He finds it most challenging."

"What do you do while Papa is working?"

"Oh, I garden, cook, mend clothes, that sort of thing. On Sundays after church, I usually read. I have a small collection of books, and I read them over and over."

"Would you care to go on a picnic with me Sunday after church?" Geffrey said, surprising himself with his boldness.

"I would love to, Geffrey. I can pack a lunch for us to take."

"No, don't do that. I have money and can purchase some items. Getting paid for one's work is a new experience for me."

"You never worked before?"

"I was my father's apprentice, so no, I never got paid." He laughed and Isolde laughed along with him. "You like living here in Brenig?"

Isolde looked at him with soft eyes. "It's a nice village. There are a lot of different people who come through here to work on the cathedral. It's fun to meet them and find out where they have come from and where they are going. And what their plans are."

"People like myself, I presume. I think you are very beautiful, Isolde."

"Thank you, Geffrey. People say I look like my mother. She was very beautiful."

On Saturday after work, Geffrey scurried around Brenig buying bread, cheese, wine, pickles, and an orange cake. When he told Byrun what he was doing the following day, he noticed a strange look descend upon him. A sneer—dark and foreboding. It was a look he had never seen on Byrun's face. Geffrey wondered why but quickly forgot it as he hurried to bathe and clean himself in preparation for the picnic.

The following day Isolde was delighted with his choice of items and packed them away neatly in a basket. Geffrey carried it to a grass covered area next to the stream at the edge of town where he and Isolde ate, chatted, and laughed. He learned she was eighteen and between beaux at the moment. Most eligible young men around the village worked at the cathedral and were raucous, crude, and drank too much ale, she said.

As they sat on the sweet smelling grass, Geffrey inquired about Isolde's mother.

"She died of smallpox," Isolde said. "A little over a year ago. Papa has never been the same since."

"I imagine not," Geffrey said. "How so?"

"He's more irritable, short tempered. Don't get me wrong, he believes the sun rises and sets with me. But with his workers, he is demanding and curt."

"Always been fair and cordial with me and my friends. I try to do an honest day's work for an honest day's pay. Jubal, who works in the quarry, says the same."

She looked at him with the queerest expression, eyes wide, glistening—almost as if the remembrance of her mother brought tears to them. To Geffrey, she appeared fragile, like a flower that had just bloomed, but beautiful, nonetheless. Without thinking, he leaned toward her and kissed her. Her lips parted slightly, she didn't pull away. Instead, she placed the fingers of her hand on his cheek and kissed him again.

Geffrey felt as if his heart was going to explode within his chest. It was difficult to catch his breath. He gazed into her eyes, looking deep. He started to speak but she placed a finger on his lips then kissed him once more.

"I didn't mean to bring back painful memories of your mother," he said. "I didn't know."

"It's fine," Isolde said.

After they finished their picnic, Geffrey escorted Isolde to her home. He said goodbye, walked the short distance to the barn where Byrun stood, watching. He had seen him say goodbye to Isolde.

"Have a nice time?" Byrun said.

"I did. Isolde is a lovely girl."

But Geffrey noticed the edge to Byrun's voice. Something wasn't right.

ᴄ◠ᴈᴄ◠ᴈ

Days turned into weeks and weeks into months. The work on the cathedral progressed at an agonizingly slow methodical pace and Geffrey's life became a monotonous cycle of laboring in the forge day after day. The bright spot was in the evenings when he spent time with Isolde. The two of them took long walks after supper, went on picnics on Sunday afternoons. He and his companions were saving their money and soon he hoped to have enough to get him on his way back to Lochwald. Or what was left of it. The only complication in his plans was Isolde. The truth was he had fallen in love with her and the thought of leaving her grieved him and sent chills down his spine. He didn't know if he could bear to be parted from her. She loved him, of course, that much was plain. She had said it, right out one night during an embrace. What her father, Breslin, thought of the idea, he didn't know. Isolde hadn't said.

It was a difficulty Geffrey had not counted on. Because, until he met Isolde, his heart belonged to Rosalind. So was his involvement with the stonecutter's daughter nothing more than an infatuation? He worried that if he was in love with Isolde how then, could he have been in love with Rosalind? None of it made sense and the answers were not forthcoming.

One evening as they strolled along the bank of the stream, Isolde stopped, smiled at him. The moonlight cast silver streaks in her golden hair.

"Geffrey," she said, "there's a fair this weekend."

"Yes, I know," he said. "Everyone is talking about it."

"And there's going to be a dance on Saturday night. Do you want to go?"

He brightened, his pulse quickened.

"Of course. What kind of dance?"

"There'll be mandolins, flutes, and fiddles. Everyone from the village will be there. It should be fun."

"I know the work at the cathedral will stop during the fair," Geffrey said. "Fortunately, I'm caught up on my work in the forge. I'm working on a chandelier for Abbot Sewell in my spare time."

"Papa talks to Howard and the builder says you singlehandedly keep the workers supplied with tools. He says as fast as they break them you have them repaired or sharpened and back in their hands."

"Well—"

"Papa says Howard is pleased with all of you. Byrun, Jodocus. And that Jubal. Papa says the man is a beast. Can lift most anything. What does Jodocus do at the site?"

They laughed together.

"My friends are important to me," Geffrey said. "We've been through a lot together. Byrun nursed me back to health after I was tortured and thrown in the dungeon at Remmelsberg. Jodocus helps with all the geometry and calculations. He is very knowledgeable with numbers."

"You've been tortured?" Isolde now had a worried look about her.

"A long time ago, my love. But, Byrun—well—"

"He saved your life?"

"Maybe not like that but I'll never forget what he did for me. I owe him a lot."

The Brenig fair brought people from far and wide. On Saturday there were arm wrestling matches, hammer throws, archery contests, races, and weight lifting events.

People set up food booths and sold cakes, pies, box lunches. Geffrey entered the ten pound hammer throw and came in second. Isolde bought him a pie.

The dance was a splendid affair with the ladies dressed in all their finery. Isolde wore a blue dress that accentuated her eyes. It had a low-cut bodice revealing an ample bosom, a fact that wasn't lost on Geffrey. They danced almost every dance together until, exhausted, Isolde begged for a rest. He brought her a cup of punch and they sat on a bench under a tree. The night air was warm, sultry. Insects chirped in the nearby trees.

"Where are your friends?" Isolde said.

"Byrun and Jodocus are inside watching the ladies and drinking the ale," he said. "Jubal isn't much for these kinds of things so he elected to remain back at the barn."

"He doesn't say much."

"No. He's the strong silent type." He chuckled at his description. "Actually, he talks more than you know. It's just that he's extremely shy. Women, especially pretty ones like you, get him all tongue-tied."

Finished with their punch, they returned to the dance. Jodocus strolled up to them, took Geffrey by an arm.

"I need to talk to you," he said. "Let's go somewhere private." He wore a frown on his face.

They went outside leaving Isolde with a girlfriend.

"What gives?" Geffrey said.

"It's Byrun," he said.

"Yes? What about him? Has the man got himself in trouble over a young lady?"

"No. He's a jealous man."

"Of who? What?"

"Of you. And Isolde. He's told me so. Not in those exact words but he feels he saw her first and you cut him out. He feels he didn't stand a chance with her because of you."

"Jodocus, are you kidding? This can't be true. Byrun is my best friend besides you and Jubal. When he was sweet on Quinn's daughter, Norène, I didn't interfere. So, how can he be jealous?"

"I don't know but he is. And it's eating him up inside. He's angry."

"Why hasn't he said something? Surely, we can talk this out."

"I dunno why he hasn't. I tried to reason with him but he wouldn't have it. Seems to think that you are now his enemy. The look on his face frightened me."

"I—I can't believe this," Geffrey said, stunned. "He's always seemed so casual about everything, so carefree."

"Are you saying you haven't noticed a change in his demeanor toward you?"

Geffrey thought for a moment. "Well, yes, Jodocus, come to think of it, he has been more sullen when the two of us are together. However, I really didn't think much of it."

"I suspect there's something about Byrun we haven't discovered. Something from his past before any of us knew him."

"Then I must speak to him," Geffrey said, undone by Jodocus's revelation.

"Not yet, Geffrey. Wait a while. I'm going to try again to talk sense with Byrun so maybe it will work itself out. I'll let you know when the time is right."

Later, after saying goodnight to Isolde, Geffrey lay in the barn unable to sleep. Jodocus's disclosure left his mind reeling. It was an unsettling development.

ℰℐℰℐ

Byrun lay on his cot and thought of his meeting with Isolde. Without Geffrey's knowledge, he approached

Isolde and asked if she would like to walk with him. That was almost a month ago and since that time Byrun had found circumstances where he found Isolde alone, without Geffrey knowing it. To Byrun she was the most beautiful creature he had ever seen.

During their brief conversations together, however, it was obvious that Isolde was not totally comfortable with the situation and voiced her concern to Byrun.

"I don't like you constantly finding me alone, Byrun," she said one day when he found her alone in the family garden. "Geffrey will not like it nor understand."

"You're beautiful, Isolde," Byrun said, moving closer. "I want more. Can't you see it clear to go on a picnic with me? Like you do with Geffrey?"

"I don't think so, Byrun. I like you, but with Geffrey—"

"Yeah," he said. "I get the picture. The big oaf always gets the girl."

He followed her into the barn, watched her replace a rake and trowel. When she turned to leave, he caught her by an arm. She tried to escape his grasp, but he tightened his grip.

"Byrun," she said. "What are you doing? Let go, you're hurting my arm."

"I wouldn't worry about it," Byrun said, putting an arm around her. "Geffrey is a big boy. He should understand the fortunes of love and war. For all you know, he's seeing another woman on the sly."

"I doubt it. Knowing Geffrey, if he was, I think he would come out and tell me. Now let me go. Please."

When he drew her close to him, the fragrance of her perfume seemed like heaven.

"You don't want Geffrey," Byrun said, consumed with Isolde's beauty. "I can make you so much happier. Now come here and give me a little kiss."

In spite of Isolde's struggling, Byrun forced her face into his and kissed her hard on her lips. She fought him, pushing against his restraint with her delicate hands. He grabbed both her wrists and shoved her against a barn wall. She moved her head as he tried in vain to kiss her again.

"Byrun!" she screamed. "Please don't do this."

She lunged free of him and tried to run out of the barn, but he caught her and threw her to the ground. On top of her he ripped open her dress, exposing the tops of her breasts.

"Geffrey isn't for you," he hissed in her ear. "I'm a much better man."

Together they fought and Isolde managed to roll out from under him. He lunged for an arm but missed. He squatted on the barn floor and watched her run out the door, sobbing, and into the bright sunlight.

CHAPTER 22

The days in the forge changed perceptively for Geffrey. Byrun was no longer his talkative self, no longer laughed and joked with him. At the end of the day, he preferred to walk home alone. Geffrey wanted to speak to him, resolve whatever issues or misunderstandings prevented their usual relationship. It pained him to be at odds with his friend.

And he noticed a change in Isolde as well, for at supper when all were gathered around Breslin's table, she hardly said a word, just ate with her head bowed. Instead, she served their supper without talking or smiling. Afterward, when they took their walk together, Geffrey inquired about the change he noticed. But she shrugged it off as a woman's prerogative to be emotional and changeable. It was just a mood, she said. It would improve if he would just be patient.

If he had been more perceptive, he might have recognized that Isolde's mood coincided with Byrun's dark manner. He was so deeply in love that it would have been difficult for him to understand that his relationship with Isolde was a matter of pain for Byrun. That they loved each other was not something that Geffrey kept secret from his friends. Not since that first evening when she cooked for them and he caught the faintest scent of lilacs. He was determined to clear the air with Byrun.

One day, as the fall equinox approached, Geffrey arrived at the barn after a long day in the forge. Waiting for him were Breslin, Howard, Abbot Sewell, and two men he didn't know. In a far corner of the barn he noticed Byrun lurking in a shadow. At once, his pulse banged in his temples while a foul taste formed in his mouth. What was going on?

The master builder stepped forward. His face held a scowl.

"Yes, Howard," Geffrey said, "What is it?"

"It's Breslin here," the builder said. "His money pouch is missing."

"Oh? I'm sorry to hear that. But—"

Howard nodded and the two strange men came forward and stood at Geffrey's shoulder.

"And Byrun here," Howard continued, glancing at Byrun in the shadows, "has accused you of stealing it."

"No!" Geffrey exclaimed. "Are you kidding? Is this some sort of joke?" He glanced toward the dark corner of the barn where Byrun stood, silent. "Byrun, tell them you made a mistake. You know I didn't do such a thing! That I couldn't do such a terrible thing! Please tell them!"

"Byrun has said he saw you put the pouch in your bag. We want to have a look, Geffrey."

Geffrey shot an unbelieving look at Byrun who had not advanced from the shadows. Byrun was his friend, the man who nursed him back to health. The man whose life Geffrey saved in the cave-in. The man he convinced Ornolf to bring out of the mines and make him an assistant in the forge. This was Byrun, who he would gladly give his life to save if necessary. What was this about?

He noticed that Breslin and Howard stood with a stiff posture, frowns on their faces. Breslin looked as if he might explode. Abbot Sewell appeared embarrassed at being with the others.

Jodocus and Jubal stood nearby, their jaws slack in amazed bewilderment at what was transpiring before them.

"Where is your bag, Geffrey?" Howard said. "May we have a look?"

"By all means," Geffrey said. "The bag is right there in the straw next to where I make my bed. But, Howard, you know me. How long have I worked for you? Have I not been honest and dependable?"

"I'm sorry, Geffrey," he said and stooped to retrieve the bag.

Howard opened the bag, reached in, and took out a small leather pouch. It was full of coins and jingled as he handed it to Breslin." "Is that your pouch?" he asked the stonecutter.

Breslin inspected the pouch, opened it, looked inside, then nodded. "It is," he said.

Geffrey protested. "It can't be!" he yelled. "I have no idea how it got there. Someone must have put it there. Why?"

The two men each took Geffrey by an arm.

"Gentlemen, I protest! I beg you to listen to me. I did not do this!"

Abbot Sewell stepped toward Geffrey with a sad look. "My son, I am so sorry," he said. "Our protector, the duke, is the one who usually hears these cases and determines guilt and punishment. But he is away at the moment. We could subject you to the trial by fire to determine your guilt, but you are not one of us, not from here. So that cannot be done."

"Please, Abbot, I beg you," Geffrey protested. "I did not do this."

Geffrey's head was in a whirl, spinning out of control. He felt like screaming, running off somewhere. Instead, he stared at his accusers, astonished at Byrun's lie.

"Then how do you explain my money pouch being in your bag?" an angry Breslin said.

"I do not know. All I know is that I am innocent. Byrun! Why have you said these things?"

Geffrey shot a look where Byrun stood.

He was gone.

"As Brenig's chief religious authority," Abbot Sewell said, "I suggest banishment." He turned to Howard. "Pay these men what they are owed, give them each a horse, and see that they are escorted out of Brenig. It is a less severe punishment than this man deserves but, under the circumstances, it is the best we can do. And do it today."

Howard nodded his understanding. He waited until Breslin and the abbot went their way then escorted Geffrey to the forge. Jodocus and Jubal followed. They were allowed to gather their possessions and weapons. At the edge of Brenig, Geffrey looked over his shoulder and saw Isolde standing alone, her shoulders shaking, weeping.

He turned his horse onto the road heading west and wiped the tears from his eyes. "Why?" he said aloud. "Why?"

Jodocus reined his horse alongside Geffrey. His soft voice was barely audible over the plodding of the horse's hooves. "I told you," he whispered. "I told you Byrun was no longer your friend."

❧❧

As they neared the River Skye the landscape took on a familiar appearance with its lush rolling hills, dotted with patches of loamy dark bottomlands. Since leaving Brenig, the trio of friends rode through several small villages each located along a tributary of the main river. Autumn was upon them and the verdant hills were interspersed with the occasional copse of aspens whose leaves began to show their brilliant orange color.

Midday saw them dismounted and resting in a stand of aspens beside a small creek. The morning chill was gone, replaced by a warm afternoon. Bright sunlight filtered through the quaking leaves.

"How much farther?" Jodocus said.

"I roamed all over these hills," Geffrey said. "Hunted and fished here so I used to know these parts like the back of my hand. But, it's been years since I was here. Things look familiar but not familiar. Does that make sense?"

Jubal shook his head but Jodocus nodded.

"Of course," Jodocus said. "As an old man my mind sometimes plays tricks on me."

"I remember," Geffrey continued, "one time when my father took me hunting. He wanted an elk for the winter. Well, there aren't any elk in these parts, haven't been in years but father had heard of a place that had a large herd of the animals. So, we lit out on foot, packs on our backs, and my father with his bow and arrows. Well, father was never a very good marksman with that bow. We stalked all around these forests, our eyes peeled for elk."

"What happened?" Jubal interrupted. "Did you find any?"

"I'm coming to that part. One night we were camped and about to bed down beside our campfire when I heard a rustling in the trees. Father heard it too. 'Elk,' he said, and gathered his bow and arrows. I sat by the fire while he crept toward the sound, notched an arrow, and readied his shot. The rustling came again. Father let fly with the arrow and it hit something for a loud roar shot through the trees. It definitely wasn't an elk. The next thing I saw was Father high tailing it my way and a dark form lumbering after him."

"Ha, a bear," Jodocus said. "He shot a bear."

"Right on. And the closer that dark shape came, the more I was able to make out that it was indeed a bear and the beast had Father's arrow stuck in his hide. He was madder than a nest of hornets."

"What did you do?" Jubal said, his eyes wide with anticipation.

"What do you think I did? I grabbed our provisions under an arm and lit out. Father passed me and you should have seen the look on his face. Scared out of his mind, he was. After running about a mile, the bear gave up the chase, and we fell to the ground, exhausted and out of breath. After that, Father never took me elk hunting again."

"That's funny," Jodocus opined.

"I would have gone again," Jubal said.

"I would never have believed that Byrun was capable of such deceit," Geffrey said, changing the subject. "He was my friend. You two believe me, don't you? That I didn't steal the money pouch?"

"Must you ask that, son? One never knows what motivates a person to treachery," Jodocus said. "And what Byrun did was certainly treacherous."

"I will squash him like a bug when I see him," Jubal said, pounding one fist into the other.

"You were betrayed, Geffrey," Jodocus said. "Betrayed and set up. Betrayal is devastating because it disrupts an ongoing, meaningful relationship in which partners have invested material and emotional resources. For most people, betrayal is worse than rejection. I would argue, however, that this conceptualization of interpersonal rejection is too narrow and misses the essential meaning of what it is to betray, and to be betrayed, within an interpersonal relationship. Essentially, betrayal means that Byrun acted in a way that favored his own interests at the expense of yours, Geffrey. In one sense, this behavior means that the Byrun regarded his needs as more important than yours. But, in a deeper sense, betrayal sends an ominous signal about how little he cares about, or values his relationship with you. In particular, when those on whom we depend for love and support betray our trust, the feeling is like a stab at the heart that leaves us feeling unsafe, diminished, and alone. In a human sense, betrayal is a profound form of interpersonal rejection with potentially serious consequences."

"I loved her," Geffrey said. "Isolde. My heart took flight when I was with her. And now, I doubt I will ever see her again. That makes Byrun's betrayal doubly hard to take—that she is gone forever."

"Well," Jubal said. "There's more fish where you found that one."

'I never thought anyone could ever replace Rosalind," Geffrey said, burying his head on an arm. "But a miracle happened when I first saw Isolde."

"You say she loved you, Geffrey. I'm sure she was committed to you," Jodocus said. "I didn't know her well, but I believe you may see her again. If anything, after a while when this calms down, you might return."

"Why didn't she say anything?" Geffrey said.

Jodocus said nothing, just shook his head.

When the sun was on its downward arc and the shadows began to lengthen, Geffrey kicked his horse into a trot. Near the river he came to a partially constructed wall and within its perimeter the scorched remains of a village. He dismounted and approached the wall. Only about several hundred yards of it still stood and from its looks Geffrey could tell it was never completed. Grass encroached on what was once a road, the dirt black as if burnt by fire. The odor of a fiery holocaust lingered in the air. A lump formed in his throat while tears welled in his eyes. Jodocus dismounted and led his horse to where he stood.

"I'm home," Geffrey said. "This is Lochwald."

Years of memories flooded Geffrey's rattled brain mixed with guilt for not saving his father or the others. That day when the Norse raiders leveled his village. The noise, the screams, the smell of smoke, visions of flames leaping high into the sky—all came surging back to him. The cataclysm that took his family and sent him as a slave to the mines. His father's burned body hanging from a tree. It all descended upon Geffrey, as a gigantic boulder would squash a tiny insect. He couldn't hold back the flood of emotion any longer.

He buried his head into Jodocus's shoulder and wept.

Guilt and rage poured from his soul as the old man held him, comforted him.

"Oh, my God," Geffrey cried. "My God, help me."

Jodocus wrapped him in his aging arms until Geffrey's grief was spent.

When Geffrey looked at Jodocus, eyes red and swollen, the old man spoke in a voice just above a whisper. "Come," he said. "Let's see what is left of Lochwald."

Jubal dismounted and followed the pair. The intervening years since the Norse raid had not extinguished all traces of the desolation the Norsemen left behind. A number of trees had their trunks scarred and burned, parts of the ground remained black, and there were two partially standing buildings, their stones crumbling and black with soot. Geffrey led the way over the grounds of where the village once stood, remembering the houses and buildings with merchants along the way.

He came to a corner of the main road, stopped. Jodocus was at his side.

"This is where my father had his blacksmith stable," Geffrey said. You can see the remains of the hearth and

forge over there." He pointed to a pile of bricks and
stone. "We worked many an hour in this place."

They strolled at a diagonal from the stable remains to
where Geffrey and his family once lived. There was
nothing remaining of their home except the stone fireplace where his mother cooked their meals. Now, it was
nothing more than a pile of stone ruble like the stable's
hearth.

"Right here was where we took our meals," Geffrey
said, standing a few paces from the fireplace. We had a
table my father built which was a rarity in Lochwald." A
sad expression once again formed in his face. "Now, it's
all gone. Destroyed by those bastards."

"The ones who imprisoned us," Jubal said.

"The very same," Geffrey agreed. "I should have
fought them. We had made weapons with which to defend ourselves but the attack came so suddenly we had
little time to do anything. I should have died with my father. Now, remembering, I understand what little courage
I possessed at the time."

"You shouldn't be so hard on yourself," Jodocus said.
"The Norsemen are experts at shock warfare, we all
know that. As a boy, you could hardly be expected to defend your village to the death. You are alive now and that
is all that matters."

At the far end of the compound that used to be
Lochwald's main center, Geffrey noticed a few homes,
standing as if recently constructed. He hadn't noticed
them earlier. He motioned Jodocus and Jubal to follow
and trudged down the road toward the houses. On closer
inspection, he noticed that they were constructed of mud
bricks, a far better method of building than his old home
of waddle and stone. To the side of one of the houses was
a small garden, enclosed within a short picket fence. A
few melons and cucumbers lay on the ground.

As they approached the closer of the houses, a man stepped out from inside, shielded his eyes from the sun, squinted in their direction.

"Hello there," Geffrey called.

The man nodded but said nothing. *We're strangers,* Geffrey thought. When they reached the house, Geffrey smiled, held out his hand. "I'm Geffrey," he said. "These are my friends, Jodocus and Jubal. I used to live here years ago."

"When was that?" the man said.

"Before the raids. My father was killed and I was taken prisoner to work in the Norse iron mines. I don't believe I remember you."

A woman ambled through the door to stand beside the man.

"Didn't come here until last year," the man said. "My friend, next door, he came with me. You were here during the Norse raids?"

"Yes, I was. I am searching for my mother and my girlfriend. Have you heard of anyone from this village living anywhere around here?"

"What were their names?" the woman said.

"My mother's name was Oriel and my girlfriend's name was Rosalind."

Both the man and the woman shook their heads.

"Those names are not familiar," the man said. "We have heard many tales about the raids from years ago."

"We are searching for a place to call home," Geffrey said. "I would like to build a house back down the road there where my old home was located. Would you have any objections?"

The man shook his head. "Can't say that there's anyone here to stop you," he said. "Haven't seen any Norsemen since we've been here. There's good farming land around here, what with the river close by."

Geffrey eyed Jodocus and Jubal, winked at them. "What do you say, men? Shall we call this place home?"

Jodocus surveyed the road, what used to be Lochwald, the hills to the north and east. He took a deep breath of the crisp air floating up from the River Skye and nodded.

"I say we're home," he said.

CHAPTER 23

Geffrey, with the help of Jodocus and Jubal, worked to get a home erected before the snows of winter descended upon Lochwald, and they were locked in its icy embrace. He took them to where stones were dug for the wall and excavated enough for the foundation and sides. Jodocus cut logs and, with a borrowed saw, hewed timbers for the rafters. From his work in the cathedral quarry where he learned how to make mortar, Jubal mixed clay, sand, and burned wood together into a useable slurry. After a week of heavy work, the shell of the house was completed except for the roof. They constructed the house on the same site as Geffrey's former house, utilizing the hearth and incorporating it into the new one. It needed work to repair its crumbling chimney but Jubal labored until it looked as good as the one Geffrey remembered.

The roof was not so easy. After putting up a series of trusses, the three men harvested wild wheat that grew in the fields around Lochwald. This was allowed to dry in the sun, the resulting straw then formed into uniform bundles. Jubal tossed the bundles up to Geffrey who steadied himself against one of the rafters. He then affixed the straw bundles to the rafters starting at the lowest level and working upward, one layer of straw overlapping the previous. This method of construction allowed water to easily run off the roof.

Jodocus built a door and shutters for the windows. By
All Hallows Eve, the house was completed and Geffrey
wanted a celebration to commemorate the fact.

He invited the two other couples residing in Lochwald
and one of the men, Herb, brought a pitcher of ale. His
neighbor, Benjamin, brought a side of wild boar that the
men roasted in the hearth while they sang and danced
about on the packed earthen floor. Their wives joined the
fun and spun Geffrey and Jubal about while they all celebrated Geffrey's new house.

"How long have you two lived here?" Geffrey asked
Herb during a lull in the merrymaking.

"Almost a year," Herb said. He wiped his dark beard
with the back if his hand. "Ben came shortly afterward.
We more or less stumbled onto this place."

Benjamin nodded. "Herb had his house erected and he
invited me and the wife to stay. It was clear that some
sort of destruction occurred here in the past. Folks passing by apprised us of the tragedy years ago. Herb told me
that your family lived here once, Geffrey."

Geffrey took a long pull on the ale. "There was a
small village here, years ago, by the name of Lochwald.
It was a thriving community. As I have mentioned, my
father was the smithy and I his apprentice. We lived a
good life and I was in love with a girl. Her name was
Rosalind. The Norse raiders killed my father and took me
prisoner. I don't know what happened to my mother or
Rosalind. I don't even know what happened to my father's body."

"It might be buried in the cemetery," Herb said. "I noticed one down toward the river."

"I doubt if there's a marker or stone," Geffrey said,
taking another pull on his ale. "There may not have been
many people left after the raid. The last I saw of it,

Lochwald was engulfed in a raging inferno. The raiders may have murdered most of the people who lived here."

"In the morning, we can wander down to the cemetery and check," Herb said. "There might be a marker."

When their guests had returned home, Geffrey kicked off his shoes and stoked the fire higher. "I would say it was a grand party," he said. "Our new neighbors seem nice enough."

"Yes, they do," Jodocus agreed. "You going to go to the cemetery tomorrow?"

"I may," Geffrey responded. "Just to be sure the folks aren't buried there."

"I imagine your father's body was left hanging for the vultures," Jodocus said. "The Norsemen like to leave warnings behind."

"How is the garden coming along?" Geffrey said, changing the subject.

"The root vegetables are ready to harvest. The potatoes and turnips. The squash and beans are about done so we may have another harvest before a cold snap kills them."

"Our neighbor Herb told me this was supposed to be a hellacious winter," Geffrey said, noticing that Jubal was asleep in his chair by the hearth. "He told me a traveling minstrel mentioned that Venus was near the new moon, which meant a hard winter. If that turns out to be the case, we'll be in for a rough time."

The following morning, Geffrey strolled toward the river to Lochwald's cemetery, accompanied by Jubal and Jodocus. What they found was a graveyard ill kept and in disarray. Stones and other markers were overturned, grass and weeds knee high, the short whitewashed fence surrounding it broken and falling down. They walked through the cemetery searching for any sign that Geffrey's parents or Rosalind were buried there but found nothing. After an hour, they returned to their home to begin their day's chores.

When winter descended upon the tiny hamlet, it was indeed, a cold, difficult one. The frost-laden wind howled through the desolate hills and bit at Geffrey's frozen skin. The bleak gray clouds overhead reflected perfectly his gray mood. The days shortened, leaving long nights, while a dampness crept into his weary bones and made him ache for summer again. Each week brought a new snowfall. His footfalls broke the iced puddles that lay embedded in the hardened earth, the ones made in the autumn, when the hooves of the horses that were ridden over the path had each sunk several inches into the then-soft soil. The world seemed to lie barren and lifeless before him as if God himself had put it to sleep.

When he and Jubal returned from a hunting trip, they struggled through the knee-deep snow to their house. With numb hands Geffrey scooped the snowdrift away from the rough wooden door and Jubal pressed his body against it to wedge it open. Inside it was as barren as the landscape outside, with only a few pieces of furniture. But there was a fireplace and kindling wood, a box of matches, some logs. He shivered in the draft that oozed in from under the door as they built the fire. Then, when Jodocus arrived, they sat around the hearth waiting for the house to become cozy and warm, so they could thaw their bodies and dry their wet clothes.

Once a fire roared in the hearth the winter weather seemed less dreary and more like a wonderland. Less barren and more beautiful and pristine. The only thing missing was Isolde.

Geffrey remembered winters as a child. The street of Lochwald was like an unfinished painting with so much of the canvas still perfectly white, as if waiting for the artist's hand to return. The morning light of those winters past struggled through the murky clouds, but even in its weakness it was enough to blind him. Moving from the overbearing heat near the hearth to the living room was like sipping on cold water in the height of summer. The tiny home was filled with delightful smells as his mother scurried around roasting winter vegetables and baking apple pie.

When at last the days began to lengthen and the warm breezes retuned from the south, Geffrey's spirits rose. A few more families settled in the area. The depression that clung to him like a heavy cloak lifted with the first crocus that pushed their tiny heads through the still-frozen crust of earth. The week of the vernal equinox saw the men planting a garden and working in the fields planting barley and wheat. One night as they sat around the hearth Jodocus spoke some news he had heard.

"Our Duke William," he said, "is enlarging his army. Word is that it will be a magnificent army. Apparently, he plans to take by force what he considers his by right."

"And what is that?" Geffrey said.

Jubal stoked a pipe, lit it with an ember from the hearth, puffed for a while as Jodocus described the situation.

"Some years ago, our duke visited his English cousin, Edward the Confessor. Edward and his brother Alfred had spent much of their childhood in exile at the Norman Court. Their mother, Emma, had been a daughter of the House of Normandy. During this visit, Edward is purported to have promised his Norman cousin the crown of England, should he die without issue.

"Last year, Edward the Confessor finally breathed his last and was buried in his foundation of St. Peter, Westminster. On his deathbed he nominated Harold as his successor. Harold is the son of the powerful Godwine, Earl of Wessex, whose sister Edith, was married to King

Edward the Confessor. The Saxon Witangemot, or council of elders, which traditionally elects the next English King, apparently has duly accepted Harold as King. Harold has assembled a Saxon militia of freemen in preparation for William's imminent landing."

"I have heard how the duke gained his wife," Geffrey said. "When Duke William sent representatives to her father's court to request Matilda's hand in marriage, she retorted by proudly, informing the representative that she was far too high-born to consider marrying a bastard. Furious on receiving this response, William rode to Bruges, where he confronted Matilda on her way to church, pulled her off her horse then threw her down in the street in front of her attendants and rode off. Whereupon it is said Matilda refused to marry anyone but William."

They had a good laugh at Geffrey's story.

"So what does all this mean for us?" Geffrey said.

"It means," Jodocus said, "that men of William's army are in the area, recruiting soldiers. The rumor is that William is mounting an army so he can invade the Britons and make himself the English King."

"I still don't understand," Geffrey said.

"We can join William's army. The bastard's army. It would be a grand adventure, Geffrey. A grand adventure."

"One that might get us all killed."

"We have such a great life here?" Jodocus pressed. "Three men living alone in an empty village without a single prospect for marriage? Digging in the dirt eking out some semblance of a living? I am an old man but you and Jubal—surely you desire more to your lives than to scrape out a meager living here in this godforsaken place."

Geffrey turned to Jubal, poked him in his side, waking him.

"Jodocus here thinks we need an adventure, Jubal. He believes our lives have become, shall I say, commonplace and mundane. He wants to join Duke William's army and invade England. Help him become king. What do you say to that?"

"What is mundane?" he asked.

"In a word—boring. Jodocus wants us to join him in this grand adventure."

Jubal shrugged. "Sure, why not?" he said. "I'm tiring of hoeing and plowing and planting."

Geffrey looked at Jodocus. "We can at least talk to them if they travel this way," he said.

Two days later, the soldiers arrived in Lochwald.

Two dozen men clad in chain mail, riding powerful destriers, and flying Duke William's banner—three golden lions resting on a red background—rode through the village and dismounted. They wore shiny helmets with a nose guard and carried shields bearing William's coat of arms. Over the chain mail they wore tunics of bright colors, red, yellow, and blue.

A small crowd of Lochwald's villagers gathered about the soldiers along with Geffrey, Jodocus, and Jubal. They pressed close to the men bearing their duke's banner to hear their message. A heavy-set man with a red beard climbed the perimeter wall. His broadsword hung at his side.

"Citizens!" he began. "I bring you greetings from William, Duke of Normandie. Our duke is the rightful King of England. He is recruiting an army to help bring him to the throne. Able-bodied men of all ages are requested to consider joining this noble cause. You will be paid a handsome wage, the food and ale plentiful, the possibility of heroism on the battlefield great. William, Duke of Normandie, desires all those who champion freedom and justice to aid him in this quest."

A murmur went through the crowd. The man continued. "If you decide to join William's army, you will move to his castle at Château de Caen. There you will be housed while you train for this invasion. You will be provided armor and weapons.

"Now, all those men who desire to join us, please step forward and affix your mark to the agreement."

When he finished speaking, the man jumped off the wall and waited. The few people dissipated leaving only Geffrey, Jodocus, and Jubal near the soldier.

The man looked them over, removed his helmet, and nodded. "You gentlemen the only ones here with enough courage to aid our duke?" he said in a raspy voice.

"We are farmers here," Geffrey said. "You will train us to fight?"

"That is the bargain," the soldier said. "William pays, you to train and fight. It will be a glorious battle."

"And if we are killed?" Jodocus said.

"You will be welcomed into heaven with loving arms. The Elysium Fields of old. The pope himself has blessed this expedition."

The three men conferred among themselves for a few moments.

"Then we will go with the duke," Geffrey said. "Anything is better than rotting away here."

"Then place your mark upon this document," the soldier said.

Geffrey signed first, followed by Jodocus, then Jubal. When they finished, the soldier rolled the paper and tucked it in his charger's saddlebag. "It being late in the day," he said, "we will make camp here for the night and continue on in the morning. You men have your horses saddled and ready to leave at sunup. Understand? Good. You are now soldiers in Duke William's army. You will take the oath of allegiance once we are back at the castle."

That night after supper, Jubal asked questions. They sat near the hearth sipping tankards of ale.

"Is it far?" Jubal said. "This place where we will fight?"

"I believe it is," Jodocus said. "Across the Channel. England."

"Will there be many of us?"

"Yes," Jodocus said. "I have heard William wants an army of over five thousand soldiers. He is putting together a navy as well."

"And if I am killed," Jubal continued, "where will my body be buried?"

"I don't know." Jodocus smiled at the big man. "That's a good question. Where would you wish to be buried?"

"Back here," Jubal responded immediately. "This has been the only home I have really known. I mean a home I helped build. I have no desire to be buried in foreign soil."

"Well, my big friend," Geffrey said, "I will see to it that you are brought back to Lochwald. That is in the unlikely event something happens to you. Let us all hope we return safe."

"Here, here," Jodocus said. "This will be a grand adventure."

A grand adventure, Geffrey thought with a sense of foreboding. *God watch over us all.*

CHAPTER 24

The horses were saddled and ready. Their saddlebags were filled with jerky and dried vegetables for the journey to Château de Caen. Geffrey closed the door of their home for the last time, glanced at the well-tended garden, then turned his attention to the center of the village where the soldiers gathered. He, Jodocus, and Jubal walked their horses over the hardpacked road as the early morning gray of dawn ripened into a sky filled with hues of orange, magenta, and purple. A cool breeze ruffled Geffrey's tunic as he approached the gathering of soldiers.

The heavy-set man of the previous day greeted them. "Very punctual," he said. "That's good. My name is Ulric. I am captain of the guard. Well, it's time to mount up and get going."

With that, the soldiers swung into their saddles and Geffrey followed their lead. As did Jodocus and Jubal. When they plodded to the edge of Lochwald, he glanced over his shoulder for what was, in all likelihood, his last look at their home and the village. A lump formed in his throat.

They journeyed northwest through low hills and plains toward the Castle Caen, located twenty miles from the coast on the River Orne. Along the way, they passed through the towns of Alençon, Macé, Falaise, which was the birthplace of the Duke of Normandie, and Cintheaux where they recruited soldiers. Two dozen joined their ranks.

When he looked upon the Château de Falaise, it was Geffrey's first sighting of a castle that large. Built on a hill, the square structure with its massive stone walls seemed insurmountable to him, providing a safe haven for those ensconced within.

At each stop they rested for the night while Ulric enlisted men from all walks of life, all ages, into William's army. Their ranks swelled as they neared their destination. Seeing the legions on horseback caused goose bumps to form on the back of Geffrey's neck, sent chills racing through his body. Some of the new recruits were mere boys while others were the age and looks of Jodocus.

Only recently at Alençon had William laid siege to the town. Its citizens had hung animal skins from the walls of the town in reference to his ancestry as the illegitimate son of Duke Robert and a tanner's daughter. On capturing the town, William had a number of the citizens' hands and feet cut off in revenge.

Falaise meant cliff, and the little plateau atop the craggy rock faces rising above the Ante and Masceron Rivers was chosen as an excellent place for a major castle for the ruling Norman family as they built fortifications around their region. Early on, it became the main base for Robert, rebellious younger brother of Richard, heir to the duchy. Upon their father's death, the elder son became Duke Richard III of Normandy, but he soon died in mysterious circumstances. Robert cast aside his young nephew to become Duke Robert I of Normandy. His eight-year reign was fraught with dissent.

Based at Falaise castle, Duke Robert fell for the charms of a young local woman, Herleva, the daughter of a local tanner. Robert spotted the young woman beside a stream and was immediately smitten. She later gave birth to their illegitimate son, William. Although the duke would not marry Herleva, she acquired power through her relationship with him, and William spent his childhood in Falaise with his mother.

Geffrey noticed the gray towers of Château de Caen from a great distance. Situated atop a high rocky knoll and surrounded by a dense forest, the castle gleamed in the bright morning sun. With their banners flying and Ulric at the head of the column, the line of soldiers and recruits snaked its way toward the castle.

When they reached the base of the knoll, a flurry of trumpets echoed down the valley heralding their arrival. Geffrey turned to Jodocus and laughed. "It seems they were expecting us,"

"The place looks impregnable," Jodocus replied. "Look at all the archers at the top."

Geffrey gazed upward and saw a line of archers ringing roof of the castle. Most held crossbows but there were a few long bows among the men.

Ulric led the column up a narrow rocky path to the castle. As they ascended the knoll, Geffrey noticed a group of hawks high overhead soaring on the thermal currents. The air was sweet and crisp.

At the castle's entrance, they waited while the iron gate was opened along with the large wooden door. Geffrey reined his horse over a cobblestone walkway that led under a stone archway and onto the castle grounds. As Ulric formed his soldiers in ranks facing the castle balcony, the recruits were pushed into a queue at the rear.

When a tall, portly man appeared on the balcony, a rousing cheer went up through the soldiers' ranks. It must be Duke William, Geffrey mused. The duke was a thick man with reddish hair, which receded quickly from his forehead. He possessed a ruddy complexion. On his head rested a gold crown circled with crosses. When he spoke, his deep bass voice resonated across the courtyard.

"My friends," William said, his voice booming. "We are soon to be united in a glorious undertaking. It will be my honor to lead you good men across the sea into battle With God on our side, who can stand against us? Now, you new recruits, take your places with your commanders and later tonight you will take the soldier's oath."

With that, William disappeared into the castle and Ulric began gathering the men into smaller groups. Geffrey, Jubal, and Jodocus were pushed into a queue of men in far corner of the courtyard. A tall, muscled, tanned soldier stood beside Ulric.

"This man beside me," Ulric said, "goes by the name of Merek. He will be your commander and will be responsible for your training here at the castle. He is a knight and holds the rank of Marshall of the Guard. You are to give him your undivided attention, loyalty, and follow his orders."

Then Ulric turned, nodded at Merek, headed for the castle. When he was no longer in site, Merek stepped forward. "All right, men," he said. "The first order of business is to get everyone here billeted in the tents you see at the other end of the grounds. You are now members of the Green Infantry and as such you will eat together, sleep together, fight together. You will take you your meals along with me in the castle's dining hall with the rest of the duke's soldiers. Your training will take place on the plain below the castle. After supper tonight all recruits will gather and take the oath of allegiance. Now, if you will follow me I will see to your getting settled."

Geffrey, Jodocus, and Jubal followed Merek along with the other men of the Green Infantry to a group of large blue and white striped tents placed together at one end of the castle courtyard. Under the massive canvas, cots were arranged in rows and at the foot of each cot was a wooden box with a lid."

"Find yourselves a cot," Merek said, "and put your personal items in the box at the foot of each one. You will notice that there are no locks on the boxes. In the Green Infantry soldiers do not steal from each other. Anyone who does so will be dealt with in a most severe fashion."

Jodocus found a cot next to Geffrey while Jubal took the one on the other side. After storing their few personal items in the boxes, they reclined and relaxed from their long journey. Many other men doing similar tasks crowded the tent. A buzz of voices filled the air and made hearing each other's conversation difficult.

"Well, my friend," Jodocus said to Geffrey, "we are finally here. Members of the duke's army."

"We still haven't taken the oath," Jubal said.

"Jubal's right," Geffrey said, kicking off his boots. "So, it's not too late to back out."

Jodocus shook his head.

"Not on your life. I've come too far to turn back."

"I wonder what kind of training it will be," Jubal said. He sat on his cot while Geffrey and Jodocus reclined on theirs.

Geffrey laughed. "Training to keep your big butt from getting killed, I imagine," he said.

"Geffrey," Jubal continued, "what is an infantry? Commander Merek said we are in an infantry."

"We will be fighting on foot," Geffrey said.

"No horses?"

"I'm afraid not," interjected Jodocus. "Time to get your feet toughened up, Jubal."

Merek entered the tent. "Listen up," he said, his husky voice booming over the idle chatter. "Supper is in the dining hall. We will march over there in orderly fashion in a column of twos. Line up and follow me."

Geffrey pulled on his boots and scrambled into line behind Jodocus as the Green Infantry marched to the castle and into the large dining hall. It was a massive room with a high arched ceiling filled with row after row of tables and benches. On each table there sat three large pewter pitchers containing ale. Geffrey found an empty table and sat alongside his companions. He looked around the large hall and guessed there must be upward of a thousand men seated. At the front of the dining hall there was a raised dais with a long table. In its center sat Duke William with a woman at each elbow. One looked as if she was near William's age and probably his wife but the other appeared younger, near Geffrey's age. He had no idea who she might be. On each side of the women a cadre of men made up the rest of William's party.

Women began circulating the hall carrying trays of food and placing them on the tables. There was roasted boar, pigeons, and venison. Large bowls of cooked vegetables and fruits of all varieties. And the ale. Loud talk soon filled the hall as the men dug into their meal. For Geffrey it was the first meal since Remmelsberg where he could eat his fill.

"I have never seen so much food," Jubal said as he helped himself to another pigeon. "I think I have died already and gone to heaven."

"The Norsemen believe in Valhalla," Jodocus said. "They say that their god, Wödan, has spirit handmaidens, the Valkyries, who ride over a battlefield and determine who lives and who dies. Those they choose to die are escorted to the hall of the slain, Valhalla."

"It's a nice story," Jubal said, "but I doubt if it's true. Only our Christian God decides who lives or dies."

"Who's to say, Jubal?" Jodocus said. "Who's to say?"

When the supper was finished, William stood and asked for everyone's attention. He wore a white, fur-ringed cloak held together with a gold clasp and chain. His crown glinted in the light of the dining hall.

"Recruits," he said in a booming voice. "Please rise."

Geffrey rose along with Jodocus and Jubal. His heart pulsed in his neck. His palms were moist.

"You will make this oath freely and without reservation," he said. "In front of my knights and God. Raise you right hand and repeat after me."

Geffrey did as commanded and out of the corner of his eye noticed Jodocus and Jubal doing the same. William recited the oath of allegiance. His voice echoed throughout the hall.

"I promise on my faith that I will in the future be faithful to William, my lord, never cause him harm and will observe my homage to him completely against all persons in good faith and without deceit."

Geffrey repeated the oath and when finished the men in the hall gave a resounding cheer. Later in the tent, Jodocus smiled.

"We're sure enough soldiers now," he said. "With sworn allegiance to Duke William. I pray our brightest days lie ahead."

Commander Merek ambled into the tent. "Get some sleep," he said. "Tomorrow we begin your training in earnest."

છેસ

It was near midnight and Duke William lounged in his bedchamber with Matilda, his wife, and daughter, Adela. The duke had changed into a long brocaded robe of purple and gray. He stood while the women rested in chairs around a small table.

"Well, William," Matilda said. "You've got your army. Does that please you?"

"Of course, my dear. Recruiting and training will be the easy part of this venture. Once the army swells to seven thousand or so men, the challenge will be to get them across the Channel."

"Aren't you building ships?" Adela asked. She had long golden hair, green eyes, a turned up nose.

"We are," William said. "But there is no way we can build enough. I am going to have to borrow from our neighbors."

"How many ships will be required?" Matilda said.

"Possibly as many as five or six hundred. Right now the fleet is forming on the River Dives. Word has come to me that we are woefully behind schedule. This is a massive undertaking, one that I am afraid I may not be up to. Not only are there the soldiers to get across the Channel, there are the horses, grain, livestock, provisions, weapons, armor."

"If you cannot build enough ships," Adela said, "where will you get them?"

"I will have to go begging from our neighbors and the aristocrats who owe me fealty. It's all I can do."

PART III

HASTINGS

CHAPTER 25

Château de Caen, 1065 AD:

Geffrey was up early before dawn, excited at what the new day would bring. He strolled alone on the castle grounds amidst a low hanging fog breathing the cool fresh morning air. The tents and castle were quiet in the early morning twilight—he was content to be alone with his thoughts. He was now a soldier beginning, as Jodocus was fond of saying, a grand adventure. One he hoped would not end prematurely with his death. He hungered for love and a family as much as he did adventure, maybe more so.

He glanced toward the castle and in the fog caught a glimpse of someone walking the far side of the grounds. The person was like a vision, not in clear focus, almost ethereal. But on closer inspection, he saw that it was a young woman. She wore a silken white robe. It was the woman on the dais in the dining hall.

Geffrey ambled toward her and when she came into sharper relief he noticed her beauty. Tall and slender with an erect carriage, her long golden hair fell in loose curls over her shoulders. Her nose turned up ever so slightly on the end. She moved across the grounds as if gliding on air. He startled her when he spoke.

"Good morning, my lady," he said in a soft voice.

She jumped, as if surprised by his greeting.

"Oh," she said. "I'm so sorry. I was lost in thought."

"You are out walking and thinking as well?" Geffrey said, his voice somewhat louder. "What a coincidence. I was doing the very same thing."

"You were?" the woman said.

"Oh yes. I find it clears the mind. Gets one ready for the day."

Geffrey noticed her slender delicate fingers, her green eyes that had the appearance of emeralds. She moved closer. "My name is Geffrey, my lady," he said. "I have joined the duke's army. Me and my friends."

"Oh?" she said. "Where do you come from?"

"From a small village by the name of Lochwald. I doubt if you have heard of it."

She shook her head.

"I'm Adela." She held out her hand and Geffrey held it for an instant. It felt small, smooth in his hand.

"Do you walk on these grounds often, Adela?" he asked. His mouth was suddenly dry making it difficult to speak.

"Every morning," Adela said. "Unless it's raining, of course."

They smiled at each other.

"Do you live here in the castle?" Geffrey said.

"I do. I'm a permanent resident here. You said you have joined the army?"

"Yes. My friends, Jodocus and Jubal traveled with me after Ulric and his men passed through Lochwald recruiting soldiers. We traveled for over a week to get here."

"Jodocus?" Adela inquired. "That's a funny name."

"Alas, he would not be pleased to hear you say that. He quite fancies his name. Jodocus hails from Silesia—a long ways away. Have you heard of it? Silesia?"

"Of course," she said, tossing her head back and laughing. "I have learned my geography. Along with numbers and Latin."

"You know Latin?" Geffrey knew no one who could read and write the strange language.

"But of course. My tutors taught me."

"I see," he said. "Tutors."

"Are you looking forward to the upcoming invasion and battle?"

"Oh, yes. It will be a grand adventure. I hope I have enough courage so as to not dishonor the memory of my parents."

"Your training should help in that respect," Adela said. "I may watch from my balcony window."

"Merek, he is the commander of the Green Infantry of which I am a member, says the training will be hard. That we will grow to hate it in time."

"I know Commander Merek. He is a tough taskmaster. But you will be a better soldier because of his leadership."

"I am glad to hear that."

"Well," Adela said. "I must be returning to the castle, Geffrey. It was nice meeting you." She turned back toward the Château de Caen.

"Will you be strolling here tomorrow morning," he said.

Adela nodded. "Unless it's raining."

Soon, she had disappeared within the castle's walls.

ℰↃℰↃ

After breakfast the Green Infantry assembled on the broad plain below the castle. The sun was bright and warm. Merek had the men line up in ranks and files. He paced the line while he talked.

"Some of you will become swordsmen, others spearmen. All of you will be provided with shields and battleaxes. Spearmen are much more effective in a formation than swordsmen are. Spearmen can attack well in formation and can do well against cavalry. Spearmen can attack well in formation, since the length of the weapon allows a formation of spearmen to have several rows that can take part in an offensive or defensive attack simultaneously. When you face a spearmen formation, you not only have to deal with the front row of spearmen, but also the second, third, possibly even the fourth row. This is not possible with a formation of swordsmen, who are effectively limited to a first row offense. The basic tactic for you foot soldiers is to close with the enemy and start using your weapon.

"Our infantry will typically be employed at the outset of the battle to break open the enemy infantry formations. Once you have coaxed the opposing infantry into breaking formation, our cavalry will be deployed in an attempt to exploit the loss of cohesion in the opposing infantry lines and begin slaying the infantrymen from atop their chargers. Once a break in the lines is exploited, the cavalry becomes instrumental to victory—causing further breakage in the lines and wreaking havoc amongst the infantrymen, as it is much easier to kill a man from the top of a horse than to stand on the ground and face a half-ton destrier carrying an armed knight. With regard to fighting the enemy's cavalry, the most obvious tactic against cavalry is the infantry square formation, which was used by the ancient Romans.

"You will learn how to attack from a defensive position. This maneuver involves luring the enemy to vainly attack a strong, well-chosen defensive position before counterattacking against the exhausted force. Expectedly, this maneuver is used if such an impenetrable defensive position is available or if a direct offensive is not viable. The advantages of this maneuver include the economic use of resources in the defensive mode and that the switch from defense to offense can produce a decisive result. One disadvantage is that the maneuver may become too passive and either be attacked from an unexpected direction or an attack may never come. Another disadvantage is that submitting to encirclement, which is sometimes required, may lead to total annihilation of one's force."

Geffrey thought it all sounded extremely complicated. Would he ever be able to learn it all?

"Finally," Merek continued, "you will practice the indirect approach. This maneuver involves distracting the enemy with secondary forces while using the main force to strategically envelop the enemy in rear and flank. This maneuver seeks to force the enemy to react and give battle on unfavorable terms for fear of being cut off from supplies or communications. This maneuver is usually attempted if an aggressive mobile force is available or if enemy supply and communication lines are vulnerable. Advantages of this maneuver include the total victory if the enemy loses a battle while cut off from his base and the prospect of alternative objectives once in the enemy's rear and flank. The disadvantages of this maneuver are few because the maneuver has so much diversity although mobility and timing are vital to its success.

"Now," Merek concluded, "I want each of you to file by the table next to me and get your shield, axe, spear or sword. When you have them, return to your original position."

Merek stepped aside and the recruits began filing by him to be assigned either spear or sword and be outfitted with a shield and battle-axe. Geffrey stood in line and when he got to the table was relieved when he was given a sword. He took the other items and returned to the ranks.

The rest of the day was devoted to the most basic of infantry battle tactics—formation of the square. Merek drilled them until they were exhausted and he still was not satisfied.

At supper, Geffrey was so tired he could hardly eat. Jodocus was totally spent.

"I'm not in good enough physical condition," Geffrey said. "Tomorrow is going to be hell."

They chatted among themselves during the rest of the meal and later as they lay on their cots. Geffrey mentioned the woman he met on the grounds in the early morning but neither Jodocus nor Jubal knew who she was. When the oil lanterns were extinguished, Geffrey lay in the dark remembering the woman's long golden hair, her soft voice, her easy smile.

The next morning he pulled himself off his cot and trudged around the courtyard grounds until he saw her. This time she was dressed in a dark green gown that matched her eyes. She smiled when he approached her.

"Good morning, Adela," he said. He yawned and stretched his arms.

"Good morning..."

"Geffrey."

"Yes. Geffrey. Tired from the drilling yesterday?" She seemed amused by his misery.

"It was murder," he said. "Commander Merek was ruthless. My legs ached and my arms felt as if they would fall off from carrying my sword and shield all day. I'm still in misery and am beginning to think I wasn't cut out to be a soldier."

Adela tossed he head back and laughed. "After only one day? My, Geffrey, are you going to let Merek get the better of you after one day?"

She laughed again.

Geffrey felt a foot tall, embarrassed. "No, it was only a figure of speech," he said. "But, I must admit I'm exhausted."

Adela wore a gold necklace with a green stone in its middle. It accentuated the bodice of her gown. Geffrey thought she was the most beautiful woman he had ever seen.

"Tell me, Geffrey," she said. "Your parents know you are here? Do they approve of your plans to help the duke acquire the English throne?"

"My father was murdered by Norse raiders who ravaged our town. I don't know about my mother. I never saw her after that day."

"I see," Adela said, the tone of her voice turning somber. She toyed with her necklace.

"When I returned to my village years later, my mother was not there. No one knew where she was or had gone. For all I know she may be dead now."

"I'm so sorry to hear that. You—you seem so nice—gentle. I like you, Geffrey."

"And I you, Adela."

Before he could say anything else she was gone, scurrying back to the castle. As he wandered back to the tents, her face and green eyes lingered with him. It would be difficult to concentrate on the drills this day.

Later, as they were queuing up in preparation for the day's drills, Geffrey passed Merek. He stopped and the commander smiled, nodded.

"Commander Merek," Geffrey said. "Might I have a quick word?"

The man stopped and looked at Geffrey.

"Yes?" he said.

"Sir, the past two mornings I have strolled about the grounds before dawn. I find it helps clear the mind and prepare me for the coming day."

"Yes, go on," Merek said.

"There's a woman, sir, who walks the grounds at that time as well. I was wondering if you knew—"

"You mean Adela?"

"Yes, sir. That's the one. She says she is a permanent resident of the castle."

A hearty scoff exploded from Merek's tongue. "I should say she is," he said, laughing. "Adela is Duke William's daughter. You've been conversing with her each morning?"

Geffrey's head spun with the revelation. Duke William's daughter? And she had never mentioned the fact? My God, he was having casual conversation with the duke's daughter. Would he be in trouble?

"I can assure you, sir," Geffrey stammered, "that I knew nothing of her identity until this very minute. If I had known who she was—"

"Calm down, son," Merek said, his laughter now only a broad smile. "You are not in any trouble. Adela is a beautiful young woman. She is betrothed to Frederic, one of our knights. They will be wed after William is on the English throne. Then she will be Princess Adela."

Merek moved on to begin the day's drill leaving Geffrey with a spinning head. No sooner does he meet an enticing woman but then learns she is the duke's daughter.

That news alone left him dizzy, lightheaded. But to then learn she was pledged to someone—his spirit fell.

The rest of the day was a fog. It was difficult to keep his mind on the training. He couldn't do anything right, kept making mistakes.

Merek yelled at him more than once. His group paired up and drilled in the proper way to engage the enemy with a sword. Each pair practiced delivering blows and the parry. It was hot heavy work with Merek striding down the lines yelling at the men. But, his heart and mind wasn't in soldiering.

It was on Adela and how she had broken his heart.

CHAPTER 26

The great hall in Château de Caen was where Duke William conducted his affairs of state. Each morning after breakfast a small group of advisors met with the duke to bring him the news and hear any pronouncements he might issue. For the past month the discussions centered around his planned invasion of England, the necessary army and naval forces along with choice of a landing site. The discussions had been lively, in fact downright argumentative and to date no firm site had been decided. The army had swelled to seven thousand men and Commander Merek was in the field holding training exercises. Even with the support of his Norman barons, William still did not have enough soldiers to defeat Harold. He therefore had to enter into negotiations with the rulers of Flanders, Brittany, Aquitaine, and Boulogne, who not only agreed to supply men but also promised not to invade Normandie while he was away.

For his navy, William had acquired seven hundred ships. In order to obtain that number he requisitioned all existing craft in Norman ports and purchased most of the rest of his vessels from Flanders.

A sly negotiator, William approached Pope Alexander II with the hope of gaining papal support for his invasion. William promised that he would grant one quarter of England to the Church. Pope Alexander, angry at the English throne for appointing an Archbishop of Canterbury without papal approval, gave William his approval and support. The prospect of gaining additional lands and wealth helped convince the pope to agree to the duke's plan.

In addition, special care had to be taken with the war-horses, as they were the key to military success. They needed shelter if they were to remain in good condition. Their minimum daily ration was twelve pounds of grain and thirteen pounds of hay per horse. The warhorses would carry two hundred fifty pounds of rider and equipment into a battle that might last all day and involve uphill charges. So their health and well-being was of utmost concern.

One of William's advisors, Robert de Beaumont, stood across from the throne and looked at William with a scowl.

"My lord," he said, "just how do you propose to get seven thousand men and seven hundred ships safely across the Channel? They can't fly."

William gazed upon Robert with affection. The man was a loyal friend, one of only a handful of advisors willing to speak truth to power.

"I have given that much thought, Robert," he said. "I propose after the ships are loaded with men and equipment, they will sail down the river Dives-sur-Mer for Saint-Valery. The sea crossing from there is much shorter. I have received information from my spies in England that the Sussex coast is undefended at the present. I am abandoning the earlier plan to land in Hampshire to march on Winchester, the capital of Wessex."

"A wise decision, my lord," Robert said. "We will need favorable winds."

"As always, my friend," William said, "success depends on the fates of weather. We will pray for good weather to speed our crossing."

Robert nodded.

"I shall go inform the ship captains of the change in plans."

When Robert took his leave, William dismissed the remaining advisors. He was weary of all the morning's war plans. After leaving the hall, he retired to his drawing room where he found his daughter waiting.

"Why Adela," he said. "How lovely you are."

"Father," Adela said, in a breathy tone, "I just came from mother. She wants to move the wedding up several months."

"Matilda, unfortunately, has no idea of the current invasion plans. Your mother may want to move the wedding plans forward but I just cannot accommodate her, Adela. It's impossible. Too much is riding on this invasion."

Adela slumped in a chair and William thought she looked relieved at the news. He wasn't overly impressed with her intended, Frederic, but the man was a loyal knight and commander of a cavalry regiment. A bit impulsive and hotheaded perhaps but William figured him for an opportunist. Frederic did everything possible to ingratiate himself to himself and Matilda. But, Adela loved him and he thought that important in a marriage, if even not his own. He much preferred another of his daughter's suitors, Stephen, Count of Blois and Count of Chartres. Upon the death of his father, Theobald, Stephen acquired vast land holdings. Now that would be a marriage of consequence, William thought.

"Father," Adela said, her eyes downcast, her hands in her lap in a picture of supplication. "Would it displease you if I decided not to marry Frederic? At least for the present? Would that upset your and Mother's plans too terribly much?"

William thought he would jump for joy at her news. He tried hard to contain his excitement but found it difficult. Keeping a straight face, he ambled to her and touched her arm. "What brought this change of heart, my dear? Only last week you were planning a great wedding ceremony."

"I don't really know, Father. It's just that Frederic— he's so...so..." Her voice trailed off as if searching for the right word.

"Overbearing?" William said.

"Yes," Adela said. Her eyes brightened. "That's it, exactly. So you do understand."

It was a statement, not a question. Of all his children, Adela was the most thoughtful, the most introspective. She loved books, excelled in Latin, enjoyed philosophical talks, unlike her older sister, Adeliza, who was outspoken on most subjects and professed a desire to become a nun.

"Yes, my daughter, I completely understand. And I bow to your wisdom in wanting to wait a while longer. Time will show if this engagement is right for both of you."

"But what about mother? She's eager to have this wedding. The sooner the better."

"Not to worry, child. I will speak to your mother. Now, let me get on with the day's business."

಩

The next morning Adela woke early, dressed, and threw her cloak over her shoulders. She ran down the castle stairs and out onto the grounds where she hoped Geffrey would be taking his early morning stroll. A thin fog hung over the grounds and mixed with a haze from cooking fires within the castle as the staff prepared the morning meal.

Adela glanced about the grounds then saw him hurrying toward her. Her heart leaped into her throat, she caught her breath up short as she hastened to him. "Geffrey," she said and she reached out with a hand and he took it with his.

"Adela," he responded. "This past month has been heaven seeing you here, each morning. But I long to see more of you. Why didn't you tell me who you are?"

"Who I am?" she said.

"The duke's daughter." Geffrey kissed her hand and let it go.

"Would it have mattered?" Adela was probing the man's motive for seeing her.

"It might have, back then," Geffrey answered. "I am humbled now, even more, my lady."

"There is no need, Geffrey, to call me my lady. I am my father's daughter by a mere accident of birth."

"It doesn't take away who you are," Geffrey protested.

"I am a poor lowly peasant. One who cannot even claim a family at present. Only true friends, Jodocus and Jubal."

"Rank and station carry no sway with me," Adela said.

"What about your upcoming marriage to Frederic?"

"You have heard of that?" Her voice sounded concerned. How did the news get to the new recruits so quickly?

"Commander Merek told me. He said Frederic has won your hand and heart."

Adela shook her head. "Merek should not speak of things of which he knows nothing."

"He spoke incorrectly?"

"He did. To be truthful, we were betrothed to each other but there have been— complications."

"Like what?" Geffrey said.

Adela hesitated. Did she dare mention to Geffrey that he was the complication? That his arrival at the Château de Caen turned her world upside down and caused her to rethink her engagement to Frederic? "You, Geffrey."

"Me? How?"

"Trust me," Adela said. "Seeing you each morning is the brightest part of my day."

Geffrey moved closer, took both of her hands in his. "It is the same with me. I have difficulty concentrating on my duties during the daily drills. Merek yells at me a lot."

"Listen," Adela said. "I have a secret place in the hills near here where I go to read and think. After supper we can go there together. We can be alone and no prying eyes will worry us."

"Until tonight, then," Geffrey said.

Adela watched him hurry toward the tents where he was housed.

That night Adela and Geffrey met outside the castle gate. The sun had gone down and the sky was a deep azure streaked with thin golden clouds. She led him along a rocky path down into the dense forest of trees to a clearing that overlooked the entire valley. Below them the River Orne tumbled its way through the valley like a black serpentine snake. It was a breathtaking view. Behind and above them, the castle's lights shined bright. Adela wore a long blue satin dress whose bodice was cut low over her breasts. Around her neck she wore her favorite necklace with the single emerald. She sat on a smooth rock and indicated that Geffrey should sit beside her.

"At last we are alone," she said.

Without a word, Geffrey gathered her in his arms and kissed her. It was a soft, lingering kiss.

Adela's heart pounded as she struggled to catch her breath. When she broke away, she fanned her face with an empty hand.

"Oh," she said. "What an impertinent boy you are, Geffrey." She tried to hide her excitement but smiled.

"Adela," he said, still holding her. "I'm afraid I have fallen in love with you. Please forgive me."

"Forgive you for speaking your heart? Never. I feel the same way, my love."

"Adela?"

"I love you, Geffrey. I don't understand how or why but it happened. I know I can't bear to not see you."

"What about Frederic? Won't he be angry? I have heard he has a temper."

"Do not worry, Geffrey. I can handle Frederic. He does not own me. And I don't think Father was all that enamored with him, anyway."

The following month saw Adela meet Geffrey on her overlook where they talked of many things, kissed, and pledged their love. She listened with interest as he described his training and how it progressed. She had no idea of the intricacies of warfare and Geffrey made it all sound fascinating. He learned swordsmanship and the art of killing with his spear and battle-axe as well as group offensive and defensive formations. Since those initial days when he returned to his tent exhausted, he was now a tanned, muscled, and confident soldier in the Green Infantry. It took her breath away to be held in his strong arms.

℮↷℮↷

Over and over the Green Infantry practiced one of the most effective of infantry tactics—the phalanx formation. The phalanx was essentially a wall of men armed with shield and spear several rows deep that would engage the enemy with spear thrusts as a moving wall by interlocking their shields. This was particularly effective because it enabled individual soldiers to multiply their effectiveness against an enemy by fighting as a unit. Moreover, it essentially defeated all cavalry and chariot charges to the front because horses were unwilling to charge into a wall of sharp sticks. When utilizing the phalanx, individual infantrymen, in order to be effective on the battlefield, need not be masters of any given weapon, but rather merely capable of some overhand spear thrusts, some sword cuts and thrusts, and the use of a shield. Of greater import to the effectiveness of the phalanx than any individual's mastery of weapon techniques was their discipline and unit cohesion. The genius behind the phalanx was its simplicity. The ease with which a unit gained a basic level of proficiency in fighting in a phalanx allowed non-professional soldiers to fill the role of heavy infantry during wartime, though they may only drill with unit and weapons a few times a year.

When a phalanx engaged with the enemy, they would not break formation and fight as individuals. It would be pointless to train in the phalanx to begin with, Merek stressed, if this were the case. Imagine, he said, drilling day in and day out in a technique where, after you've marched to the battlefield from your home polis, you use this technique to assemble before the enemy, march toward them, and then abandon the technique to fight as individuals. Ridiculous. Merek went to great lengths to ensure the men remained in that formation because it gave the individual a better chance of living and killing the enemy than fighting alone. Once an enemy broke before the phalanx, great efforts would be made to keep the soldiers in formation in the phalanx during the pursuit phase of the battle. Cavalry and chariots, archers and slingers were better during that phase than the heavy infantry. The moments directly following the victory in a skirmish or battle were when the victorious troops were at the greatest threat of defeat because of potential counterattacks. Anyone breaking formations even after the battle was won, Merek threatened, was likely to be punished.

One afternoon Commander Merek stood next to Geffrey's cot while Geffrey pulled on his boots. After doing so, he jumped to attention while Jodocus and Jubal sat on their cots.

"Geffrey," Merek said in a voice that sounded official. "You have proved yourself an apt pupil in the Green Infantry. You have learned the tactics of infantry battle well. Yes, there were times I had my doubts. At first I thought you nothing more than a farmer but you proved my initial suspicions wrong. In fact, you surpassed my expectations."

"Sir, I am honored," Geffrey said.

"Do not speak until I am finished, young man. My, the impertinence of youth. As I was saying, you are the top soldier of the Green Infantry. Without a doubt, you are the best recruit I have seen in all my years training troops. I say this not to swell your head, which it probably will unfortunately, but to inform you that you have been promoted. To the cavalry. I have spoken with the duke, and he agrees. You will begin training with the cavalry in the morning. That is all. Good luck."

Merek shook Geffrey's hand and slapped him on a shoulder. After the commander left, Geffrey collapsed on his cot, dumbfounded.

"The cavalry," he said. "Wow. All he ever does in our training is yell at me."

"Is it all right if I touch you now?" Jodocus said. "Are Jubal and I still allowed in your presence?"

"Oh, stop it," Geffrey said.

"I am glad for you," Jubal said.

"I can't wait to tell Adela," Geffrey said. "She will so impressed."

"Are you still seeing her?" Jodocus said.

"Yes, all I can. She's the most wonderful lady I have ever known."

"Including Rosalind?" Jubal asked.

"Including her."

"Tell me, Geffrey," Jodocus said. "You seem to be a young man who falls in love easily. First, it was Rosalind. Then it was Isolde. Now, a few short months later, it is Adela. Are you sure she is the one for you?"

"I swear by all that is holy, Jodocus. This woman is the only one for me."

"But that is what you said about Rosalind."

"Rosalind is most likely dead," Geffrey said in a stern tone. "Don't you think I should move on with my life?"

Jodocus ignored the question. "Does her father, the duke, know about you?" he said.

"I doubt it. But Adela says she will tell him very soon, before we sail for England. I welcome the chance to meet him."

"He will probably eat you for his lunch," Jubal said.

"I don't doubt it," Geffrey said, his stomach revolting at the thought.

༺ঙৎঙৎ༻

Frederic found Adela crossing the castle courtyard and caught up with her. It was early evening and she wore a dark burgundy cloak to ward away the chill that hung on the air.

"Adela, my love," he said, softly. He touched her arm and felt her turn to face him. She did not smile. "Adela," he continued, "why haven't I seen you these past few weeks? Have you been avoiding me?"

Adela looked at him with a curious expression, one he had not seen before. Then, the furrows on her forehead softened and she smiled.

"Why no, Frederic," she said. "It's just that I have been extremely busy."

"I have missed you," he said. He took her in his arms, felt her stiffen in the embrace. "We used to have many long walks on these grounds, my love. You've been too busy to see your betrothed?"

"No, it's not that."

"What then?"

"It's just that...that..."

"Your heart is growing cold toward me, Adela? Is that why you have avoided me?"

"Frederic—" Adela stopped and Frederic sensed that something serious lay behind Adela's beautiful eyes.

"Yes?" he said, prodding.

She shook her head, turned, and started to walk away. Frederic stopped her.

"I have heard rumors, my love," he said. "That I possibly may have a rival. Could that be the reason for this sudden coldness?"

Adela said nothing.

"Oh, yes," Frederic continued. "These castle walls have prying eyes and ears. They see and hear much. And they tell me that the new soldier named Geffrey of Lochwald has gained your attention and favor."

Adela's eyes flashed. She stared at Frederic. "I will not lie to you, Frederic," she said in a low voice. "Geffrey and I have talked on a number of occasions. I find him charming and witty."

"The man is nothing more than a mere peasant!" Frederic howled. "Adela, how could you?" The revelation that his intended found another man charming and witty exploded in his brain sending shock waves coursing through his body. How could the woman he loved betray his feelings so easily? He lay awake at night dreaming of the time they were married and William was in the English throne. Adela would be a princess and he a duke. Surely William would cede him a great quantity of land and servants. He would be wealthy beyond his wildest expectations. All this seemed to be evaporating because his betrothed was temporarily infatuated with some poor peasant? He would not let it happen.

"Frederic," Adela said, "you do not own me. I will do as I please."

He grabbed her by an arm, pulled her closer to him. "What will your parents say, my love, when I tell them of your betrayal? Your breaking of your promise?" His fingers dug into her soft flesh, and he felt her try to pull away.

"We had no legal contract," she said. "We were pledged to each other, yes, but that pledge can be broken. It carries no legal weight. Now, please let go of my arm. You're hurting me."

With that, Frederic let her go and watched her hurry into the castle. He stood in the courtyard for a long moment trying to process what had happened between them. Adela's revelation hit him out of the blue, left him reeling and confused. He would have to see what the duke and Adela's mother thought about this sudden turn of events. Frederic had her mother's ear.

CHAPTER 27

Training in the cavalry was much more rigorous than in the infantry. If that was possible. The cavalry was made up of men from the aristocracy— they usually had a title or were knights. Most came from landed families. A quarter of William's force was mounted. It was a source of pride to be chosen to serve in the cavalry and the men who did carried themselves with a certain enviable air.

For William to persuade so many titled and landed men to involve themselves in his grand adventure indicated what a good job he did in acquiring papal support. These elite troops were the best protected of all. Like the English housecarl, they wore a haurberk or shirt made of chain mail over a leather undergarment, usually split from the waist to below the knee for easy mounting and dismounting. Sometimes it extended to cover the neck and head on which would be placed a conical metal helmet with a nasal guard. A slit was cut in the left side to hold the sword scabbard.

Geffrey's shield was kite shaped and held behind him with a leather thong when riding. It was made of wood with reinforcing pieces of metal around the perimeter to absorb blows. It had William's coat of arms on it—three gold reclining lions on a field of red. His destrier was a stallion but not large. The mount fielded him no protection. During the rigorous training he learned to ride upright with his legs straight and angled forward to avoid being thrown off his mount during a charge. A personal stable boy assigned to Geffrey cared for his mount. When asked who from the foot soldiers he wanted for the task, he chose Jodocus. Unlike the Saxon force that did not rely on horses to do battle, the cavalry were an integral part of Norman strategy.

Geffrey practiced with the cavalry attacking in several different ways, implementing shock tactics, but always in formations of several knights, never individually. For defense, a formation of horsemen was as tight as possible next to each other in a line. This prevented the enemy from charging and also from surrounding them individually. The most devastating charging method was to ride in a looser formation at a gallop. This attack was often protected by simultaneous or shortly preceding ranged attacks of archers or crossbowmen. A most important element, and one not easily mastered, was to stay in one line with fixed spaces while accelerating and having the maximum speed at impact. They practiced attacking in several waves, with the first being the best equipped and armored.

Heavy cavalry in William's army had been reduced to roughly equal value on the battlefield in comparison to missile and foot troops. The futility of charging well-emplaced and disciplined infantry was well understood. The rules of warfare had changed. Stakes, horse traps, and trenches were routinely employed by armies to protect against cavalry charges. Charges against massed ranks of pikemen and archers left only a pile of broken horses and men. Knights were forced to fight on foot or wait for the right opportunity to charge. Devastating charges were still possible, but only when the enemy was in flight, disorganized, or out from behind his temporary battlefield defenses.

Geffrey's cavalry unit was divided into the typical

three divisions, to be sent into battle one after another. The first wave would break through to disrupt the enemy so that the second or third wave could rout the adversary. Once the enemy was running, the real killing and capturing could take place.

As they practiced, Geffrey learned that knights often followed personal agendas to the detriment of any commander's plan. Most were interested primarily in honor and glory and jockeyed for positions in the first rank of the first division. He noticed that to many of William's knights, overall victory on the field was a secondary concern to personal glory. It was common knowledge that in many a previous battle, the knights charged as soon as they saw the enemy, dissolving any plan of attack.

Geffrey sat on a new form of saddle that was a more supportive wood-framed saddle imported from Persia. This new saddle had breast and crupper straps around the front and rear of the horse with doubled girths beneath the animal's body. It was designed, at least in part, to keep the saddle in place during the stresses of mounted combat. The breast-strap was of particular importance along with stirrups. The raised pommel and cantle of the deep saddle gave the rider with a lance or spear greater support when he, his weapon, and his horse came in contact with their target.

Geffrey's destrier was an Andalusian stallion. The Andalusian was named for where he originated— Andalusia on the Iberian Peninsula. Engravings and wall paintings found in parts of the Iberian Peninsula dated centuries before Christianity and were the oldest known reference to the Spanish horse. The Andalusian horse dated back to the Moors who were fine horsemen and brought their Berber horses into the conquered territory where they crossed them with the native horses of the Iberian Peninsula. The Berbers were noble horses, esteemed for their stamina and courage. The resulting cross was an unparalleled warhorse. The horse they developed was sturdy, with a long sloping shoulder, short back, rounded strong hindquarters, wide chest, deep girth, with a well crested, naturally arched neck and very sturdy legs.

Geffrey sat astride his destrier, Midnight, and listened while his cavalry commander, Gaylord, spoke. He was a tall, well-muscled man who sported a full, blonde beard and a hawkish nose. A scar ran the length of his right cheek. Gaylord's booming bass voice carried across the training grounds.

"The most important quality of a cavalryman," he said, "is discipline. Personal self-discipline and discipline within the ranks. The lack of order among the Frankish cavalry at the Battle of Suntal led to their defeat by the opposing Saxon infantry. If a cavalry unit does not remember its training or listen to the orders of its commanders they will charge in piecemeal fashion and be easily repulsed by archers or infantry. And if the cavalry goes down, the battle is lost. If the unthinkable happens and the cavalry is undone, then it is imperative to have a clear head and regroup quickly so a series of coordinated counterattacks can follow. Under adverse conditions, the fact that you don't immediately turn and run, or surrender, is the first proof of your discipline. This is why we train so hard and will continue to train until the day we board the ships. It is so that when the chips are down, you will act and react automatically without thinking of your fear. And by so doing, we will prevail."

At supper, Geffrey extolled his admiration for Gaylord. Jodocus and Jubal listened with intent ears.

"The man is one of a kind," Geffrey said. "He commands respect. He knows what he is doing and what he wants from his men. I am honored to serve under him."

"Let us hope that in the heat of the battle," Jodocus said, "he doesn't forget to show courage in front of his men."

Jubal nodded his agreement.

"He is a knight," Geffrey said. "In fact, most of the cavalry are knights. I am one of the few men who are not. I feel—inferior—when I am among them."

"You don't have to hang your head to anyone," Jubal said. "You showed your courage back in the mines."

"And in the dungeon," Jodocus added.

"Maybe so, but still, I am not one of them. And when I am with Adela, I feel that even more. I am sure she wishes I was more than a peasant."

"I doubt that," Jodocus said. "If that were so, she would never have loved you in the first place."

"But, affairs of the heart, my friend Jodocus," Geffrey said, "are not always rational."

The following morning Duke William was scheduled to give a speech to his army in the courtyard of the castle. The men were abuzz with thoughts as to what he would say. Some thought he would announce plans for the invasion while others thought he wanted to watch the drills of the combined cavalry and infantry.

Geffrey watched Jodocus brush, then saddle Midnight, in readiness for the morning maneuvers. The destrier was compact and powerful, had carried Geffrey with his armor and weapons without faltering once. He had come to love the stallion.

A cheer rose among the men and Geffrey noticed William hurrying out of the castle and into the courtyard. Geffrey signaled for Jodocus to follow and the pair ambled closer to where William stood. Out of the corner of an eye, Geffrey saw an ill-kempt man scramble toward William. It seemed the man, whom Geffrey had never seen before, was intent on speaking to the duke. But as the man closed on William, Geffrey noticed his hand.

It held a long dagger.

The man pounced on William, the knife flashing in the morning sunlight. A roar of surprise erupted from the crowd gathered around the duke.

No one moved.

The men were frozen, as if disbelieving.

The dagger plunged toward the duke, and Geffrey heard him grunt, saw him clutch his shoulder. The dagger raised again, poised for another blow.

Without thinking, Geffrey flew toward the scuffle and threw himself upon the assailant, wrestled him off of the duke. The two grappled. The man was stronger than he appeared. As the man raised his dagger at Geffrey, he grabbed the man's arm holding the dagger and bent it over his other arm.

The man fought to keep from losing the dagger. He kicked Geffrey in the groin, doubling him over, thrust the dagger at his belly.

Geffrey dodged the thrust, grabbed the man's knife hand once again. This time Geffrey's own strength prevailed. He bent the hand back on itself until the dagger fell to the ground. Several knights jumped on the man and contained him.

William, holding his right shoulder, struggled to his feet. A large bloodstain covered his tunic. He looked at Geffrey, smiled, then staggered to where Geffrey stood.

"I don't know why that man persists in thinking I have been sleeping with his wife," William said. "He refuses to listen to the truth. Well, maybe a few months in the dungeon will cool him off." He turned to Geffrey. "I am grateful, young man. If it weren't for your quick thinking I might be dead meat right now."

Geffrey removed his helmet, wiped the sweat from his brow with his sleeve.

"I was honored to be of service, my lord," he said.

"Are you badly hurt, sire?"

William smiled, waved a hand.

"A mere flesh wound, my lad."

William waved his hand again and the knights led the man away. As they did, he shot a nefarious look over his shoulder at the duke.

"Well, I must attend to this wound," William said. He turned to face Geffrey.

"You have my undying gratitude," he said. "Thanks."

Geffrey bowed slightly and watched the duke take his leave to the castle along with a cadre of knights.

At supper that evening Geffrey noticed William sitting on the dais, his shoulder bandaged. As the plates and other dishes were being cleared away, Gaylord rose on the dais and made an announcement.

"All men are to report to the great hall immediately following the evening meal. Geffrey of Lochwald, you are to come with me."

A buzz went up among the men and all eyes turned toward Geffrey. He could tell the men were talking about him and wondering why they were ordered to the hall. Jodocus looked at him with a questioning look.

"What's this about?" he said.

"I have no idea," Geffrey said. "All I did was take a knife away from a man intent on killing the duke."

Geffrey found Gaylord on the way to the great hall.

"What's this about, Commander?" he asked. "Am I in some sort of trouble?"

Gaylord laughed. "Hardly," he said. "But you will soon see. Come."

When everyone was assembled in the hall, Geffrey glanced around and noticed Adela sitting next to William who sat upon his throne. He wore his white robe and his crown glittered in the light. He stood, surveyed the men and women gathered. It seemed to Geffrey that all of Château de Caen was assembled in the hall.

"Geffrey of Lochwald," William said in a booming voice. "Please step forward."

Geffrey felt Gaylord take him by an arm and escort him to the throne. He stood before William, knees shaking, mouth dry.

"Geffrey of Lochwald, since joining this duke's army, you have shown intelligence, quick thinking, and leadership. Today, in saving my life, you displayed courage and honor in front of everyone. In recognition of those qualities and in saving this duke's life, tonight you are to be knighted in my service. Kneel, sire."

Geffrey felt Gaylord's hand on his shoulder pushing him to his knees. Which was good, because his knees were like pudding—weak and shaking. His mind was in a whirl. Was this really happening?

"Geffrey of Lochwald, please clutch this Bible, the word of our Lord and repeat after me the oath of knighthood."

The duke handed Geffrey a large leather-bound Bible, which he took and held with two hands.

"I do solemnly swear by Almighty God
and His Name, and in free and voluntary
desire, to serve as a Knight of William,
King of Normandie and of the most holy empire.
I do swear by the Eternal Power of the Trinity,
to be both a true and chivalric Knight, to obey
my Commanders and to aid my brethren.
I also swear by all that is holy and dear unto me,
to aid those less fortunate than I, to relieve the
distress of the world and to fulfill my knightly

obligations. This oath do I give of my own free
and independent will, so help me God!"

William retrieved the Bible and took his sword, a
long, two-handed broadsword, placed the blade on Geffrey's shoulder.

"I, William, Duke of Normandie, dub thee, Geffrey of
Lochwald, a knight in the service of William." He
touched the blade to the other shoulder. "And I bestow
upon thee, Geffrey of Lochwald, all the rights, privileges,
and responsibilities attendant upon knighthood." William
set his sword aside and touched Geffrey on his head.
"Arise, Sir Geffrey," he said. "And greet your fellow
knights."

With that, Geffrey turned around and a raucous cheer
greeted him. His knees, although still wobbly, seemed
much stronger, his mouth no longer dry.

A cry erupted from somewhere in the crowd.

"Three cheers for Sir Geffrey!"

"Hurrah! Hurrah! Hurrah!"

Following the cheers, great quantities of ale flowed
freely. Men and women of the castle as well as the
knights, now his comrades in arms, gathered about him,
toasting him and his knighthood.

Geffrey felt a tug at his shoulder. He turned to see Adela standing next to him, her smiling face radiant. She
was beautiful.

"Oh, Sir Geffrey," she said. "I am so happy for you."

CHAPTER 28

A week went by and Sir Geffrey's head was in the clouds. His feet barely touched the ground as he went about his daily duties. He felt light as a feather in the saddle. His new knight comrades welcomed him into their midst as if they had known him for years. Even Jodocus's position as his horse tender reached a new height, which impressed the old man. The cavalry training progressed well into the summer, the heat forcing the men to shed their armor and leather vests for the sake of comfort.

As a knight, Geffrey's billet was reassigned to the knight's dormitory within the castle. Located in the east wing the dormitory housed the hundred or so knights in the service of the duke. As Sir Geffrey's assistant or squire, Jodocus was allowed to live in the dormitory as well, albeit in a different sector. Women were employed to wait on the knights, do their laundry, bring them fresh water with which to bathe, keep the living quarters clean and fresh. Most were matronly types but a few young girls gave him an occasional smile or nod.

One definite advantage of living in the castle was that he had free run of the place, which meant he saw Adela daily. It was easy to see her and plan their next tryst, usually at her secret overlook on the hill.

Geffrey turned a corner as he hurried to breakfast. Blocking his way were Frederic and three burly men.

Frederic stared at him with an evil sneer. The three men grabbed Geffrey by the arms. Frederic stuck his head in his face.

"What's this all about, Frederic?" Geffrey said.

"Shut up, you bastard," Frederic hissed.

Geffrey struggled against the strong arms that held him but could not move.

"Take him away," Frederic said.

The men pushed Geffrey down the wide hallway to the nearest stairwell then down two flights to the basement. There, one of the men lit a torch and they proceeded down a dank tunnel that smelled of must and mildew. The light of the torch flickered off the walls giving the dark tunnel an atmosphere of dread. After a while they came to a heavy wooden door. One of the men took a key ring from his belt, unlocked the door. Inside, the wide dark room illuminated by a single torch, felt cold, smelled of urine and decay. On two of the room's walls, Geffrey saw there were more doors, each containing a small barred window.

After one of the men opened another door, Geffrey was shoved into a tiny darkened cell. His wrists were fastened to leather bindings attached to chains that were affixed to the stone wall of the cell. After checking his restraints, the men left. He heard the key turning in the lock.

Memories of his previous incarceration at the mines came flooding back, tormenting his reeling brain. Why had Frederic done this to him? Where was Adela? Jodocus?

The cell was black as a moonless night. The odor of urine, sweat, and vomit nauseated him. In the dark he could hear the rats scurrying about. He tried to move but the chains prevented much movement. He attempted to sit but found it was impossible.

How long he stood in the dark he had no idea. His legs and back ached from standing on the stone floor. His hands were numb and his fingers tingled. A bitter taste filled his mouth.

The door opened and Frederic entered—alone. He sported a sneer, his face contorted in an evil grin. He approached Geffrey until he stood face to face with him.

"Did you think you could get away with it?" he growled.

"What did I do to you, Frederic? What?

"Adela, that's what."

"I don't understand."

Frederic's eyes were red, menacing. "You thought I would just sit idly by while you took Adela away from me? You're beneath contempt. Our chivalric code means nothing to you. You're nothing but a peasant. And one without honor."

"Frederic, listen to me. I never knew you were betrothed to Adela until it was too late. We fell in love. We didn't plan to betray you. She didn't speak to you?"

"She did. And she told me all about the two of you. I was going to be the King of England's son-in-law if all went as planned. A duke. But you spoiled everything."

"Frederic," Geffrey said in his most imploring tone. "If I had known of your and Adela's relationship I would never have spoken to her more than a casual hello. You must believe me."

"A peasant. You came stealing into our lives and turned them upside down. How you arranged to save the duke's life I will never know but now even he sings your praises. Did you really think a peasant could become a knight so easily? You shall live to regret it, I assure you."

"Frederic," Geffrey pleaded. "Please believe me. Never once did I know you were Adela's intended. Never once did I seek to do you harm. In any way."

Nose to nose with Geffrey, Frederic seethed. "Well, my contemptible knight, Sir Geffrey. I doubt you will ever see the light of day. I will see to it that you rot in this place." The way Frederic said Sir Geffrey made the name sound evil.

Geffrey stared into Frederic's glowering eyes. Anger welled from somewhere deep within his gut until it spilled over.

He spat in Frederic's face.

Then slumped back against the wall.

Frederic sneered as if horror-stricken for a moment, wiped his face with a sleeve. Without warning, he punched Geffrey in the side. A bolt of pain shot through him and he slumped against his restraints. As his head spun, he watched Frederic turn and leave the cell. Geffrey was again alone in the darkness.

With his thoughts of how it all happened.

ତ⁄ତ⁄ତ

Sir Frederic reclined on his cot, seething with incalculable anger. The impudent peasant dared to spit in his face! How dare he? How Adela could find the man interesting and attractive was beyond his comprehension. What was it that she called him? Charming and witty? But he would show her the error of her ways. He would show her what a coward, what a yellow-livered coward her new found love interest was. And when she finally realized her mistake, he would be around to console her.

The duke was busy with the invasion plans and overseeing the building of his armada so Frederic decided to approach Adela's mother, Matilda, with his concerns. The woman had been shocked to learn of her daughter's seeming fickleness and casual disregard for her favorite knight. She promised that she would speak to the duke about it. It just wouldn't do, she said, for Adela to marry a common peasant, even if he was now a knight in her husband's service.

He knew, however, that Geffrey would soon be discovered. One couldn't hide in the castle indefinitely, especially locked up in the dungeon. He would be missed from the daily exercises. When Adela discovered her peasant missing, the dungeon would be the first place she searched. He was going to have to move the man to a location away from the castle, a location no one knew but him.

Another possibility was to goad him into a sword fight and simply kill the man. If done in front of witnesses, no one dare accuse him of murder. He reasoned Geffrey wasn't that skilled a swordsman as he had only been in the duke's army a few months. He should be easy enough to rouse his temper where Adela was concerned—enough to have him draw his sword. He hoped the man had a temper and would defend his woman's honor if challenged.

The more he thought of the idea the more he liked it. Killing Geffrey would give him complete satisfaction. And by doing it front of Adela she would see what a hotheaded peasant he was. Unworthy of her love.

He downed a tankard of ale in one long gulp, wiped his mouth with a sleeve, and closed his eyes. One day soon they would all be gathered in the courtyard and Frederic would have his chance at revenge.

And hopefully redemption.

ℰↃℰↃ

Jodocus was worried.

Geffrey was not at breakfast and he had not seen the knight all morning. The cavalry maneuvers proceeded without him and when Gaylord inquired as to Geffrey's whereabouts, Jodocus pleaded ignorance. He had no idea where the newly dubbed knight had disappeared.

After the day's training exercises ended, Jodocus hurried to Adela's bedroom chamber hoping she would receive him. They had never spoken directly and he counted on the fact that Geffrey mentioned him and that Adela would remember. As a knight's squire no one intercepted him demanding to know where he was going but a lady's bedroom was off limits.

The entrance to her bedroom was alive with activity. Maids in waiting scurried in and out of the room, chattering and gesturing. One of the women saw his approach, stopped, frowned.

"Sire," she said. "You are not to be in this part of the castle. If you are caught—"

"Please," Jodocus said in his most serious tone, "I must speak to your lady. It is a matter of utmost importance."

"I'm sorry, sire. She is dressing at the moment."

"Please—"

A voice from within the bedroom chamber called out. "What is it, Rawanda?"

"A man, my lady," the woman replied. "He wishes to speak with you. He says it is extremely important."

"Show the man in, Rawanda."

The woman escorted Jodocus into Adela's presence, where, with the wave of her hand, the other women departed.

"Yes?" Adela said.

"Please forgive the intrusion, my lady, but I am Jodocus, Sir Geffrey's squire."

"Yes," Adela said. "He has spoken of you often. He values your friendship."

"I come here with an anxious heart. Sir Geffrey was

not at breakfast and has not returned to his quarters. He was not at the training, either. He seems to have disappeared. I am worried."

"When did you last see him, Jodocus?"

"Just after dawn yesterday. We woke and dressed and he left our quarters. He never returned."

A frown formed on Adela's forehead. Deep furrows. Her eyes narrowed. "I have a feeling I know what happened to him," she said.

"Happened?"

"The knight I was once betrothed to is an extremely jealous man. He has been hounding me ever since I broke our engagement. I fear he's done Geffrey harm."

"What can we do?" Jodocus said, now more worried than he was earlier. "Where could he be?"

"If I know Frederic," Adela said, "he's locked Geffrey up in the dungeon. He'll say he has no idea where he went, and if no one goes down there and checks on him—" She paused.

"No one will ever know what happened to Geffrey. Is that what you were going to say?"

Adela nodded. "I need to find him," she said. "If he's down there, my father will free him."

"I will accompany you, my lady," Jodocus said.

"No. I must go alone."

Adela wrapped her cloak about her shoulders and left Jodocus standing outside her bedchamber. After watching her round a corner, he returned to the living quarters where he hoped he could explain Geffrey's absence to Gaylord.

❧❧❧

Adela hurried down the narrow stone tunnel that led to the dungeon. Dimly lit by only a single oil lantern, her shadow danced on the moss-covered walls. At the wooden door of the dungeon, she glanced to her rear and breathing a sigh of relief that no one followed her, rapped loudly. From behind the door she heard a man grunt then shuffle to the door. Keys jingled on the other side and soon the door opened revealing a large brutish man with a black beard. His eyes widened at the sight of her.

"My lady," he said, obviously surprised by her presence in the dungeon. "What are you doing here?" The man had large hairy arms and crooked teeth.

"Is Sir Geffrey here?" she said.

"My lady, I cannot—"

"Shall I have the duke down here to check?" she said, anger and impatience rising in her voice.

"Oh no, my lady. It's just that Frederic—"

"Frederic?" she screamed. "I might have known. So Sir Geffrey is here. Take me to him."

"My lady, you shouldn't be down here."

"Take me to him. Now!"

The jailor shrugged and stepped aside, allowing Adela access to the castle's dungeon. She breezed past him then waited for him to show her to Geffrey's cell.

"I wish to see him alone," she said.

The jailor fumbled for his key ring and led her to a cell at the end of a row of heavy doors. When he had the door unlocked, she hurried inside. Geffrey was shackled with chains to the wall.

"Light the lantern," she commanded the jailor.

After there was light in the cell, Adela was shocked at what she saw. Geffrey was naked to the waist and dripped with sweat. He looked exhausted from standing but when he saw her, his eyes widened and sparkled.

"Adela," he said.

She crossed the room and took him into her arms. His skin felt hot, clammy.

"This is Frederic's doing, isn't it?" she said, her eyes welling with tears.

"How did you know I was here?"

"It wasn't hard to figure. Frederic has been pestering me to marry him and forget you ever since I broke our engagement. Jodocus came to my bedchamber this morning and told me you were missing."

"Good old Jodocus," Geffrey said.

Adela looked at him then reached up and kissed him. "We are right for each other aren't we, Geffrey?"

"Of course we are, my love. Such a silly question."

"It's just that I have searched a long time for a man who I thought was a soul mate to me. One that didn't care about my money or station. Just me."

"It doesn't much matter at the moment," Geffrey said. "What with me locked up in here."

"I'll get you out of here. I'm going to find Gaylord, and he'll free you. And if not, then I'll go to my father."

"That bastard, Frederic," Geffrey seethed.

"They say my father is a bastard, Geffrey."

"Matters of your father's birth are not of any concern to me. A man makes his reputation by what he does, not the by the particulars of his birth. Adela, I owe who I am today to the generosity of your father. I will defend his honor with my life, if necessary."

Adela covered her head with the hood of the cloak. "And Frederic has made his by his actions here. Do not abandon hope," she said. "Hopefully, by nightfall you will be free."

She found Commander Gaylord on the castle grounds readying his horse for the ride down the hill and the training maneuvers.

He looked up from his work and smiled as she hurried to his side.

"Commander," she said, almost out of breath. "I come

bearing sad news. Sir Geffrey has been abducted and is chained in the dungeon."

"Abducted?" Gaylord said. His tone sounded suspicious. "Dungeon? By whom?"

"Frederic," Adela hissed. "He's been mad and jealous since I broke off our engagement. Geffrey and I plan to marry. Frederic wants his head."

"I have been wondering where my new knight had disappeared to. Well, if that's the case," Gaylord said, securing the horse's reins, "let's go get him outta there. If what you say is true, I'll deal with Frederic."

ᘓᘔᘓ

On a warm sunny morning, Duke William traveled to the River Dives to check on the progress of his fleet and its construction. He arrived on horseback with his retinue of advisors and immediately sought out Lothar, his master shipbuilder. He found the man aboard the skeleton of a longboat that had the appearance of a Norse design.

"Lothar!" William called to the man who stood on a wooden beam a good twenty feet above the ground. "Come down and give me an appraisal as to how the fleet is forming."

The stocky man with a bulbous nose and stubby hands climbed down from the ship and strolled to where the duke stood. A master shipbuilder would set the design for the Norman ship, and he started with the keel. However, it was the two curving posts at the front and the back of the ship—the stem and the stern—that would determine what sort of shape the finished vessel would be. It is from this vital first stage that he got his name—the Stemsmith.

The stemsmith was responsible for making sure that the hull was the correct shape. This involved cutting planks in ways that seemed counter-intuitive. However, the stemsmith was an expert in taking a two-dimensional plank and turning it into a three-dimensional ship. The Norman ships, patterned after their Norse neighbors, did not have deep keels, because there were few harbors that could accommodate them. This meant that, when sailing with the wind anywhere other than right behind them, there was a tendency to be blown off course. By changing the hull section of the boat, a negative keel could be formed, effectively using the boat's speed through the water to increase the effect of the keel.

"Sire," Lothar said, "the building goes on, although at a snail's pace. The construction of these boats is complicated and time consuming."

"In what way?" William was fascinated with the art of shipbuilding. He walked around the ship's frame studying and watching the laborers at work. Lothar followed him, explaining.

"Since most of the trees in this region are oak, that is what we are using. All the planks are radially split, meaning it goes with the grain of the wood. It is the strongest way that you can process wood because it works with the grain of the wood—it gains strength by following the way that the tree grows. The log is split using an axe to make a cut, running up and down the trunk. The split is widened and extended by driving wedges into it, until eventually the whole trunk splits in half."

He pointed to a group of men doing what he described.

"At this point, if we were using a pine tree, the splitting stops. Only two planks can be made from a pine tree with any success, and the two halves of the log are shaved down along their length. Oak trees can be split further. Each half is split into quarters, each quarter split into eighths, and so on. In fact, from a two hundred year-old tree, with skill, about sixty-four planks can be obtained. They are all slightly triangular, and quite rough, so they are smoothed down a little, like the pine planks."

The two men strolled around the ship with William gazing with admiration at its massive form. Lothar continued his description of the process.

"For the frames inside the ships, we use another type of timber—the grown timber. A grown timber is simply one that has grown to the right shape. The grain runs in the direction that was needed, making the timber incredibly strong. The stem and sternposts will be taken from large, curved branches. Where two parts of the frame are to meet we use a single timber, cut from a branching element of a tree. On smaller vessels, where the oars don't pass through oar holes, the holes or rowlocks are made from the junction of a branch with the trunk—putting the strongest part of the wood at the point of most strain."

"I knew it was complicated but never realized how much so," William said. "But you say the building goes slow?"

"It does, my lord. There is no way we can build enough ships for your entire army."

"Yes, it is as I feared, Lothar. That is why I have asked all my fellow lords of Normandie and my Flemish friends to help in this holy undertaking. I expect them to send ships any day now."

"The first strake to go on is called the Garboard strake," Lothar continued, "and it is nailed onto the keel. We use iron rivets. Nails are used where the end of the rivet cannot be reached—usually at the stem and stern, where space is tight. The next plank is riveted on to the garboard strake, so that it overlaps it when seen from outside. The rivet passes through the outside of the plank near its bottom edge, through the garboard strake near its top edge, and it is bent over a washer inside the boat.

"Caulking is used to stop water from getting into the boats. No wooden boat can claim to be entirely watertight, but we do our best. The caulking is made from sheep's wool that has been dipped in a sticky pitch made from pine resin. It is laid in the groove on the plank and, when the plank is riveted to the rest of the boat, creates an almost watertight seal, while still having the flexibility to move with the boat."

"The pitch is made right here on site?" William asked. He tried to show an interest although he was interested only in the date his ships would be ready to sail. Lothar however, seemed determined to complete his education.

"As each plank is riveted to the next, the boat begins to take shape. To get the boat to the correct profile we must cut the planks into some fairly strange shapes. The way that the ends of the planks join onto the stem and stern helps determine the profile of the boat—whether it will be a beamy cargo ship or a knife-thin warship. The larger the ship, the more planks will be required. These longships will require that several shorter planks be joined together by scarf joints—some of which could be quite elaborate. As the planks are added one above the other, clamps are used to hold them in place and the frame inside can be added."

CHAPTER 29

When Harold broke his oath to support Duke William's claim to the English throne, it fell on two members of the church to find a solution from which the Church would most benefit. Abbot Lanfranc of the Abbey of Bec, a trusted servant to Duke William, was entrusted to go yet again to Rome to gain papal support for William. While in Rome, Archdeacon Hildebrand, the political power behind the papal throne, had his own plans far beyond assisting the Norman Duke.

It was probable that these two formidable ecclesiastical politicians had met on Lanfranc's earlier mission to Rome to obtain papal sanction and blessing on the marriage of Duke William and Matilda. This mission was successful and the two similar clergymen established a strong and useful partnership.

Archdeacon Hildebrand's plan was to establish a temporal power base throughout Italy and beyond, by using those newly seized lands established by Norman mercenaries, such as Robert Guiscard, Conqueror of Naples. Some of these new nobles had sworn themselves as fiefs to the Holy Mother Church, thus these priest-knights obtained political recognition through the Church. By increasing the number of devoted Normans willing to conquer new lands for the church and establish new fiefs, Rome could obtain a massive power base not only in Italy but also over the Alps and indeed wherever such fiefs could be founded. The Archdeacons only problem was the lack of Normans capable of seizing such lands. It would further these plans greatly if the Duke of Normandy and perhaps the future King of England would give his support as well as his available nobles. There also arose the question that if Duke William was willing to submit to the authority of Rome on a temporal matter, namely the question of the succession, would William be willing to submit England as a fief to Rome?

It was with these prizes in mind that Archdeacon Hildebrand used his considerable power within the Assembly of Cardinals to promote and support the claims of William Duke of Normandy. Abbot Lanfranc presented the arguments in support of William, while Hildebrand brought about the decision. For not only was Harold of England on trial as an oath breaker and a violator of sacred relics but also the Church and State of England was brought under question. The King of England had not sent the levy to Rome known as Peter's Pence. The Church in England had allowed the act of simony to spread within its body, and it was argued that the state of England had descended into a near barbarous condition. Only by the appointment of a king who was a God fearing, dutiful son to the Holy Father, would England be restored into the brotherhood of the Christian World.

It was clear that some of these charges were unreasonable. Harold failed to send a clerical spokesman to Rome, due to the fact that Harold's supporter Archbishop Stigand would not be recognized by the papacy.

With such evidence and interests, the excommunication of Harold was foregone. Papal support in the form of the Papal Banner, a relic of Saint Peter, and a papal blessing were issued. Copies of the papal blessing were made and sent from the Abbey of Bec to all those heads of state who might wish to join William in his crusade. It clearly indicated the position of the Church.

꿍ꚉꚉ

At the approach of sunset, Geffrey found Frederic strolling the castle grounds. A few soldiers were lounging in the courtyard waiting for the evening meal to be served. He closed on the knight and drew his sword. "Frederic!" he yelled across the courtyard.

The knight turned and saw Geffrey crossing the grounds, sword in hand.

"Prepare to defend yourself, you lowlife bastard!"

Frederic dropped the bag he carried and drew his sword. In three large steps Geffrey was on him, his sword held high.

"There was a time, Frederic, that I believed in the chivalric code of knights. But you, sir, have all but destroyed that faith. And for doing that, I can never forgive you. For being a small man without honor when you could have talked to me, I can never forgive you. But most of all, you scum sucking pig, for all the grief you have caused Lady Adela, I am going to kill you."

With that, Geffrey charged Frederic and swung his sword. The two weapons collided with an ear-piercing *clang*. The blow sent Frederic reeling back on his heels. Geffrey pressed the action and the two knights fought, their swords hitting each other with such force and noise that Geffrey thought his ears would burst.

Men gathered in the courtyard to watch the fight. Out of the corner of an eye, Geffrey noticed Adela standing silent, her hand at her mouth, eyes wide in obvious horror. A large crowd stood in silence as they two men attacked each other.

Frederic feigned a blow, charged with a swing of his sword. Geffrey blocked the blow, parried, and delivered one of his own but Frederic managed to dodge out of the way. They continued the struggle, moving to an edge of the grounds where a wooden horse rail stood. Frederic raised his sword, brought it down in a wide-swinging arc but it missed its mark and hit the horse rail, splitting it in half.

Memories of his father and mother, Rosalind, and the iron chair at Remmelsberg overwhelmed Geffrey unleashing a fury within that he didn't know he possessed. The image of the Norsemen riding through his village, burning it to the ground, followed by his father's charred body hanging from the tree, empowered a strength that welled up from a place he thought long buried. He knew that fighting among knights was forbidden but his blood was up and he was powerless to stop it.

While Frederic regained his grip on his sword, Geffrey saw his chance and moved in with a slashing arc. At the last second Frederic managed to block the blow that would have ended his life.

Beads of sweat formed on the back of Geffrey's neck, his stomach turned sour, his arms weakened. He didn't know how much strength he had left.

A slashing blow from Frederic caught him on the arm drawing blood. Pain shot into Geffrey's shoulder and, for a moment, he thought his knees would give way. He prayed for the strength to continue. *In the name of God and my father, let me not falter at this critical time.*

The crowd that gathered to watch was much larger now. Men and women stood four and five deep in a large circle surrounding the combatants. Geffrey thought he spotted Jodocus and Jubal among those present to see which knight would prevail. No one seemed inclined to step in and put an end to the fight. Was it possible Frederic wasn't well liked by the men?

Frederic thrust his sword at Geffrey's midsection. Using an upward swing, Geffrey hit the knight's blade and knocked the sword from his hand. As his sword went flying, he tripped and fell backward, landing on his back. Geffrey was on him in a second, his blade at the man's throat.

He stood there for a long moment, staring at Frederic, his chest heaving, arms aching.

"Go ahead, man," Frederic hissed. "Finish it."

Geffrey stood as if paralyzed. He glanced over at Adela who wept at the sight. The duke stood beside her.

Then, in an instant, his fury was spent. Geffrey relaxed his blade, letting it fall away from Frederic's throat. He stepped back a few steps.

"Go on," he seethed. "Get outta my sight. Go away."

Geffrey returned his sword to its scabbard, turned his back on the fallen Frederic, and walked away.

❦❦❦

He sat in the duke's solar, the family drawing room. Located on the top floor of Château de Caen, it was smaller than the great hall whose walls were adorned with luxurious heavy tapestries depicting different landscape scenes. Dark woodwork framed a large hearth wherein a fire glowed orange and red.

Geffrey figured he knew the reason he had been summoned to the duke's private quarters—fighting with Frederic.

He expected to be punished, or worse, relieved if his knighthood and banished. The solar was where the duke and Matilda lived, and he felt awkward being in their private abode.

William and Adela entered and Adela rushed to Geffrey's side, touched his wound.

"Does it hurt much?" she said.

"Not much," Geffrey lied, wincing when she touched his arm.

Duke William eyed him and his daughter as they stood next to each other. Geffrey noticed him and stiffened. "My lord," he said. "I apologize for my display of unknightly behavior. I have no excuse. I allowed my jealousy of a man to get the better of rational thinking. I am willing to accept whatever punishment the duke feels appropriate. If you wish, I can leave the army and return to my home."

William waved an arm, strolled to a chair, and sat.

"Come now, Sir Geffrey," he said. "You apologize for defending my daughter's honor? She has told me the whole story, my lad. Frederic, for his unchivalric behavior toward Adela will be dealt with in a most severe fashion. He is to be banished from the castle and his knighthood stripped from him. He will be placed in the infantry. Any further trouble from him, and he will be executed."

"Still," Geffrey said, "I am sorry for the part I played in this sordid affair."

"Never apologize, Sir Geffrey," the duke said, rising. "It's a sign of weakness."

"Papa?" Adela said. She seemed to be imploring her father about something.

"Ah yes," William said. "Now, to business. Adela has mentioned to me that the two of you wish to be married. Is that right?"

Geffrey hesitated. "Well—"

"No hesitation, my boy," William blurted out. "Either you love my daughter or you don't. I ask you again. You wish to marry Adela?"

"That is my fervent wish, my lord," Geffrey said. "I love her beyond description, beyond mere words."

"Then it shall be so," the duke said. "When I am on the English throne, you shall have a wedding that people will talk about for a long time to come."

"You are most gracious, my lord," Geffrey said, taking William's hand, kissing it.

"Oh, posh," William said, withdrawing his hand.

"My lord, please let me show my gratitude in a more practical way," Geffrey said. "Before I was a soldier, I was a blacksmith. While I was a Norse captive, I learned a revolutionary new process for making weapons, allowing for a stronger steel to be forged. Please allow me to make you a sword, sir, that you can take into battle. I will fashion you a sword such as the world has never seen. It will be my pleasure to do so."

William was obviously touched by this display of affection, for he sat back in his chair and looked toward Adela.

"Oh, Papa," she said. "Let him do it. A new sword for your conquest of the Britons. A wonderful idea."

The duke smiled, nodded. "You have my permission, Sir Geffrey. I will so inform Sir Gaylord of my decision to allow you time away from your training. How much time would you require?"

"A week, my lord. Maybe a day or two longer. May I have my squire Jodocus as my assistant?"

"You may. Now that is settled, I have an invasion to attend to. I will take my leave. I am sure you two have ways in which to occupy your time."

After William left the solar, Adela threw herself into Geffrey's arms.

"What a glorious day," she exclaimed. "A grand glorious day."

But Geffrey's mind wasn't on his bride to be. It was now on the forge and the crucible process he learned while in Remmelsberg. It had been over a year since he had made a weapon of any sort. Now that he had opened his mouth, would he be able to deliver a sword worthy of

Duke William? Worthy of a grand invasion? Worthy of a future king?

He prayed that he was up to the task.

CHAPTER 30

The blacksmith stable was hot and stuffy. Jodocus worked the forge's bellows, stoking the glowing charcoal into a hotter mass of coals. Over the hearth hung an earthen pot that Geffrey filled with pieces of wrought iron.

"The secret of the crucible process," he told Jodocus, "is to heat the iron until it is completely liquid. To do this the fire must be extremely hot. Something happens to the iron when it melts. I don't know what it is, but it's magic, Jodocus. The high heat and melting somehow transforms the metal into newer, harder steel unlike anything seen up to now. We'll pour the liquid steel into ingots and let them cool. Then I can begin fashioning the duke's sword."

"It is nice of him to allow you to do this," the old man said.

"Yes," Geffrey said. "I want to make him a gift of the finest sword possible. In a small way I hope it repays him for his kindnesses."

"This process has been a secret then?"

"This is the process I learned in Remmelsberg. I don't know about a secret. But it is absolutely essential to melt all the iron. Completely."

"Why is that?"

"Gets rid of the slag," Geffrey said. "In order to do that, one needs a crucible that can withstand extremely high temperatures. Ordinary clay crucibles will not work.

You must use a special clay strengthened with rice chaff. It's absolutely crucial to the making of crucible steel. I hope this pot is up to the task."

Jodocus pumped on the bellows while Geffrey inspected the contents of the crucible.

"You really need a furnace to produce that kind of heat," Geffrey continued. "I'm hoping this hearth along with those bellows gets the temperature high enough to melt all of the iron. On top of the iron go some plants. Don't ask me why, it's part of the magic. We put a lid on the crucible and let it cook for several hours."

"And hope the whole thing doesn't explode," Jodocus said. He laughed at his humor.

"Yeah, I suppose. Then we cool down the crucible."

"So," Jodocus said, "you take wrought iron that has already been heated once and heat it again, this time until it melts."

"Yep, that's essentially it. Once the steel has cooled, you have a cake or an ingot, whichever you choose to call it. Then I take the cake and reheat it until it's soft and begin hammering and shaping the sword. I'll fold the blade over several times on itself to give the blade more strength."

He stood while Jodocus pumped on the bellows, creating a glowing white pile of coals.

The crucible creaked and popped, and Geffrey thought at one time Jodocus's prophecy of an explosion might come true. It seemed that the earthen post itself was glowing the color of the coals.

"I never said anything after your fight with Frederic," Jodocus said. "When I informed Adela you were nowhere to be found, she knew immediately that Frederic was responsible. She told me that he continued to harass her after she dissolved their engagement. He wouldn't leave her alone."

"On one hand, Jodocus, I understand. I would be dev-astated if Adela loved another. But he should never have tried to posses her. Jealousy is a harmful thing."

"If it had been me holding your sword, I would have run him through."

"The thought did cross my mind."

After an hour, Geffrey looked into the crucible and found the iron was in a liquid state. He tossed in the green plants, covered the crucible, and he and Jodocus sat in the stable and waited while the iron cooked. As they sat, Jodocus produced three dice made of bone and the men played chuck-a-luck. During the afternoon, Adela stopped in to check on the progress. Her maidservant, Rawanda, was at her side,

"Is it going well?" she said.

"We are about to open the crucible," Geffrey said. "We should have a cake."

"A what?" Adela said.

"A cake," Jodocus replied. We're baking a cake."

ↄↄↄ

William's advisors gathered in the great hall, and the duke listened to their opinions as to the best date for the invasion. Outside, a rainstorm beat against the shutters.

"The fleet has gathered in the River Dives," Robert de Beaumont said, "ready to sail. The shipbuilder sent word that he believes there are enough longships to carry all the necessary men, horses, and equipment. But the weather has been miserable the past few days with the wind out of the north. It would be impossible to attempt a crossing at the present."

"And my ship?" Duke William said.

"Your flagship, *Mora*, is the fastest of the fleet and is loaded and ready to sail. Her crew is waiting for the order. Your wife, sire, traveled to Dives this morning to look her over."

The *Mora* was a gift from his wife, Matilda. The ship's name came from a word for an edible root, like a carrot or parsnip. The sea carrot grew abundantly along the southern coasts of England, bloomed from May until September, and was noted as a cure for various ailments. The Anglo-Saxon word suggested that, like the plant, the ship had a remedy for the Saxons. The *Mora* displayed numerous religious symbols affirming William's divine election. The mast was topped with a cross and the pope's flag emblazoned with a cross, symbolizing the blessings of God and the pope for William's cause. Its prow had the gilded statue of a child pointing toward England with his right hand and blowing a horn as white as ivory with his left. The stern of the *Mora* bore the head of a lion, a symbol of strength, stability, and royal power.

It was Matilda's idea to place the religious symbols at the top of the mast, the prow and the stern. They formed a religious trinity protecting the ship and the expedition. The cross and papal flag symbolized God's blessing and His divine will, acknowledged by the pope, God's representative on earth. The head of a lion on the stern represented Christ the Heavenly King and William, the future earthly king. The gold statue of the child symbolized the Holy Spirit, God's spirit at work in the world, linking past and present with Virgil's Fourth Eclogue prefiguring William's reign and the new lineage of William and Matilda in their children. William would save England as Christ saved mankind.

"Do we know what Harold is doing at the moment?" William asked. "Where his armies are?"

"Our spies tell us that he has moved to the north," an aide said. "There is a rumor that an invasion of Norsemen is immanent and King Harold is moving his army to repulse the. Harold's Saxon army is having a busy autumn. We hear they marched from London to Yorkshire to repel the invading forces of the Norse ruler Harald Hardrada and his ally, the English king's brother-turned-traitor, Tostig."

"So," William said, "when the weather begins to clear, I want our troops to move to the ships on the Dives. As soon as we have favorable winds and a tide, we sail."

ℯ∕ℑℯ∕ℑ

The following day after making the crucible cake Geffrey began hammering it into something that began to resemble a sword. Jodocus kept the forge hot by working the bellows. Periodically, Geffrey would stick the weapon in a bucket of water and, after the steam cleared, placed it back into the forge.

"This sword gonna have a name?" Jodocus said. "Every ruler's sword must have a name."

"I don't know," Geffrey said. "I suppose it should be something from the Norsemen, because I learned this process from them."

"Yes, that would be appropriate." Jodocus leaned on the bellows' handles and continued pumping.

"You know anything about their religion?" Geffrey said.

"A little. While I was in the mines, I learned a few things from the guards."

"Like what?"

"Well," Jodocus said. He stopped working the bellows and stroked his chin. "Among the many Norse deities who inhabit Asgard, the fortress of the gods, Wödan plays the role of chieftain. But he is not the creator, nor the first god to come into existence."

"Tell me more, please," Geffrey said. He took the

steel from the forge using a set of tongs and began hammering. At this point, he had a long slender piece of steel.

"Before humanity existed and even before sky or ground or wind, there existed a gaping abyss. At one end of the gap flamed elemental fire and at the other end there blew elemental ice. The cold and the heat met within the gap and the drops formed a frost ogre. As frost continued to melt in the gap, a cow emerged. She fed the ogre with her milk and she was in turn nourished by salt licks that formed in the ice. Later, she uncovered Buri, the first of the Norse gods. Buri had a son named Bor, who with the giantess Bestla had three sons—Wödan, along with his brothers Vili and Ve. The three brothers killed the frost ogre and constructed the world with his corpse. The frost ogre's blood became the seas and lakes, his flesh the earth, and his bones the mountains.

"Wödan is not an omniscient god. In fact, his chief characteristic is that he's always seeking wisdom, even at great personal cost. He also often spoken of in poems and is credited with giving poetry to humanity. This happened when he stole and consumed the Mead of Poetry, which unsurprisingly required a great deal of effort and sacrifice. Beyond just poetry, this mead was truly a source of knowledge and inspiration—it even came to be nicknamed the stirrer of inspiration. Drinking this mead not only gives knowledge and words to the mind, but the ability to inspire and persuade and arrange those words in meaningful ways.

"Finally, he is a god of war and death. As the god of war, Wödan watches over warriors who fall in battle. Valkyries carry the fallen ones straight to Valhalla. There, Wödan feasts with them and prepares them for Ragnarok, the final battle in which the gods and the world were doomed to perish."

"Perfect," Geffrey said. "Wödan is the perfect name for my sword. I shall call it, Halvor. Which in the Norse language means, sword of god. The Sword of Wödan.

"Sure," Jodocus said. "Wödan always wielded a sword during battle. How long is the sword going to be?" He watched as Geffrey continued to hammer the steel, slowly forming it into a weapon.

"I've noticed that all the cavalry's swords are thirty-three inches long. Any longer would hinder a knight riding horseback and hang too low over the animal's side. The duke will be on his destrier so I'll make it thirty-three inches long."

"How does the duke feel about you and Adela being together?"

"I think he likes me, Jodocus."

"No question about it. When you came to stand between his daughter and Frederic I believe you rose significantly in his estimation. Speaking of Frederic, have you seen him lately?"

"Not since the duke banished him from the castle. He may be lying in wait for me somewhere out on the plains waiting for me to ride by. And spear me."

"Surely he wouldn't be that foolish," Jodocus said. He stopped working the bellows again, wiped his brow with a sleeve.

"Don't bet on it. Those kinds of people have no honor. It would be just like him."

They spent the rest of the afternoon fashioning *Halvor*. Geffrey worked the steel longer and thinner until it was the approximate length he desired.

The blade Geffrey envisioned was broad, double edged with both edges being sharp, and tapered in two ways—its profile tapered, meaning the sword got narrower closer to the tip and distal tapered, meaning its thickness decreases from the base to the tip. The sword was a dedicated cutting weapon, well balanced and re-sponsive, made for use by only one hand since the other one held a shield. It would have a fuller, a groove down each side, to lighten the sword's weight.

As he worked, Geffrey began to think of the hilt and pommel and what decoration he would use. Also what inscription, if any, he would mark in the sword. The size and weight of the pommel was important for it needed to balance the sword. The hilt and it covering, the grip, needed to be comfortable in its users hand. He knew he wished the hilt and pommel to be encrusted with precious jewels so he would ask Adela if she could part with the ones he had seen on a necklace she wore. For the inscrip-tion which he would place across the quillon, or cross guard, and quillon block, it would read—*Lux veritas et honorem*—Light, Truth, and Honor.

The following day, Geffrey fashioned the hilt and pommel. On the pommel, he inscribed a cross patonce, where the ends of its limbs were trifurcated into leaf shapes, and the limbs gently widened from the center.

Adela, after hearing that Geffrey needed a handful of jewels with which to decorate the sword for her father, gladly gave him a necklace that contained a number of rubies and emeralds. Heating the sword once again, he encrusted the jewels into the end of the pommel and in the quillon block above the blade. Geffrey fashioned the fuller that ran the length of both sides of the blade, end-ing a few inches from the tip of the double-edged sword.

When the difficult work of forging the weapon was completed, only the more delicate polishing remained. It took Geffrey three days of meticulous work with the various grits to put a mirror finish on the blade. He and Jodocus took turns wiping the various rouges with a piece of moistened leather. As the blade began to gleam, Jodocus's eyes widened.

"It's a work of art," he said. "I can't believe it. We started with only a hunk of iron and you have made a weapon that is truly magnificent."

"You think the duke will be pleased?" Geffrey asked as he put the finishing touches on the sword.

"If he's not, then he's not the man I think he is," Jodocus said.

Adela was amazed at its beauty. Her jewels gave the sword a regal touch, she said. Her father would be excited and proud to carry it with him.

While Jodocus was polishing, Geffrey worked at making a scabbard of leather tipped with steel. The sword fit effortlessly into it.

That night during the evening meal as William and his family ate with the soldiers, Geffrey approached the dais. He carried the sword in his hands.

"My lord," he said, after making his way to stand in front of the duke. "I have the sword I promised for you. I call it *Halvor*, which is Norse for sword of god. It is the sword of Wödan. It was from the Norsemen that I learned the process of making this exceptional blade. Wödan is the Norsemen's god of war. I hope you are satisfied with my efforts. I put an inscription on the quillon."

Geffrey handed the sword to Duke William who took it and removed it from its scabbard. The blade flashed in the light of the dining hall, reflecting thousands of sparkles from its mirrored surface. From the look on his face Geffrey knew the duke was pleased.

"I—I don't know what to say, Sir Geffrey," William said. "It's beautiful. An amazing work. You have given me a gift I will cherish forever."

"Read the inscription, Father," urged Adela.

Matilda moved closer to look over William's shoulder.

"*Lux veritas et honorem*—Light, Truth, and Honor. Such a fitting motto for the future King of England." William held the sword high above his head for all in the dining all to see. Its jewels and blade glimmered in the lights. "Behold the Sword of Wödan!" William said, his voice booming throughout the hall.

A rousing cheer rocked the room.

Sir Geffrey blushed.

CHAPTER 31

Harold Godwinson sat on his throne and surveyed the throng of people who gathered to wish him well. He had just been crowned King of England after he was elected by the Witenagemot and anointed king at Winchester Abbey by the archbishop of York. In his heart, however, he knew he was an imposter. Even his wife mentioned it the night prior to his coronation.

Edward, the previous king, on his deathbed designated William of Normandie as his heir, an act that enraged Harold. But almost immediately on ascending the throne, he faced opposition. First from William, then by Harald Hardrade, King of Norway, and finally by his own brother, Tostig.

Tostig was the previous appointed Earl of Northumbria. As Earl of Northumbria, Tostig enforced the laws and taxation of King Edward. Unfortunately for peace loving King Edward, Tostig pursued the taxation of Northumbria with great and violent zeal, which benefitted himself, his friends, and his agents in the region. Oddly enough, Tostig's relentless and forceful tax requisitions had made him a very unpopular governor among the citizens of Northumbrians who actually had to pay the king and Tostig's taxes.

In October of 1065, the citizens of Northumbria had had more than enough of Earl Tostig. Being greedy, violent, and unsympathetic to rich and poor alike, Tostig had pushed Northumbria's citizens with property and peasants too far. During a brief journey outside Northumbria, the citizens rose up and replaced Tostig with a new earl. King Edward had mixed feelings about this usurpation, not liking most of the Godwinsons, but he chose Tostig's older brother Harold to investigate and judge the situation. Rather surprisingly, Harold's interviews in Northumbria caused him to advise King Edward that Northumbria was better off with the new earl and much better off without Tostig. The king quickly agreed with Harold Godwinson and banished the infuriated Tostig from all of England. Tostig sought allies overseas and eventually latched on to the King of Norway, Harald Hardrada. With Tostig's enthusiastic support, Harald had gathered a fleet of three hundred Norse long ships, filled with ten thousand experienced Norse warriors.

Harold mobilized his fleet and a peasant army of the south to guard the coast against an expected invasion by William. At the same time, he was forced to repel Tostig's raids on the eastern coasts. But, in September Harald and Tostig invaded from the north, forcing King Harold to move most of his troops to the northern coast.

Years earlier, Harold's father, Godwine, earl of Wessex, refused to obey a royal command of King Edward to punish the people of a town friendly to him. Both sides rallied their troops, but Godwine's rebellion collapsed when powerful nobles supported the king. Godwine and his sons were banished for defying royal authority, and Edward sent his wife to a convent and designated William of Normandie as his heir. Eventually, Harold invaded England and forced the king to restore his father and his family to their previous positions.

Having established himself as the preeminent figure in England, Harold expected to ascend the throne after the passing of the childless Edward. His designs, however, were complicated by certain events. Much to his dismay,

Harold was sent by Edward to Normandy to confirm Duke William as the king's heir. While en route, Harold was shipwrecked and captured by one of William's vassals but the duke demanded Harold's release and ransomed him.

Harold was warmly welcomed by William and joined him on a military campaign in Brittany. While in Normandie, Harold swore an oath of fealty to William and promised to protect William's claim to the English throne.

But once safely ensconced on his throne, Harold had no intention of honoring that promise.

"Albus," Harold said to his chief advisor on military affairs, "what is the current situation in the north. I am anxious to hear."

"My lord," Albus said, a frown on his face. "It is dire. The Norse raiders threaten to invade. Our southern troops have mostly disbanded because they ran out of supplies and needed to return home for harvest. The bastard Hardraade and your brother are poised for a victory if nothing is done."

"What would you suggest, Albus?" Harold said.

"There are still a few thousand troops left in the southern region, sire. Move them northward at once to repel the Norsemen."

"But, at any moment, William threatens to invade us from across the Channel. We will be defenseless."

"Move them, my lord." Albus's voice was emphatic. "William is still acquiring ships with which to cross the sea. You have time to strike the northern invaders and still make it back to the south to face William."

"My army will be exhausted!" Harold shouted, his anger rising.

"You have no other choice, my lord king," Albus said in a resigned tone.

ɛ৲১ɛৎ১

Normandie Coast, August 1066 AD:

William's army gathered at Dives-sur-Mer, a small community on the River Dives estuary. Located halfway between the River La Vire and the Seine, the port swelled in size and activity when the duke moved his naval fleet into its waters. In addition to the soldiers and cavalry, the sailors and horses increased the invading forces to around ten thousand. Add another five to seven thousand men and women providing support services such as cooking and cleaning, the ranks surrounding William was a truly awe-inspiring sight. The small community had never seen such raucous activity in its many year existence and while Geffrey, Jodocus, and Jubal mingled with others of the army and navy, the work of provisioning the ships continued day and night.

"I am required to stay with the Green Infantry," Jubal said. "So, I won't see either of you until after we land." He grabbed Geffrey, gave the man a hug, and did the same with Jodocus. Geffrey watched the man with whom he had shared many a campfire, walk away, and disappear in the crowd.

When he was no longer in sight, Geffrey noticed Gaylord approaching. The man was hurrying, his frame stiff, his head erect.

"Sir Geffrey," he said after he reached the pair. "Please have your squire stable your horse at the church. There's a large patch of ground nearby and all the knights are to keep their chargers staked out there. The women of the village will feed them for you. One more thing. Duke William has issued an order. There will be no, absolutely no looting, stealing, abuse of the women or children while we are here at Dives. Any violation will be dealt with in a most severe fashion. Roll call is at dawn tomorrow."

With that, Gaylord moved on, heading toward the port.

Geffrey knew from overheard conversations, that William bore serious cause for apprehension with respect to the effect that this long-continued storm might have on the success of his enterprise. The delay was a serious consideration in itself, for the winter would soon be drawing near. In another month it would seem to be out of the question for such a vast armament to cross the Channel at all. Geffrey reasoned when men embarked in such dark and hazardous endeavor as that in which William was now engaged, their spirits and their energy would rise and sink under the influence of very slight causes. He knew that nothing had greater influence over their spirits at such times than the aspect of the weather. Jodocus mentioned that the ardor and enthusiasm of the army were fast disappearing under the effects of chilling winds and driving rain.

The feelings of discontent and depression, which the frowning expression of the heavens awakened in their minds, were deepened and spread by the influence of sympathy. Waiting was their immediate enemy. The men had nothing to do, during the long and dreary hours of the day, but to anticipate hardships and dangers. As they watched the clouds driving along the cliffs and the rolling of the surges upon the coastal shores, the anticipations of shipwrecks, battles, and defeats, and all the other gloomy forebodings haunted the imagination of a discouraged and discontented soldier.

The encampment of the army was spread out over two hundred acres, more or less, each cavalry and infantry unit given their own space to bivouac. Several days' work consisted of loading the ships, making sure one's armor and weapons were clean and sharp, meetings with commanders going over strategy once on English soil.

Somewhere in the massive encampment Geffrey knew Frederic waited with his fellow infantrymen. He wondered if the man's thoughts were on the upcoming battle or on his former love. He had not caught as much as a glimpse of Frederic since arriving at the ships. He hoped it would remain so.

Being away from Adela was difficult on Geffrey. Every day he wrote her a letter, sealed it with candle wax, and sent it by daily horseman to Château de Caen. In them, he pledged his undying love for her and imagined what their life would be like after the duke's coronation as King of England and she joined him. He hoped he could show bravery in battle and be rewarded by a large estate.

Her letters were of a similar nature. She longed to be with him. A few of her letters mentioned how much William loved his sword, how he showed it to everyone before they left for Dives, and how pleased he was with her choice of a future husband.

ϾᴣϾᴣ

Harald Hardrada was considered the greatest warrior in the North, if not in all Europe. Said to be seven-feet tall and broadly built, he had been a fighting man since old enough to wield a sword. As a young man in exile from his homeland, he had ventured to the distant Court of Byzantium. There he won a great renown and an ever larger fortune as a leader of the famed Varangian Guard—the Scandinavian *corps de elite* of the East Roman Emperors.

Returning to Norway, he seized the throne that had once been his older brother's. His subsequent reign had

been a period of war and centralization; as he brought the
turbulent and independent Norse landholders under royal
authority. For years, he campaigned in Denmark as well,
in an attempt to unite the two countries under his sword
and recreate the Empire of Canute.

After his banishment, Tostig Godwinson found in
Hardrada a patron with ready ear for intrigue. Between
the two men, a scheme was hatched to invade England
and unite Norway and England as one. What Canute had
wrought two generations earlier, could not the Champion
of the North do as well?

Meanwhile, in England, Edward the Confessor's long
reign finally came to an end. On his deathbed, he was
said to have named Harold Godwinson as his heir. However, in Normandy, William openly disputed this claim
as an invention of his rival. The English proto-
Parliament, called the Witan, met and elected Harold
King of England. Harold was fully aware that William
was prepared to contest the English throne. Throughout
the summer of 1066, the English militia, called the Fyrd,
stood ready on land and sea. Watch was kept along the
coast, with the strong English fleet patrolling the English
Channel. That year Haley's Comet appeared over the Eu-
ropean sky and was called in England, the Fire-Drake.
Throughout the North, men saw this as an omen, heralding momentous events to come.

Harald was subsequently excommunicated by the
Pope, and a papal legate delivered a Papal banner to Wil-
liam, symbolizing the support of Holy Mother Church.
This religious sanction gave William immeasurable polit-
ical and psychological advantage. The morale of his vas-
sals grew strong in the fearsome undertaking to come.
Papal support encouraged pious adventurers from all over
Northern France to flock to William's banner, in order to

win religious indulgence by smiting the Usurper, and perhaps new land in a conquered England.

England was a far larger and, in theory, stronger country than the Duchy of Normandy. Her fleet controlled the channel and William had nothing that could be called a navy to oppose the English Sea Fyrd. Harold's navy was manned by experienced seamen, captained by men who were in many cases former Norsemen. His ships were filled with detachments of axe-wielding housecarl, who were experienced at fighting aboard ships.

All that summer of 1066, England held its breath. Harold found himself in the unenviable position of having to surrender the initiative to his enemies. He was able to do nothing but wait, and try to keep his levies in the field. Unfortunately for him, summer turned to fall and still his enemies failed to materialize. Feudal obligation demanded he disband the Fyrd, both by land and sea, so that this country militia could return to their farms and bring in the autumn harvest.

No sooner had the levies gone home, than word arrived from the north of England that the opening salvo of a three-way campaign had arrived—Harald of Norway landed near York. In September, Harald Hardrada and Tostig Godwinson invaded England, coming with a large invasion fleet of Norse longships and experienced Norse warriors. By the time word of the incursion reached Harold in London, the Norse had already met and routed the Northumbrian levies at the Battle of Gate Fulford. York was on the verge of surrendering.

In response, King Harold force-marched north with an army composed of his housecarl and levies hastily gathered along the way. He arrived on September 25th, in time to intercept Hardrada and the Norse army as they marched unarmored to accept the surrender of York. At a

river crossing called Stamford Bridge, the two armies
met.

For a while, a single, gigantic Norse warrior held the
narrow bridge. Time and again, Harold sent forward
champions from his own housecarl to clear the bridge.
Each time, the Norse champion sent them back reeling.
Finally, a housecarl in a small boat worked his way under
the bridge and with a spear stabbed between the boards
and under the Norse champion's mail skirts. The warrior
fell, mortally wounded allowing the English army pas-
sage across the bridge.

Hardrada used the time gained to prepare his army for
battle. As the English approached the Norse shields deployed beneath King Harold's banner, Tostig Godwinson
arrived to parlay with his estranged brother. King Harold
offered his brother clemency if he would surrender himself. But when asked what terms he offered Tostig's ally,
Harald of Norway, the reply was "Six feet of English
earth to be buried in."

With that, a ferocious battle erupted. Though mighty
warriors, the Norse suffered from their lack of armor and
few archers. An English bowman struck the decisive
blow when an arrow struck Hardrada in his unprotected
throat. In spite of the death of their famous lord, the
Norse fought on. Reinforcements arrived under Hardrada's Marshal, Eyestein, who poured off their ships but
the men were exhausted by their long run from the coast
to the battle. These too were defeated and within hours of
its beginning the battle ended with the routing of the
Norwegian army, with both Hardrada and Tostig Godwinson slain. The Battle of Stamford Bridge was so decisive that only twenty-five ships returned to Norway form
the original fleet of over three hundred. Harold's victory
was total, but at the cost of the lives of many of his best
officers and men.

അൈഅ

The weather was miserable. A cold north wind blew a rainstorm over Dives-sur-Mer, forcing William and his army to retreat into tents and under canvas tarps. The duke sat in his tent and fumed with his commanders, Gaylord and Merek among them.

"If this infernal storm doesn't let up soon," William said, "we'll be waterlogged and the men will have no desire for the fight." Wind rattled the tarps, pulling hard on the guide ropes.

"They are already getting restless, my lord," Gaylord said. "The farmers of the area are beginning to have difficulty securing enough hay for the horses."

The other commanders raised a similar concern—idleness produced restlessness that invariably led to a loss of focus in addition to the dwindling feed for the animals.

"We can attempt to cross the Channel during a rainstorm," William said, pacing the tent, "but as long as the wind is from the north it is impossible. The morning outgoing tides will change soon and not be ideal either."

"Maybe we should all pray," Merek said and laughed at his idea of a joke.

William stopped. Looked at his commander.

"You may have the right idea there, Commander," he said. "Gentlemen, I propose a Mass tonight in the church. Someone wake up the priest and bring him here."

Several men scrambled from the tent and a half hour later the village priest stood before William. He appeared as if he had been drawn out of bed for his hair was plastered against his head and he wore his housecoat.

"You're the priest here at Dives?" the duke inquired.

"I am, sire. May I help you?"

"You can. I would like you to say a Mass in your church. My men will attend. I wish for this godforsaken storm to end. Maybe your Mass will help."

"Sire, do you really think—"

"What is the name of your church?" William said.

"The Eglise Notre-Dame," the priest said.

"Is it a good church?"

"It is just a small chapel, sire. Much too small for your entire army."

"Whoever cannot sit inside can remain outside," William said. "It's important that a Mass be said so this storm might abate."

The priest smiled demurely. "There is a legend told of a miraculous Christ, bleeding from a knee wound. It was found in the sea. The figure was not attached to a cross. However, a few years later, the waters also yielded a naked cross that perfectly matched the Christ. You can view that cross in the Church chapel."

"See there," William said, brightening considerably. "Miracles can occur here. Please Father, I beg you to hold the Mass. Tonight."

The priest nodded, pulled his housecoat tight about his neck.

"As you wish, sire," he said. "Have your men gather at the church at midnight."

The priest scurried out into the dark and rain back to his home.

Later that evening, Mass was celebrated in Eglise Notre-Dame.

ຂໆຂໆ

Jubal tried to sleep but it would not come. His thoughts were on the upcoming battle and his role in it. Since Geffrey and Jodocus had left the Green Infantry he felt totally alone. He rarely saw his friends, a fact that depressed him. Although he did his best in the training exercises, the large man was slow afoot and somewhat clumsy, a fact that irritated Merek.

It wasn't that Jubal was a coward. In fact, he could be a downright bully at times—he remembered his bullying of Geffrey with some remorse. He had fought many a man in hand-to-hand fistfights and won most of them. But he had never fought in a battle and that fact caused him much worry and consternation. To march into a fight with nothing more than a shield and spear didn't seem to Jubal as much weaponry. To be sure, his Green Infantry unit had trained with the square and phalanx formations, trained until he saw the maneuvers in his sleep. It was his self-control that worried him. Did he possess the courage to remain with his men and fight as trained?

He reached under his cot, retrieved his earthen water bottle, took a long slug. His dry mouth felt much better. He turned on his side, closed his eyes. And prayed for courage.

CHAPTER 32

Two days later the rain stopped and the winds shifted from out of the west. William gave the order to board the boats and set sail for England.

The invasion was underway.

Geffrey climbed aboard the *Maiden,* a Norse inspired boat seventy feet long and fifteen feet wide. There were sixteen fittings for oars on each side with an inclinable mast in its center. Cavalry were crammed into the ship until there was hardly room to move and Jodocus held the reins of Midnight, soothing the charger as it fought for solid footing on the pitching deck.

Up ahead in the gray evening, Geffrey could make out the mast of the fleet's flagship, William's *Mora.* It was a ninety-foot vessel, eighteen oars to a side, a mast whose sails were different colors. Upon them were painted, in various places, the three lions, which was the device of the Norman ensign. At the bow of the ship was an effigy, or figurehead, representing William and Matilda's second son shooting with a bow. A cross and a standard especially ordained by the pope were fixed to the top of the mast of the *Mora.* The red color of the standard referred to the St. George's Cross and the cross referred to St. Peter's Cross. William had received the Pope's blessing for his endeavor. He had promised the Pope to take England as a fiefdom for God and St. Peter and to pay taxes to the church.

They made their way down the River Dives and into the Channel. Once out in open water the *Maiden* pitched and rolled as the waves crashed over her bow and sides. The horses' eyes were wide with fright and Jodocus worked frantically to keep Midnight calm. Before dawn, he gave up and wrapped a shawl over the charger's eyes, which seemed to help. At least Geffrey no longer had to look at the fear in the animal's wide eyes.

Geffrey clung to the ship's gunwale and stared northward into the inky gloom. He could see nothing in the distance but a velvet curtain. Seventy miles away lay the coast of England, whose soil his duke believed he was destined to rule as king. If all went well, by midmorning the fleet should make landfall and the difficult job of disembarking would begin. The plan was to gain a foothold on the beach, then establish the order of battle. Once everything was in order, the infantry would begin marching inland, followed by the cavalry.

Jodocus found a spot in the shelter of the wheelhouse and as they two men stood out of the wind, Geffrey spoke of Adela.

"She's wonderful, Jodocus," he said. "She's beautiful, smart, and knows Latin. She read the inscription on the duke's sword without any difficulty. I believe she will make a fine wife."

"You have told me this many times, Geffrey. I believe I understand. She might even produce many fine children, eh?" Jodocus said and winked.

"That as well, old man."

Although he could barely see Jodocus, Geffrey noticed the man sported a broad smile.

"Are you afraid?" Jodocus said.

"Of course. More excited than afraid. But the thought of death has crossed my mind, yes it has. The thought of never seeing Adela again weighs heavy on my spirit, Jo-

docus. I have to be honest with you. Your friendship and
that of Jubal's has given me something I never thought I
would own. And that is the love and respect of men other
than my father. And I cannot begin to describe how that
makes me feel."

He paused momentarily then continued.

"I love you and Jubal. I may not have the opportunity
to say this to you again but you have meant the world to
me. I would give my life for you, if necessary."

"I feel the same way, my friend. I was lost in the
mines until I met you. But not to worry, we will not die. I
do not believe it is our time. Not yet."

"I do hope you're right, Jodocus."

❧❧❧

The crossing didn't last long for right before dawn the
wind changed direction again, booming out of the north.
The fleet was forced parallel along the French coast until
it reached the safety of Saint Valery where William
weighed anchor.

Once again a storm blew and prevented the fleet from
sailing. Days past and the weather didn't clear. William
was losing patience.

Geffrey and Jodocus paced the deck of the Maiden,
hoping any minute the sky would clear.

"The weather might clear, Jodocus," Geffrey said as
the morning dawned gray, with low black clouds threatening rain blowing in on a north wind. "Is it possible that
God himself is trying to tell us that this invasion doesn't
have his blessing? That although it has the Pope's, He
does not condone it? Is that what is happening?"

"How should I know, my friend? I am not a man of
the cloth. Not a theologian. I do know the ship smells of
a pigsty. The men are grumbling. I can only imagine

what Jubal must be thinking. If we don't cross the Channel and soon there's going to be hell to pay."

Gaylord appeared on deck and issued an order.

"The duke wishes all men to be assembled on the shore after the evening meal," he said.

"What's up?" Geffrey said.

"Don't know. But it's an order. Be there."

Gaylord turned to leave but Geffrey stopped him.

"I have heard the storm wrecked many ships," he said. "That many lives were lost."

"Sadly, it is true," Gaylord said. "The duke is distraught. Be on shore later."

"What's it about do you think?" Geffrey asked Jodocus after Gaylord left the ship.

"Could be anything. I hope it's not another Mass. Another one of those and I'll be the most religious squire in the cavalry."

"Ha, that's funny, Jodocus. I guess we'll find out soon enough."

After supper, the soldiers gathered on a great expanse of sand. Torches burned bright giving light to the meeting. Geffrey and Jodocus stood at the side of the gathering with their cavalry unit.

William stood on a flat rock. He had a container beneath his feet. What was in it? Geffrey wondered.

William raised his arms to the heavens. "Listen to me, you Norman warriors!" his bass voice boomed. "Tonight we are marooned on this small spit of land called Saint Valery. We wonder if our Father in Heaven has abandoned us. We pray for fair weather." William stooped and picked up the box and signaled to two men who took the box and began circulating among the gathering.

"Look upon the bones of Saint Valery," William continued. "When you do, each of you utter a silent prayer for the weather to change and allow our crossing. Saint Valery lived the Benedictine Rule perfectly."

As the bones of the venerated monk moved among the men, Geffrey reflected on their chances of success. If the prayers were successful, maybe they were even. At best. Duke William was a believer of the effect of holy relics on people, so he had the bones of Saint Valery exhumed from their resting place in the church and had them carried in procession through the men.

"It was soon visible to all," William continued, "that God destined Saint Valery for some high purpose in the Church. He left this place for a more distant monastery where he lived a life more angelic than human. A rich lord of the region, after talking with him one day, disposed of his entire fortune without even returning home, to embrace religious poverty."

When Geffrey looked upon the dried desiccated remains of the monk, a new conviction renewed his spirit. Maybe everything would work out for the best.

The following morning the rains stopped. The winds changed—now they blew from the south. The tide was outgoing. It was time to sail.

Geffrey gathered with the army for William's parting orders. They stood on the beach while he stood high on the gunwale of the Mora. The morning sun glinted off his steel helmet and his chain mail.

"My friends," he said. "We stand here on the precipice of a great journey. Normans! Bravest of nations! I have no doubt of your courage, and none of your victory, which never by any chance or obstacle escaped your efforts. If indeed you had, once only, failed to conquer, there might be a need now to inflame your courage by exhortation, but your native spirit does not require to be roused. Bravest of men, what could the power of the Frankish King effect with all his people, from Lorraine to

Spain, against Hastings my predecessor? What he wanted of France he took, and gave to the King only what he pleased. What he had, he held as long as it suited him, and relinquished it only for something better. Did not Rollo my ancestor, founder of our nation, with our fathers conquer at Paris the King of the Franks in the heart of his kingdom, nor had the King of the Franks any hope of safety until he humbly offered his daughter and possession of the country, which, after you, is called Normandie.

"Did not your fathers capture the King of the Franks at Rouen, and keep him there until he restored Normandie to Duke Richard, then a boy with this condition—that, in every conference between the King of France and the Duke of Normandie, the duke should wear his sword, while the King should not be permitted to carry a sword nor even a dagger. This concession your fathers compelled the great King to submit to, as binding forever. Did not the same duke lead your fathers to Mirmande, at the foot of the Alps, and enforce submission from the lord of the town, his son-in-law, to his own wife, the duke's daughter? Nor was it enough for you to conquer men, he conquered the devil himself, with whom he wrestled, cast down and bound him with his hands behind his back, and left him a shameful spectacle to angels. But why do I talk of former times? Did not you, in our own time, engage the Franks at Mortemer? Did not the Franks prefer flight to battle, and use their spurs? While you reaped the honor and the spoil as the natural result of your usual success. Ah! Let any one of the English whom, a hundred times, our predecessors, both Danes and Normans, have defeated in battle, come forth and show that the race of Rollo ever suffered a defeat from his time until now, and I will withdraw conquered. Is it not, therefore, shameful that a people accustomed to be conquered, a people ignorant of war, a people even without arrows, should proceed in order of battle against you, my brave men? Is it not a shame that King Harold, perjured as he was in your presence, should dare to show his face to you? It is amazing to me that you have been allowed to see those who, by a horrible crime, beheaded your relations and Alfred my kinsman, and that their own heads are still on their shoulders.

"Raise your standards, my brave men! Set neither measure nor limit to your merited rage. May the lightning of your glory be seen and the thunders of your onset heard from east to west, and be ye the avengers of noble blood."

With that rousing battle speech ringing in his ears, Geffrey followed Jodocus back to the *Maiden*, where they helped prepare the ship for sailing. With the wind at their backs, the ships started out across the wide waters of the Channel once again. Geffrey thought of Adela back at the castle Caen, said a quick prayer for her continued safety, then took up a position at the rail where he could get a good look at the ships ahead of them. The sun glistened like pearls off the wakes as the ships plowed through the blue-green waters.

The weather was warm.

The sun bright.

It was September 27, 1066.

CHAPTER 33

"Land ho!" The lookout scrambled down the mast to report the sighting to the ship's captain.

Geffrey woke with a start, rubbed his eyes, and looked around for Jodocus. He found him at the rail, straining his eyes at the dark mound on the horizon. The ship's bow pushed through the waves, sending showers of spray onto the deck. The sun was high and the storm a distant memory.

"A great day for a landing," Geffrey said as he came alongside Jodocus. "Those old bones of that saint really had some power in them."

Jodocus ignored Geffrey's last comment. He smiled and nodded. "A good day," he said. "I wonder if the Brits will greet us in force."

"We may have to fight our way onshore," Geffrey said, shielding his eyes from the sun as he gazed at the spit of land in the distance.

The dark mound was now noticeably greener. With the word filtering through the ship of the impending landfall, men aboard the Maiden gathered at the rail. The soldiers created quite a buzz among themselves at the realization that the battle was close at hand. Geffrey felt a palpable excitement at the thought of finally setting foot on foreign soil and bringing William's vision to fruition. His pulse throbbed in his neck, his palms moist.

The cavalry, made up of some of the finest men and knights he had ever known, had trained daily on the plains below Château de Caen, their final maneuvers in a coordinated exercise with infantry and archers. Geffrey felt confident but this would be his first battle—he had no idea what to expect. Some of the knights who had fought alongside William in prior battles calmed the younger men's fears by laughing and joking. Geffrey wondered on which ship Jubal traveled and how his friend was faring. Would they meet up once they were on land?

Up ahead in the distance, the *Mora's* banners flew regally in the morning sunlight. A shout went out though the men.

The first ships had reached shore.

The rest of the day and evening was spent involved in the agonizing chore of off loading the ships. Men, horses, equipment, armor, weapons, foodstuffs, grain—every item needed to support a massive invasion was unloaded and stacked on shore. The commanders were in charge of keeping everything organized and placed with their respective units.

When the *Maiden* came close to shore, Geffrey and Jodocus jumped over its side and ran to the beach. Geffrey knelt and ran his hand through the sand feeling its warmth. Gaylord happened by them, stood over Geffrey. He looked at his commander, the sun silhouetting the man against the azure late afternoon sky.

"What is this place called?" Geffrey said. "Do you know?"

"Yes," Gaylord said, kneeling beside him. "It is called Pevensey. We tracked in an almost straight north direction. Our ships made good time."

"Where are the Saxons?" Jodocus said. "Why aren't they here to greet us? Why aren't they here to fight?"

"That I don't know." Gaylord said. "It is odd to be sure. I am on my way to a commander's meeting so maybe there will be news. Stay with the unit till I return."

Later, Gaylord gathered his cavalry around him. Geffrey and Jodocus listened to what news he brought.

"Apparently," Gaylord said, "the Saxons have been busy. They have been fighting north of here as the Norsemen attacked. There was serious fighting but they managed to kill and repulse the invaders. But Harold surely knows we are here and in all likelihood is making his way back here to greet us. It will be a long march for him and his army. They will be tired. It will give us an advantage."

One of the knights raised a question.

"Will we wait her for them to arrive or what, Commander?"

"We will move inland and set up our bivouac. It will be a late supper tonight. Tomorrow, the duke wants to push forward and seek out the Saxons. If we locate them, we will engage."

The cavalry unit busied itself in relative quiet as the men moved their horses, equipment, and weapons beyond the shore to the lush green interior of England. Geffrey was lost in his own thoughts and he surmised that each man was the same. Thinking of home, hearth, and family. That night, around a dwindling campfire, Geffrey pressed Jodocus about his family.

"Under the Roman emperor Otto, Silesia became incorporated into Poland. Life wasn't bad until Casimir became ruler. A civil war erupted and Casimir fled and Silesia came under Bohemian rule. Casimir, who fled earlier, returned and began pillaging the countryside. We Silesians, aided by the Bohemians, fought back.

"My wife and I grew weary of the constant fighting. Our daughter and granddaughter lived with us as my son-in-law was killed in a skirmish with Casimir's troops. So, we began our westward journey. At first we lived off the land, catching small game in snares I laid out. But as time went on, the food became scarcer and my wife took sick. My daughter, Kristina, had knowledge of medicinal leaves and roots so she made her a tea of some ground roots. It tasted terrible but after several days my wife's condition improved. Enough for us to continue our journey. We had no idea where we were heading, just away from all the war and fighting.

"We were camped along a beautiful stream when they came. Out of the north they rode. It seemed as if their destriers snorted fire for smoke billowed from their flared nostrils. They swooped down upon us and before you knew it my wife, daughter, and grandson were gone. Just like that. In a twinkling of an eye. The Norsemen that remained bound me, threw me backward on a horse, sold me at the Remmelsberg mines. I think I was there ten years before we made our escape."

"A lot of us have similar stories, Jodocus. But we are blessed to be here at this moment in history. I have a feeling our presence here will be remembered by the Saxons for a long time to come."

ၔၣၔၣ

Harold's army, although victorious at Stamford Bridge, was weakened by the fatigue of the march and by the losses suffered in the battle. Harold himself was wounded, though not so severely as to prevent his continuing to exercise his command. He pressed on toward the south with great energy, sending messages into the surrounding country, calling upon the villagers to arm themselves, and to join his army with all possible dispatch. He hoped to advance so rapidly to the southern coast as to surprise William before he was aware of their approach and could fully entrench himself in his camp.

Along the way however, William sent out small recon-
noitering parties of horsemen on all the roads leading
northward, that they might bring him intelligence of the
first approach of the enemy. Harold's advanced guard,
seeing these parties, sped back to the camp to give the
news to Harold.

The hope of surprising William evaporated.

Harold found, as he drew near the enemy, to his utter
surprise and happiness, that his forces were four times as
numerous as William's. It would, of course, be madness
for him to attack an enemy in his entrenchments with
such a weary force, no matter their superior numbers.
The only alternative left him was either to retreat or take
some strong position and fortify his army. In doing so, he
might be able to resist the invaders and arrest their advance.

Some of Harold's counselors advised him not to hazard a battle at all, but to fall back toward the country's
interior, carrying with him or destroying everything
which could afford sustenance or aid to William's army.
A scorched earth in retreat. This would soon reduce William's army to great distress for want of food, for it
would have been impossible for him to transport large
quantities of supplies across the Channel. In addition, this
plan would compel William to make so many predatory
excursions among the more distant villages and towns,
where the inhabitants would become incensed and join
Harold's army in great numbers. Harold listened to these
counsels, but said, after consideration, that he could never adopt such a plan. He could not be so derelict to his
duty as to lay waste a country that he was under obligations to protect and save.

In the end, Harold decided on giving William battle. It
was not necessary, however, for him to attack the invader. He perceived that if he should take a strong position

and fortify it, William would have to attack him, since his army could not remain indefinitely on the shore without adequate support from his rear. Harold chose a position six or seven miles from William's camp. Neither army was in sight of the other nor knew the numbers, disposition, or plans of the other. The country between them erupted into one of consternation and terror. No villager knew at what point the two vast clouds of danger and destruction that were hovering near them would meet, or over what regions the terrible storm which was to burst forth would sweep in its destructive fury. The inhabitants, therefore, went scurrying about in dismay, moving the aged and the helpless by any means available. They took with them such treasures as they could carry. They hid in rude and uncertain places of concealment. The region that lay between the two encampments became one of quiet and emptiness.

As soon as Harold had completed his encampment, he expressed a desire for his commander to ride across the intermediate country and take a view of William's lines. The only danger was of being pursued by a detachment of horsemen from the camp or surrounded by an ambush. To guard against these dangers, Harold and his commander took the most powerful horses in the camp. He called out a small but strong guard of well-selected men to escort them. They rode over to the enemy's front lines, advanced so near that, from a small hill, they could survey the whole scene of William's encampment. Harold was astonished by what he saw—the palisades and embankments with which it was guarded, extended for miles. The long lines of tents within, the vast multitude of soldiers, the knights and officers riding to and fro, glittering with steel, and the grand pavilion of the duke himself, with the consecrated banner of the cross floating above it. Harold couldn't believe his eyes. He had never seen such a spectacle.

After gazing on this scene for some time in silence, Harold said that perhaps, after all, the policy of falling back would have been the wisest for them to adopt, rather than to risk a battle with so overwhelming a force as they saw before them. He did not know but that it would be best for them to change their plan, and adopt that policy now. But, his commander said it was too late. They had taken their stand, and now for them to break up their encampment and retire would be considered a retreat and not a maneuver. It would discourage and dishearten Harold's entire army and those families within Briton.

After surveying the situation and extent of William's encampment, Harold's party returned to their own lines, still determined to make a stand there against the invaders, but feeling great doubt and despondency in respect to the result. Harold sent over in the course of the day, a number of spies. The men whom he employed for this purpose were Normans by birth. These Norman spies disguised themselves, and mingled, without attracting attention, among the thousands of workmen and camp followers that were coming and going continually around William's encampment. They did this so effectively, that they examined the whole of the fortification. When they returned to Harold with their report, they gave a formidable account of the numbers and condition of William's troops. There was a large corps of bowmen in the army, who had shaved their faces and heads in such a manner that the spies thought they were priests.

They told Harold, accordingly, that there were more priests in William's camp than there were soldiers in all his army.

∽∾∽

William's moment had arrived. The bastard son had accomplished the improbable—he had landed an enormous army on Saxon soil. Now, it was time for the impossible. It was time to vanquish the enemy.

Years of thinking and planning followed by months of arduous work by thousands of supporters got him to this day. He and his trusted advisors thought out every conceivable contingency, every possible complication and incorporated them into the battle plan. He was prepared and confident.

He knew the upcoming battle was just the beginning. After defeating Harold's army he would need to conquer the entire country, a task, he sensed, that would be more formidable than the battle with Harold. However, according to his spies, he had superior numbers, so victory should be theirs.

William wished to write Matilda and Adela a letter but was so anxious for the arrival of dawn he decided against it. Better wait until the battle was won. Soon after their marriage, the Pope expressed his displeasure at this marriage between cousins and excommunicated them. William indignantly appealed to the Pope who finally relented but with conditions. They must build two abbeys. And so William founded St. Stephen's Abbey for monks, and Matilda, the Abbaye-aux-Dames for nuns. King Philip I of France treated William's idea of annexing England as absurd, even had the temerity to ask him who would be left in charge of Normandy while he was running a kingdom. To this William confidently replied that he had Matilda and his subjects, who were capable of securing the duchy during his absence. He hoped his wife would not let him down.

Before retiring for the night, William knelt beside his cot and said a prayer, asking God for His protection. It was short and to the point.

"O God, You are the preserver of men, and the keeper of our lives. We commit ourselves to Your perfect care on the journey that awaits us. We pray for a safe and auspicious journey.

Give Your angels charge over us to keep us in all our ways. Let no evil befall us, nor any harm come to our dwelling that we leave behind. Although we are uncertain of what the days may bring, may we be prepared for any event or delay, and greet such with patience and understanding.

Bless us O Lord, that we may complete our journey safely and successfully under Your ever watchful care."

CHAPTER 34

Geffrey stood with William's commanders under the rustling canvas of the duke's bright colored tent. He didn't know why but Gaylord wanted him to accompany him to the meeting. The sun was high and warm and Geffrey, perspiring heavily under his chainmail tunic, was thankful for the shade the tent provided. William paced as he gave his orders.

"We will continue offloading the ships for the rest of the day," he said. "By nightfall everything should be on shore and stacked in organized areas. As you know, we brought three dismantled wooden castles with us on the ships, each ready to be erected. They are all shaped and pierced to receive the pins that we brought with us, cut and ready in large barrels on board one of the ships.

"I want the infantry to help the support crews in erecting one of the castles up near that grove of trees there." He pointed to a small copse of trees several hundred yards inland. "We need to get it up and the stores moved into it before supper tonight. The cavalry will ride sentry duty and create a safe perimeter within which we can work. Once that is accomplished, we will eat and thank God for a safe journey. Any questions?"

Merek spoke. "Any news of the Saxons? They seem to be absent. I fully expected them to be here in full arms to greet us."

"Our spies have not returned," William said. "Maybe by supper will have some news. Anything else?"

There was nothing.

"All right then," William said, "let's get to work."

The rest of the day was spent unloading the hundreds of ships, a massive undertaking in itself. The longboats were brought close to shore a dozen at a time where their contents were offloaded into small skiffs where their contents were stacked on land.

As Geffrey saddled Midnight, the destrier pranced as though thankful to be on firm footing. Geffrey jumped into the saddle and rode to join the other knights and receive his orders from Gaylord.

Geffrey headed north for a few miles keeping a sharp eye out for Saxons then turned east. The soft breeze from the Channel cooled him as he rode. As he approached a thicket of bushes he heard a rustling sound. He reined up, listened. Hearing nothing more, he continued on.

There it was again. A rustling. This time there was also the sound of a horse pawing the hard ground. He kicked Midnight closer to the thicket, drew his sword.

"Come out of there," Geffrey commanded.

No one emerged from the clump of bushes.

"Outta there or I'll run my sword through you," Geffrey said impatiently.

The thicket rustled again and a disheveled man appeared, his hands held high, a sword in one of them. He wore chain mail and a tunic, no helmet. His tunic was filthy and smeared with mud.

"Throw down that sword," Geffrey commanded again.

The man looked at him with a hate-filled glare. He complied with Geffrey's order and threw his sword onto the ground.

"Now," Geffrey said, "who are you?"

The man stood silent. He glared at Geffrey.

"Answer or you won't speak another word."

"A Saxon," the man replied.

"You came to spy on us, eh?" Geffrey said. "Well, we'll see about that. Who is your commander?"

The man's eyes brightened. "King Harold," the Saxon said.

"Ho, ho!" Geffrey laughed. "My duke, who is the rightful heir to the throne of England will have something to say about that, I'm sure."

"I have seen your army," the Saxon hissed. "We outnumber you Norman dogs at least a hundred to one. You don't stand a chance in battle. Might as well surrender before you are all slaughtered."

"We will see," Geffrey said, grabbing the reins of the Saxon's horse. "Now, move along with you. The duke will want to see the prize I bring him."

Geffrey pushed the man southward back toward the Norman encampment. The man stumbled over the rough terrain while Geffrey led his horse behind them. Once William's brightly colored tent came into view, his soldier's let out a shout, ran to greet them. They talked wildly and gathered around Geffrey and the Saxon.

William stepped from his tent as Geffrey dismounted and pushed the man toward the duke.

"Sir Geffrey," William said in an excited tone, "who is this?"

"A Saxon prisoner, my lord. I thought you might wish to interrogate this spy. He comes here from Harold's army."

"You don't say?" William said. He stuck his face in the Saxon's and sneered. "What do you have to say for yourself, Saxon?" he said.

"You Norman dogs," the Saxon said, spitting out the words as if they were poison on his lips, "will burn in hell after we slaughter each and every last one of you. Our God will see to that."

"Your God?" William scoffed. "We pray to the same God, Saxon. Do you think he values your lives over ours?

"Satan has a special place for you," the Saxon prisoner said. "You will see him sooner than you think."

"Where is Harold?" William said. "I am here as the rightful heir to the throne. I wish to avoid bloodshed."

Geffrey noticed the man's quick glance to the north-east.

"He waits for you," the Saxon snarled. "He waits."

William turned and addressed one of his commanders.

"Put this man in irons and guard him. Do not let him out of your sight. We march as soon as the castle is built."

William headed the march along England's southern shoreline heading eastward over a road abandoned by the Romans centuries earlier. The sun was warm and bright for an October day and Geffrey rode alongside Gaylord basking in the day's warmth. Once, he glanced over his shoulder and noticed the soldiers and support crews stretching out for miles behind them. What a grand accomplishment, he thought, to move all these people and supplies across the sea.

In the late afternoon, two of William's scouts came galloping up and reined their chargers to a stop. William halted and the entire column came to a stop while the scouts gave their reports.

"My lord, there is a small fishing village not far up ahead," one of the scouts said. "A few women and children are about. The men seem to have vanished."

"What is the name of this village?" William inquired. He strained in his saddle for a better look ahead.

"The small sign on the village's outskirts said Hastings, sire. The village is called Hastings."

William turned, nodded at Gaylord.

"Sir Gaylord," he said in a matter-of-fact tone, "split your cavalry into two divisions. Have one of them circle to the north and approach the village. The other will continue on this road. Kill anyone that you meet or that resists and burn every home and building."

"Have you noticed the peasants fleeing our advance, sire?" Gaylord said. "They know we are here."

William nodded. "It matters not," he said. "I want this village sacked and burned. No one is to escape alive. Bring me a few of the women. I wish to find out where Harold is lurking, waiting for us."

"Yes, my liege," Gaylord said and turned horse to give the orders.

"When the village is no more, we will erect the other castle and make our encampment there," William said.

To Geffrey's right or south was the Channel, while to his left or north was a series of wooded rolling hills interspersed with thickets. After getting Gaylord's order to proceed northward, Geffrey kicked his destrier into a trot and joined the others of the northbound division. His pulse quickened at the thought of confronting the Saxon enemy. His group rode to the north of the fishing village then turned south and spread out into a single line. Geffrey drew his sword. His mouth was dry.

A few women and children sprang from hiding places in the thickets and began running in all directions. Their screams and yells pierced the otherwise quiet afternoon.

Geffrey spotted a young woman fleeing with a small child. He kicked Midnight into a gallop and ran them down. Once he was upon them, he wielded his sword in an arc and slashed the woman's neck. She fell to the ground bleeding. Her young son veered off to the east forcing Geffrey to run him over with his charger. He glanced over his shoulder—neither woman nor boy moved.

The other knights found similar targets for their swords and cut them down as they fled. Geffrey located another woman holding two babies in her arms and he quickly ran them through with his sword, killing all three.

The line of knights pressed into the village of Hastings and soon met up with Gaylord's division. The homes and other buildings were aflame. Black smoke billowed into the brilliant blue sky, soot choking Geffrey's lungs. Only an occasional scream was heard over the roaring flames. Two knights stood nearby with three young women at sword point. Waiting for William, Geffrey surmised.

It had taken less than a half an hour and the village of Hastings was no more. The knights queued up in what was the village center and waited for William to arrive. Geffrey dismounted and stood by Midnight stroking the animal's nose and patting his neck, calming the charger with a soothing word.

A realization hit him like a whirlwind. Standing in the middle of the carnage and firestorm brought back a nightmare, the morning the Norse marauders ransacked and pillaged Lochwald. *My god!* He was part of a slaughter that was no different than the one that killed his father and scattered his mother and Rosalind, to where he couldn't know. His stomach convulsed at the realization that he was no different than the Norsemen he reviled. He fought the urge to vomit but it was no use.

He stumbled to the nearest tree; stood behind it; and vomited a thin, dark green, foul-tasting bile. The thought of what he had done sickened him but he knew it was what William had ordered. Had not he volunteered for this? Had he not sought the glory of battle? But the wholesale slaughter of innocents was not what he envisioned. But it might be the only way, he reasoned, to win the country for the new king. Could their Christian God, the God of the pope who had given his sanction for this quest, approve of the wholesale slaughter of innocent women and children? The problem was too complicated for his rattled brain at the moment to figure out.

William rode up and began barking orders as to where he wanted the castle to be erected. The three women were brought before him. They looked frightened as if they knew they would later be killed.

"Do any of you know where Harold and his army are located?" William said.

One of the women looked at William with sad eyes. She pointed to the north. "To the north," she said. "About ten kilometers. A place called Senlac Ridge. They are well fortified. You will all die."

"We shall see," William said.

"You will kill us now?" one of the other women said.

"I haven't decided as yet," the duke said. "Place them in irons with the other prisoners and take them away."

Later that evening Geffrey found Gaylord alone and wanted to talk to his commander.

"What is it?" Gaylord said, lounging in his cot in the commander's tent.

"I'm sick, sir. Was it imperative that we kill all those women and children? I mean they weren't combatants or anything."

Gaylord looked at him with sympathetic eyes. "Geffrey," he said, "sometimes it is necessary to do things we hate, or that are morally reprehensible to some people, for the greater good. You need to understand this. These Britons have been subjugated and lorded over ever since this Harold crowned himself king. We may have killed a few but, in the end, the country will be better served under William's rule."

"But I killed helpless women and children, Gaylord. Just like the Norse marauders who ransacked my village and killed my father. Possibly my mother. How does what we did today advance William's moral imperative?"

"I don't try and understand it," the knight said. "I just don't think about it."

CHAPTER 35

King Harold stood on an outcropping of Senlac Ridge and gazed down the sloping hill toward William's army. Dawn was an hour away and, in the distance, the fires of the Norman encampment flickered like tiny fireflies. He rose early, unable to sleep, and wandered alone to this jut of land, attempting to collect his thoughts.

He remembered approaching Stamford Bridge, moving his army into position. Before the battle commenced, Harold sent one of his officers to his brother, Tostig and offered him the title of earl of Northumbria if he would desert. With neither side willing to yield, the army advanced and began the battle. The Norse outposts on the west bank of the River Derwent fought a rearguard action to allow the rest of the army to prepare.

A desperate delaying action by the Norwegian outposts kept the Saxons from crossing the Derwent while the main army frantically donned their gear and took up position. One anonymous Norwegian held the bridge alone until he was stabbed from beneath the planks of the bridge with a long spear. The Norse formed a shield wall in the shape of a triangle, to present a narrow front. The Saxons battered at the wall in a fierce hand-to-hand fight that lasted all day, before the legendary Harald Hardrada was felled by a Saxon missile. Earl Tostig tried vainly to rally the demoralized men, but the Norse resistance crumbled and the battle became a rout. Pushing across the bridge, Harold's army reformed and charged the Norse line. A prolonged melee ensued with Hardrada falling after being struck by an arrow.

With Hardrada slain, Tostig continued the fight, aided by reinforcements. As sunset approached, both Tostig and his commander were killed. Lacking a leader, the Norse ranks began to waver and they were forced back to their ships.

Harold's army suffered a large number of killed and wounded. Hardrada's was nearly destroyed. But the long march from Stamford Bridge to Senlac Ridge left his troops exhausted and Harold wondered if they had enough left in them to face William.

He turned and ambled back to his command tent at the rear of the bulwarks. Harold knew his army vastly outnumbered William's but the condition of his men worried him. It wasn't their willingness to fight that he doubted, for they had proven that many times over. No, it was the constant war, the constant fighting that he knew would eventually take its toll on a man's spirit. Sooner or later, they would want to return home to see their families, their wives. To face the Normans so soon after Stamford Bridge and the forced march to their present location was a condition his troops had never before faced. He prayed all would go well.

His commanders and advisors gathered in his tent as the sky was beginning to turn a dirty gray. Most were dressed in their chain mail and held their helmets at their side.

"A bad day for a battle," Harold began. "I wish the men had more time to rest but the Norman dogs won't give us the opportunity, you can count on that. What is the latest report on their troop placements?"

A sleepy soldier stepped forward, ran a hand through his dirty hair.

"They are spread out at the bottom of the hill, sire," he said. "The Bretons on the west end while the Flemish are on the east. The Normans occupy the center. Archers on their flanks and cavalry at the rear of the infantry."

"Rouse the men," Harold said. "I have a feeling there will be an early start to this battle. Be sure and have them eat something. This may turn out to be a long day."

Alone in his tent once again, Harold reflected on events that led William to Senlac Ridge with his army. When Edward the Confessor died he left no direct heir. Harold, through some calling-in of favors and chicanery, got himself elected King of England. William claimed that, before his death, Edward promised the throne to him. And now he was on English soil to claim his title as king.

When Harold was shipwrecked near Normandie, he became a guest, if not a prisoner, of Duke William. Harold was forced to take an oath to the effect that he would marry William's daughter thus reinforcing William's claim to the crown of England. William then allowed Harold to return to England. Harold was now betraying that oath. He justified himself on the grounds that his oath to William of Normandie was taken under duress and therefore invalid. William protested against what he referred to as the bad faith of Harold and proclaimed his intention to assert his rights in battle by the sword.

In his heart, Harold realized that Edward, in all likelihood, did promise the throne to William, as the duke was always a favorite of the king. This knowledge infuriated Harold beyond his ability to rationally cope with the rejection. In fact, he despised William. After duke amassed a large army while in Normandie, William devoted his early adult life to enforcing his authority in a succession of ruthless campaigns, meanwhile building his dukedom into a fearsome mini-state, efficient both administratively and militarily. Harold knew his greatest mistake would be to take William for granted and assume his army was nothing more than a group of ill-trained guttersnipes.

He mounted his charger and rode back to the head of the front. Harold's brother, Gurth, joined him. Harold smiled as they sat on their destriers and looked down at the Normans.

"My brother, my king," Gurth said. "Take this last moment to reconsider this battle. I beg you to return to London and gather your army there with reinforcements from the realm. If William chooses to move toward London, you would prevail. Either by force or by starvation once his stores run out, William would be defeated."

"Gurth, my dear brother," Harold said. "I cannot. My blood is up, and I am eager for this fight. I will destroy the Norman dog here this day. I will not be persuaded otherwise."

"Then do me this favor," Gurth pressed. "You cannot not deny that, either by force or free will, thou made Duke William an oath on the bodies of saints. Why then risk yourself in the battle with a perjury hanging over you? To us, who have sworn nothing, this is a holy and just war, for we are fighting for our country. Leave us then alone to fight this battle, and he who has the right will win."

"I cannot look on while others risk their lives for their king," Harold said. "You would not do so yourself if you were in my place. My men would deem me a coward and blame me for sending them where I refused to go. Therefore, my precious brother, I will fight and fight in person. Besides, our position here is a good one. We have the woods at our back and I have ordered sharpened stakes along the front of the line and a ditch between the Normans and us. And they will have to charge uphill, always an unenviable tactic."

King Harold and his Saxon army had made camp seven miles outside Hastings at Senlac. He had no cavalry and only a few archers but they struck a defensive position at Senlac and formed a tight shield wall with their battle-axes at the ready. Their main weapons were the Danish battle-axe, a two-handed, long-handled battle-axe with a heavy chopping head, and a long double-edged sword.

ଏ୨ଏ୨

Adela finished her bath, rubbed perfumed oil on her skin, and wrapped herself in a luxurious soft robe. Rawanda brought her a cup of warmed glögg, a mixture of wine, sugar, and spices. She sipped the drink as she lounged on her bed thinking of Geffrey. Her lady-in-waiting stood beside her bed, an expectant look in her face.

"Yes, Rawanda?" Adela said. "You may speak. I know that look."

"I was wondering, my lady," her maid said, "if you have received word from the duke or Sir Geffrey?"

"Not since they sailed for England. And I suspect I won't hear anything until after the campaign is over. Both Sir Geffrey and Father wrote while they were at Dives-sur-Mer."

"This Sir Geffrey, my lady, you love him?"

"With all I can muster, Rawanda. He is the sun and moon of my life."

"And you will be sad if something happens to him in the battle?"

"Rawanda! Hush your mouth. My life would be over if Geffrey did not return. Father, too."

"He is a good man, yes?"

"Who Father or Sir Geffrey?"

Rawanda laughed and easy laugh. "Sir Geffrey, of course."

"He is a very good man, the best. He has honor—he fought Frederic for my honor. He made the sword he gave Father. Rawanda, it is the most beautiful weapon you have ever seen. Father took it with him."

"Have you…you…you know…"

"Rawanda!" Adela said, her voice rose in surprise. "Shame on you. No, we haven't. But—" She stopped, contemplated the possibility, and then laughed. "Someday."

Rawanda left her alone. She sipped her glögg and her mind rested on her maid's risqué suggestion. The battle was won and Geffrey was back at Château de Caen. The wedding ceremony was finished and they basked in a hidden meadow under the afternoon sun and out of sight of prying eyes. He took her in his arms, kissed her gently on her lips, felt her breast. She thought her heart would explode.

Slowly, Geffrey unbuttoned her bodice and kissed her neck. His lips felt as if they were hot coals on her skin. He kissed again, this time lower. Her head was in a tailspin.

There was a knock at the door.

She sat up, struggled to focus.

"Yes?" she said in a faltering voice, her mind still lingering on Geffrey.

It was Rawanda. "I'm sorry, my lady, but I thought you would want to know."

"What, Rawanda?"

"The battle, my lady. It has begun."

CHAPTER 36

Geffrey and Gaylord stood in Duke William's tent as he outlined his plan. The sun was breaking the horizon sending shards of gold and red into a pale violet sky. A light breeze rustled the tent's walls.

"I want you two to take a small cadre of knights under a flag of truce and go to see Harold. Take this offer of peace. Tell Harold that I have no desire to fight a battle if it can be avoided. Tell him that if what I consider as rightfully my kingdom can be delivered to me without bloodshed, that is what is preferable to me. And that I am determined to make one final effort to obtain a peaceable surrender of it, before coming to the dreadful resort of an appeal to arms."

Geffrey wondered if they would survive such a mission—riding into the enemy encampment. He shot a smirk toward Gaylord who shrugged. William continued.

"Here are the propositions I make so that Harold might avoid battle. It is up to him to choose one of the following options. First, that he should surrender the kingdom to me as he had solemnly sworn to do over the sacred relics in Normandy. Second, that we should both agree to refer the whole subject of controversy between us over to the pope and abide by his decision. Or third, that we would settle the dispute by single combat, the two claimants to the crown to fight a duel on the plain, in presence of their respective armies."

"My Lord Duke," Gaylord said. "Do you think the man will accept any of these terms?"

William smiled a wry grin. "It is obvious that Harold cannot accept any of these propositions. The first gives up the whole point at issue. As for the second, the pope has already prejudged the case, and if it were to be referred to him, there could be no doubt that he would simply reaffirm his former decision. And in respect to single combat, the disadvantage on Harold's part would be as great in such a contest as it would be in the proposed arbitration. He is himself a man of comparatively slender form and of little bodily strength, while I, on the other hand, am much larger and stronger."

Gaylord and Geffrey mounted their destriers and rode north toward the Saxon lines. They wore their chain mail and helmets, their swords and shields at their sides. With the sun beating down on their heavy armor, Geffrey found himself perspiring as they rode along.

"Do you think this mission will be successful, Gaylord?" Geffrey said.

"I doubt it. Why would the man just hand over his kingdom to the duke without a fight? If it were me, I would go down fighting."

"Wouldn't the duke be generous if he acquiesced? Provide him with an estate?"

"That's hardly the same as King of England, is it?"

"I suppose not. But I have found the duke to be a warm generous man," Geffrey said as they approached Harold's encampment.

"Don't let that calm exterior fool you, Geffrey. Underneath that warm, sensitive facade beats the heart of a ferocious tiger. I have seen him when provoked. Be glad you haven't been on the receiving end of his anger."

"I hope they don't take us for spies and kill us before we've delivered the message," Geffrey said.

When they reached the Saxon bulwarks, Geffrey noticed the condition of Harold's army. His men looked
haggard, exhausted. It didn't appear they were eager to
fight.

Two soldiers escorted them to Harold's command tent
at the rear of the bulwarks. The king looked small, hardly
presenting a commanding presence, Geffrey thought. A
stark contrast to William.

Gaylord saluted King Harold and in a terse clipped
voice presented William's proposals and hope that war
could be averted. When he was finished outlining them,
Harold sat silent for a few moments before he let out with
a hearty laugh.

They received Harold's courteous answer to William's
propositions—hell no. Forget them. The Saxons would
fight.

On the ride back, Geffrey commented on the Saxon
army. "They looked exhausted, Gaylord. I didn't see a
single man that looked like he was eager for a fight."

"They repulsed the Norsemen on their north shores recently then underwent a forced march to get here. It's no
wonder they are tired. Too bad Harold didn't accept the
duke's offers."

When they reported back to the duke, he was not surprised. He paced in his tent. "I wish you to return with
one more proposal. If Harold consents to acknowledge
me as King of England, I will assign the whole territory
to him and to his brother Gurth, to hold as provinces, under my general rule. Under this arrangement, I will return
to Normandie and make the city of Rouen, the capital of
the whole united realm. However, if he still persists in
refusing my offers, then you shall tell him, before all his
people, that he is a perjurer and a liar. That he and all
who shall support him are excommunicated by the mouth

of the pope, and that the decree to that effect is in my hands."

The two knights rode out again, carrying William's proposal to Harold who, once again, turned it down. One of his advisors expressed sentiment for all who heard William's offer.

"We must fight, whatever may be the danger to us. For what we have to consider is not whether we shall accept and receive a new lord, as if our king were dead. The case is quite the opposite. The Norman has already given our lands to his captains, to his knights, to all his people, the greater part of who have already done homage to him for them. That said, they will all look for their gift if their duke become our king and he himself is bound to deliver up to them our goods, our wives, and our daughters. All is promised to them beforehand. You come, not only to ruin us, but to ruin our descendants also, and to take from us the country of our ancestors. And what shall we do? Whither shall we go, when we have no longer a country?"

This time, however, Harold had a proposal of his own. He was willing, he said, to compromise the dispute, so far as it could be, done by the payment of money. If William would abandon his invasion and return to Normandie, giving up his claims to the English crown, Harold would pay him any sum of money that he would name.

When Gaylord delivered Harold's proposal, William burst out in a fit of laughter. "Is the man serious? Daft? I cannot accept this proposal," he bellowed. "I am the true and rightful heir to the throne of England, and there is a point of honor involved here as well as a dictate of my own personal ambition, which I freely acknowledge, to be obeyed. Now, while these days have passed in fruitless negotiations, my officers and counselors begin to be uneasy at the delay. They say that every hour new reinforcements are coming into Harold's camp while we are gaining no advantage. As a result, the longer the battle is delayed, the less is the certainty of victory. So, we will attack King Harold in his camp at daybreak."

Gaylord and Geffrey looked at each other, a gratified look on their faces.

"Prepare your men," William said. "Tomorrow will be a busy day."

ഇൗഇൗ

Near Hastings, 14 October 1066:

Geffrey was up long before sunrise, unable to sleep. Most of the men in his cavalry unit were up also, warming themselves around the campfire. The morning was chilly with a hint of frost in the air. Jodocus labored getting Midnight saddled and ready for the upcoming battle. The stallion snorted and pawed the ground as if sensing what was about to unfold and his role in it.

As the men talked softly among themselves, Geffrey looked out over the encampment, noticed other fires with other groups of men gathered around them. An eerie silence hovered over the camp, the hushed tones of conversation centered on the battle and possible death. Sobering words. Not the usual raucous chatter of knights.

William appeared in their midst, dressed in his finest white tunic and trousers, his chain mail gleaming from the light of the nearby fire. His sword, Halvor, hung loosely on his hip, its jeweled hilt glittering. He strode to Geffrey, putting an arm on his shoulder.

"Walk with me, lad," he said.

When the two were out of earshot of the men, William stopped and eyed Geffrey for a silent moment.

"Today, I carry my cherished sword with me into battle, Geffrey," he said finally. "I know it will bring me luck and victory." He enveloped Geffrey in his arms, hugged him for a long moment. "You are the son I wished I had. The heir to whom I would gladly pass the throne."

Geffrey didn't know what to say to this revelation. His throat tightened, his eyes filled with tears. "But Robert. Your son—"

"Robert is a fool and spendthrift. No, you are my son, Geffrey. I came here to tell you that if I should die today—I love you. We have never spoken of it," he continued, "but I sense that you feel as I do. And Adela is wise to choose you for her husband. You both have my blessing."

William again clutched Geffrey in a tight embrace. Choking back tears, Geffrey responded and hugged the only man that he ever respected as much as his father.

After a quiet moment, the duke broke away. "Courage and honor," he said and strolled beyond the light of the campfire to the next group of soldiers.

Geffrey stood motionless for a long moment as he savored the duke's words. A lump formed in his throat. He dried his eyes and went to check on his mount.

The first order of business was to convene the army for a grand celebration of Mass. It was a curious mingling of the religious and superstitious sentiment of the times. In the spirit of war, the bishop who officiated in this solemn service wore a coat of mail under his pontifical attire. The attendant who stood by his side while he was offering his prayers, held a steel-pointed spear in his hand, ready for the battle as soon as the service ended. Accordingly, when the religious duty was performed, the bishop threw off his surplice, took the spear, and mounting his white charger, rode on to the assault of the enemy.

When Geffrey later saw William, he was struck with admiration at the splendid figure which their commander made—his large and well-formed limbs covered with steel, and his horse, whose form was as noble as that of his master, prancing restlessly, as if impatient for the battle to begin.

Geffrey found Jodocus, took the man by an arm, and stood eye to eye with him. The old man's eyes were wide, bright, expectant.

"Jodocus," he said. "I have a request to make of you. If I should die and you survive, I want you to burn my body."

"Burn your body?" Jodocus said in a surprised voice.

Geffrey nodded.

"But why?"

"I don't wish the wild dogs to dig me up or the enemy to desecrate my body, pissing on me or scattering my bones to the winds."

"I—I—" Jodocus stammered.

"Promise me, my good friend. Promise."

Jodocus's eyes filled with tears. He hugged Geffrey for a moment before releasing him. "You have my word, Geffrey," he said.

"Now, old man, the battle awaits. Courage and honor."

A trumpet sounded in the distance.

Just after the sun rose over the horizon, William's army broke camp and headed to battle. The Bretons, soldiers from west of Normandie, took the lead, followed by the Franco Flemish while the Normans brought up the rear. The march to Senlac Ridge took a little over an hour.

Harold positioned his army atop the ridge behind a wall of shields several hundred yards in length. The heavily armed housecarl were to the front while the less well-armed fyrdsmen stood at their rear. As the household troops of Harold, the housecarl owned the crucial role as the backbone of Harold's army. Although they were numerically the smaller part of Harold's army, their superior equipment and training meant Harold hoped they would strengthen the militia, or fyrd, which made up most of his troops. The housecarl formed in the center, around their leader's standard, but also in the first ranks of both flanks, with the fyrdsmen behind them. The densely packed formation was eight ranks deep. Their position was well-suited to defense, unable to be outflanked due to the steep, uneven ground on either side— any assault had to be frontal. To the front, the ground sloped away to the south making it an uphill charge for William's troops. Harold raised his standards, the Wyvern of Wessex which was a golden dragon on a red background along with his personal banner, The Fighting Man, on a slight rise near the center of the line. His personal banner was of heavy wool, needlework on canvas, a deep blue field on which a warrior, richly devised in gold wire thread, stood with a battle-axe upraised to strike. About the four borders, like the stars over the stilled field, the jewels gleamed against the faded wool.

William formed his army a little more than a hundred yards away on lower ground from the Saxon position, out of range of the few Saxon archers. The right division was made up of French and Flemish troops where they straddled the road facing Harold's left. On William's left, on flat and boggy ground there formed the Bretons. The center, twice the size of the flanks, was made up of the Normans under the delegated command of Merek of the Green Infantry. It was here that William raised his personal standard and the papal banner.

Each division split into three sections of similar composition. The first rank was composed of archers and spearmen, the second of infantry, and the third cavalry. Geffrey sat astride Midnight and gazed over the field of infantry ahead of the cavalry unit. He searched for Jubal but didn't see the giant of a man. Jodocus wanted to grab a spear or sword but neither Merek nor the other commanders wanted an old man in their unit. He was incensed but headed back to the encampment after taking his leave of Geffrey.

It had been a tearful goodbye. The old man blubbered a few nonsensical words as they hugged each other. When Geffrey mounted his stallion, the man turned, walked down the hill without looking back. He was alone with his thoughts, his skill, and his memories. Inside his gloves, he could feel the wetness of his hands, his stomach rolled, a nausea rolled over him. He fought the urge to jump down and vomit. He said a silent prayer for courage and honor.

A shout rang out and the three divisions began their slow advance up the ridge toward the Saxon line. When they got within range of the archers, they stopped and William's bowmen let loose with their arrows. Geffrey watched in awe as over two thousand arrows soared through the air. The Saxon shield wall braced for the onslaught by raising their shields over their heads. The Norman arrows fell on the shields or harmlessly elsewhere. A few of the enemy fell dead by an arrow.

To Geffrey's way of thinking they were attacking at an odd angle, more from Harold's left flank than head on.

The archer's arrows spent, they scrambled back to await resupply from the rear and the infantry moved forward. The odd angle of attack allowed their left flank, manned by the Bretons, exposed to a counterattack by Harold's forces. The Saxons moved forward engaging the Bretons, killing many of them. Fires flared on the flanks of the divisions but Geffrey was unable to see through the thick black smoke that billowed skyward, rolled down the hill. Engulfed in a thin haze of smoke and soot, his breathing became difficult. A charred taste filled his mouth.

The Saxon infantry and their axmen began butchering William's left flank. Geffrey could only watch although his heart begged to gallop to their defense. He remembered his training and held his ground with his fellow knights, waited for orders from Gaylord.

Off to his left in the distance, he heard the screams of men as they were cut down by the swords, spears, and axes. How horrible it must be, he thought to be hacked to death by a battle-axe. Or have a limb severed by a heavy blow.

At the head of the center infantry division Geffrey saw William on his white destrier conferring with a couple of commanders pointing to the west where the Saxons were having their way with his infantry. Gaylord galloped back and soon the center column of infantry and cavalry were on their way to support the routed soldiers.

CHAPTER 37

A small break in the fighting allowed William to rally his army's faltering morale while the dead and wounded were attended. Hauberks were removed from the dead for reuse in the next attack. The Saxons meanwhile, plugged any gaps in their defenses, moved their dead and wounded to the rear and piled up any dead horses in front as an added obstacle.

The second phase of the battle began around midday, which was slower and much better coordinated. Again, it began with an ineffectual archery barrage. Lasting for two hours, attack after attack was repulsed by the Saxons with the dead of both sides piling up. The bodies caused a further obstacle to the attackers. As casualties mounted, gaps began to appear in the shield wall but men rushed to quickly fill them. Shortly after noon, the French division began to falter. William galloped through the fighting holding the papal banner and moving men around. His efforts managed to halt a rout.

Geffrey's unit moved into the fray to reinforce the flank division. He kicked Midnight into a trot, headed to where he saw the Bretons being overpowered. Off to his right, William, now on foot, removed his helmet to show his face. Thank heaven, Geffrey thought. The rumor was not true—William had not been killed.

As each attack by the Saxons was repulsed, the Norman army broke ranks only to be rallied by their commanders. It was only by the strength and ability of their leaders and their training that they rallied enough to counterattack any Saxons foolish to break ranks. At this point, William ordered another withdrawal, covered by the cavalry.

In the early afternoon, Merek and Gaylord wanted a conference with William to discuss a change of tactics. Geffrey accompanied them to the duke's command post at the rear of the fighting.

"My lord," Gaylord said, his helmet under an arm, his brow covered in dust, sweat, and soot. "The situation is precarious. One quarter of our army is either dead or lies wounded. We have been fighting for five hours and our losses are mounting. The Saxon line is still intact. If our next attack fails, it is likely to be our last."

"If that happens," Merek added, "we would be slaughtered. Harold would show no mercy."

"You have analyzed the situation perfectly," William said. He still carried Halvor in his hand. Geffrey noticed the blood on its mirrored surface. "The Saxons are making their own adjustments," he continued. "They are moving their forces to the slightly higher ground toward the center and the east."

William drew a sketch of the battle area in the dirt, explaining as he did.

"So," Gaylord said, pointing, "we should attack from here. From the west."

"It would be no easy going, but that seems to be our only option," William said. He sheathed his sword, took a drink of water from an earthen jar. "How to do it?"

"I suggest, my lord," Gaylord said, "to form a single line of infantry interspersed with cavalry. Put the archers at the rear and when they fire their volleys have them land their arrows in the middle of the Saxon ranks. This morning they were way off target. They will provide the distraction and confusion we need when we engage the enemy."

"Then that is what we will do. God go with you," William said and he remounted his horse and headed to the west. "Courage and honor," he called over a shoulder.

The next wave of assaults was the fiercest of the day, each one preceded by arrows. As the Normans broke through the Saxon line, fighting was reduced to hand to hand. Geffrey rode through enemy soldiers slashing them with his sword. The smoke and haze was so thick it clogged his throat gagging him. He forced down the metal taste in his mouth.

At the far west end of the skirmish line he noticed Jubal with a sword and battle-axe. The giant man's eyes were bloodshot and there were numerous cuts and other wounds on his body. He had lost his helmet and his long dark hair was matted with blood. As he spun to engage another attacker, a Saxon plunged his sword into Jubal's midsection. Blood gushed onto the ground. Jubal looked momentarily stunned, then swung his sword on a great arc landing across the man's neck, decapitating him.

Geffrey galloped to his side, jumped off his destrier, and went to Jubal's aid but it was too late. The man lay on his back as Geffrey cradled his head in his arms. His eyes didn't move, they were fixed in a vacant stare. He gasped several times.

"Jubal," Geffrey said as he kept an eye open on the battle raging around him. "It's Geffrey. Can you hear me?"

Jubal turned his head toward Geffrey's voice but it was obvious he wasn't in the present. Geffrey took one of his large hands in his, squeezed it.

"Jubal, hang in there," he said. "I'll try and find help."

Geffrey scanned the battlefield for any unengaged Norman soldiers but there were none. When he turned his attention back to Jubal, the man had stopped breathing. Black blood gushed from his mouth.

Geffrey laid his friend's head on the ground and stood, a fury welling inside. Jubal, although a giant of a man, was the kindest and most soft-spoken person. His friend was gone.

He returned to the fighting, wielding his sword at several Saxon soldiers. Late in the day, weaknesses began to appear in the Saxon line, which the Normans pushed to exploit. The cavalry assaulted the weakened left flank, and they broke through. The Saxon line split apart and became a series of isolated groups fighting for survival.

☙❧

Jodocus paced the inside perimeter of his tent located in the Norman encampment. A runner staggered into the camp and Jodocus pressed him for details. The man talked in excited tones as he spoke of the day's happenings.

"The Norman line advanced. Straight up the hill they charged. 'God help us!' they shouted while the English veterans cried, 'Holy Cross! Holy Cross!' Harold had laid his plans well. The palisade, the wall of shields, the solid ranks of men—as long as these were unbroken the Norman onslaughts were as powerless as a shower beating upon an oak tree. Duke William and his men fell back. The ranks were in disorder. The whole invading force was panic-stricken.

"'Flee, my duke, save yourself!' shouted a soldier.

"'The duke is dead! The duke is dead!' cried another, and the wild cry ran through the lines.

William removed his helmet to show to all that he was still alive and pursued his men.

"'Come back,' he called. 'Why do you flee? I live, and by the grace of God I will conquer. Come back, or with my own hand, I will strike you down.'"

Jodocus listened, fascinated by the man's description of the battle.

"Leading his Normans," the man continued, "William dashed forward for another attack. His horse fell under him. No matter, he could press nearer on foot. He struck down Harold's brother and now the English fought for vengeance. William mounted another horse. It was slain. He mounted a third. The Norman forces pressed on. The wooden palisade was beginning to yield but behind it were the deep ranks of brave Englishmen. Their firmly grasped shields made for a stronger wall than any palisade.

"Something more than daring was needed. Part of the invading force advanced, turned, broke ranks and fled. The raw troops of the English rushed from their position and pursued, though the veterans at their left shouted 'Back! Back!' for this was the old trick which the Danes had played upon the English two centuries before, and which William had played upon the king of France. The Normans wheeled about, formed their lines anew, and cut down their scattered pursuers. As—"

"Tell me," Jodocus interrupted. The man's eyes were wide with excitement as he recounted the battle. "Have we suffered great losses?"

"It was almost twilight," the man continued, not acknowledging Jodocus's question. "Since nine in the morning the battle had raged. To attack the English behind the firm line of shields was like making an assault upon a fortress. William ordered his archers to shoot straight up into the air. There fell upon the English a storm of the deadly steel, the most terrible event of the day. Men held their shields high up to protect their heads.

Then was the moment for the Norman lance and the Norman sword.

"Harold fell, his eye pierced by an arrow. His own veterans fought to the death. Not one was captured, but the less disciplined troops fled madly over the hills to the northward. They knew the country, but their pursuers were lost in the morass or fell headlong over the precipice. The land itself was avenging the death of her heroes. The English turned and took a fearful revenge on the invaders but this was only a momentary turn—the battle was lost. The battle was lost, I tell you! If those Englishmen who left their lines to pursue the pretended retreat of the enemy had been as true to Harold in deed as they were in heart, if they had been as obedient as they were courageous, then might the battle of Senlac have been an English victory instead of an English defeat."

Finished, the man collapsed, spent, on the ground.

"You mean the battle is won?" cried Jodocus.

"It is soon won," the runner said. "It is soon won."

Jodocus flopped onto his cot. Was Geffrey still alive? Jubal? It would be hours before he knew for sure. But, the battle was won. The battle was won! Would they be returning home anytime soon? Questions. All he had was questions.

℘⅋℘

Saxon swordsmen surrounded Geffrey. A mace hit him from behind and knocked him off Midnight, the animal charged off in the distance. On foot, he clutched his sword with a tight grip, looked about for enemy soldiers. They were all around him.

A soldier charged him with a spear, eyes wide, mouth spewing spittle. Geffrey sidestepped the man and ran him through with his sword. The man groaned and fell bleeding to the ground. Another Saxon confronted him, both hands grasping a heavy broadsword. When he swung the weapon and hit Geffrey's sword with a loud *clang*, the force almost knocked it from his hand. He felt the sting all the way into his shoulder. He spun around, parried another blow, then countered with a thrust of his own that found its mark in the man's chest. The Saxon backed away, stumbled, and fell.

Geffrey felt as if he was outside his body. His head was in a fog, his body reacting as a result of hours of training. Reflexes, conditioned by hours of swordsman-ship instruction, took over. He was on automatic. He had pledged his fealty to William, and he would give the duke his very best efforts.

Dead Saxons and Normans lay all around and the stench of blood, vomit and excrement repulsed his sens-es. From his left, three Saxons fell upon him, their swords slashing. As he parried a blow, he felt a sting on his left arm, felt the warmth spread under his gambeson. Spinning toward the direction of the hit, he saw the man lunge with a sword. Geffrey's own sword clanged against the attacker's steel and the sword went flying into the dirt. The man ran off.

The other two men charged Geffrey with a fury in their eyes. They squared off and began a deadly fight, swords clashing and clanging, sending sparks spewing off the blades. As he parried the blows from the Saxons, Geffrey turned toward a loud sound and saw two more Saxons coming for him, their battleaxes held high.

Geffrey clashed with the four men as they locked in a death struggle, swords and axes clanging loudly on the hill. The four Saxons surrounded him. He sensed this was his last fight. One of the men charged, swing his axe and Geffrey managed to sidestep his attacker and plunge his sword into the man's belly. Two more raced to engage him and he was able to deflect their blows and kill them. The fourth man disappeared in the confusion of the battle.

It wasn't long before the fighting wound down. When Harold was killed, the news of his death spread like a wildfire. The Saxon army disintegrated. After a day of fierce fighting, the Normans showed no mercy to the dying and wounded, slaughtering them where they lay. Those unable to escape and hide in the forests were pursued and cut down by cavalry. One group fled, pursued by Gaylord and fifty cavalry in the fading light. In near darkness and unfamiliar with the terrain, they rode straight into a steep gully and a Saxon ambush. William arrived to take command of the situation and beat off the attack before returning to the battlefield. The Normans won the battle and every remaining Saxon killed.

Harold's mother, upon learning of her son's death, petitioned William to give up her son's body for a payment in gold equal to the King's weight. William refused, saying the man ought to be buried on the soil he chose to defend.

CHAPTER 38

Geffrey stood exhausted, surveying the carnage around him. Dead Saxons lay all about, their blood running in large rivers down Senlac Ridge. Fires still raged filling the air with smoke. The remnants of Harold's army had fled leaving William's forces victorious. The infantry and cavalry began to gather up the dead and wounded. A familiar voice rang out behind him.

"Sir Geffrey!" The voice pierced the din of battle. "Sir Geffrey! I await your pleasure!"

Geffrey turned and saw Frederic standing a few yards away. His face was bloodied, his sword in his hand. His eyes burned with hatred.

"There you are, you bastard," he hissed. "Now, I will have my revenge."

Frederic lunged, his sword slashing the air in wild arcs. Momentarily stunned by the situation, Geffrey took several steps backward and drew his sword.

"Frederic," he said. "This neither the time nor the place. Surely we can work this out."

Frederic said nothing, kept coming, his sword cutting the air. Geffrey had no choice but to defend himself.

He took Frederic's first blow with his sword, the noise splitting the noise of the battlefield as Normans gathered around. He parried with a blow, which Frederic caught and the two engaged in a dance of clashing weapons, each man trying to wield a deathblow to the other.

One of Geffrey's blows hit Frederic on the thigh, cutting a gash in the man's flesh. But the man fought on as if unfazed by his injury. A lunge pierced Geffrey's chain mail and came dangerously close to his chest.

A blow knocked Frederic's sword from his hand and it landed in the dirt a few meters away. Frederic's look was one of confused amazement.

"Pick it up," Geffrey hissed. "I'll not kill you without a sword in your hand."

Frederic scrambled to pick up his weapon and once again came at Geffrey. This time the two swords locked together at the cross guards and the two men stood facing each other, mere inches apart.

Geffrey felt a sharp pain in his side, looked down to see that Frederic had stuck a dagger into his side. It was in up to the hilt. Where the dagger came from he never saw. The pain was intense.

He shoved Frederic away along with the dagger and noticed blood staining his tunic. When Frederic rushed him, he parried the blow. Geffrey felt his legs weakening but he continued to fight. Blow after blow the men's swords clanged against each other. Out of the corner of an eye he noticed the crowd of Norman soldiers had grown larger. Most stood in silent amazement at the battle before them.

Geffrey stumbled to a knee and Frederic raised his sword above his head. Seeing an opportunity, Geffrey plunged his sword deep into the man's chest. With a huge expulsion of air, Frederic gasped and fell back onto the ground, his hands wrapped around the blade of Geffrey's sword.

He didn't move.

Geffrey staggered, his legs rubber. Pain seared his brain, a pain never felt before. His knees buckled. He fought to remain on his feet. Ahead of him, his Norman friends, stunned at seeing him stumbling about, gave him a wide berth.

His head felt light as a feather and the battlefield blurred. The vision of Frederic lying dead in a pool of blood darkened. He struggled to remain erect. Blood filled his mouth and he spat it out. A Norman infantryman hurried to his side but Geffrey shrugged him away. The battlefield began to whirl about him.

He staggered a few steps then fell to his knees. Blood continued to flow from his wound. He dropped his sword, grabbed his side with his hands. They filled with blood.

He collapsed on his back.

As he lay in the dirt, the memory of Adela floated through his reeling brain. A vague vision of her in a green dress wearing an emerald necklace. Their first kiss. He saw his father running to meet him, his mother at his side. He struggled to raise an arm, to reach out and touch them but his strength failed him. Breathing became difficult, the world about him darkened. He felt the grains of dirt in his mouth and wondered about his own burial. Would Adela grieve his passing?

His lungs filled with blood. He coughed up a glob of bloody froth, spit it out. The Norman and Saxon infantryman around him blurred. He felt weak, lightheaded. Why wasn't Jodocus at his side? He was weak, so very weak.

Then everything faded to black.

 exer

When word of Geffrey's death reached William, he went immediately to view his knight's body. Gaylord and a few others brought Geffrey to William's command tent and laid him on a cot covered with furs and blankets. Jodocus came and stood at the entrance. When William saw him standing there, he summoned the man with a wave of his hand.

"You were his squire," William said. "How you must grieve for him."

"I was more than his squire, my lord," Jodocus said, tears streaming down his cheeks. "I was his friend. And he was mine."

"I hope I was his friend as well, Jodocus."

"I would like to take him home to Lochwald," Jodocus said. "But, in the event of his death, he requested that his body be burned."

"He will not go home. He was a knight of the realm. As such, he will be buried on the spot he died. It is the best honor a knight can claim. We will bury him tomorrow at sunrise."

William retired to his private quarters where he penned a letter to Adela. He struggled to find the words.

My dearest daughter Adela.

Words cannot express my remorse for the reason I write this letter.

Our beloved Sir Geffrey, your intended, was killed in battle today by Saxon soldiers. He died swiftly and I do not think he agonized more than a few minutes. He suffered a mortal wound from a sword that pierced his body at the hand of the jackal, Frederic. But Frederic died along with our knight. Geffrey died fighting for our cause. I will never forget his sacrifice. I have an idea what Geffrey meant to you—he was something special to me as well. He was destined to become my son-in-law but with his fashioning the sword he presented me, he became a son.

We shall both grieve his untimely death, you and I. But hopefully one day we can remember Sir Geffrey without the pain. We will remember what a good and noble man he was. A true knight of the realm who displayed courage and honor in the face of adversity. That he was a member of our family.

Your loving father,
William

ະຈະຈ

Jodocus spent the evening washing Geffrey's body and anointing it with sweet smelling herbs and spices in preparation for his cremation and burial. His friend was gone. Jubal was gone, listed among the missing, presumed dead for he was not counted when William had all the commanders perform a head count of their troops.

Jodocus dressed Geffrey in clothes Duke William provided. He had never seen such finery, cloth so smooth to the touch. The carpenter hastened by to measure Geffrey for his coffin that, he said, would be ready by midnight. Jodocus would be up—he didn't figure on sleeping this night.

He wondered how Adela would take the news. Devastated, he was sure, for she loved the man beyond all reason. He saw it in her eyes, the way she looked at him, spoke to him. But Adela seemed a strong woman so she would deal with this blow in her unusual feminine way. He wished her the best.

For him, he didn't know what lay in store now that William would be crowned King of England. His three best friends in the world were gone. Byrun, lost somewhere, due to his treachery and callousness of heart. The man who betrayed Geffrey's trust and didn't seem to care. Jubal, the quiet giant man, the one they always could count on when strength mattered. And Geffrey, the knight. For whom he would have gladly laid down his own life so that Geffrey might live to serve William and Adela.

He was alone and the world didn't seem worth living in any more. Where his wife, daughter, and grandson were he had no idea. Maybe he would return to Normandie and renew his search for them. It had been so many long years ago since he had last seen them.

They might still be out there.

Somewhere.

౬౨౬౨

Dawn came on the wings of low dark clouds that threatened rain. A bitter wind blew across the blood-stained battlefield. Four of Sir Geffrey's fellow knights, including Gaylord and Merek, bore his coffin to the spot where his grave had been dug. The wooden box was made of polished pine and the carpenter adorned it with fine scrollwork of mahogany. William's army turned out to mourn Geffrey's passing. Jodocus stood erect at the front of them.

William was dressed in his finest. White trousers and shirt with an armor chest plate decorated in gold and silver. A burgundy cape draped over his shoulders, its edges trimmed with golden needlework.

A bolt of lightning shattered the sky and thunder rumbled over the plains. William asked that the coffin lid be removed and the carpenter scurried to obey the command. The duke moved to the coffin, stood silent for the longest moment.

"This noble knight was a soldier of Normandie," he said. "He died fighting for my right to be crowned King of England. For that sacrifice, I will forever be grateful." He choked back the tears and the lump that formed in his throat. He struggled to continue. "We come today to pay homage to a great man, a man who was more than a friend to me." William retrieved his sword from its scabbard, held it high for all to see. "He forged this sword, Halvor. He called it the Sword of Wödan and he fashioned it especially for me and this campaign. He used a special secret process, wouldn't even tell me what it was. But you can see that it is a sword like no other. Today, the day of a great victory, I am returning it to its rightful owner."

William stooped and, with a trembling hand placed the sword upon Geffrey's chest. The carpenter nailed the lid closed. The pallbearers lowered the coffin into the grave.

William stood, tears on his cheeks.

"He was nothing more than a peasant," he said. "A peasant who became a slave. A slave who became a knight. And a knight who became my son."

As a fine drizzle began to fall on the gathering, William bent slightly, touched Geffrey's coffin, and then disappeared into the foggy mist.

Jodocus piled peat and boughs on top of the coffin. With a torch he lit the wood, watched the flames and smoke billow into the dark sky. He stood silent until the last of the coffin was nothing more than a heap of ashes. Tears streamed down his face.

William was right, he thought. Geffrey was nothing more than a mere peasant.

But what a peasant.

He lived the words he inscribed on William's sword.

Lux veritas et honorem—Light, Truth, and Honor.

Historical Notes

Although a work of fiction, this story is set in an historical period. The Battle of Hastings in October of 1066, was an event so significant, it completely changed the course of English history.

After Effects of the Battle of Hastings.

After the Battle of Hastings, William still had to conquer England. He marched from Hastings, crossing the Thames then on toward London where he received the surrender of the city. His coronation took place on Christmas Day 1066 and was held at Westminster Abbey. William kept the promises he had made to the barons who fought with him to give them English land. He gave them lands taken from the Saxons. In exchange, the barons were required to be loyal to William and provide knights to fight for him when he needed them. Every person owed his or her living to the people who had allowed them their land and was paid in service, money, or goods. This feudal system was the basis of society in the early middle ages. William also gave lands to the Church because the pope had supported William in his claim to the English throne.

William, the bastard, Duke of Normandie,
Later William the Conqueror.

William died early on the morning of September 9, 1087. He was fifty-nine years old and had ruled England for twenty-one years and Normandy for thirty-one more. He died after sustaining an injury from a fall from his horse. When it came time to bury the heavy body, it was discovered that the stone sarcophagus was not long enough to accommodate his body. There was an attempt to force the bloated corpse into the coffin and the swollen bowels burst, issuing forth an intolerable stench. Even the frankincense and spices of his physician were not enough to mask the smell and the rites were hurriedly concluded.

Adela, William's daughter.

Her birthdate is generally believed to be between 1066 and 1070, after her father's accession to the English throne in 1066, much too young to be an adult during the battle. I made her Geffrey's love interest for the sake of the story. She was the favorite sister of King Henry I of England; they were probably the youngest of the Conqueror's children.

William's son, Robert.

Robert, Duke of Normandy, nicknamed Curthose for the shortness of his legs and hence his leggings, was the oldest, nicest, and least effective of William the Conqueror's three sons. Brave, generous, good-natured, and trusting, he was easily outmatched in statecraft, ruthlessness, and cunning by his younger brothers—William Rufus and Henry. Their father had no confidence in Robert as a ruler and arranged for Rufus to succeed him on the throne of England.

Remmelsberg Mines.

Mining was done at Remmelsberg as early as 900 AD. Iron and silver were the chief ores. When silver was discovered at Remmelsberg in 1005, the King of Germany expanded its operation and built a fort nearby. Historically, there is no evidence that slaves manned it.

Lochwald.

A fictional village in medieval Normandy.

Crucible Process of Forging Steel.

The crucible process was a process for melting metals and alloys in pots, or crucibles, made of refractory materials. The crucible process is the oldest known method for melting metals. It was described by Aristotle in the fourth century BC and was well known in India, Persia, and Syria. Crucible steel was used for producing sharp knives, strong tools, and such steel weapons as damask blades. In later centuries, the secret of the process was lost. Whether it was used in the Remmelsberg mines is unknown.

About the Author

Richard Edde was born and raised in Oklahoma. After graduating from Central State College, he attended the University of Oklahoma College of Medicine, where he earned his medical degree in 1971. After spending a few years in family practice in two rural Oklahoma towns, he completed a residency in anesthesiology. Following a long career in academia and private practice, he retired to devote time to writing. His first novel, *The Photograph*, was released in 2014. Dr. Edde resides in eastern Oklahoma with his wife.